IN PAGES LEFT BEHIND

JESSICA NOELLE

In Pages Left Behind

By Jessica Noelle

ISNB/SKU- 979-8-218-50412-0

EISBN- 979-8-218-50414-4

This is a work of fiction. All characters in this book are fictitious, and any resemblance to actual persons, living or dead, is purely coincidental. The names, incidents, dialogue, and opinions expressed are products of the author's imagination and are not to be construed as real.

Published by Jessica Noelle

Cover design by Molly Camacho

Visit my website at jessicanoellebooks.com

Instagram @jessica.noelle

PRAISE FOR JESSICA NOELLE

"Jessica Noelle does it again. . . her new Novel, *"In Pages Left Behind,"* made us feel all the things!! She hooked us from the dedication, if we're honest. . . This is a story about addiction and grief, but also ultimately about love, adventures and even forgiveness. *In Pages Left Behind* shows us that life isn't black and white and that sometimes relationships are complicated. Noelle demonstrates through her FMC, Jenesis, that strength and vulnerability can coincide, and that sometimes healing is not linear. We cannot wait to read about where Jules ends up. Jessica is 2 for 2 so far, so I think we can safely say - if it has Jessica Noelle's name on it, you can count us in!"

— TIPSY BOOK READS

"Like Finding an old mix tape full of memories, *"In Pages Left Behind"* had me COMPLETELY hooked. This story follows Jenesis as she discovers her father's journal from the 80s and 90s (hello nostalgia!), leading her on an epic journey that's giving major "Eat, Pray, Love" vibes! This beautiful blend of wanderlust, romance, and self-discovery is the kind of story that stays with you long after you have read the final page. Why you need this book: 1. Dual timeline that hits harder than your first AIM heartbreak. 2. Travel adventures across places like Maui & London. 3. A wanderlust romance that'll make you swoon. 4. Family secrets that are more surprising than the end of "The Sixth Sense." 5. Character growth that'll remind you of your own coming-of-age story. The way Jessica weaves between past and present? Seamless! And don't even get me started on Adam - this free-spirited wanderer will have you catching feelings faster than dial up internet! Trust your local millennial book bestie - this one's an instant click author!"

— SHE'S ALL BOOKS

In *"In Pages Left Behind,"* Jessica Noelle takes us on a journey of healing that is as unexpected as it is rewarding. In an attempt to come to grips with the untimely death of her father, a complex man at once flawed and wonderful, a daughter retraces his steps, taking us on a trip across the globe. The journey Noelle vividly describes, though, is as much internal as it is external. This is a book about facing our grief and not letting it ruin our capacity to love. Her heroine must learn to forgive past hurts, and her own shortcomings, in order to open her heart. *"In Pages Left Behind"* is a moving and honest testament to the power of forgiveness to heal even the most deeply wounded of hearts. *"In Pages Left Behind"* is a powerful bulwark against the temptation to shrink and disappear in the face of great pain and loss. A must-read for anyone trying to navigate the turbulent waters of loss, grief and love.

— ALFRED BOTELLO, AWARD WINNING
AUTHOR OF 180 DAYS.

"In *Adopting Secrets*, Jessica Noelle viscerally explores the themes of pain, guilt, love, and ultimately hope. Her prose deftly mirrors the evolution of Kat, a stoic young woman who has locked herself in a state of emotional exile to avoid the pain of a very difficult memory. But you can't outrun your past. As people and circumstances help her pry open the door to this self-constructed prison, Noelle reminds us that sometimes the most powerful way to cope with guilt and shame is to be brave enough to share it. Sunlight trumps the dark. *Adopting Secrets* is an elegant, compelling testament to the healing power of trust and vulnerability."

— ALFRED BOTELLO, AWARD WINNING
AUTHOR OF *180 DAYS*.

"Adopting Secrets spans the inner depths of pain and escapism at the hands of abuse. Regret, self-understanding, and, ultimately, the power of love and connection that make it all worthwhile aer felt profoundly through this mind-bending novel that leaves you wanting more. Jessica Noelle has given us a fantastic story. Please read it and feel deeply."

— DIANNE C. BRALEY, AUTHOR OF *THE SILENCE AND THE SOUND*, WINNER OF THE NYC 2022 BIG BOOK AWARD

"A heartfelt exploration of the unbreakable bond between two sisters, forged in love and tragedy, and the secrets that survive the grave."

"The twists and turns in this book made it absolutely impossible to foresee the ending. Jessica Noelle wrote such lovable characters that dealt with such real-life trauma. She really put her characters and us readers through the wringer. We were hooked from paragraph 2, but our jaws literally **DROPPED** when we hit chapter 8, and from that point on we stayed on the edge of our seats. In future books, we would love to see the story (going) more in depth (on) Alice and Lily's relationship along with their meeting for the first time. This book was truly bingeable, and we hope to read more from Jessica Noelle."

"This book took me on the wildest of rides and I couldn't put it down! The author did such an amazing job weaving in the past with the FMC's present and it had so many twists that I did NOT see coming! Every time I thought I knew the "twist", I was wrong.

This one hurt my heart and stitched it all back together by the last page.

And that ending. My gosh that ending was so perfect in a way I would have never expected. The last line of this book is one that will stay with me forever because it was so beautiful."

— DANIELLE MORRIS, AUTHOR OF
BIRDS OF A FEATHER

"Babe, you're going to want to read this!

SO thankful I dove into this book blind!

This debut book by Jessica Noelle will satisfy all of your suspense, mystery, twist and turn cravings! With each turn of the page, I found myself grasping my kindle a little tighter and reading a little quicker. The end will shock you and the ride is so twisty that it may leave you dizzy but it's thrilling and addicting!

To be honest, I sat with this review for a while because it is pretty difficult to write one without giving anything away. So what I will say is that the female character is SO badass and two male characters are so perfectly written. The plot is THICK & Jessica Noelle hit the ball out of the park with this debut book. If you like books that make you want to finish in one sitting, and can leave you shocked... this is for you babe!"

— SHE'S ALL BOOKS

"For the girls untangling complicated father-daughter relationships- a.k.a daddy issues - this one's for you. "

playlist
In Pages Left Behind

Strangers
Jonas Brothers

What Was I Made For?
Billie Eilish

I Will
The Beatles

My Greatest Fear
Benson Boone

The Climb
Miley Cyrus

Lost Boy
Ruth B.

Enjoy artists like the Jonas Brothers, Death Cab For Cutie, The Doobie Brothers, Dashboard Confessional, The Beach Boys and more. Scan QR code to visit full playlist.

PINTEREST

Scan the QR code for a more visual experience with the In Pages Left Behind Pinterest board.

"Write hard and clear about what hurts."

— ERNEST HEMINGWAY

PROLOGUE

"Hey, wanna play mermaids?" I gurgle the pool water and ask the young boy splashing next to me to join me in my delusional little world.

"I'm a mer-man. Not a mermaid." He corrects me, but I am already submerged so it comes out more garbled like, *"IIIII ammmmmm a mmmmerrrmannnn."*

The fact this stranger is willing to play pretend with me is astonishing and feels warmer than the direct sunlight.

The water shimmers around me, reflecting the rays in a dance of glistening green and gold. I revel in the sensation of my silky scales, alive with iridescence, as they sway with the gentle currents. Roseate strands of hair cascade around my face, kissed by the warm Hawaiian breeze, framing my vision in a delicate halo. I try to catch the bubbles that leave my mouth in a gravity-defying trail to the surface.

I am a mermaid in all her glory. Or at least that is how my six-year-old mind perceives my appearance as I toss (not as gracefully as I imagine) in the waters of Hawaii. Sure, it is the pool waters at the resort on Maui and not the ocean, but my imagination sees coral and seaweed galore. The goggles pinch my nose in the most uncomfortable way, as water both expels and swells into lenses, completely blocking my sight underwater. However, this doesn't hinder my imagination, so I refuse to remove them. Seeing isn't the primary reason I wear them; they're my gateway to a whole new reality. To remove them would be to welcome myself back into the present, which I most definitely am not ready for. I am the master of my multiverse.

With them, I can escape into another world or another time because at this moment, I know I am safe in the real one. I asked that boy to play with me, but I didn't need him to have a good time. He joined in the beginning, but he is surely older than me and his loss of interest occurred pretty quickly. Doesn't matter. The pool is an undersea mecca and I am the prettiest mermaid there ever was. Rainbow tail and all.

"Don't swim too far away, Jenesis." A loud voice booms above me, both in authority and kindness.

I can feel his eyes on me from up above, can see his large arms cross across his chest as he watches me splash about so freely. Large tattoos decorate every inch of his arms, but even so, the prominence of his stature is steadfast. I am safe.

MY DAD. A COMPLICATED MAN WHO, IF I AM REMEMBERING correctly, didn't stand much taller than my mom. Mom wasn't alive long enough for me to accurately remember how tall she stood against his bodybuilder frame, though he carries himself with an embodiment that makes him seem like he envelopes the entirety of the room. Sometimes it is the safest place to be, wrapped up in his arms. And other times it is the scariest place on earth. A place I need to retreat from.

His emotions are so big, there can only be capacity for what *he* is feeling and no one else. Sometimes it is love, and that love can consume you. Other times, it is a temper that feels like the walls will come down in a violent shake. And then there are moments when it's all confuddled in a narcotized blur.

This was before all of that, though. Before, the pain eclipsed me, and my childhood still had magic in it. Whether I was a mermaid, a fairy, a pirate alongside him, or just me. He looks like a pirate, which was made even more prominent when the tattoos came around. His white long hair touches his shoulders in a wisp and his handlebar mustache commands attention. His green eyes glimmer against the hues of the sky at sunset. A flash of green before the sun finally sets. His hair is pretty straight now and a shade of off-white that I know he doesn't care for, but he swears it is better than the dark curly hair he had in his youth. I still have his dark hair, albeit less curly, but I've never minded the waves.

"Just be grateful God gave you straighter hair," he would

always say as he brushed my hair in the mornings before school.

He didn't always have his tattoos, but when he got them, they just solidified his look as a pirate or even more uncannily, *Hulk Hogan*. People would swear up and down they were long-lost twins.

Ironically, tattoos were extremely taboo for me as a young child, so it was surprising when he got his. They not only covered his arms, but his entire back and torso as well. He used to loathe when I would do the gum-wrapper tattoos. I would have to scrub my skin raw if I ever painted on my skin with a Sharpie, but even in his hypocrisy, I love those tattoos of his.

"I am nearly fifty years old, Jenesis. When you're my age, if you still want a tattoo, then I will allow it."

As if I will need permission to do much of anything past the age of eighteen.

I would just nod.

"I've had my whole life to figure out what is worth permanently putting on my body."

And now you won't have much of your life left to enjoy them.

I would think but never say it out loud. I didn't know then just how right I was.

"Okay, Daddy." That is all I would say in an out-loud response.

"Your skin is so beautiful and pure, just as it is. My baby girl."

I would always be his baby girl. Even as I got older. In his mind, I would always be the little thing that fit from the palm of his hand to the crook of his elbow.

The tattoos weren't worth an argument. There was nothing I could think of that I wanted on my skin permanently, except my freckles. Maybe a mermaid tattoo! I always wished for scales. But looking back, there is a reason you have to be of a certain age to get one.

I HOLD MY BREATH UNDER THE WATER UNTIL MY LUNGS BURN, the chlorine that manages to get into my goggles stinging my eyes, and I see his shadow hovering over me. Protecting me and just. . . there. I hold my breath until I can't last another second. Another reminder that I am not really a mermaid and can't actually breathe underwater. One surge upward and I will be back into reality. I plunge out of the water to see him hovering over me, but instead of meeting his protective open arms and a warm sunbaked towel, my body jolts awake.

Twenty-nine years old, not six. A woman and not a mermaid. Curled up in bed in a small-ish apartment and not splashing in the pool, though I am wet with sweat. Gasping for breath, not because I am underwater, but because my face is buried in my pillow and lastly, not welcomed by a protective, loving father, but rather all alone. A dream, a nightmare, or a memory - my startled self can't be sure. Deep breathing revives my lungs from my near-pillow suffocation and calms the cortisol/adrenaline pulsing through me from being awoken so abruptly. I want to see him. I want to be a child again. I was reaching for him in my mind, but when I breached the reflective water and opened my eyes, I was left deserted.

There is no one here. Not even the crickets outside are awake to continue their chirping. I am alone and Dad is still dead.

1

NORTHERN CALIFORNIA

2022

"I'm sorry. It's going to be just a little while longer. Your dad, um, he won't, um. . . he doesn't fit in the body bag."

The paramedic looks sheepish when he says this.

"You're kidding, right?"

"Sadly, no."

What am I supposed to say to that?

"We also need to wait for a little more. . . assistance."

"For what?" Now I am agitated. *Out with it already.*

"My partner and I can't seem to lift him on our own."

No duh, they couldn't lift my 260 pound bodybuilder father out of his house by themselves. Especially since one of them is a slender woman, who I am sure can bench press more than I currently can, but still.

I exhale a large puff of air. "Take your time. It's not like he is going anywhere."

What else can I say to them? No, please, drag him out without a

body bag and hope for the best in getting him into the ambulance. I sure
as hell am not offering my additional aid. I've seen enough of this mess
to scar me for life as it is.

It had been a few days since I had heard from him. His
phone was off and he missed our date to get together a few
days prior. None of this was circumstantial. No flags went
up in my mind because it was so common for him to be too
high to remember what day it was, let alone any plans we
made.

It wasn't odd that I hadn't heard from him. It wasn't odd
that he stood me up. I had gotten used to that cycle of his
life by now. One day he was the dad that I knew and loved
and the next day, the pills had him swirling in a tempest of
lethargy and intoxication. I learned to take it all just one
day, one hour, one moment at a time.

It wasn't weird until days had gone by with nothing but
calls that went straight to voicemail. It got especially
concerning when a week went by and he hadn't paid his
rent. I got a text from his landlord. All of this should have
tipped me off, but what got me to come tonight was the fact
he hadn't called to confirm what day he could come down
to store his motorcycle in my garage for winter. His cabin in
the woods barely provided any protection for himself
against the harsh seasonal elements, let alone any vehicle
that presides outdoors.

I had worked myself up into fits so many times before. I
would scream and cry so adamantly that he was dead, and
every time I went to check on him or had an officer beat
down his door. It was always the same outcome. . .

He would emerge from his bedroom, having just been stirred from an opiate-induced deep sleep. Regardless, though, he would turn on his charm and charismatic narcissism and schmooze the logic out of any law enforcement persons who entered his home. I saw it time and time again. I recall many autographed photos being signed for whoever fell for his enchantments and then having that same someone look at me like I had wasted their day calling a well check on a "celebrity" who was very clearly "fine."

The tug-of-war I allowed my emotions to go through was brutal and made me question my sanity from time to time.

Was I really worrying so much about a man who was completely fine? Was I actually the problem?

This specific day felt like all the others, only this time I didn't allow myself to panic. Every incident like this in the past proved he was just watching a movie or taking a nap. I had only my fears to prove anything otherwise, and it was my lack of fear that proved me wrong.

It had been the story of *the boy who cried wolf* one too many times, but this time it blew the house down.

Bright red and blue lights flashed up the driveway filled with a hundred potholes and a man in uniform parked after a cloud of dust. Once it settled, he set out and crossed under the trees to get to me. He wasn't in any particular rush. He wasn't the one who would be of any help medically speaking.

"Why do you suspect an overdose?" Sheriff Roberts asks.

Why does that question sound so stupid? I hadn't heard the conversation leading up to the question either.

Um…because he was always going to die from an overdose. Because taking the pills was the vice that had been slowly killing him for over two decades now, and because anytime I didn't hear from my dad, I expected nothing else.

I just stand still, dumbfounded. No one can blame me for my actions. Shock can blanket a multitude of inappropriate behaviors.

The officers may not have been in a rush, but the ambulance that tore through the mud up the hill was hell-bent on saving a life. Little did we all know at that point it was futile. I should have known when screaming his name into the void of his broken front door didn't elicit a response. I could have walked in by myself, but there was something in the air and I just knew I shouldn't enter the premises alone.

I watched as the paramedics bolted into his home, blazing in a rampage of medical supplies and urgency. Then I watched as every single one of them in a split instant set down their instruments and meandered back outside the busted door. What was a moment of pressing crisis had just as quickly turned into hopelessness.

There was nothing they could do. Death had already come and laid its claim many days prior. Any revival was an option long gone.

The one time I didn't fear he was dead was the one time I actually should have. And now I trust myself a little less than before.

I look back on the last week and wonder to myself how I could have been so blind to all the signs, but I guess that's what happens when your father is an addict. He primed me for this. All those "scares" I had in the past had desensitized me to this very moment. Only it wasn't at all what I thought it would be like.

I walked in with the paramedics, but seeing him lying there, having already been dead for what they assumed was a week, was unbearable. The empty shell of the human body that was lying there was in no way, shape, or form the father I knew and loved. The soul had departed, leaving behind nothing but the beginnings of decay and a post-mortem posture.

My stomach turns as I relive it over and over, and I excuse myself from the presence of the paramedics and Sheriff Roberts. I am not sure what might happen. If I cry or vomit or both, I don't want to be around anyone for whatever reaction my body concocts. The great outdoors is safe even though my body crumples on top of a pile of dirt and stones before the tears begin to fall.

When I said I was going to go check on him tonight, no part of me thought he was dead. I had felt inclined to "check" on him too many times before.

Where do I go from here? What happens now?

Death is very good at feeling final. I watch as the police and the medical professionals call for the coroner and rifle through his small cabin in search of all the little orange bottles with white labels printed "Gideon Haynes." I watch as everything, with a point or needle, is delicately placed in an evidence bag and removed from the premises.

"Is this him?" A scrawny, rookie-looking officer asks me as he holds up what is my father's most recent driver's license. I guess it is hard to tell now because of the swelling and in a manner of respect, I don't think he wants to remove the white sheet currently covering his body. Even if it is just to confirm identity.

"Yeah. . . that's him." My throat feels like it is swallowing a bowling ball.

Gideon Haynes, sixty-eight years old, has green eyes and white long hair that encircles his head in wisps like a cloud. I remember making fun of him for that picture and telling him he should have worn one of his bandanas like he normally did in his genuine leather and biker fashion. At least his eyes weren't completely bloodshot and open in slits like they were during so many of our conversations. He managed to pull himself together whenever there was an audience to perform for.

"So, do you have questions?"

I didn't even realize someone was speaking to me. A badge, Sheriff Roberts. The officer in charge.

Could you repeat everything you just said? I think to myself.

I can't bear to ask him to reiterate the entire spiel for me all over again. So I just shake my head in a non-emphatic "no" and continue to look at my feet.

"Would you like to sit in my squad car for a minute while we wait for backup? I have some seat warmers and can give you a minute to process everything."

His kindness surprises me. I drove here and could hide out in my own car if I wanted to, though his offer for seat heaters is clearly not an option in my beat-up Volkswagen.

I am only shivering from the horror of it all. It is yet another side effect I didn't expect. This week, in particular, has been the hottest week of the year. It has been unseasonably warm for the beginning of September, especially for this part of Northern California. Degrees well into the hundreds. There is no excuse for my chills on one of these last few summer nights aside from my nervous system trying to process the trauma.

I also can't deny him. One indicator of adult children of alcoholics/addicts is that we cannot say no to anyone in a position of power.

"Thank you," I mumble as he opens the door to the SUV for me. His lights are still on and he has no intention of turning them off before the scene is all over. Once inside, my uncomfortableness in the front seat of the Sheriff's vehicle overpowers my desire to sob. The people-pleasing part of my brain overtakes my grief. It's like it is all on pause. All I can do is fidget with my fingers and try to cease the shivers. He didn't bother asking me not to touch anything. I wouldn't dare.

Time moves in fast forward all around me in a blur, as if I am in a *Brittany Murphy* movie. I possibly blink all of three times before another coroner arrives, even though it is at least forty-five minutes. Sheriff Roberts is true to his promise and leaves me alone the entire time. His team is still busy making sure that all the prescriptions are in their care. Even the bottle of extra-strength ibuprofen is snatched. Not sure what kind of investigation is about to take place, but I blankly watch them in their thoroughness.

A knock on the window snaps me back into the reality of it all. I don't realize that the reflection of the emergency lights has hypnotized me, reflecting off of all the outdoor surfaces. I crack the door to let Sheriff Roberts in.

"How are you doing?"

How am I doing? Isn't that the question of the hour?

"Fine, I think." I can barely look at him and my fingers have gone numb from gripping them in a clenched hand-hold. My nails were piercing the skin, and I had not felt its sting. Mentally I have been floating aimlessly. "The coroner is having an issue removing the body. Your father was a muscular man, and he doesn't exactly fit in the body bag." Sheriff Roberts looks amused, but also sensitive that this is not exactly a common occurrence.

"So I heard." The paramedics had already told me that. I didn't know the coroner was still having issues.

I can just see my dad now with his cocky arrogance beaming with pride that all his years of bodybuilding made it so that he was too large to fit in a standard-sized body bag. He hated being ordinary and so, in many ways, he was extraordinary.

"The deputy is also calling the funeral home for a few other guys to come help him. I don't know why he thought he could carry a six-foot-tall bodybuilder with only two of them. . . I told them all this when I filed the report. They were supposed to come with additional aid. . ."

Sheriff Roberts' voice trails off like he's audibly frustrated that they did not listen to him. And now we all have to just sit and wait for even more team members to wrap this all up.

He may not have felt it appropriate to laugh. I, however, cannot contain the burst of laughter that explodes out of me. My emotions are all extreme at the moment, but this is all too much.

"He doesn't fit in the body bag!" I exclaim like it's the funniest anecdote I have ever heard in my entire life. If the man wasn't dead, he would beam with satisfaction.

I'm still laughing so uncontrollably that my face turns red. I don't think Sheriff Roberts finds alarm in my outburst at all, though; he seems like a veteran in this sort of grief behavior, even though he is probably only mid-thirties.

"Sheriff Roberts, have you heard of anything so ridiculous in your entire life?" I ask mid-hilarity. He reaches over the center console and places his hand on mine, releasing them from their clenching. I still haven't allowed myself to release my fingers from their self-imposed prison.

His touch is gentle and emanates an energy that is full of concern. He doesn't know me. He is just the one on duty, unfortunate enough to respond to the call, and yet he is the kindest person I have come across in what feels like years. His touch subsides my burgeoning emotions and the volatility I have felt this entire evening.

I found Dad around seven tonight, and now it is already approaching eleven. Time has moved unbearably fast and I just can't get over the fact that he has been lying there deceased for so long. This process is a bit gut-wrenching, there is no other way to put it. Had he died in a hospital bed, it may have been more civilized, but because it was so graphic and unforeseen, I am sure ruling out foul play is necessary and time-consuming. I know it isn't anything nefarious or self-inflicted. This is simply an overdose that has been inching its way towards my father for the last two decades. It just finally caught up to him.

The warmth from my hand instantly leaves, along with

the rest of the heat from my body. It all drains from me the moment I see it. It is almost worse than finding him initially. Seven men - SEVEN - are all stretched evenly around the gurney, with every one of their muscles defined in straining under the massive weight of the figure now shrouded in a much larger white zipped bag.

2

NORTHERN CALIFORNIA

2022

I am completely alone now. It feels much like when I first arrived at the cabin, although this time I am not searching for anyone. I know without a doubt I am alone. It is well past midnight, but the adrenaline that is pulsing through me still works better than any caffeine I consume to keep me alert and awake. My mind, wired and buzzing, constantly bouncing around thoughts of. . .

Your dad is dead. Where do you go from here? What do you do next?

The thoughts are nagging and incessant and leave virtually little space in my brain to contemplate just what my next move should theoretically be. I really should sleep and revive myself for what inevitably will be a challenging day once the sun rises, since it already is technically tomorrow.

I cannot believe the amount of crap in here.

Once the paramedics removed all the translucent orange bottles, the space felt emptier, and yet there were still piles of boxes and shelves of random junk I knew I personally would have to go through. When Sheriff Roberts left, he informed me that he couldn't locate any will or trust, but as next surviving kin, I am entitled to his entire estate.

Yippie Me!

Little did he know that most of his belongings were memorabilia of "the good old days" peppered in with lots of debt and about a whopping six hundred dollars in his bank account. I will walk away with nothing after cremation, funeral services, and all other end-of-life costs. Who knew death could be so expensive? He owned his motorcycle, so I might potentially find a buyer and make a tiny profit from that sale, but it just feels like wishful thinking. The thing has well over 100,000 miles on it. A byproduct of being used as a daily driver. I just need to clean out his rental as quickly as I can.

All six hundred square feet of space, coated in floor-to-ceiling framed pictures ranging from me as a kid, to autographed photos from celebrities, to Gideon's literal hall of fame. He had medals hanging from thumbtacks and banners from bodybuilder shows. If there was any accolade in his life worth bragging about, he would promptly frame and hang it on his walls. I take pride in knowing that I am on the walls alongside all his other accomplishments. I know he was endlessly proud of me no matter what I did, or did not, accomplish. It's like a displayed time capsule and I can visualize us immortalized in time from childhood to the present.

For most of his life, Gideon looked like a burly Santa Claus who liked to wear leather and had giant tattoos of pirate skulls and Celtic crosses encasing his entire upper body. However, in his early thirties, he looked more like a lean movie star with tight, curly hair and muted green eyes. The two images don't resemble the same person at all.

I guess there is no time like the present to rummage through all of this.

It's easy to grab one of the many boxes cluttering the so-called living room and remove the lifeline off of the walls one by one. This project will take the longest. The photos and clutter of clothes he hoarded from the early eighties will inevitably consume most of my time and energy. I may as well get a head start while I am still fueled by my shock. As soon as it feels real, I know I won't be able to do this alone.

I have dedicated the last few years of my life working as a newspaper editor and taking care of him to my best capacity. Mom died when I was five, which was another catalyst into the deep end of intoxication for Gideon. Because I have had no time to spend with anyone else, it's not like I have a boyfriend to rely on. I am twenty-nine years old and I never heard the end of the nagging from my father about having kids and settling down.

"Don't wait until you're thirty-eight like I did." He would always punctuate his thoughts with this anecdote.

Like being in your thirties is too old?

I could have dedicated more energy to my love life had I not been so consumed by his drama, a fact that I liked to remind Gideon of often, though he conveniently always forgot.

He sometimes said the right things but rarely meant them and as long as my attention was on him solely, he was pleasant with me.

Rifling through a lot of his memories, I have to wonder who my father was before the pills altered him completely. We never spoke much about the past. After my mom died, it just became too hard to even share the good things. She remains a mystery to me and now all hope of ever conversing with him about her died when he did. Dead men indeed tell no tales. Not even ones of loving mothers and memories you can't recall.

I feel like I am playing detective as I throw things gently into boxes. Most of his pictures on the walls are moments I either lived with him or he was proud enough to share with me. None of these are an enigma to me. It's the polaroids in the back of his sock drawer and the stack of prints that I uncover under his bed that have me engaged for the next several hours of the early morning. Time and that pesky number on his calendar don't seem to matter anymore. Time ceases to exist as I gaze upon photograph after photograph. It's like finding a time portal to the past and I freeze, staring at the smile of a man I had grown to know and love, but the person looking back at me isn't anyone I recognize.

I also don't know anyone from the photos. They tell the story of a completely different lifetime for my father and I digest every image like I am a detective in a crime investigation. I strive to read between the lines and understand all the moments of this person's life that he refused to share. As if I could uncover all I want to know by simply studying intensely one photo at a time, but it all feels like uncovering clues to a larger picture.

I am ravenous. If my father's cabin was a mess before, it will be uninhabitable by the time I finish throwing everything out of the cabinets and nooks. I had no clue there was so much hidden past in secret compartments all around the tiny home. I "left no stone unturned," as they say.

"Oh, my gosh!" I shout out loud when I uncover some nude Polaroids I wish I hadn't. At least he had the courtesy of hiding them in the back of his dresser drawer. Based on the faded edges, I am assuming the picture is much older than I am. I could have gone my entire life without visualizing the bush on this woman that was obviously taken in the late sixties of *peace, love, and no shaving.* She was definitely all-natural. It didn't even look like she was completely naked, if you know what I mean. I also didn't need to imagine the sensual acts my father was engaging in at the time these photos were taken.

Blech, yuck, and hell to the no!

No one likes to think of their parents having a sex life. EVER! However, it made him seem more like an individual person and not just my paternal figure whom I had a complicated relationship with. While I hate thinking about him having any sort of sex life, it is nice to envision him as his own person; a different person than the troubled addict I came to know so well. A man in love maybe.

Those are fortunately all the photos of that nature that I manage to scrounge up. The only other indecent photos I uncover are silly ones of my dad and his group of friends "mooning" the camera as reckless high school students who undoubtedly thought they were the funniest people to inhabit the earth. The maturity level of teenage boys is astonishing.

My emotions are still so high and volatile. I cry at every

photo he kept of the two of us and I laugh at all the ones that confuse me, but make me smile. Starting the clean-out process in his photos is the right call, and it also makes me realize the officers were incredibly thorough in their search for medications. I continue to uncover about thirty different "hidden" spots where my dad stored his memories, but not a single pill bottle remains. That is probably why it took so long for them to conduct their search.

I wonder if they found the naked flower power brunette in the drawers as well?

If they did, they said nothing. It probably wasn't as shocking for them as it was for me. What would have been worse would be finding naked photos of him in the same "come hither" poses. I should count my blessings. She is a perfect stranger, and it's not like I have never seen a vagina before.

I dwell on that one insipid photo for far too long and I try to sort out my thoughts, only to realize that the sun is rising and the small sparkle of new daylight is just beginning to peek through the heavy foliage outside. The cabin is still a mess and there are a few choice photographs placed on the couch that I know I either want to frame or use in some important way. Maybe for a memorial service pamphlet.

One is this old-school photo booth strip in black and white that has me mesmerized. Some faces are silly, some serious, and I just can't get a grip on this gnawing feeling that I didn't know this person at all. Some of that is stemming from the fact that I literally didn't exist when this photo was taken. Gideon was in his late twenties, I assume. The other part is the person in these simple photos is uninhibited, carefree, maybe a little reckless, and overall pretty happy-looking. It's like staring at a raw image of who Dad was supposed to be; what his soul was like before opiate use dampened it.

The surrounding universe still has a vignette filter on it when I hear a faint knock on the door. Of course, the shattered door remains mangled. Kicked in and broken in half from the last month of abuse the poor door endured, so I can see right away that it is Jules standing in the entryway with two venti somethings steaming in her hand.

"Hey girl, how are you doing?" she says sympathetically as she navigates around the broken wood and the piles of personal items strewn around her feet. It's like an estate sale obstacle course to get to where I sit and not spill the beverages in her hands.

"What are you doing here?"

I totally forgot I texted her last night.

"You texted me saying your dad died and then didn't respond for the rest of the night. I was worried about you. I wasn't sure if you went home or not last night and when you still hadn't responded, I pulled up your shared location on my phone. When I saw you were still here, I figured that meant you had been up all night and needed a caffeine boost. Based on the state of your eyes and your hair and no offense girl, but your breath, I take it I am right." She says as she hands me the warm paper cup.

Her snarky comment is much warranted. My breath is rank. I haven't stopped to take an inventory of my personal hygiene. I have no hesitation in admitting it isn't the best, but I am not about to use my dad's toothbrush. I do, however, take a swig of the drink, which has now been determined to be a chai latte, and hope that the spices mask some of the morning breath for a little while. Probably not, but it's all I have to go on right now.

"You know, anxiety makes me smell funny." It's true, but I would only admit it to her.

Jules sets her latte on the kitchen counter and comes to sit next to me on the floor. My legs have gone all tingly from sitting in "criss-cross applesauce" all night long. I groan as she wraps her arms around me in an embrace.

"I am so, so sorry, Jen. I can't imagine how you feel right now."

My full name is Jenesis, but I have insisted everyone call me Jen since I was six years old. My parents both had admiration for the famous *Phil Collins* and his band *Genesis* but wanted to be more original and spell it with a J. I, too, love the reference. Being named after a rock band is so unique in my mind, but I get annoyed that no one ever spells it right and the first time kids started making biblical jokes at my expense, I simplified and now just go by Jen.

"How are you coping right now?" She asks as she gently pulls away from me, but plops herself on the floor still right beside me. Her eyes haven't moved from me awaiting my response. I know she wants to be helpful to me in my time of crisis, hence her just showing up.

"Overall, I think I am handling things pretty well." I actually think I believe it too.

"How can I be helpful? Just tell me whatever you need? I brought you some caffeine and. . . have you eaten? I think maybe I should run out and get us some breakfast burritos?"

I don't realize how hungry I am until she says breakfast burrito. Now all I can think about is the mess in front of me and how badly I want extra guacamole on the side of something filling.

I think I have earned the extra dollar that the side of guac costs. I am still in shock. I like to make myself laugh when I am incredibly uncomfortable. Even just to myself.

"I see the look on your face. . ." Jules points her finger at me. "You want the chorizo?"

Jules stands up and grabs her keys and latte off of the counter in a flash. "I'll be back and will bring extra chips and guacamole. Is it too soon for margaritas, because we might need some tequila too? I'll stop at the store and buy supplies," she says, looking around at the colossal mess I created on top of the mess that was already there. "By the looks of it, we are going to be here a while."

The sip of latte I swig almost sputters out of my mouth with a chuckle. She doesn't underestimate the magnitude of the crap in need of sorting.

A "thank you," is all I can muster. I laugh/cry when I am overwhelmed and even though Jules is here in a very invaluable way, I am still so overwhelmed by the events of last night and the tasks ahead of me I might just burst into a fit of tears and chuckles before she exits.

"I'll be back in less than an hour with extra guacamole and tequila!" She says as she practically sings out of the cabin. I love how well she knows me and her bubbly attempts to lighten the mood. Not much to salvage when a parent dies, but Jules has known my turbulent relationship with my father since we were six. It's been over two decades of calling her my friend and I don't know if I would have enjoyed life as much as I have these last few years without her friendship.

She's always been a shoulder to cry on and a confidant when I needed to share the lowest moments of my and my dad's relationship, but she was also there when the pendulum swung and he and I were in a really good place. She never questioned the roller coaster and, in many ways, understood the back-and-forth better than anyone else in my life. The closest thing I have to a sister is Jules.

I can feel the laughter bubbling under the surface as she navigates around the broken door and haphazardly placed furniture. It's all too ridiculous.

How is this even a reality?

None of this feels real, but as soon as Jules leaves, the heaviness of my emotions fills me again and the tears fall free, making it hard to see the details in the photographs I have set aside.

There will be time for this later, Jen. Get to doing something productive.

I finally pull myself off the floor. Wobbling like Gumby and almost falling to the ground face first, but because my dad had moved his couch to block the broken door, I have a cushion to break my fall. The cushion comes down with me and thank goodness I got most of the pictures off the wall, otherwise the ricochet would have added broken glass to the mix of mess on the floor. My hip stings and my legs still have pins and needles, but it is what lies under the couch pillows that grabs my attention.

Thrust into the room with my fall is a small, leather-bound journal that looks like it has seen a lot of places in life. The cover of the small diary is battered and worn, and the pages contain pictures, scribbles, and journal entries dating as early as 1983. My dad was twenty-nine in 1983, the same age I am now.

Why did I not think to check under the couch cushions? I checked under his mattress.

Every part of me wants to sit still and read every entry. It is like a sneak peek into all the parts of my dad's life he wouldn't share, or the parts that he simply died too soon to reiterate to me. Either way, this may be my book of answers. I found his words. His deepest innermost thoughts and I wish I could tap it into my brain and know all of it at once. Maybe download it into the hard drive of my mind like the digital cloud. However, I know Jules will be heading back soon with food and I should, at the very least, make a pathway for her to enter the cabin easier. If she spills my food on the ground from tripping, it won't be salvageable and will only add to my heartbreak. I really need to get my blood sugar regulated. Aside from his darker hair color, hypoglycemia is another genetic trait my dad so lovingly passed down to me.

I need to take a deep breath and concentrate on the priorities at hand here. I need to get my dad's stuff together, clean, and rent a U-Haul because all of this junk will not fit in my car. It would take a minimum of fifteen trips on my own in my Volkswagen Beetle, and I don't think Jules can haul too much, either. It's not like either one of us has a beefy bro truck. I don't even know of anyone who has one that I can borrow. Again, a boyfriend would be ideal here.

How much of this stuff do I realistically plan on keeping? A lot of this is garbage. I think to myself, although I instantly feel ashamed. These items that were my father's treasures may not have meaning to me, but they held so much importance to him and here I am contemplating just casting it all aside. There is a reason we do not take our belongings with us when we pass on, but just because I view the piles in front of me as junk, doesn't mean that they weren't valuable to someone else. To him. As much as my dad was a sore spot in my life, he was my only family, and I adored him. *Adore him.*

I can feel the tears beginning to push past the barrier of my lower lids and pool before I allow a few to fall. The stinging sensation from crying practically nonstop for hours has taken a toll on my face. I am puffy and raw, and I honestly don't want to cry anymore.

I organize a few of the boxes in hopes they might fit into a moving truck and place them out of the way of the door so Jules can safely make it through with breakfast when she arrives back with the goods. I sit down on the couch rather than on the floor now to read the first journal entry. The wood floor was making my tailbone ache and, for someone who has spent most of their later years as a shut-in, my dad at least bought a really comfortable couch. I read the first few pages before the fatigue overpowers me and I doze off for a quick power nap. That is until I smell chorizo and Jules' perfume waft in and my stomach rumbles me awake.

3

JOURNAL ENTRY
1983

J une, 15 1983

The pain was unbearable. I remember feeling like all I wanted to do was fart. Yes, fart! If I could just fart, maybe I would feel so much better. Much to my disappointment, though, I could not fart. Nor do I believe now that it would have eased any of my pain.

There is nothing quite like having appendicitis while working on a cruise ship in Alaska. There was nothing but water as far as the eye could see. The boat rocking didn't help too much either.

No one got their hair done by me that day. No bee hives to tease and no caustic hairspray to choke on. I felt like my insides were about to burst. It was a very appropriate feeling, considering something on my inside was actually preparing to burst. Not going to lie, I felt the fear start to creep in. I love my nomadic lifestyle, but I didn't ever intend to die in such a youthful prime. Taken out by my appendix on a ship in the ocean is poetic, but also a tad pathetic. I might like to be buried at sea. It's a romantic concept. Though my mother would never forgive me.

I clung to my side on my bunk as the boat rocked back and forth while I waited to call into Juneau. We weren't too far off, and I crossed my fingers, hoping by some miracle I would make it.

Spoilers. . . I survived, hence this journal entry, but not without many obstacles in my way. I could barely stand erect when we did finally dock. Denny, my cabin mate, helped me off the ship and into a taxi by resting me under his shoulder while I limped and held pressure on the right side of my body. My thought process being if I held it tight enough, I could keep everything at bay. I could feel my logical mind slowly slip into nonsense as the pain grew more and more intense.

Denny was there to place me in the taxi, briefly described the emergent nature of my situation, and urged the driver to take off towards the hospital immediately. He would have gone with me if we could have spared any crew members. My muffled cries and groans of agony should have been enough to tip the driver off. However, he was void of all haste. Instead, he babbled on for thirty minutes as he took the "scenic route" of historic Juneau in order for me to "see the sights." I guess I should have been grateful. At Least if I had died, I would have died seeing ALL OF JUNEAU. There's a check off of my bucket list, though my annoyance and searing pain kind of dampened any sort of enjoyment of the involuntary tour. Finally, I made it to the hospital, paid my leisurely tour guide, and slunk into the door of the Emergency Room.

Fortunately for me, the doctors didn't care whether I got my Alaskan tour, they only cared that I lived to see another day. Praise God. I was very grateful for their swiftness and I was on the operating table before I could even utter fully what symptoms I was experiencing. It had been over twenty-four hours of pain at this point and delirium was setting in. I haven't eaten a full meal and my only real resting was anesthesia induced.

Sure enough, as I was going under, I felt a POP in my abdomen. I wasn't coherent enough to realize what happened because the drugs worked quickly, but when I woke up, the surgeon explained my appendix had burst right on the table. My first thought was to that obnoxious taxi driver. Had he been a little faster, I would have not experienced my appendix legitimately exploding. The other thought was to thank God that my fate was so timely. Had it popped any sooner, I would have surely died.

All I wanted at that moment was to call my mom. An almost thirty-year-old man pining for his

mommy was a little sad, but I had broken both literally and a bit spiritually. I just wanted to hear her
voice. I am not ashamed.

I couldn't stand up straight, but once I could do
a lap around the hospital floor, I went to the phone
to give my mom a ring. She said the exact opposite of
what I thought she would. I would have bet money
she would have told me to come home on the next
available jet and run into her arms. Instead, she
gave me a hearty dose of tough love mixed with her
genuine care for me. She said, "While I don't understand the way you have chosen to live your life,
Gideon, you have indeed chosen to be a world traveler
and not sit still. If anything, I respect you for your
decision. This kind of stuff comes with the territory."

It wasn't what I wanted to hear, but she knew
it was what I needed to hear.

"Just add it to the long list of adventures you
have sought out to have. Be the powerful man I know
you are, the man I raised you to be, and remember,
the silver lining of it all is that it at least cannot
happen again." She ended her thought with a
chuckle. I knew she didn't like my untraditional way
of life. She wanted me to get married and give her
grandchildren and settle in the Bay, close to her and
close to all things familiar. She was right. I do thrive
in the unfamiliar. Rougher experiences like this are
just part of the adventures. I knew calling my mom
would make everything better. I kind of wanted her

to tell me to come home. I might have if she had co-dependently endorsed my fleeting want, but she was right. I would be a coward had I chosen to abandon my calling.

Once I had received enough stitches and healed, the hospital released me. My only current predicament was that my job had sailed away days ago. Being a hairdresser on a cruise means I kind of need to be on the ship if I am to work. It's not like the cruise could have halted every passenger's plans just for one employee. So embark it did. Headed back to port and then onto Hawaii. I was supposed to continue on to Hawaii. That is still the plan and I have arrangements to board when they make port in Seattle. That is, if I can get a plane in time to make that docking.

The doctor said I was already making excellent strides and should be back to my livelier self in no time. I'm not so good at sitting still. My mother would always say that I was born with more energy than she could keep up with, which is why she never had any other children. I know that isn't why, but I do know she was worried I would never find a constructive outlet to place all of it. She was hoping for me to place my incessant energy into a family, wife, kids, career the whole shebang! As first generation immigrants from Ireland, she wanted me to have the quintessential "American Dream." However, I told her, "It's called settling down for a reason and I am in no state to settle or go down."

I am a wanderer. I flit from one place to the
next to see how adaptable I can make myself in an
unfamiliar environment. Always succeeding and never
tiring of the next adventure. To settle down sounds
like losing all the joy and vibrancy of life. It may not
be in the cards for me ever.

If I died tomorrow (or a few days ago, like I
almost did) I don't think I would regret not having
children. I would talk to God and praise him for the
gift of seeing what the world He created has to offer.
My only regret would be if I died and didn't see it all.
Corner to corner or round part to round part. As
much as I would love it if the world had clear edges,
sadly, that theory was debunked a long time ago by
the ancient Greeks. That reminds me, I need to put
Greece towards the top of my bucket list. Any place
that makes me warmer than I am now is what I
need next. Not that the cold usually bothers me, but
I am ready to feel the sun on my skin. Hawaii should
thaw me. I love the snow, but having watched it fall
from the sterile hospital room made me feel like I was
being whitewashed away. Like all the white might
consume me into the opposite of something. I guess
I'd become. . . nothing.

My biggest fear in life is being nothing. I have to
be somebody. I am Gideon Haynes. I want that name
to mean something. Someday. Maybe. Life is worth
living and living to the fullest.

Snow usually has such a gratifying magic to it. Like a memory you try to hold on to, but instantly melts away in your touch. Each flake dusts by us, kissing whatever they land on. Our eyelashes tickle under the weight of a blizzard. I can reach out and feel their gentle descent onto my skin. Each crystal is perplexing. I don't like thinking of snow as anything less than a friend.

I hope the Doc is right about me getting back to my normal self soon. I can feel the depression smothering me like a wet blanket. I gotta shake this off, and fast. I was discharged and couldn't get a flight out today, so I found a bar called the Red Dog Saloon to pass some time in. I need to feel like me again. One pitcher of beer later and I already have some friends and feel more like myself. Cheers to the next chapter.

Hawaii here I come. . .

Gideon Haynes.

4

NORTHERN CALIFORNIA

2022

"You sure you want to do this?" Jules takes my hand as I head to the security line at Sacramento International Airport. She is concerned I am not handling my dad's death so well. She is right, but that's beside the point.

When Jules came back with breakfast and saw his open journal prostrated on the floor, it intrigued her. When I told her I was going to use the journal like a map and retrace his life from it, she looked amused and then uneasy.

I have rarely set foot out of my home in the last several years, let alone taken a vacation. I don't think I can ever convince her it is a good idea that I travel alone. She knows how bad my anxiety can get when I am placed in uncomfortable situations.

My boss was surprisingly sympathetic and understood when I asked to take some time off for this. I told her it was open-ended, and she replied, "Your job will be here for you when you get back." It's not like editorial jobs are hard to find, but I like my newspaper gig.

I plan on taking at least the rest of the year to comb through every landmark I can find within these pages. Of course, they have to hire a freelancer for the time being to take over. I can hardly be surprised and I appreciate the willingness to hire me back, even though I guess I am not quitting nor am I being fired. Limbo is a weird state to be in. I just hope they don't fall in love with my stand-in.

Job security is exactly the safety net I need right now.

"I am very sure I want to do this." I added the "very sure" in response to Jules because I cannot stress enough how confident I am in my decision. She strains to hear me over the static airport announcements.

My dad never told me much about my mother after she passed and the pills he consumed took parts of him away little by little. I lost one parent rather quickly and another slowly withered away for years in front of me. Even though I spent most of my life around that man, I feel like I never truly knew him. Oddly, it makes me feel like I don't know myself. I have to follow his story to learn where I come from. Maybe I will understand why the pills took over. Like, maybe there is a good reason. I don't know. . . maybe there is a scenario out there where I can forgive him.

"I need to do this, Jules. I know I sound certifiably insane, but I swear I feel like my brain is thinking clearly for the first time in a decade. Does this make any sense at all?"

She just looks at me and says nothing, but her eyes tell me everything I need to hear. She can't relate to my grief to understand why this is so important to me. Yes, she thinks I am a loon for leaving my entire life behind on a whim to chase after a man who only exists in the past. However, she knows I will never begin to recover from my grief if I don't try.

"I understand," she finally modulates as she releases my hand and nudges me toward security. "Go."

She may not honestly understand one iota, but what she does grasp is that I need her blessing for me to feel secure enough to take the first step.

"I'll call you when I land." She doesn't need me to check in, but I like that I still have someone to check in with. When both your parents are now dead, you gain the opportunity to cherry-pick which people replace that "family" presence in your life. Jules has been like family for the past twenty-three years and I am so grateful to have her.

She watches me take my shoes off and place them in a bin on the conveyor belt before spinning on her heels slowly and waving goodbye. I know she will be here waiting for me when I return. Part of me wishes she were coming with me, but I know what lies ahead I need to do on my own.

"Miss. . . miss. . . is this your bag?"

I was watching Jules descend the escalator when the TSA attendant taps me on the shoulder. My carry-on is stuck before the rollers that lead it into the unknown scanner and I need to push it in.

"Push it through. Well done." The condescension is palpable. What is it with TSA and DMV agents? So moody. What did I do to you?

Here we go. There is no turning back now.

Of course, in reality, I could just turn around and leave,

but every step I take feels closer to the answers I am so desperately searching for and I cannot permit myself to chicken out. Like my dad said in his first journal entry, *"Life is worth living."*

"I haven't done this in a while." I nervously say to the older lady behind me. I rarely engage with strangers, but she looks kind and I could use a smidge of comfort right about now. I am so very wrong. She just simply rolls her eyes at me, clearly not in the mood to talk. Quite honestly, that one is on me for assuming a woman of a certain age would want to play the role of comforting grandma to anyone who approaches her. You know what they say about people who assume. . .

I never really understood the travel bloggers who love the atmosphere of the airport. It's grimy and there are a lot of people all anxious to get anywhere they aren't presently. It feels like cattle herding with a lot of rules and regulations and I am a lost little lamb with no clue how to do this. I haven't flown in so long that I almost forget that it's custom to take your shoes off in security. I wear sandals because it is warm in Sacramento, but I regret that decision when my bare feet touch the floor of the international airport. I can feel the germs settling in between my toes and don't want to put my sandals back on. I, of course, do, with a mental note to always wear socks when traveling, and head to my terminal just in time for boarding. Thank goodness I didn't store any liquids or weird items in my carry-on. I just packed a book, my noise-canceling headphones, and a few snacks.

It's imperative that I get better at this punctuality thing before I make travel my entire identity for the next several months of my life or I might be missing a few of my connections and spending more time in airports which instantly makes my anxiety skyrocket just thinking about it.

I honestly have no idea what is in store for me. I feel more anger than sadness. I haven't cried in a few days now; I laugh anytime I think about what happened. It's all so ridiculous to even fathom, but I have noticed that bursting out in laughter randomly startles strangers. The giggles begin to surface yet again as I find my place in line for my boarding section and I know my face is turning red from holding my breath. I try to keep the chuckles at bay.

A small tap touches my shoulder from a young man in a suit and tie who is very clearly not headed to a week-long beach vacation, but probably rather puddle jumping to LAX, which is my first layover. "Are you okay?"

Even perfect strangers can sense my rigidity in trying to hold back my inappropriate humor outburst.

"Yes, I am fine, thanks. . . just. . . nervous." I choke out in between a few laughs. It's the best, most valid excuse I can come up with. It's not a lie either. I am nervous, but not about flying. I am not anxious about air travel. I am nervous about what my life is going to look like after this year is over.

I also can't help but notice how hot he is. He very clearly works out and I can see his button-down puckering ever so slightly around his pecks. It's not an ill-fitting suit, most likely it is bespoke with how it complements his physique.

"Do you fly a lot for work purposes?" I ask as we stand in our prospective queues at the Southwest boarding poles.

"I do." His curt response doesn't give much.

"What do you do for work?" I think I might be beating a

dead horse, trying to force a conversation. Also, what a horrible phrase, "beating a dead horse."

The edges of his mouth twitch upward and I have to admit I feel a little flutter low in my stomach.

"I am a consultant for a major financial firm and I travel around the world."

"Oh consulting," I mutter, "I always thought consulting was just a fancy word for getting paid a lot to do basically nothing." I instantly wish I could put my words back. You remember that tube of toothpaste metaphor? Well, I have effectively made a minty mess.

"I'm so sorry. That's not what I meant. I mean, I didn't mean to offend." I ramble.

"It's ok." He puts a hand up gently. "You're not entirely wrong." I think I even see a hint of a smile.

"Thanks." I wait maybe five seconds before the next phrase fumbles out of me. "Hey, are you single by chance?" I can feel my cheeks heat. I don't know this person. I don't even know if I would like to be around someone who travels all the time. I know I don't look my most alluring self, donning sweats and deep eye circles. All I have to go on is that he's kinda totally hot.

"I'm not." He turns to give the agent his ticket off of his phone and heads down the jetway, leaving our conversation at that. Of course, he's not. I am completely mortified as I hand over my paper ticket, feeling less than and knowing full well the airport employee just witnessed me botch that exchange miserably. I'm just grateful she doesn't laugh at me.

I've been so out of practice around the opposite sex that

I quite brutally don't even recall how to interact with them. *Maybe I should start by downloading a dating app before I randomly ask men if they are single in cities they might not even live in.*

My entire identity has been wrapped up in my dad for so many years. I don't know how to resume any form of normalcy now that he is gone. I have no (active) job, no parents, no boyfriend, and no plans after my spontaneous (or delusional) adventure. How did *Elizabeth Gilbert* turn her delusion into *Eat, Pray, Love?*

You are heading to Alaska. Can you just chill for five seconds? It's okay to be alone. Or so I tell myself.

My inner monologue has a point. I need to step back from my life to rediscover who I am. Thank goodness my dad spent his late twenties/early thirties in such thrilling locations. The alternative could have been somewhere very far or very undesirable. Cruising with whales and glaciers sounds like a dream right about now.

I chose the cheapest flight. Of course fully booked, leaving essentially only middle seats left for those of us who are solo travelers. Not sure how I am going to stretch my finances currently, so I need to be as frugal as I can from the get-go. It's a solid mindset to be in. I slowly slip into my middle seat in between two gentlemen headed to LAX for business in their suits. Thankfully, not the gentlemen I awkwardly blushed at.

I can see the stiffness in their posture and mimic them, afraid I might wrinkle their attire if I don't adopt the position. It causes an immediate stiffness in my neck. One that hinders my ability to sip on my overpriced latte from the airport Starbucks. *Yes, I couldn't help myself buying the coffee. I know it is expensive, but caffeine is life. I will just have to make do with factoring that in. So what if caffeine makes my anxiety worse?*

Overall, the flight is pretty easy and I even get one of the "Bluetooths in a button-down" to say a few words to me right before landing. It isn't the greatest conversation by any means. I chronically over-share when I am uncomfortable. So when I tell him all about my sudden travel plans and the gruesome reason behind them, all I elicit from him is an awkward nod and a pitiful, "Oh, I'm sorry for your loss." I know that I can make people feel uneasy when I ramble. It is T.M.I. for sure, but once I start, it is incredibly difficult to stop. Even when my social radar starts sending me red flags. I can see the sympathy behind his tenseness, and it just makes me feel pathetic rather than justified. Maybe I am being impetuous and a tad bit insane. Thirty thousand feet in the air is hardly the time to start rethinking my actions.

Landing isn't difficult either. I am pleasantly surprised by how smooth everything is. The only thing turbulent is my attempt at being social, but just as I suspect, the unwilling seat buddy rushes to deplane as soon as the wheels hit the runway. I like to think that it has to do with an upcoming deadline or meeting rather than a hurriedness to escape me and my budding lunacy.

I hate layovers.

I do. I can't stand the incessant waiting just to repeat the sequence of events recently accomplished at a separate terminal. My only concerns should be about getting on one plane, landing, and arriving at my destination. One, two, done. I am overwhelmed by the sheer number of gates and finding the correct one on the correct side of the airport.

Hoping it doesn't change randomly. It feels very daunting to someone who travels very little. Finding my gate listed on the screen is a challenge in itself. Not to mention, once I finally do, I now have to know where the hell Gate C27 is and what tram or shuttle or bus I need to take to get there. Because, of course, the arrival gate is nowhere near the connecting one.

After a maze of confusion and a few wrong turns, I finally find where I need to be. A few people are kind enough to point me in the right direction, but it is merely a passing glance and then I am freaking lost again.

I need caffeine or a drink or something. Again. Should I really just be consuming liquids? Maybe food is a better idea.

I can feel my head swirling, but luckily there is a Coffee Bean right next door. I don't have to search and risk getting lost again. My need for additional caffeine intake is strong, but my fear of missing my flight is also present. I gamble it and end up buying yet another latte, knowing full well it won't calm me, but that hit of serotonin from a vanilla latte will satiate me temporarily.

Miraculously for me, the line for coffee is short and I snatch the liquid magic with little to no anxiety about yet another jaunt in the air. However, hearing the dang speaker system list off several announcements makes me jump every time. The barista with a massive septum ring assumes I am annoyed at her because I keep fidgeting until I have my coffee in hand. In hindsight, it's borderline irresponsible to add jitters to my already overloaded nervous system, but I need a fix. *Junkie.* Hopefully, my latte can help me focus on the task at hand. *Get on the plane.* I had no issues leaving Sac.

Well, duh. . . if you missed your flight in Sac, at least you would be stranded at home and not in a city you don't know.

My brain has a point. I can be logical and set the emotion aside. With every step I make, getting me closer to my first destination, I don't feel more at ease like I thought I would. Instead, I feel more and more out of my mind the closer I get.

What am I doing?

I can easily hop on the next flight back home. No harm, no foul.

Quit being a chicken and see this through.

The angel and devil on my shoulder are working overtime, and I have no idea what the right move is. Jules might be relieved if I come home and I did leave a few details of my dad's estate unresolved. . .

Before my brain catches up to my body, I find myself responding to the boarding call for the 3 p.m. flight to Alaska. Once again, I have to recite the mantra of the moment. . . *There's no turning back now.*

5

ALASKA
2022

Well, *that sure was one hell of a bumpy ride.*
Thank goodness I remembered to pack Dramamine patches. One wasn't cutting it so I put two on. One behind each ear and laid on my bed praying that the jostling would stop.

"This is your captain speaking." The speakers in my headboard chime as soon as the sun is high enough in the sky to justify a universal announcement. It still startles me out of bed like a cat dodging aluminum foil.

"Sorry about the bumps folks, we should have calmer waters from here on out." Much like an airplane announcement the speech isn't coming in that clear, but I press my ear to the headboard, crossing my fingers that I hear the words smooth, calm, still. . . anything to convince me that being tossed around like a ping-pong ball is officially over. You don't mess with the ocean! It yields to no master.

"We had to divert from our normal route and instead tucked into a nearby peninsula for a bit of a reprieve. This, however, will not affect our path and we still should call into Juneau on time tomorrow morning. Sorry for the inconvenience, and I'm certain the duration of your cruising will be smooth sailing." The static ends instantly.

Luckily, I pick up on exactly what I need to hear and collapse on the bed, still swirly and nauseated, but also craving a starchy breakfast and a cup of coffee.

I crawl out of the unmade bed and slip on my cozies, bundling up to fight the chill in the air. Even in the halls of the ship. I haven't been this cold in a while. It's been even longer since I have seen snow. Dad's cabin got it a couple of times during his duration of living there, but never much and I don't get snow even just a short distance down the hill from him. It's almost magical to watch the whips disappear into the vastness of the ocean.

I manage to pull myself out of bed just long enough to get sustenance and then meander back into my room as a shut-in until the next morning when we dock in Juneau. There is no one to talk to, no service, and I actually enjoy mindlessly watching TV under the blankets of my bed. I settle on an episode of *Gilmore Girls*. One of my comfort shows.

Much like the character Lorelai Gilmore, I too need coffee in an IV every morning. I wish I had a Luke Danes of my own. I relate to that show in a lot of ways. Except, I never had a "Rory" as my best friend and confidant. Not sure I will ever have children. The thought saddens me, like I might be running out of time.

Remember when Lorelai Gilmore says her iconic line, "I

smell snow?" I think about it every time I see the beautiful white flakes fall.

My dad was obsessed with snow. A trait he passed on to me. He had such an intrinsic relationship with the frozen flakes. As I stand where he stood and look over the vast Pacific heading to the small town of Juneau, I can feel him in every snowflake that hits my cheeks. His presence and his soul.

THE MAN WHO WALKED THE STREETS OF JUNEAU WAS NOT the man I ever had the privilege of knowing, but that doesn't mean he didn't at one time exist. Being off the ship feels nice, but my legs haven't quite caught up to me.

"It's rare to see this much snowfall this time of year." A deep and unfamiliar voice echoes from behind me.

I have been standing still in the same position for a while now. Still hypnotized by the flutters. This stranger either approaches me to be friendly or to make sure I am not frozen in place like the Tin Man.

"Oh," I say back to him. I am only being courteous in my response. I am not planning on starting a conversation.

"It's kind of magical. I stop in my tracks every time I see it. Like the snow is my old friend coming for an unexpected visit. Where are you from?" He continues.

My still swaying sea legs prove to the world that I am most definitely not an Alaskan local.

"Not from around here." My response comes across as more direct than I mean it to, but I am not exactly in a talking mood. If I learned anything from my very first plane ride, it's that I tend to gush too much to people who are merely asking for pleasantries.

Add being unpleasant in my pleasantries to things I need to work on socially.

The kind stranger simply laughs at my response. Unfazed by my rudeness.

I move my attention from the snowfall to his face. He is much younger than his voice makes him sound and, quite honestly, very attractive.

Don't ask yet another stranger if he is single. I cringe recalling how inappropriate that was.

I don't think I have ever seen eyes so blue. I have to step back a little and observe his features. I am thrown off by how much he reminds me of a younger version of my dad. Albeit a blond version.

"You look familiar," I say to excuse my strange staring. I almost want to blurt out "who's your daddy" just to rule out any possibility of an unlikely familial relation. He looks like he might be younger than I am or quite possibly the same age, which would make the possibility of him being my brother impossible. Dad couldn't have fathered anyone here in Alaska who is younger than twenty-nine.

"I get that a lot, actually. I have a face that people seem to relate to." He isn't bothered by my fixation and if I reach out to touch him, I think he might let me. "Can I help you find where you're going?"

His kindness is off-putting for some reason and I don't want a guide except that of my dad's journal.

"I am all good, thanks," I say as I start toward town. "I'll stumble across what I need to, eventually. It was nice to meet you." I wave a cursory hand gesture in his general direction without looking back at the boy in a beanie. My words are kind, but my body language is unapproachable. Even after that awkward introduction. Fortunately, the snowfall is light enough. I am not uncomfortable in my down jacket and I can still see street signs far up ahead of me.

With each step I take, I hope I am going the right way. Dad's journal spoke mostly of the hospital and a *Red Dog Saloon*. Since I don't plan on a hospital visit, I choose to see what lies behind those antique swinging doors. That is where I am headed first, but my soul feels heavier as the snow begins to stick on the ground and I press my head back with a whisper or a prayer.

"Hey Dad. I can feel you here with me. Please be my guide and show me a little piece of you I never got to know. I miss you with every flake of snow that falls to the ground. I still can't grasp that you are gone. Help me find you."

"Who you ah. . . mumbling to there?" There's that voice again.

My shoulders fall as I twitch in surprise. I thought I was alone. I want to be alone so I can feel the spirit of my dead dad, for crying out loud, but I recognize that voice now. Sure enough, the stranger from only a few minutes before is yet again standing behind me.

"Are you following me?" I don't attempt to veil the

annoyance in my tone this time. I want him to get the hint to leave me alone before I have to say it out loud.

"Hard to follow someone who has no idea where they are going." He smirks.

The wit this boy has is hard to keep up with.

I've never thought of it that way. I am following the past ramblings of a man who later in life succumbed to addiction, like a worded map in pieces of paper, and this intruder is following me. What does that say about the chain of stalking?

"I know where I am going. Just maybe not exactly how to get there and before you ask, no, I don't need help." I cut him off, holding up a finger as his mouth opens to interject.

"That's not exactly a map there." He says as he points to the leather-bound book cradled by my chest.

All I can think of is how nosy this man is and how stubborn or oblivious he must be. My hints to back off are not landing.

"Well done, detective," I say sarcastically, "no, this is not a map in the literal sense."

"Well, what is it? You are clinging on to it pretty firm."

I don't know where he gets the audacity, but I refuse to spill all my secrets to another stranger on this journey of mine.

"I don't really see how that, or anything about me for that matter, is any of your business."

Still as unfriendly as before, though this time on purpose, and he again seems unfazed.

"No problem, *Wanderlust*. I'll see you around." He says with a wink.

"Did you just give me a nickname? You don't know me?"

"Exactly, I don't know your real name yet, so yeah. . . a nickname will just have to do."

"First," I hold up my fingers in his face as I count, "I met you like thirty seconds ago. And second, you never asked for my name."

I don't know if I am impressed by his banter or appalled, but it can't require any more of my time to dissect my emotions towards an intruder. I have a journey to set out on and a bar to find. A drink wouldn't be the worst idea right now. All of which has been slowed down by this nameless, handsome nobody. In hindsight, I probably should have at least asked him which direction I should go in instead of maundering the streets in hopes of finding what I seek. No matter. I don't care for him to know my destination, anyway.

I spot a bookstore and a coffee shop on my right. They will most likely have a map of the town, or at least know the direction I should head in. And I refuse to ask the pushy person offering to show me the way because I am stubborn. Plus, nothing sounds better during a dusting of snow than a good book and something warm to sip on. The waters were calmer last night, but still a little too rough to rest well. Clearly sleep deprivation has made me moody and I need a pick me up. I can't be so dismissive to every person who crosses my path today. Alaska is large, but Juneau is not.

The cruise will depart later this evening and I have a lot of past to uncover, so I will make my stop brief.

"I'm going in there," I point to the tiny bookshop/cafe, "and I will probably not be seeing you. Have a good one."

"Toodaloo Wanderlust."

I plod off into the shop, occasionally looking back to make certain I am not being followed. Immediately, I am warmed by the fireplace and cozy atmosphere. I can't help but look back again just to see if he follows me inside, but he's gone. There is a lack of relief that surprises me.

"Could I get an almond milk latte with an added shot and no foam?" I ask the barista while placing a tip in the jar that looks like a ceramic orca whale. I saw only a few outside my deck this morning, real orca's that is. The majesty of seeing a whale in person was definitely noteworthy.

"Here you go," the barista says with a smile. She, too, is kind. Maybe everyone in Juneau is just extra engaging with tourists because they see so many.

I take my latte and peruse the bookshelves while I let my fingers and the tip of my nose warm up. One thing I did not get from my dad is his ability to be temperate in any climate. He loved the snow and the beach just the same and was comfortable in his skin in both environments. I, on the other hand, overheat with sun-sickness very easily and also freeze to death any time the temperature dips under fifty degrees. I am not a chameleon with alternating weather. I like it temperate and overcast or temperate and sunny with very little on the extremes. Hence living in California.

The bookstore is adorable and not like the large Barnes & Noble's that decorate the cities with multiple stories. I've seen closets bigger than this store and yet I want to study every shelf for the treasures they hold. The front of the store has a spinner rack of pamphlets and maps of the town, which I eagerly grab, while a table beside it has some more

sturdy books on Alaska and the history of Juneau itself. I
grab the one with the prettiest cover and review its contents
while enjoying every sip of my extra hot coffee. I am one of
those who absolutely judges books by their covers, but I also
know it's what is inside that counts. I add the history book to
the stack that is growing in my arms.

"Can I help you find anything?" A sweet older woman
asks me as I look over each display. My arms are drooping
with the weight of the books and the latte I am still savoring.

"You know, I am looking for the Red Dog Saloon and
was hoping you could point me in the right direction."

"Oh sure, honey." Her voice is smooth like warmed-up
molasses, and I find comfort in her sound. (Unlike the
woman from the airport, she comes across as a maternal
type figure.) "You are very close. It is only two blocks over to
the right of us off of S. Franklin Street."

I like her direction much more than I would have liked a
guide with the handsome stranger. Of this, I am certain.

"Are you ready to check out, hun?"

As much as I am enjoying the warmth and the coziness I
feel surrounded by books and her temperament, I know my
time is short and I haven't come all this way to just read
about Juneau. I need to experience some of it.

"Yes, thank you."

Of course, at the counter are knick-knacks and souvenirs
for impulse purchases. I grab a holographic bookmark with
an orca whale on it and then I see a stack of journals to the
side. I've been asking Dad to give me a sign he is with me all
day and this feels like it. Right on top of this stack of journals is one that is leather bound and could be a much

younger relative of the journal I now hold in my hand. I could almost hear him say audibly, *"Now it's your turn."*

"How much for the journal?" I ask as I pull it off the pile. It's the only leather one in the stack, so I am certain it is the most expensive one. Price is a moot point. I don't even hear her response. It could be a hundred dollars and I would still buy it. It's a sign from my dad. A hint that his spirit is along for the ride. Just holding it feels magical or supernatural in a sense, and I have to have it.

"Honey, are you alright?" she asks, concerned as she rings in my total.

I don't even realize a tear has fallen in my amazement over a stupid journal.

"I'm fine," I say half convincingly. "Just cold."

She places each book in a bag for me and sends me lovingly on my way. I also grabbed *Where'd You Go Bernadette by Maria Semple* for some light reading on the ship.

This stop was exactly what I needed to revive my spirits and continue on my path. The kindness from this stranger felt more like an angel than a pest, and I start toward what I now know is the correct direction of the bar that changed my dad's life in many ways.

It's just a short jaunt to the spot in question and before I know it, I am standing just under the illustrious sign. I walk through the saloon doors that swing and just barely miss my buttocks on the ricochet back, but I stop and stand still. My dad is standing right in front of me.

How can this be? Am I seeing a ghost? Am I hallucinating from exhaustion?

The vision of my father, before he was my father, is seared

into my brain. His (what I now assume must be his ghost) presents in front of me and beckons me inside as he balances a pitcher of beer on his head. He is the spitting image of my father from the early 1980s. A man with a short afro of curls tight on his head and a laugh that can hypnotize anyone into joining the party. I am under the spell of the apparition in front of me. He may as well call me over with a wave of his fingers. I haven't even had a drink yet and I am projecting the physical manifestation of a dead man. Was something slipped into my coffee? People must think I am insane, but I haven't bothered to turn around. I am still in the doorway of the saloon, just waiting for the swinging pendulum of the entry to snap me back into reality. I don't want to go back though.

Have I traveled through time? The man standing before me is confident, boisterous, the life of the party, and, most importantly. . . sober. Or at least kind of. I completely understand the irony of that thought. How could he be sober? My vision looks like he might as well be three pitchers in, but it is a different sort of intoxicated than the man I loved so tumultuously. He isn't slow and stuttering, but rather enjoyable. Flat out, I want this person to be real so badly and what's worse is I know he existed at one point in time. I just wasn't privileged enough to be a part of that chapter. The rise and fall of Gideon Haynes should have been the title of his journal, but the fall is the only part of that story that is etched on my soul.

I am clearly so desperate to study the rise that I can actually alter reality. Finally, I begin to move inside to introduce myself to the spirit when he vanishes in front of me.

What once was real is no longer present. Kind of like the greatest smack in the face to the parameters of death. Even so, my body shivers with the vision. It just felt so real. In its place is lo and behold. . . him.

"Get lost on the way in Wanderlust?" I hate how his wit is well-timed.

Why am I smiling?

"I need a drink." I don't declare it loud enough to make it a full-on declaration, but the "handsome stranger" matches my movements and meets me at the bar.

"What are you drinking?" I stare at the bartender like he is speaking any language but English.

"She'll have a Duck Fart and a Glacier Margarita." I hear the voice come up behind me and a hand presses on my lower back. A chill slowly creeps up my spine, and I don't need to turn around to know he just ordered for me.

"What the hell is a Duck Fart and why do I want to drink one?" Even if the drink is delightful, the name is incredibly off-putting. "I can also order for myself. . . thank you very much," I say with what I hope is equal wit, but I am afraid it is just coming off as bad flirting.

"Trust me, no one walks out of this bar without having a Duck Fart, and you look like you need something stronger than a beer. The Glacier Margarita is blue and matches your eyes."

"My eyes are green actually." I correct him.

"Green/blue."

Now I am not so worried about *my* bad flirting. Turns out his flirting is just as cringy as mine.

If I had my drink in front of me, I might have done a spit take of blue curaçao all over his white puffer.

"That was just about the worst line I've ever heard," I say between sputters of laughter. His eyes fixate on me in a completely neutral stare. I can't imagine he would lose at poker. He has such a good poker face. Is he hurt by my outburst? Does he agree with me? I can't tell, but I find myself getting a little self-conscious.

"Here you go." The bartender is not enthusiastic or bubbly. He doesn't need to be. He will get tips solely based on location and not customer experience. I throw a few dollars in the jar that's the shape of a bear this time and abjectly thank him while I double-fist the drinks that were ordered on my behalf. The infamous Duck Fart is a shot.

I figure my offense is enough to leave my awkward conversation behind. He will go his way and I can finally go mine, but he places that troubling hand of his at the base of my spine yet again and guides me to his table.

"Come sit with us, Wanderlust."

It doesn't sound like a demand, though it most definitely isn't a question. I know I can leave at any moment I choose, but I find myself drawn to him. Not only because his hand is guiding me. I am not used to someone taking control or calling the shots (forgive the pun). I am used to having to make every decision and taking care of myself. It is all very unsettling, and I don't trust him. Yet I follow.

"Since we can't help but interact with one another, isn't it about time I learn your name?" I have to shout, because the closer we get to the table in the center of the room, the harder it is to hear even my own debasing thoughts.

"I kind of like the mystery." He says, but doesn't even look at me. His confidence is so high I don't even feel I need to be present for him to have a conversation.

"If you don't tell me your name, I am going to have to start calling you Wander Boy."

"Wonder Boy. . . how did you come up with that?"

"I didn't say Wonder Boy! I said WANDER Boy. Don't flatter yourself too much."

He laughs at my embarrassment. I am so unbelievably annoyed at how often I find myself feeling awkward around this perfect stranger. Cute or not, I usually can hide my emotions better than this.

"Okay fine," he chuckles, "again though, how did you come up with that nickname?"

"Well. . . you call me Wanderlust so I added boy to the wander. I could call you my freaking shadow because you always seem to be wherever I am. Stalker has a nice ring to it, too."

He stops my rant with an "Okay, okay, okay. ADAM." He says a little aggressively, but it's only because the noise level is at its peak now. "My name is Adam Greene. Although I kind of like Wander Boy," he notes, looking to the side, like maybe he would put that name on a travel mug and sell them to invested tourists.

"Adam." The name rolls in my mouth and sticks on my tongue like chewing gum before blowing a bubble. "It's nice to meet you, Adam. I am Jenesis."

The shocking realization that Adam was the first man recorded on Earth in the first book of the Bible entitled

Genesis is incredibly amusing. Yet it feels like it was designed that way. Of course, his name is Adam.

"Genesis as in. . . in the beginning, God?" he asks.

"More like Genesis, the Phil Collins band, but also spelled with a J. So basically Jen, my name is Jen." I don't know why I even bothered telling him my full name. No one can wrap their heads around the fact that it is Jenesis with a J. I always introduce myself as Jen, but I guess subconsciously, I want him to make the correlation between the first man and the first book of the Bible. It's funny.

"Jen. . . hmm. . . I think I'll call you Wanderlust."

I am blushing. *Why?! It's just a freaking nickname.*

I blame the cold. My skin instantly pinks in this weather, but the body heat of a hundred people makes it anything but cold in this crowded saloon. I like the nickname. I like it all. I like him, Adam, which isn't how I felt towards him outside of this bar.

After a minute of pause, Adam breaks the silence. "So are you going to shoot that Duck Fart or what?"

There's a sentence I never thought I would hear.

"I can't in good conscience ingest something with such a foul name. I don't even know what is in it. Why is it called that?"

"Rumor has it an old lady drank it and felt it was reminiscent of that," Adam speaks rapidly and without haste. Urging me to ignore the name and shoot the three layers back.

"One. . . two. . . three. . . Down the hatch." I reply as I finally stop dissecting the drink and just go for it. I can feel the burn. The whiskey burns, but then is followed by the bitter coffee liquor and is finished off with a creamy Bailey's. Overall, it is a pleasurable experience despite the face I make in the aftermath. I am not the biggest whiskey girl.

"By the way your mouth is twisting, I assume you are not a fan." Adam seems a little disappointed that I am not jumping up for joy at the unusual combination.

I can't fault him for his assumptions. I swallow hard like I ingested gasoline. Nevertheless, the alcohol has already started to make me feel sassy. "I was about to ask for another, and also there is nothing about this that remotely resembles flatulence from a fowl."

6

FLASHBACK

2019

I hadn't been feeling like myself, taking extra long naps in the afternoons on my day off. WebMD made it sound like I a possible autoimmune disease, which I guess it could be, but I have battled anxiety since I was ten and it's taken over my life. However, it is hard to be anxious when you're not conscious.

I couldn't believe the fatigue that washed over me around eleven in the morning. It's become routine now to be alone, which is why I was surprised when I heard the doorbell ring over and over with hasty repetition. No delivery driver would be so brazen and I hadn't ordered anything lately to expect a delivery.

"Who's there?" I shouted from my bedroom, holding the only weapon I could scrounge up, which to my dismay was a coat hanger. I really should have something a little more threatening since I am a single woman who lives *alone*.

"It's Dad!" I could hear the aggression in his voice before I even saw his face. I knew his eyes would be in slits, darting from side to side. I knew he would be leaning against the doorframe because he couldn't keep his balance. I knew he would be putting all of his strength into the knock on my door, trying to, but insisting he wouldn't break it down. I knew all of this before I so much as stared through my peep-hole. As much as I didn't want to open the door, I knew if I didn't quickly, the situation would only escalate. I should have known better than to shout, giving away any hope of stealth. Now he knew that I was home and I couldn't pretend otherwise. The more I stood there, debating what to do next, the more anger would bubble under his intoxicated surface, which would make diffusing him that much more difficult.

"Open. . . the. . . door. . . Jenesis!" He enunciated every syllable.

He only cursed when he was truly in a rage. Since he didn't throw in any expletives to the sentence, my pulse slowed just enough to stop shaking. I never understood why I panicked most times I saw him. He had never actually put hands on me in his volatility, but that doesn't mean I wanted to place myself in his way to do so. He often just hit things around me. The not hitting me was almost worse. If he did hit me, I'd have a legal reason to excuse myself from his presence. I don't though. He's the only family I have left and I planned to stick it out through the hard. This was not my first encounter and it wouldn't be the last. It was like talking directly to the pills when he got like this and I dissociated my dad's person from the one taking meds. Very much like Jekyll and Hyde.

"Hey Dad, what are you doing?" I said, a little bubblier

than normal as I opened the door. Giving the facade that I was not apprehensive.

I was right on all counts. He was leaning against the frame and his eyes were barely open.

"Dad! You drove here?!" I was mortified. I expected to see a taxi or something, but no. He acted so unbelievably negligent. He could hardly stand up and yet I could see his car parked just outside my half-duplex. He barely parked it straight into the driveway.

I did not expect my dad to be hardly clothed. It wasn't exactly cold out, but he showed up at my home, which is about thirty minutes away from his, with no shirt and no shoes. He also forgot his belt and was desperately trying to hold up his baggy jeans.

"I needed to bring you candy." He mumbled out under his breath, which also had a soft hint of alcohol on it.

Oh. . . Ok. . . We're talking nonsense. Who did he think he was, Willy Wonka? Though the resemblance to Gene Wilder was uncanny, my sweet tooth did not request any candy.

"What do you mean you NEEDED to bring me candy?" I asked speculatively. "Did you bring me candy?"

My dad looked around like a kid looking for a lost sock; with very little expertise and enthusiasm. I was beyond certain that he did, in fact, not bring me candy. He had no shoes and unless a chocolate bar was stuffed in the pockets of his jeans, there was no place to hold candy.

"You are the one who asked me for candy, Jenesis! You called me asking me to rush because you needed it now." The agitation was rising.

"I did NOT, Dad. I am sorry if I gave you that impression. I am not feeling very well and the last thing I want right now is candy. Plus, it doesn't seem like you are feeling well either. You are sweaty and not wearing shoes, Dad. Did you know you aren't wearing any shoes? Not to mention, you don't have a shirt on either. I wouldn't ask you for anything at this moment." I was deep into a monologue, but very genteel in my tone so as not to trigger the monster I knew was lying dormant, waiting for any excuse to erupt like a volcano headed straight for me.

Gideon didn't respond to me. He hadn't acknowledged his lack of footwear either. The way I saw it, I had two options. I could invite him in to sleep off whatever he had taken (I couldn't pinpoint the culprit of this kind of high), or I could send him home and hope that whatever dark magic that got him to me safely would rear its nonsensical powers in the opposite direction.

"Oh, well, um. . ." His words growled into disintegration. A ramble like he was embarrassed and couldn't keep a trail of his thoughts straight. "I guess I will just go."

"Dad! You are in no condition to drive." I said as he stumbled away, back toward his car. He tripped over his dragging pant legs and bare toes. I partly watched him tiptoe over the gravel in my yard and half screamed at him. I may as well have yelled, "Don't you dare!"

He ignored me or didn't hear me. I was not sure, but I said nothing else as he slowly hobbled over to his car and slid inside the driver's seat. I said nothing as he let off the parking brake and started to roll down my driveway.

You're a coward. I thought to myself about myself. Maybe about him, too.

I had my phone in my hand the entire time. I was always ready and on alert when I was around my dad under some sort of influence. However, my fingers lifted into view and then fell back at my hips. I could have easily called 911, and alerted them of an intoxicated driver that was a harm to himself and others, but I didn't. I walked back inside and crawled under my covers, silently wondering which phone call I would receive. The one from him saying he got home safe or the one from the hospital alerting me as next of kin?

What if he did die? Wouldn't life be easier? I repulsed myself at the thought, and yet I couldn't banish it from my mind.

Fully prepared for either one, I fell back asleep, contemplating my thoughts and partially loathing myself for desiring the latter.

7

JOURNAL ENTRY
1983

J uly 4, 1983

It was a scorcher today on the island. A lot of people flew in to join in the holiday festivities, which meant a lot more customers in need of rental cars and a very busy day for me and the guys at work. It made the day go faster, but all I could think about was getting out of these khakis and hitting the beach with my boys when our shift finally ended. We didn't even head back to what we call the "stud shack" for anything. I always carry my swim shorts with me so there was no need to go home before the adventure could begin. We just piled into my small yellow Volkswagen and headed straight for the waves.

The beaches were over packed and crowded for a busy Independence Day celebration, but I know a spot off the beaten path that is usually pretty chill. I call it my secret cove. If there are people there, it is usually only a few because it is a bit of a hike to get to. Luckily, it's not near any of the touristy locations, which gives us a better shot at some choice waves.

I've been working on my tan since I got here and even the locals are starting to call me Kama'aina, which translates loosely to a Hawaiian resident, regardless of racial background. It feels like I have just joined the best club. I've always had a knack for fitting in.

My mother always refers to me as a gypsy nomad, and it's the nicest thing she has ever said to me. Not that my mother has said many unkind things to me in the past. She is my biggest supporter, even when I know she wishes I would just settle down already. My relationship with my parents is probably the ONLY thing I miss from back home. Seeing as how I am an only child, I know it pains my family that I became the rebel of the group. Coming from a traditional family, I am anything but. I don't really believe in rules. Rules are in place to be challenged and, dare I say, to be broken. Boundaries should be pushed, otherwise there are pieces of life that we miss out on. I don't want to miss out on anything life has to offer. If I were to breeze through life without experiencing anything meaningful, I think I would simply drop dead.

The minute I turned that tassel on my flat graduation cap, I was taking off as far as I could possibly go. I wanted to see something. I wanted to see everything. I packed my meager duffle and sought out any place that wasn't Alameda. The Bay Area always has such a gloom to it, so when my cabin mate in Alaska mentioned that a car rental shop he worked for on Maui would ship my car overseas for me and offer me a job, I didn't hesitate. On to the next adventure. It was an opportunity that presented itself and I wasn't in any place to turn down anything, let alone something as great as this. I chose not to chase the ship after my surgery, and the idea of staying on land somewhere warm was taunting me. I'll go back to Alaska one day.

I could already feel the tropical breeze. The company shipped my small yellow van that I love so much, and I hopped on the next jet out of Oakland Airport. I wasn't well enough after my surgery to make it in time to get on the ship in Seattle. So I flew home with a guarantee that my job would be there for me when the next sail season was upon us.

I barely had two pennies to rub together, but my buddy Allen was kind enough to lend me his living room to crash in. He already has two roommates and his girlfriend living with him, but the laid-back vibes of Hawaii are as true as people say and we all meld together nicely. It's not the Ritz, but it's good enough for a traveler like me.

We are back home now, but the party followed us

here. I am writing this from a small cushion on the floor and a sleeping bag. I have never felt more alive than I do right now. I recognize that my possessions are few and what I own is practically nothing, and yet what I have gained in life is already so much more than wealth could bring. I am twenty-nine and I want to have done so much more already, but I know I am still young and there is still time.

College was fun, but my soul's desire is to see the world. Allen says he is going to take me hang-gliding over the island soon and cliff diving shortly after. I already cannot wait and wish we were going tomorrow, but since the fourth of July is a busy time for us all at Rent-O-Car, my shifts are stacking up for a little while. Even though I occupy a very intimate space and Allen has offered me shelter for practically nothing, I still feel the need to chip in my share of the space I am taking up.

I can hear the fireworks going off all around me and the celebration ensuing as I write this. I am about to head out there because I am not about to miss out. Life is meant to be lived. Plus, Allen might drink all the beer I bought if I don't get out there soon. I also shouldn't leave Kailani all alone. Oh yeah, I have a sweetheart. She is kind of just a homegirl right now, but she is a total Betty and I plan on asking her to be my girl tonight. I act like a total ditz around her. It's mental. She is very much out of my league, but hopefully, she sees something in me.

It's all so new and I don't want anyone else stepping in her direction. She is easily the most fly babe on the entire island. I met her when Allen and I drove around in search of some tubular waves. It was like a sign from God when we pulled onto the most radical beach and there she was. It felt like my heart stopped. I had to ask her out at that moment and, much to my surprise, she agreed to have a low-key dinner with me. I took her to the private beach for a picnic and some body-surfing. She taught me a few things, but I am also a natural talent, (I say humbly.)

I've picked up body surfing pretty quickly and my friends have started to call me Gideon "The Wave" Haynes. I've always liked having nicknames. It isn't my first and it won't be my last, but when Kailani calls me honey, it's the greatest nickname of all. Turns out I am a total mush, but the guys haven't teased me much for it. Probably because every single man in Maui wishes they could be Kailani's man. Even if it's for a brief period, I am grateful that I get to hold that title in the present.

Well, it's time to go get my freak on. Talk to me later.

Gideon "The Wave" Haynes

8

MAUI
2022

Choking on air didn't seem like a possibility until I stepped off of that small jet and onto the tarmac in Maui. Dad warned about it in his journal. Though he wrote about it fondly, I find myself struggling to enjoy the gulps of air that seem hard to swallow. I went from one extreme to the next. Alaska was a blizzard of ice-cold air that bit my throat as I inhaled, but Hawaii is quite the opposite. The air here doesn't bite or sting, but it does heat as it goes down and almost expands, compressing airways and settling into lungs like wet moss.

I think I prefer it to the cold, but can't be sure just yet. That being said, the rest of my body feels wonderful. My skin is already dotted with beadlets of sweat, but instead of being uncomfortable, the humidity is symbiotic with the perspiration making me feel dewy and moisturized rather than rashy and irritated, like the dry heat at home makes me feel.

"Aloha, welcome to Maui." a beautiful native Hawaiian

woman, who looks to be around my age, wrapped in a hula skirt and simple bikini top, places a wreath of alternating plumeria flowers and yellow hibiscus over my head. A lei. Her voice is as warm as the air around us and even heavier, like molasses. So sweet. Everyone else waiting for their luggage on the carousel has one on as well. I am not special, just one of the many, but I feel special and that counts for something.

As quickly as she comes up to me, she dances her way over to the next tourist to give them the same treatment. The complimentary Mai Thai on the airplane loosened me up just enough to remind me of how good of an idea this is. Step two of my journey has begun and I have to admit to myself that I did rather enjoy part one. I still think this journey of retracing my dead dad's footsteps to better learn who he was in life is the most rational idea that has ever struck me. Others may not agree, but that's okay. They aren't me, are they?

I'm a woman traveling alone, so I booked in advance a private shuttle to take me to the resort.

"Aloha, miss." again another welcoming voice directs towards me, only this one is male. "May I take your bags?"

I don't know how I managed to pack for both Alaska and Hawaii in one suitcase, but the strain on my driver's face, as he lifts the behemoth into the back of the van, proves to me that I didn't get away with as light of a load as I had originally thought. I won't be needing the down jacket that takes up the majority of the space in my bag, but I don't tell him that. Though it would be clever,

I don't like it when I don't feel clever. I've always admired my cleverness, deeming it my most likable trait.

"You are here for a long while, yes?" My driver chortles as my luggage falls with a thump. I sit inside the car with complimentary water bottles, chilled lavender washcloths, and, most importantly, air conditioning.

"I'm here for a bit, yes," I say, knowing I am full well about to give away too much information. "and then I'm off to the next place. You see, my dad died. I sort of found him, you know. . ." I cross my eyes and make a grotesque face. Not exactly appropriate, "and I have decided to take the next year off to travel." I leave out so much, but I can tell by the scrunch on his face that I have definitely made our fifteen-minute drive to the resort awkward. With that, I figure I'll let the conversation die. Until he speaks first.

"Mourning is a beautiful journey. I do hope that the islands speak to you in your grief."

Stunned by his words and a smidge of travel exhaustion, my eyes well up against my better judgment.

"Many people come to these islands and find that they can commune with spirits that have passed. They visit in other forms, such as a mighty stingray or majestic sea turtle. These are not simply just creatures, but rather the spirits of our ancestors inhabit these beings as they travel on to the next life. Perhaps you will find your loved ones in these waters. Or if not, perhaps you will be able to find some peace."

Who knew I paid for a means of transport and the most profound therapy session I've ever attended? Believe me, there have been many.

"Thank you, Keone." I peek at the name tag on the dash. This conversation is too deep not to at least attempt to remember his name.

"Here we are, miss." The next several minutes we chat and it makes the drive feel like it only lasts a couple of seconds. I am almost sad to leave his company, but then I look out the window and see the structure before me. The marble is magnificent and the water features are mystical, looking almost as ethereal as the waters made by God. I am going to be very, very happy here. Just like he was.

Keone hands me a card as he takes my hand out of our ride.

"If you need anything miss, please call me. I will show you the island like a local."

"I may take you up on that Keone. Thank you and you can call me Jen."

If I am to be on a first-name basis with Keone, I can at least give him my name so he can stop calling me miss.

"Aloha." His tanned skin glistens as he gets back into the driver's seat and drives away. Either the island keeps you young or he can't be much older than me, but I have lost all sense of judgment here. Everyone looks no more than thirty-two.

"Aloha," I whisper back in his general direction. I may never get used to the fact that hello and goodbye are the same word here. They mean two very different things. How is this entire island not bound up in confusion? Too much aloha, I guess, which also basically stands for good vibes.

I get why Keone struggled with my bag. As I drag it to the check-in desk, I too find myself briefly out of breath. It didn't feel so heavy in Alaska. The cruise line dealt with my bags for most of the trip. I didn't have to do much dragging until now; I guess. It feels like a metaphor for my life. Everything just feels heavier as time goes on.

I hate that I ever thought Gideon's death would unburden me. What I hate even more is that a part of me is indeed more free. Living in this limbo of being broken that he is gone and also free of his chaos is the weirdest emotion, with little to no navigational system. I want a GPS for grief.

"Checking in?" The hostess behind a large bamboo desk looks like she has never been burdened by anything in her life. Not a wrinkle or enlarged pore exists on her complexion. If this is the spirit of aloha, I hope I catch some.

"Yes, last name Haynes." Her eyes continue to sparkle in rhythm with the waterfall trickling behind her. A masterpiece that has me questioning if I am indoors or outside. It is a combination of both, but it is hard to tell what is the organic landscape and what is man made amongst the plants, rocks, and multiple shallow pools. Obviously, those are tiled to reflect the vibrant blue of the ocean and the sky, but the rest is rock and natural. Orchids grow out of the gardened walls and I am certain those are real. Each one has dew drops on them like they are adorned with diamonds. Everything here sparkles.

"Yes, Miss Haynes. It looks like we have upgraded you to a suite, compliments of your friend Jules."

"What?"

I very intentionally booked the cheapest room here. Of course, Dad managed a stay at one of the ritziest resorts because he knew somebody. I want to stay here because he did, but am also on a budget.

"She left a note for you as well," she says as she hands me a printed piece of paper, like a fax or a card that goes along with flowers.

```
Hey Jen. I may not understand your
need to do this, but that doesn't mean
I don't agree. It's something you need
to do. You should at least do it in
luxury. I miss you and hope to see you
soon. I support you always.
```

My heart pinches when I finish her note. I miss her. She has always been there for me in my darkest and brightest moments. This is both a dark and a bright moment that she made even brighter. I can't imagine how much more I would enjoy this if she were beside me.

Luckily, my bag is taken up to my room for me, so the only baggage I carry now is emotional.

Wow Jules, this is way too much. I think to myself as I enter into the now fully chilled room with an ocean view. No part of me feels I deserve her generosity, but Jules has always been the one to show her love with gifts. All meaningful, this just seems like more than I can accept.

The fatigue of travel washes over me, pressing me into the bed briefly. Do I nap or do I stay busy? I will be exhausted either way. I can lay here and my mind will take me to a place of incessant thoughts and loneliness, or I can silence those by getting out of bed and feeling the feebleness in my body.

Laying in the room makes me feel lonely. My thoughts go to Jules and how much I miss her, then the reason I am here, and how much I miss him. I am tired of missing people. The point of this journey is to find people. To find the person my dad used to be and to find who I am without him. I don't have time to be missing what's not with me.

Stay present Jenesis! Go enjoy the island.

I crawl my weak body out of the most comfortable bed I have ever plopped on and throw on my little yellow bikini and floral sarong I found in my dad's dresser drawer. Why he had it I don't know, but it matches my swimsuit, so I brought it with me.

Even just a walk will do me some good. The more time I spend in the humidity, the more my body will acclimate to its weight.

I grab my seashell purse that jingles every time I walk, alerting everyone to my whereabouts, place my keycard inside, dab my face with zinc oxide, and head out the door.

What adventures await me?

I wonder.

9

FLASHBACK

2017

Red and blue lights flashed and I watched my dad get handcuffed against a cop car and placed into custody. I could see it, but I couldn't hear it. All my blood was in my ears, making it so the only audio I picked up was the swooshing against my pounding heartbeat.

This wasn't the first time I had to call the cops on Gideon, but it was the first time the result was an arrest. He could usually negotiate his way out of trouble. (A trait he had before his addictions rooted into his life.) However, this time was different. Breathalyzers don't lie and even if it had, his slurred speech was a dead giveaway that he was well over the legal limit to drive.

My heart felt like it was in my throat.

"Are you okay, miss?" The officer was attentive. I was very clearly having a panic attack. "Are you able to recall the events of tonight for us to make a formal report against your father?" It was a simple enough question. And justified. I had every right to indict my father for what had just happened. It was the furthest his aggression had ever gone. It was reckless and endangering. Yet still I felt guilty for it having to be me. I didn't want to be the one to put him in handcuffs. That's how he would see it. He did the action, but it would be my fault. The cops are the ones who arrested him for it, he'll hold it against me that I called the police in the first place. Let alone sealed his fate by filing a report.

DUI isn't something they hold you in a cell for for long and even though this was not the first time he had been behind a wheel on the verge of unconsciousness, it was his first time he got caught. First time offenders are usually released once they sober up. He'll go home and blame me for being dramatic. I'll get an earful depending on how many (and what) pills he's taken and the aggressive behavior will only continue before it ends with a heartfelt, "You know I would never hurt you, Jen," which will only leave me feeling nauseated when I begrudgingly reply, "of course Daddy, I know."

"Do I have to?" I asked the officer. His eyes tell me that he's seen others in my exact situation before. I needed help, but I was afraid of what harm the help would do.

"We can file a report without your statement, but it will be much more effective in potential future events if we have your account of the incident."

He was right. He had seen this before, knowing full well that "future events" are inevitable. If I was to have any armor to guard myself, I needed to have this as ammo.

"Gideon called earlier tonight. He was definitely on something. I could tell he had been drinking too. He was threatening to come over, saying things like he 'owned my space' and 'how dare I have the audacity to set boundaries.' Also 'do you know who you are talking to?' And 'you exist because of me, therefore your life is mine,' etc.

"I got scared, so I got in my car to go to a friend's house, but he was pulling into my driveway when I started rolling out. He tried to wave me down to stop, but I didn't. I wasn't in a public place and knew with his attitude that I needed to get somewhere populated. Somewhere with witnesses. Just for the record, he has never hit me."

I feel the need to explain this as I paint him out to be a monster.

"That was when he started to drive erratically. I would speed up to avoid him, but he would drive faster, cut me off, then break hard. It seemed like he was trying to run me off the road."

I was erratic and a lot of what I was saying wasn't conveyed the way I would have liked it to. I tried to take the emotion out of it and just stick to the facts.

"I dropped my phone by the gas pedal when I tried to dial 911, so I just kept on in the direction of the police station. It's only about ten minutes away. I don't think he was trying to harm me."

"Whether he intended to harm you or not right now is irrelevant. The fact is, he put you in harm's way and broke many laws in doing so. You did the right thing."

You did the right thing. That's not something I hear or feel often.

Most of the time I'm being told how insufficient my best effort is. What a disappointment I constantly am. Of course, I was always then met with high praise and lots of compliments. How I was the greatest blessing in Gideon's life. His angel. The pendulum swung both ways, but Gideon had no problem reminding me that I only existed because of him.

All of this turmoil and I was still more concerned about him and what the repercussions might be *for him.*

Gideon was taken into the station by the time I was done talking, and I was told that if I felt up to it, I could drive home now. Still a little shaky, but left in the dark without the squad car's lights to light up the lateness of the night, I decided I'd rather brave the streets and get home than sit in an empty parking lot.

Memories of events like this from the past often creep into my mind like a reel. Incessant and on a loop. This one was one of the worst. I wanted to escape the whirlpool. I allowed myself to cry in the car on the way home, still anxious and riddled with anxiety about what might happen next. I couldn't play any music.

In an attempt to calm myself, I told myself to get over it. And breathe. No matter what happened next. I took measures to protect myself, like locking my door and parking in my garage so he wouldn't know I was home. I'd give myself some time off. Ignore the reality of it all for just a bit. I gave myself permission to ignore him.

I called my friend to inform her I was no longer coming and to not worry about me. I apologized for the lateness of the hour, which she totally understood. Jules, duh. She knew the roller coaster it was to have an addict in the family.

Part of me thought about sleeping with one eye open. I could have waited for a text chime with an excuse for his behavior or a knock on the door. Instead, I checked my deadbolt about fifteen times. Pulling on the door each time with immense effort just to make sure. When I was satisfied that it was indeed secure and all the windows closed, I laid back down in bed, having never gotten out of my pajamas in the first place, and pulled the covers over my head. Completely shut out the entire world around me and within me until I drifted into slumber with nothing but the TV on to drown out any unwanted noise. A habit of mine I tried for years to break before giving in to the routine. It did a really good job of overruling the incessant voices in my head that refused to let me rest.

10

MAUI

2022

I am like the Grinch when his heart grows in size though for me it's my lungs growing in capacity with every breath I take in this incredible atmosphere. I rather enjoy it now. With my feet in the sand, I decide to walk along the beach, stopping at the pool bar for a cocktail mixed up in a real pineapple before setting off.

"It's called a hurricane." The bartender informs me because I just point to the pineapple another pool guest is sipping on and ask for that.

The drink itself is dangerous. I'm not even sure they put any alcohol in here. It tastes like straight juice, but I can feel each grain of sand between my toes and I am not quite sure where I left my sandals, so I guess they put *some* in here.

My mind wanders with each sip and before I know it, I am pretty far down the beach by the time my pineapple is reaching empty. Much to my luck, a snorkel shack is directly to my right and I think a little swim is just what the doctor ordered.

The hyper fixation of getting somehow into the crystalline waters is all I can dwell on. It's my only purpose. I stumble up to the small palm-covered shack. I'd say I am hiding my drunkenness well. I'm tipsy at best.

Good idea. If you lie to yourself, then absolutely no one will be able to tell the difference.

"How much for a rental?" I slur slightly. Completely ignoring the fact that I only have a key card as payment and this shack is not affiliated with the resort, so I have no way to pay.

"Jenesis?" The stranger manning the snorkel booth is handsome, but I have no idea how he knows my name.

"Am I wearing a name tag?" I look down, fumbling. More entertained that he knows my name than alarmed, which would have been my normal response if I weren't currently under the influence of some aloha with a smidgen of alcohol.

"How was that Duck Fart?"

Drunk or not, my brain puts two and two together in a flash.

"Adam?" The alarm bells blare in my mind. "Are you for real stalking me?" I am kind of scared.

"Yes." His voice is stoic. "I came all the way from Alaska to Hawaii just because I met you in a bar once. I knew you would wander down Sugar Beach and demand a snorkel. I just had to make sure I was here when you did."

"Really?" Now suddenly aware that the booze makes me sound stupid.

"No." Adam laughs amidst his sarcastic disbelief. "Are you drunk?"

His voice carries a hint of amusement. He isn't at all surprised to see me. Like the universe brings people together in all manner of crazy coincidences often.

"I am not drunk." I once again slur a bit, giving myself away despite my protests. I think I lose my footing a bit as well.

"Oh yeah, okay," he basically snorts out a laugh. I may be drunk, but I have enough social awareness to see he doesn't believe a word coming out of my mouth.

"If you're not stalking me, then how do you explain how you're here?" I can hear my arrogance, but cannot stop my words from falling from my inebriated self. "Are you also not real?" I whisper loudly.

Adam bypasses my hallucinogenic confession that I sometimes see a ghost.

"You think very highly of yourself, huh?" He poses it as a question, though it doesn't translate as such. I don't have a response.

"When the season in Alaska is over, I follow the ship to Hawaii, where I work here for a bit. Then I take some time off to travel a little for myself and then I head back to Alaska. It's not a bad gig. . . for a nomad."

I knew he seemed familiar and now I know why. He outlined my dad's agenda from the early 1980s. He is the ghost. I want away from this person immediately. I can turn and walk away, but instead, I double down.

"So how much for a snorkel? You know. . . since you work here and all." I say all too flirtatiously. The drink giving me courage I don't normally possess.

"If you think I am letting you anywhere near that water

in your condition, you are more out of your mind than I thought."

"I am a paying customer and you are not my keeper." Then I remember I don't have a way to pay him unless he accepts an empty pineapple husk or a random resort key card.

Adam notices my futile reach for any form of currency.

"Oh, you're a paying customer, you say?"

"You know what?" I say a bit mightier than I have a leg to stand on.

"No, I don't. What?" He's baiting me. Teasing me with a smile stitched onto his face.

"I don't need a snorkel. I'll just go for a dip without one!" With my declaration, I spin on my heels and head for the waves. Slowly leaving my sarong and a few belongings behind on the sand. I don't need or ask for an audience, but I can feel Adam's eyes searing into the back of my head. I am challenging him. Curious to see what he will do. Either he will come after me or I will achieve my goal of feeling the blue waters kiss my skin, which is all I've wanted since before our unforeseen reunion.

"Like hell you will!" Adam shouts as he tears after me. I just reach the edge of sand and water when I hear him running behind me. The sand feels stickier, like weights to my ankles, but the water is as magical as I imagine. Lapping my skin as I brave into it further. Calling my name like a siren song. My balance is almost nonexistent and with one more step I can feel myself beginning to fall, but every plod of wading into the ocean balances me with the way my body begins to float. Weightless in the teal blue. It's what I imagine heaven must feel like.

Adam reaches me mid-wade. His arms lasso around my waist, causing me to stumble, splashing us completely, full bodies into the ocean.

"What are you thinking?" I exclaim, now frustrated. My hair is sopping and stuck to my forehead.

"I could ask you the same thing." Adam retorts in a fit of hysterics. Still holding me up above the waves with one brawny arm, while the other aids me in moving the hair and saltwater out of my face and eyes.

"You made me fall!" I shout, sounding pretty angry. Maybe I am angry. So what if the ocean claimed me? Why is it his responsibility to protect me?

"You have got to be kidding me, right?"

"Um no. You made me fall. Facts are facts. The evidence shows. I am all wet!"

"At least you are wearing a swimsuit." He snickers out between sputters of salt water escaping his mouth.

I'm serious, but coy. "Let go of me" His body is still glued to mine. I am almost floating in his arms, my body beating against his chest with every wave that crests us towards the shore. I can feel every muscle through his now wet shirt and it warms me in places I didn't think I still had feeling.

"Do you know how to ask nicely?" He says, still wrapped around me. Hindering me from escaping. In my desire to push away from his now wet and almost bare chest, I look up to see him staring me in the eyes as if all our surroundings are inferior to my face. Impossible in this atmosphere, but it makes my breath blow cold.

"This is not the moment we kiss and fall in love, Adam," I say as I push him off of me.

"Sure," he laughs as he releases me and allows me to trudge to the shore. "Will you at least tell me when that moment is? So I can be prepared for it." He is reveling in the sarcasm. Laughing with every uneasy step I take as my body weight begins to return to my ligaments. "For the record, I rarely share a first kiss with women who aren't sober."

"Don't hold your breath," I scoff, breathless. "I don't fall in love."

"No? You just fall into the ocean then?"

"Ugh!" I audibly explode.

Part of me is mad at myself. If I wasn't interested in flirting, I would have just left when I recognized him at the shack. Part of it feels good. Like exercising a muscle that atrophied a long time ago. I can't even remember the last time I even contemplated flirting. Not a relationship. Those were too difficult to maintain with how integrated in Gideon's chaos I had become, but flirting, I now realize, also disappeared. Sad people can't flirt, or at least don't flirt well. This could mean two things:

1. I am becoming less sad, which is miraculous on many counts. . .

2. I am sad and flirting badly, but it doesn't seem like Adam minds if it is, so. . .

I stand quickly from our drenched sandy entanglement

and feel all the vertigo from my drink rush to my head. The world grows blurry and is hard to grasp onto as it fades into darkness. For a blip, all I can see are the palms around the shack and Adam's hands as he grasps my waist to stabilize me. Acting as a savior or a shadow. I can feel that now familiar rush to my skin where his hands pressed into my sides. Every touch leaves a slight singe as it moves up my back to brace me. What is my body saying that my brain isn't translating?

"Woah, you okay there?" Still sarcastically said, but there is a slight twinge of concern in Adam's inflection.

"Yesssss," I assure him with an elongated lisp of my s. My fingers reach to my temples. "Just a head rush."

"Mmmhmmm." I could almost taste his disbelief. "Let's get you back to your hotel, shall we." Again, not a question and as much as I want to hide the effects of the hurricane on me, I can't feign how I am slowly drifting into definitely drunk territory.

"What do they put in the drinks over here because they are str. . . strong?" I may as well have hiccuped.

"Well, you went with the heavy hitter on what I am assuming is an empty stomach. What do you say to some food, Jenny?" Adam, calling me Jenny, feels all too familiar. Like it has been on his tongue for years. Truth is, only Dad called me Jenny. Save maybe once or twice by random strangers who more than likely misheard my real name. I like it. It feels comforting.

"I can't eat at the hotel?"

"Are you telling me there's no food at the resort? How will you gain sustenance?" Gosh, he never lets up on the sarcasm.

"They do, but it's pricey," I say as I rub my fingers together. "What do the locals eat around here, anyway? I've had a big day and I am not sure I can stomach Spam and eggs just yet?" The thought of the unknown meat and foreign food customs, along with the alcohol sloshing in my stomach, makes me gag.

Adam had assumed correctly. My stomach is beyond empty, having only had a bag of airplane pretzels and a cookie to satiate me during my day of traveling.

"Hey!" Adam acts all offended. "Don't be hating on Spam and eggs. Don't let any locals hear you hating on their island delicacy either. It's quite tasty. A staple around here." My face gives away that he is not going to convince me right now to try anything out of my comfort zone. "But for today, we can stick with a burger and fries. I know a place."

"I'm sure you do." I sneer. Mocking him on his obvious social charisma. Not sure how I am still walking, but I do notice the arm I am hanging onto for dear life. "Are you asking me out?"

"Pretty sure you invited yourself."

I am definitely drunk now. "You have really soft arm hair." And with that statement, all barriers and filters fade with all my other inhibitions.

"Okay, Wanderlust, save your energy until we get you fed."

Ah, there it is. The nickname he gave me back in Alaska when we thought we would never cross each other's paths again. I don't believe in fate. I am going to let him help me sober up. Maybe buy me a burger and then I am out of his life for good. No more chance snorkel meetups or shots in snowy bars. I am sure there is another rental shack on this beach that I can use if I ever get to wade out into the water more than a few feet.

We aren't at the beach anymore, but somehow I have my sarong back and Adam is dry in a clean snorkel shack tee-shirt. There seems to be one thing missing from my belongings that I just recall as he places me in his car.

"Wait, my pineapple!"

"Leave it Wanderlust. She belongs to the sea." I think I hear him giggle.

"Your ego! You must find yourself very amusing?" I come across as annoyed by my outspoken thoughts.

"I do, thank you."

"That isn't a compliment." I huff.

"No? Sure seems like one to me." I see a grin creep across his face, exposing straight white teeth. Obviously he had braces as a kid.

"I don't usually get in cars with strangers when I am drunk."

"Ha! I told you, you were drunk." He exclaims like he has just been proven right. I guess he has. "And don't worry about it, Jenny. You and I aren't strangers anymore."

"So which one is it, Jenny or Wanderlust?" My snark softens just a bit as we pull out of the mostly empty parking lot.

"Who says you can't be both? It depends on what mood you're in."

"What mood am I in? It seems more like you call me whatever name matches your varying range of sarcastic criticism." I say back. I guess a little coquettish with my lowered inhibitions.

"I never criticize. They are just observations." Adam says with a more serious tone, but the smile still spreads across his face, like butter on a bagel. I catch myself looking too long.

"Oh, yeah. . . well, what do you *observe* about me?" I'm not sure I want to know what an outside perspective has to say about my exterior in either a physical or a mental capacity.

"You'll just have to stick around to see."

11

FLASHBACK

2003

"Hey, Jen?" I heard the whisper that stirred me from my slumber. I hadn't been asleep for long.

"Daddy?" Although I had only been asleep for about half an hour, my voice was raspy from hitting rem. Sleep as a child came quickly and deeply. "What's wrong Daddy?" I was concerned that being woken up in the middle of the night was a bad thing, but as my night light illuminated part of his sharp features, my anxiety eased when I noticed his cheeky grin.

"Want to go to Neverland?" He asked with as much excitement as a young boy. Not unlike Peter Pan himself.

"What do you mean?" My body perked up as I sat back against my bed frame. Dad and I had been reading Peter Pan together before falling asleep. I loved when he would read to me. I could go anywhere in the world, real or not, and never leave the comfort of my covers.

"We already read our chapter for the night." I wasn't

sure what he meant. I could transport my mind to Neverland any time he opened the book. *James M. Barry* would be so pleased his work is still so magical in the lives of others to this day. That's the true magic of books. Dad and I always said that when I grew up, maybe we could write a book together someday. A book of all our adventures. I was his Wendy Darling.

"I mean, do you *really* want to go to Neverland? For real."

I couldn't believe my ears. Was it all a dream? Should I have asked him to pinch me just to be certain?

"How?" I asked with more glimmer in my eyes than ever before. It's contagious. Both of us were simply giddy with childhood imagination. It forced its way between us. In and out and all around us like pixie dust. With one happy thought, we might fly into the air.

"I just had a chat with Peter Pan and he said that Neverland is looking to recruit its very first lost girl." Girls were never allowed on the island except for Wendy. Or so Dad told me, but I was to be the very first lost girl in Peter Pan's band of miscreants. Or at least that was the news my prepubescent self was woken up for.

"You mean it!" There was no more sleepiness left in my body. I pleaded with every single cell to come to life with this incredible news.

"Now there are some rules before we go." I was all ears and eager to obey. "Peter Pan has never let a lost girl come into his home, so you'll need to put this over your head so no one can see you." I took from his hands a sheer pillowcase to place over my head and did so without question. I could still see shapes and shadows. I could still "see."

"And we will need to get you there safely, so Peter Pan has already put some pixie dust on this board. You will sit on it and fly to Neverland with me and your Uncle Max."

"Ello, darling." I could hear my Uncle Max's welcoming British accent come into my room. My dad's best friend from London had arrived earlier that day. I loved him so much that calling him uncle was more fitting than any blood relative. He was Uncle Max from the start.

"Uncle Max!" I exclaimed through the pillowcase. "We are going to Neverland!"

"I know darling." I loved when he called me that. Made me feel extra special. It is Wendy's last name, after all. "Let's get going."

Without hesitation, I sprang from my bed and hopped on a wooden plank my dad had assured me had already been enchanted. I felt them climb onto the plank as well with a thud, and off we went into the night. To Neverland.

I could hear sounds of Neverland and lights of color flash before my eyes. I recognized the pirate ship song from the iconic Disney Cartoon. Even Peter Pan's voice, "here we gooooo," sent us off into flight. I could feel the spray of water as we flew over the mermaid lagoon and the air grew colder when we passed Skull Rock. Pixie dust sprinkled all around me, and I could feel it between my fingers. I snuck a peek under the pillowcase and sure enough, the sparkles stuck to my hands in pure glittering magic. There was no hoax. I was flying in and around Neverland. I could see it all, even with my face covered by the pillow casing. I couldn't let Peter Pan get in trouble for bringing a new girl to the island, the second star to the right, so I was good and kept my coverings on the entire time.

It felt like we had been gone for hours. The night must have continued on without us. Dad and Uncle Max landed first. They had been to Neverland before; they said. Originally lost boys who decided to grow up. Though looking back, neither one of them ever really lost that boyishness about them.

We landed softly, but I heard someone slide through the gravel driveway before flying off. His shadow gave it all away. It was him. It was Peter. He thanked us all for visiting and wished me happy thoughts before he flew off again with his Peter Pan crow. It was finally safe to slide my blindfold off. There it was. A skid in the gravel where Peter had landed. Did I see his shadow not too far behind? Had the pillowcase really blinded me, though? I felt like I saw it all. Like the magic had seeped into my skin and my vision.

"Well, honey, you just went to Neverland. How do you feel?" Dad asked with still the same grin on his face. The clearest I had seen in a long time.

My words failed me as I yawned with exhaustion, but he knew exactly how I felt.

"It was pure magic, Daddy." That was all I could say with the yawn still in my throat.

"Let's get you to bed, baby girl."

I was certain the night was over with. We had been gone for so long, but when I looked at the clock, only a few minutes had passed from when he had woken me. Could all this be real? For a moment, my childlike brain chalked it up to my imagination. That what I experienced couldn't have occurred. I made it up. I must have, but as my family tucked me back into bed, I looked back on the events and the proof that had been undeniable. I couldn't doubt myself. I knew it was real. And just like that, Tinker Bell flew to my window, illuminated by a brilliant gold as she fluttered around outside. Tinker Bell had come to say goodnight and my youthful eyes didn't see the string. All I knew then was that my daddy made life magical.

12

MAUI

2022

"This might just be the best burger I have ever eaten." I very un-lady-like talk with my mouth open. Juice dribbles down my chin as I bite into the teriyaki pineapple beef in a sweet and sticky bun. I am certain the food and drink over here are far superior to anywhere else in the world. All of it has such vibrancy and brightness. The flavors all make my taste buds sing. A pineapple back home can be sour and bitter, but over here they drip gold in color and taste. The sweetness is unmatched.

Juices run down my hands, soiling the plate underneath as I inhale the meal in front of me. The starches swell my belly and curb the wooziness of earlier. And yet I am completely fine with how I must look to Adam. The pit in my stomach that was left from the cocktail is slowly starting to find reprieve. I also have an entire boat of sweet potato fries all to myself, which might be helping the most. I am a slut for any french fry.

Every time Adam reaches his hand over to sneak one, I swat him away. Maybe it's playful or maybe I just come across like a ravenous bear fresh out of hibernation. It is dangerous to have fingers near my food. I may have accidentally bitten him and not in a fun way. I snarl at him. To be fair to myself, it is the first proper meal I have eaten in over twenty-four hours. Airplane snacks do not count as part of a balanced breakfast. Not that a burger and fries are the equivalent of a high-nutrient meal, but it is a ton more protein than my stomach has encountered in days.

"Slow down there Wanderlust, I can't save you from drowning and choking all in the same day."

I swear everything that comes out of his mouth he punctuates with a snicker.

"Why is everything so funny to you?" I ask, either in annoyance or endearment. It's hard to tell what I feel when I am around Adam.

"Not everything is funny to me, Jenny. However, I do feel like life should be met with joy and laughter, so why not find amusement in as much as we can?"

This is the second time I have witnessed him be this serious, so I know he can be. The first time was when he told me I could be both Jenny and Wanderlust. As I sober up, I think I get it. When Adam is being real with me, he calls me Jenny, and when he is being flirty or sarcastic, I am Wanderlust.

"No offense, but you look like you haven't smiled or laughed in years." Adam inspects my face as if he were looking for something specific, something sad.

"You know when people say 'no offense' before starting

their thought, it is always a dead giveaway that what they are about to say is, in fact, *offensive*. You're just covering your own skin in case I do get offended by your statement. That way you can say, 'I said no offense' and wash your hands of it." I use my hands for air quotes more times than I ever had in one sentence. Emphasizing just how ludicrous the precursor "no offense," really is.

In fact, I'm not offended. I haven't laughed in years. I have contemplated botox even. It's painfully obvious on my face. That's the only part that has me saddened. I thought I was hiding my hurt well. If a complete stranger can read it all over my face, then I am not concealing my feelings as well as I had hoped.

"You're right." I place my burger down and dab the sauce from the corner of my mouth. I don't know why I suddenly feel the need to be polite. "I haven't had a reason to laugh in a long time." My face falls.

"I'm sorry, Jenny, I didn't mean to upset you." Adam reaches his hand across the rickety table in the small island bistro and brushes the back of his hand to the back of mine.

"No, just possibly offend me."

His touch is so tender and genuine, but then the thought enters my head that my hands are covered in food, so maybe he is just trying to show sincerity without actually having to hold my greasy fingers.

I'm wrong. He brushes the back of my hand several times before grabbing it. His thumb rubbing into my palm. It is more amorous than I believe he intends it to be. Though it isn't necessarily romantic, my brain can't differentiate. He is just really, really kind.

I stare into his eyes. His skin has darkened since Alaska and his olive tone seems to soak up the sun's rays and glisten back a reflection of its warmth. His eyes are crystal blue. Just as blue as the glaciers in Alaska and the Pacific Ocean here. I can understand how he seems to meld into both places. So different in landscape and climate, but his features adapt beautifully to both. It is like his entire makeup doesn't belong in one place, but the planet as a whole is where his home resides. His forearms and nose are dotted with freckles, like a map of the places he's seen and the hours he has spent basking in the outdoors. I find myself jealous. I don't feel like I particularly fit in anywhere and here is this beautiful man who has an entire body of evidence that he never takes a single moment of life for granted.

Even when he looks at me with such empathy, his eyes still shine the most brilliant hue. His hair looks lighter than it did in Alaska, but I imagine that is only because his skin is darker now. It still is a dirty shade of blond. I spy a few highlights, but those as well look like they have been born from the sun. Everything about him resembles being at peace. Peace with oneself and one's surroundings. I find myself wishing it to be contagious. Maybe I can siphon some of his tranquility and regain some of the composure I lost long ago.

My eyes dart from his features to his hand, still caressing mine. I almost don't notice his other hand reaching for a fry.

"You sneak!" I shout as he jabs the fried potato into his mouth.

"Oh, come on!" he laughs with his mouth full. "It was just too easy."

I grab the dipping sauces that are between us and hide them on my side so he can't quite reach. "What ya going to do now?" I dare him to battle me for them.

"Excuse me?" He sticks his arm out and gently nabs the attention of the server nearby. "Could I get another house dipping sauce when you get a second?" He pauses for a moment. "And another basket of fries, please."

"You cheat!" I laugh. A whole-hearted kind of laugh. This game is fun and I haven't let myself have fun with anyone like this even in my childhood years. This must have been what it would feel like. . . to be childish and free.

"You can laugh." Adam notices and smiles. "I like your laugh, Jenny."

I let out a deep breath. The kind that comes from deep inside you and with it a weight I have been carrying for so long seems to expel. I didn't realize I was punishing myself by refusing to see any joy in the mess my life slowly turned into.

When did it end? When did all the enjoyment of my life seem to stop? I feel like it was sucked out of me, leaving me an empty sarcophagus. The feeling of fulfillment with just one little ounce of amusement has revived me in a way I didn't know I needed. It wasn't like joy waved goodbye and announced its departure. I just stopped noticing its absence, completely content with the hole I placed myself into. As much as I'd like to blame Gideon, he didn't shove me into it. I willingly jumped in with both feet, trying to cling to the concept of family as much as I could. He may have moved the ladder, making it harder to get out, but I could have escaped my prison at any moment. I put myself there and then let myself be miserable. I'm not an addict, but I was allowing my entire world to be dictated by someone who was. I was on the carousel of chaos right alongside him. He, the conductor, and I the willing passenger. I kept telling myself I wanted more, but I couldn't even muster up enough change to laugh at the small things. To laugh at myself on occasion.

My small laugh turns into a fit of hysterics. Nothing said was quite that funny, but I haven't laughed (or slept) in so long that it all tries to make up for lost time. I can't inhale. I am laughing so hard.

"What's so funny?" Adam asks, laughing alongside me like a contagion.

"Nothing. . ." I still can't stop. "It just feels good, is all."

All I want to do from here on out is play and laugh and feel joy. What is just simply a conversation and food for Adam is a pivotal moment in my existence for me.

I will never place myself in darkness again. I vow.

I might still be drunk. Nothing else explains my unabashed vulnerability when I am in the same vicinity as Adam. My walls are down and it feels freeing. I know myself. Only inebriation would allow for this to feel so comfortable.

"Eh, Bruddah!" a voice echoes from behind me and a man, a staggering six foot five at least, towers behind me with his hands on the back of my seat. He gives a new definition to the phrase, tall, dark, and handsome. "Long time, Adam. How long are you back on this end of the Pacific, man?"

"Hey, Zeke! Yeah man, I'm back for a bit before the

breeze takes me away, but you know me, I always loop back." Adam is so confident when he speaks.

"I never understood your nomadic existence. I am an island man; never can tempt me to leave."

I have yet to be introduced, but Zeke is by far the tallest human I have ever seen, and my body twists in my chair to strain and look up at his face rather than just his chest. He's even leaning on my chair for support and I still cannot meet his face. His skin smells of salt water and coconut sunscreen. I imagine he has seen his way around a wave or two.

"We are hitting the morning surf tomorrow. You're welcome to join us."

I love it when I am right. My guess is barely even a question before Zeke confirms it by inviting Adam surfing. I didn't, however, know Adam could surf.

"I'll let you know." I swear Adam winks at Zeke.

"Hey girl, I'm Zeke. How you doing?" I think he might have been watching one too many episodes of *FRIENDS*. He sounds exactly like *Joey Tribbiani*. Zeke takes this opportunity to leave the backside of my head and come into view by sitting in the empty chair next to us. His face is stunning. There's a darkness to his skin like perfectly tempered chocolate. One of the most beautiful humans I have ever laid eyes on. Every inch of him glimmering. Like the opposite coloring of *Edward Cullen*, but the same sparkle.

"Hi, I'm Jenesis."

"Oh cool, as 'in the beginning God?'" He laughs but shakes my hand with familiarity. Same thing, Adam asked.

"Yeah, that and as in 'Phil Collins.'" Everyone always gets a kick out of that little detail, and Zeke is no exception.

"Way cool, sis."

Zeke has just called Adam "bruddah," I know they defi-
nitely aren't related, but I quite enjoyed being called "sis."
There is a sense of familial camaraderie here on the island.
I guess everyone here is family.

"Bring your girl tomorrow. She looks like she could use
some waves."

"I'm not (*She's not*) his (*my*) girl." Both Adam and I echo
at the same time. Different pitches, same point we want to
make clear. Neither one of us belongs to the other.

Also, apparently, every man I have come across in the
last few days has an opinion about something "I need." I
need laughter, I need a cocktail, I need to relax, I need to
surf. Not sure I am a fan of men telling me what "I need."

For the first time since Zeke's arrival, there is a moment
of silence where no one has anything to say after the
awkwardness of our outcry. Zeke just simpers like it is only a
matter of time before all of that changes.

"Invites are always open. Just holla." Zeke says to both
of us before he saunters off to the counter for his order
pickup with a Shaka.

He is a whirlwind. A sea breeze that almost knocks you
off your feet, but cools you off at the same time. I like him.

Adam seems to ponder his invite and brushes the
crumbs off his fingers before deciding where to lead the
conversation next. I interject his thought process with my
ideas as I mimic his de-crumbing process. Only I use a
napkin.

"Where do we go next?" My question surprises Adam.
His eyebrows raise, leaving a white spot where the sunburn

on his forehead stretches. I'm a little surprised by my question myself. I originally thought I'd call it an early night, but what do I have to lose? I'll waste a day having some fun. Potentially see a bit of the island. Maybe it's not a waste of time and Adam doesn't seem to be in a hurry to get back to the snorkel shack.

"Oh. . . um. . ." Adam's eyes dart from side to side. Not in a way of avoidance, but in a way like he is diving deep into his mind to figure out where the best place to go next is. In an instant, his face lights up. A mischievous grin creeps slowly. If I didn't feel so safe with him, I'd think it was nefarious. I mean, he saved me once already today. Or so he believes.

"I know the perfect place, but you are going to need different shoes."

13

JOURNAL ENTRY

1983

D

ecember 24, 1983

    Christmas on the Island is so unlike any holiday I ever spent back home. Where I would usually down a few mugs of hot buttered rum and watch the snow fall out my window while the fireplace crackles, I have now learned how to string twinkle lights on my front yard palm tree all while wearing Santa Claus board shorts. I have the whole getup. A fake white beard, which in no way matches my dark tight curls, but I have to give off the Santa look somehow. I covered my curls with a hat. I also have a shirt that says Mele Kalikimaka. Santa's on a surfboard and looks like he's enjoying his island holiday.

    I too am enjoying my holiday in the sun even though my body is begging for winter weather. On occasion, I swear I can feel a chill from the north and I know there are places on these islands where people can go to ski. I just haven't ventured there yet. My roommates are making a traditional feast in order to bring some nostalgia into the small hut. It smells incredible. Roasted honey ham and mashed potatoes and gravy. It's a trick of the senses because Kailani is slicing up papaya and pineapple for a bit of a fruit salad on the side. There was none of that back at home, but I am happy to accept a new tradition. She is everything. Still can't believe she chose to be with a goober like me. I am one lucky guy.

If it would only snow, the magic of this entire experience would be unbeatable. I'll take her to the snow someday. I mean the real snow. The kind that piles up until it's so tall you can walk directly onto the roof from the ground. She won't know what to do with herself having lived on the island her entire life. I don't think a down jacket will be enough to warm her, but I will one day show her the beauty of a white Christmas. Maybe in Tahoe where I taught ski lessons. I can teach her to glide on the powder at my old stomping grounds. Show her a bit of Gideon pre-Kailani.

Speaking of White Christmas, Rosemary Clooney is blaring in the background as we all get ready to shuffle into the "dining room" for a Christmas Eve dinner. It really isn't a dining room. It's the living room that we moved the cots out of and put a fold-up table in the center. Kailani was kind enough to let us borrow a tablecloth, from the hotel she works at, to try and class it up a little bit.

The hut is a bit overcrowded. Five of us in a three bedroom. Two of us on the floor in the living room. I happen to be one of the sorry suckers who didn't nab a bedroom. Allen swore we could rotate each season, but I got here in the summer and now it's winter and I am still on a pad next to the front door. I can't complain, though. The rent is cheap and I'm able to save my money for my adventures and spoiling my girl.

The holiday practices aren't so different here when I think about it. We have a tree that we decorated. It's small. Charlie Brown would be proud we saved it, but it still makes the season magical. We all made ornaments to place on its rather pathetic branches, but it screams Christmas. Mine's a hodge-podge picture of Bob Cratchit placed on a wood plank. It's kind of heavy, but it's okay. There are a few presents under the tree. One very special one in particular, but Kailani is unsuspecting. I placed it in the middle of the branches and didn't put a name on it. It'll be the last gift she opens tomorrow.

The only other person I told was my mom. She's so excited that I found someone to settle down with. I told her that's not what we are doing. We both talk about seeing the world, not rooting in one place. I know my mom hopes we come back to the Bay Area and start pumping out kids, but I assured her that is far from the game plan.

Buying that tiny diamond caused a hit to my savings, but she is worth even more sparkle than what I could afford. I expect we will stay on Maui for a bit until I can beef up my savings to travel. My rental car gig isn't so bad and Kailani makes decent money as a maid. She wants to be a surfing instructor full-time and I plan on making that happen for her at some point. Surfing instructor during the summer, world-traveler the rest of the year. Sounds ideal to me.

This is quickly turning into the best Christmas of my life. I close my eyes and listen to the warm rain pitter-patter onto the roof, and it's all I can do not to run out into it pretending it's snowflakes on the sand. A sand angel is a thing, right? I'd look ridiculous, but I am ridiculous. I am a man in love. Men in love do stupid things like run out into rainstorms and ask the woman they have only been seeing for half a year to marry them. When you know, you know.

Allen has all but worn out the vinyl record to the Beach Boys Christmas album, but I will say that pineapple goes down smoother with Mike Love more than Bing Crosby.

I wonder if I can send Mama a pineapple for Christmas? I think it is a marvelous new tradition. One she would be honored to adopt. Her Christmas gift this year is a new daughter in-law and it's more valuable to her than anything I could have bought for her. Even though last year she loved the knit sweater with Alaska across the front. Or so she said. This she likes more, even though it doesn't come with wrapping paper.

And speaking of new traditions. . . Allen is overall a crazy man and even in December we went out scuba diving earlier this evening. It was something Allen was adamant about, and since the sun was out, I wasn't keen to argue. However, we were out there for a while and as soon as we docked (after dark I might add) I was cold and ready to get back to Kailani, who, by the way, has been cooking all day. I just got my wetsuit off when Allen yelled at me that he and his buddy were going back out and I was to join them, no questions asked. I balked. Was he kidding? We had just spent what seemed like hours in the ocean and I was cold and wet and ready to celebrate Christmas with my girl.

All he said was, "If you don't put that suit back on and join us, you will regret it for the rest of your life." Allen doesn't have a flair for the dramatics so I was inclined to listen.

So what did I do? I put that cold damp suit back on, albeit with much struggle, and got back in the waves. He also may have taunted me to "earn my nickname." It's hard for me to back down from a challenge. I am Gideon "The Wave" Haynes.

When I said he wasn't exaggerating, he wasn't

exaggerating. It didn't take long before the water lit up with blue magic. I mean, it was bioluminescent plankton, but it was blue magic. With every glide of my hand, little bursts of underwater fireworks went off. They clung to my skin and illuminated the shoreline off in the distance. It felt like a sign from the heavens. It felt like maybe the heavens fell into the ocean; I don't know, but it didn't feel a part of this world. If it weren't for Kailani, I would have stayed in the water all night long to watch the waves sparkle. When it comes to little traditions, this one is high on my list. Though maybe I will just send Mama a pineapple.

I miss Mama. That's the hardest part of being so far away during Christmas. I want her to meet Kailani more than anything. Home is many places for me, but my mother has been where my heart has felt at home for so many years. Hawaii feels a lot like that. Or rather, Kailani feels a lot like that. She makes me feel like anywhere can be home. She is now where my heart resides.

So Merry Christmas. As Tiny Tim said, "God bless us, everyone."

Mele Kalikimaka! See you on the surf and in the magic blue waters.

Gideon "The Wave" Haynes.

14

MAUI
2022

"Where is this magical secret place you are taking me?" I ask Adam as we hike up a fairly muddy trail lined with wild orchids and random streams. The journey to wherever we are going takes my breath away. I feel like Adam is trying to tell me that it isn't about the destination, but the journey there that matters.

The more time I spend around him, the more I think he is wiser than the average man still in the prime of his life. I don't know how old he is exactly. He looks 24, but by the demeanor of his behavior and stories of his travels, he has to be older. I'm 29 and I can't imagine he is older than me. For someone who lives outside, the sun has not aged him, or at least not yet. His skin is still soft, with only a few lines that crease around his eyes and mouth.

"How old are you, Adam?" I ask as we navigate a rather dicey part of the trail. Adam had us stop at a store before hitting the trail so I could buy a better pair of hiking shoes.

Or rather, he bought them for me, but I promised to reimburse him the second I have my wallet and phone back. I'll make him download Venmo if I have to. If he hasn't already.

They aren't the boots I would use to hike in the foothills of California, but they are grippy and waterproof. My sandals, (which were indeed found), would have been a disaster in the slick mud. I make a conscious effort not to slip too much. This is not an invitation for him to hold me. Again.

"How old do you think I am, Wanderlust?" I kind of hate how everything I ask is met with a question back at me. Can he ever just answer a simple question?

"I don't know. . . um. . . twenty-four?" My guess makes him sputter, choking on a swig of water he takes at an inopportune moment.

"Are you serious?" his question comes out offended, but his smile says otherwise. Not sure if Adam could be offended. "I'm thirty-two."

We both laugh at the discrepancy. "No way," is all I can muster to say.

"Mother Nature has been kind to me, I guess."

Obviously!

"Well, the two of you seem to have a symbiotic relationship, so that doesn't surprise me at all."

Adam looks pleased by my compliment. I probably couldn't have given him higher praise. He looks young and fits in with the world around him. I'm jealous. I don't dare ask him how old he thinks I am. If I already look like I haven't laughed in years, then my age must reflect that negatively. If Adam is indeed in his thirties, like he says, then he also knows better than to ask any woman their age.

I step cautiously around boulders and breathe in the purified air. So much foliage around me makes me fantasize I'm in a remote jungle, making my way through Survivor.

"So, you never answered my question," I reiterate to the back of Adam's head as I fall into step behind him. "Where is it you are taking me?"

"To Neverland." His answer is so matter-of-fact. He cannot know what that means to me; the significance of that fictional place. I had learned Neverland wasn't an actual place shortly after my adventures with Dad and Uncle Max. I never had the heart to tell him that part of the magic died, but here I am again with someone telling me that Neverland exists and I am headed there now. A lost girl.

"Wait really?" I sound so silly. Of course not. The Neverland written in the timeless novel was made up in the psyche of a brilliant man with a mind of magic. However, my face says otherwise. My eyes bug out, wide and open, and something in my voice causes Adam to turn around and face me.

"You'll see," is all he says in return, but he reaches his hand back for me to take. I do and we walk hand in hand as the trail widens for both of us to fit side by side. His hand is warm and much bigger than mine. If hands could hug, that is what mine in his feels like. You know how sometimes fingers don't fit nicely together? It's too tight or awkward or just not a good fit. This is nothing like that. It is like my hand is meant for his.

"How much farther?" I ask in anticipation. Adam has

no clue what the symbolism Neverland has in my life, but I want to know the meaning it has in his.

"It's just a little farther." He reassures me.

Thank goodness. Not only do I have anxiety to see this magical place, but I also am starting to feel the aching in my feet and wobbly ankles. Truthfully, it is amazing my pronated self hasn't broken a shin yet.

The jungle becomes more and more dense as we travel forward making it almost impossible to walk without the dew drops from large leaves wetting your arms as you pass by. Like the plants are giving gentle kisses on our skin as we trek onward. No longer are we in stride side by side. When it feels like it can't get any narrower, that's when the clearing opens into Neverland. Truly Neverland.

Mist brushes against my face as we enter into the backside of a majestic waterfall. A staggering seventy-five feet tall. Not the tallest in Hawaii by far, but the tallest I have ever seen in person. My hands reach out to touch the water spraying into us. I am already dewy from the hike, but the stickiness my skin holds from the humidity is slowly washing away.

We went from hot and gummy to a swift change in temperature. The air is now cool. Goosebumps rise on my flesh from the immediate difference, but like a moth drawn to a flame, I cannot stop my face from turning towards the spray. Droplets make their home on my eyelashes, making everything blurry. I'm wrapped in a romantic haze, though the only romantic feelings I carry are towards the landscape itself. I honestly forget Adam is standing next to me, watching me take it all in rather than absorb the natural masterpiece himself. He must have been here time and time again, but how could he not gasp at its beauty every single time?

"I don't think I could ever tire of a place like this," I say, mouth still agape.

"Welcome to Neverland." Adam uses the palm of his hand to scratch the stubble subtly growing around his chin.

Heat leaves my body, except for my eyes, which burn with the promise of tears to fall.

I wish you could see this, Dad.

"It really is Neverland." I choke a bit on the words. And a slightly grown Peter Pan brought me here.

Watching the waterfall hit the pool below is like being in the mermaid lagoon straight out of the Disney movie. The way the light reflects off the ripples is like watching fairies leave pixie dust behind.

In my childhood, I was blindfolded so that I could not see the strings my dad and uncle were pulling, like puppet masters, creating magic for an imaginative child. It's like getting déjà vu or like walking into my past imaginations. I've traveled back in time.

This is what I saw all those years ago as I desperately tried to see through the sheerness of the pillowcase.

Looking down at my body is the only proof I have that I am no longer adolescent. The body of a woman stares back at me in the reflection of the water and I am grounded in that much of reality, at least. The rest is off into a fictional world. One where I can experience magic again and wash away the ache of grief. I add to the ripples in the streams as a singular hot tear falls below me. The rest I wipe away quickly.

There is literally no reason to cry.

I've been telling myself this a lot lately. Unaware if I actually buy into my internal narrative or if I am just so tired of trying to hold back tears, I will tell myself anything to make it stop. I don't even know who I am crying for. I didn't shed this many tears for him while he was alive, nor for myself. So who is the benefactor of these tears, really? It's best to dam them up all together.

Adam doesn't see me wipe away my emotions or if he does, he doesn't draw attention to it. Rather, I see him in my peripherals kicking off his shoes and shirt before swan-diving into the golden waters.

"Come swim, Jenny. It's one of the closest sensations to flying a person can have. There is just one rule." His voice is serious as his arms wade back and forth to tread the deep water.

"And what might that be?" My arms cross. I want to vet what rule he has before I join him. Luckily, I am still in my bikini from earlier, so this isn't some sort of skinny-dipping situation.

"You have to let go of the thoughts that hurt you and only think happy ones."

My arms uncross immediately. He has read my mind as if I journaled it all down for him.

"Can you do that?" He asks timidly, like he knows I haven't allowed myself a happy thought in a long time and doesn't want me to strain a muscle or something.

I don't answer. Instead, I kick off my new shoes and dip

one toe in at a time. Confirmation that I can let my nega-
tivity go, even if only for a brief moment of floating. One
portion of my body at a time slides into the water. First my
feet, then my knees, then I pause because the water is chilly
and feels like small needles brushing against my skin now
turning red, not from the sun, but from the bite of the cold.
I let the pain settle for a moment and then I dive, ignoring
all sensibility and plunging forward. Adam is right. I feel like
I'm flying and can only imagine the magic of this natural
spring under the starlight. It must be the same as flying
among the stars because as clouds wisp by, I feel just that.

The usually talkative Adam is simply letting me breathe
it all in. All the healing swirling around me in these waters.
Every once in a while I can see his shape out of the corners
of my eyes, but he knows he isn't what has captivated me
and I think he brought me here knowing that. A time-lapse
spins around me. What feels like five minutes is in reality
more like an hour and I have the prunes on my fingertips to
prove it. I feel soggy. The sun is beginning to set, and the sky
is lit up with the colors of a childhood ice cream sorbet.
Pink and orange decorate the sky. Small hues of blue/green
streak the sky that I haven't let my eyes fall from since. The
only movement has been the occasional dip into the edge of
the waterfall.

I do this once more and brace myself on some rocks
against the powerful force of the water as it hits me. Nothing
will stop it from entering the water below. It forges its path,
undeterred by anything in its way. I want to feel like that. I
want to feel powerful within my destiny, blazing a future for
myself that has some magic to it. However, for now, I just

want to let its influence wash over me, like showering in a pressure washer. Maybe it will strip away all the pain and confusion.

A tap on my shoulder wakes me from the best daydream I have ever had. Not sure what Adam has been doing this entire time. He's acted more like a shadow, but just like when I was a child, time seems to stand still.

"Wanna go watch the sunset?" he asks louder than usual for my ears to hear over the drum of the waterfall. I nod emphatically so as not to strain my voice. My hand cradles in his as we wade out of the water. I have gotten so used to its chill that now the outside air feels even colder. Adam doesn't release my hand but hands me my shoes and leads me barefoot up a path away from the comforts of the bath left behind. I have a feeling I will miss it but also know that the place we are walking to will be warm and spectacular. Hawaii has delivered nothing less.

Just as the plant life tries to consume us, so it releases us onto an open cliff side just as quickly. If I wasn't flying before, I am one hundred percent flying now. The sunset is all around me. I can taste the pink in the air as the sun begins its rest in the ocean for a nice nap. Ducking into the horizon, I am able to witness the changing of colors go from bright to hazy. I can't guarantee I see it, but a flash of green right before the sun vanishes from sight seems to flare where the sky meets the sea.

Adam pulls me in closer to him, his arm clutching my waist. None of his touches toe the line of discomfort. More like a steady guide, leading me to what I need to witness.

Silent with his words, but expressive in what was unnecessary to be verbalized.

I wish so much that the green flash was Dad's soul reviving. A way for the man who wrote in the journal all those years ago to stand before me and tell me where it all went so tragically wrong. A way for the aged version to whisper how sorry he is for ever hurting me and even more so for completely shattering me in his death, leaving me to figure out how to cope with the loss of hope. What could have been, never will be. Not even his ghost could stand before me and right the wrongs, but losing all the opportunity for that to even be a fantasy is the hardest reality to bear. More so than any loaded and painful incident wrought.

I can see him in the sunset; Can feel his spirit finally uninhabited by the suffering. It's the first moment since it all happened that I finally feel some peace. Not even the tears turn on. A weight lifts from my chest that I am certain will return, but I accept the moment as the gift it is.

"We should probably head back." Adam looks up at the sky and then back at me, knowing full well we already have stayed too long to avoid walking back into darkness. I feel grateful that he allowed me to stay in this moment for as long as we did.

I nod and his hand moves from my waist to lead us back. Like a habit, I accept his instigation to lead me onward.

15

MAUI

2022

Last night, I slept better than I ever have in my entire life. Turns out the best remedy for an aching soul is salt water and a sunset. Adam must have known this somehow and brought me into the medicine. I can't say that I feel fine now, but there is a miraculous difference between grief with a good night's sleep and grief with sleep deprivation.

I wake up just as the sun is peeking over the horizon. The morning is still hazy. Dawn emerges as a paradoxical blend of darkness and light, where the fading night casts lingering shadows while the first rays of the sun delicately paint the world with a pale luminescence.

I never wake up for the sunrise. I have seen almost every sunset of my lifetime, but I can count on one hand the amount of sunrises. Had I known they could be this beautiful, I might have made a point to become more of a morning person. My anxiety ramps up in the night. So I watch every sunset in anticipation of the darkness and what that feels like. This is the only place where the sunset hasn't brought extreme panic.

The hotel room is stocked with a small espresso pod machine and instead of opting to put on appropriate outing attire and head to the lobby for a proper latte, I decide to make do with a little cuppa from the room. I don't want to miss a single moment of the sunrise that is rapidly warming the sky.

With a yank, the sliding door opens to the heat of the day like a solid wall between the humidity and the air-conditioned room I leave behind. I keep it ajar behind me, knowing full well that it will change the perfectly tuned thermostat and I will have to finagle the dials again like a mad scientist trying to reconfigure the perfect living conditions. It feels too good to care too much. I take my short espresso, which is in desperate need of vanilla syrup and some cream, to my balcony and breathe in the silence.

It isn't really silent. My mind just is. The birds are all awake and the waves crash onto the shore. The world is alive, but what's silent are my incessant thoughts and feelings I haven't been able to shut up. My anxiety born out of everyday life seems to wash away and I find myself wanting to pull out my phone and research how to move here permanently.

Maybe I can ask Adam for a referral and work on a cruise ship with him. Not sure what I would do on the ship seeing as I am a writer, but the thought brings even more heat to my face and I catch myself pressing my palm into my cheeks to hide it. Not one soul is around to see me blush, but I don't even want myself to witness such a visceral reaction.

I like him, that much is obvious. I think he is a strange and curious man who shows me amazing natural pools and takes me to waterfalls, but do I fancy him in a romantic sense? The jury is still out on that. He makes me feel more alive than I have in years. What does that translate to?

The small bench on my balcony provides the perfect VIP seating for a front-row view to the beginning of a new day. A clean slate and I can't help but wonder if Dad had found a way to sobriety, maybe we would have shared more moments like this. I used to dream that we could travel just the two of us and share special moments. We could have marveled at the majesty of the surrounding creation together. He probably would have enjoyed the hotel room coffee, whereas I am struggling to choke it down. The heat from the styrofoam cup makes me feel even hotter and he would have poked fun at the fact that I don't drink any black coffee ever.

Once again, I can manifest his ghost before me. Sitting in the seat next to me. He is again his younger self and I become the ghost to this apparition. He doesn't turn to look at me, doesn't reach out to touch and I just observe as he heads to the edge of the balcony. A deep sigh expels from his spirit as he takes in the very last few seconds of the sunrise. All at once, he looks at me and smiles. The sun, now blinding my vision, engulfs him in the light. I want so badly to follow him. To find the person, I never knew in the peace of the beyond.

A knock on my hotel door brings me back to reality,

shaking off any ghosts I might have envisioned, including the one I made of myself. A quick knock again alerts me. Why would an employee of the hotel be knocking so early? Did I miss some sort of alarm? I am not meant to checkout for a few more days. It's barely 6:30 in the morning.

I've learned from previous mistakes not to announce myself before checking the peephole. If I am quiet enough, I can feign absence.

Still in my pajamas, the knocking persists, though gentle. I choke down the anxiety that creeps in. *This is not a repeat of the past.*

Adam's head is distorted through the hole in my door. It looks a million times bigger than it is with his eyes large and longing. I am transfixed by how adorable the new proportions make him look. Without giving a thought to my attire, I open the door to a very normal and well-proportioned Adam.

"What are you doing here? It's barely morning." I find myself grateful I have been awake for a while. My body has had time to settle into an energetic rhythm rather than the haggard way I usually climb out of bed. My voice is clear and free of all gravel, making it apparent I am annoyed by the early intrusion, but I was not disturbed from slumber.

"Get your swimsuit on Wanderlust," he smirks, handing me a venti-something warm in a cup. "We are going surfing."

I don't question him. He never poses his wants as questions. This is a statement. I am going surfing and, quite honestly, I don't want to waste valuable time pretending to argue about the interruption to my morning. Truthfully, I am thrilled, and after my ghostly morning kind of shook me, I am ready for another one of Adam's nature distractions.

I spin on my heels, not sure if I am anticipating Adam to come in or stay in the hall. When the door begins to close, his hand catches it before he even makes the decision. I get the impression that he wants to be invited in before just welcoming himself into my room.

"You can come in if you'd like." There it is. The invitation. "I'll just be a minute," I say as I grab my swimsuit and head to the bathroom.

"We're meeting Zeke and a couple of others," Adam shouts towards the bathroom door. "So it won't just be us today."

Not sure why he feels the need to tell me this, but I am grateful to be behind the door so he can't see the shade of disappointment come across my face.

"Oh, so you mean, this isn't our second date?" I sarcastically shout back through the door while I finagle my bikini straps into place.

"Our *second* date?" Adam responds questioningly and I become immediately flushed with embarrassment. I was trying to be coy, but maybe through the door, it's harder to detect a joke.

"I'm just kidding."

"Believe me, if yesterday had been a date, I would have tried to kiss you at the end of it."

I can almost feel Adam touching the door as he whispers it through. I take a moment and stare at myself in the mirror. It's taken me longer to put on my swimsuit because it is still damp from yesterday and the bottoms stick to my thighs as I try to slide them up. Thank goodness he can't see me. My entire body is flushed with unease. I can't pass it off as too much sun.

Something has changed in our conversation. We both were so snarky yesterday and played off each other with sarcastic jabs. It was like that in Alaska, too. Maybe he isn't much of a morning person either, but even in his laissez-faire demeanor, there is an essence of seriousness when he talks about trying to kiss me at the end of a date. Part of me wants to know what that would feel like. Before I get too caught up in thinking whether his kiss would be cool or warm across my mouth and how his cupid's bow might feel brushing my skin, I exit the bathroom, ironically less dressed than I was before entering.

"I don't think this is going to be the best thing to surf in." I envision my top popping off with a wave and drifting off to sea. I imagine Adam is thinking the same thing.

"Don't worry, I brought you these." Adam smiles as he hands me a woven bamboo bag with a wetsuit inside. I hadn't noticed it before, but simultaneously he hands me the bag and the coffee he has been holding for me.

"Thank you." I'm polite as I cautiously sip the latte. A small "mmmm" escapes my lips like a moan. It might be the most delicious coffee I have ever tasted. Not surprised. Everything about Hawaii is the best thing I've ever immersed myself in.

"It's a macadamia nut milk latte. You won't find macadamias like this anywhere else," Adam says, proud to have guessed a beverage that elicited such a response.

"You must spoil all the girls like this?" I nod to the wetsuit while raising the cup to my lips to take another sip.

The wetsuit clearly is not Adam's. It is a woman's cut and far too small to get over his calf muscles even if he tried. Of course, he would have a girl's wetsuit in his possession. I'm sure he lets all the girls he takes around the island use it. I am probably one of the many falling for the same routine he plays out every season he is in Hawaii.

"All the girls?" Adam seems confused until it clicks in his head that I am asking him in a non-direct way if I am being played.

"I don't care. I'm just curious." It's always a dead give-away that someone cares when they preface a thought by announcing they don't care. I hate myself for being so transparent.

"The wetsuit is my sister's." Adam doesn't laugh this time. "She leaves it here for when she comes to visit me. She doesn't have a lot of water sports where she lives in the desert."

"Oh." is all I can muster. I feel bad for assuming and very clearly offending him.

"As for the latte, it's my personal favorite, so I thought I'd take a gamble, see how you like it. Evidently, I made a good assumption." He points to the beverage, now almost half drunk. It's a brilliant cover for how shameful I feel.

"You don't have to defend yourself to me." I am desperate for this conversation to end and go back to the version of Adam that makes everything in life feel light-hearted.

"I do," he crosses his arms. "I have to tell you that I have never taken another living soul to Neverland. It's been my secret hiding place for three years now. I stumbled upon it when I got lost one day. I go there when I need to feel grounded. It seemed like you needed that as well."

"Is that supposed to make me feel special?" The words come out a lot harsher than I intend. I'm uncomfortable with the admission. As much as I don't want to be one of the many, I prefer it to being singled out. I can't handle his attention focused solely on me.

"Yeah Jenny, it is supposed to make you feel special. You are special. So just accept it." Adam's arms uncross and a laugh slips from an open-mouthed smile. "So go put on that wetsuit and let's get you in the water. Come on, the guys are waiting for us."

16

MAUI
2022

The Beach Boys' songs make surfing sound like it is the greatest pastime in the universe. Let me just preface by saying I am so glad that every state doesn't have an ocean for "Surfin' USA." Being pummeled by water repeatedly is starting to feel personal, like the ocean is laughing at how hard this girl is going to try to ride a wave. So much for hoping that Gideon "The Wave" Haynes would be a genetic trait. A part of me daydreams I look like *Anne Marie* in *Blue Crush*. It sucks to say that I am no *Kate Bosworth*, much to my chagrin. Not sure why I thought I'd be pro-level on my first go around, but I at least thought I'd be able to stay on the board.

Paddling out to catch a wave has my lungs on fire, only to get knocked off and have my lungs fill with stinging salt water. Every inch of my body is sore and my eyes are blazing red from desperately trying to see through sea spray.

Zeke and the rest of Adam's surfing buddies are kind. It's obvious that every single member of their group does this often and possibly have been surfing since infancy. I stand out like a neon crayon in a box of baby blue and can only imagine how much I am holding everyone back.

Why did Adam bring me out here? When Zeke invited us both, he was probably just being nice or had no idea I'd only set foot in the ocean a handful of times and never once on a surfboard.

"I'm sorry." I sputter out to Adam as he paddles up next to me.

"The ocean isn't exactly taking it easy on you."

"That's the understatement of the century." I spew salt water as Adam gives me a hand up onto my board. Luckily, the safety strap is still looped tightly around my ankle.

"Why don't we give your board a break, she's been through an ordeal this morning," Adam slaps the shallow water on the surface of my surfboard almost like he's petting a racehorse who just had a brutal training session and needs a good wipe down and a rest. "You can surf with me for a while."

Adam is playing it off like my board is just having an off day, when we both know the unspoken truth that I just suck at surfing. I can't even say I am not that bad for my first try. I am *that* bad.

"Tandem surfing?" I ask with as much skepticism as I should have approached surfing in the first place. "Is that going to be any easier?" One eyebrow raises so high it might get stuck in my hairline.

"Probably not," Adam snickers, "but if we can find a good rhythm, we might be able to ride at least one wave before we convene for lunch."

Lunch. *Ah*, lunch sounds so good right now. The

macadamia nut milk latte was delicious, but not satiating enough to tide me over without a true and proper breakfast. I find myself daydreaming about that burger I had yesterday, then nervous this group will want the Spam and eggs that Adam is adamant I will like if I try.

"Maybe I should just cut my losses and head back." I remember I still have the number of the driver from the hotel and theoretically could hitch a ride back to the resort with him.

"Where's your sense of triumph, Wanderlust?" Adam looks at me with eyes that make me feel like I don't have a choice in the matter. "Are you going to let the ocean win this one?"

Once again, Adam puts the answer in the question itself. What is there to say? *Yes, I will let the ocean win this one. I am tired and a coward and just done.*

I can already see the look on his face and I don't like it. It shouldn't matter what he thinks, and yet still I find myself not wanting to let him down. I also imagine going back to the resort and looking at myself in the mirror. Who do I want to be staring back at me? A girl who tried and gave up or a girl who kept going despite the adversity in front of her. Bruises and all.

My mind flashes to Gideon. Metaphorically speaking, he was faced with his own ocean. Beaten down over and over again, but he got tired and released the victory he could have had to the conditions of his surroundings. Even if this is a small win, I have to choose to take it. I know too well how it all snowballs, and it's a far cry from losing a battle with addiction, but if I can surf at least one wave, then maybe I can stave off the rest of the battles I will soon face for a short period.

As if my thoughts are on display, I start to hear a chant of the seven friends bobbing up and down in the motions of the ocean, "JEN-A-SIS. . . JEN-A-SIS. . . JEN-A-SIS. . ." Each syllable of my name emphasized like a valiant march. A chorus almost louder than the waves themselves, cheering me on. Or at the very least, begging me to try.

"Okay." I drawl out with a smile and all seven of my new friends erupt in a symphony of jubilance. Adam leads me back to shore where we drop my board and I hop onto his.

"Kneel on the front and paddle." I listen to Adam's instructions, so fearful of more humiliation, of sending both of us into the tumultuous waves. I can feel the heat of his breath behind me as he pants in the exertion of paddling for two. Even with my help. The rhythm of his breathing is distracting, but in a good way. His torrid inhales and exhales are like a meditation, and I focus on what I need to do to conquer this next wave.

We dip under the water together and the sudden loss of oxygen jostles me into a minor panic. Suspended in peace under the loud surface, Adam places one hand on the side of the board to maintain control and one on the small of my back. The pressure in his touch grounding me beneath the waves and guiding me back to the surface. I did it and it feels incredible. The burst of air as we break from the water makes the oxygen taste different. It is sweeter, almost as if I have earned it. Adam promptly removes his hand from my back and spins us around to face the beach.

"Here we go." he sings out, "I want you to paddle like your life depends on it when I say go. Then when I yell to stand, don't hesitate."

I wish I had thought to pull my hair back in a ponytail. Strands of my brown locks are continuously blocking my face. Adam's entire body is directly behind me, bracing me into an upright position. "Oh, and try to find your center of gravity. One foot forward, one foot back. If you lean too far to the front, we fall and if you fall back into me, I might like it, but we will also fall."

"I'm going to try," I say as more of a reassurance to myself.

You are going to give this wave all that you have!

"PADDLE!" Adam shouts, and I don't dare look back at the wave that is inevitably chasing us. Taunting me and hoping I succumb to its prowess.

My shoulders sting from the friction of trying to pull the water to propel us forward, but I refuse to be defeated despite the pain. Adam's doing most of the work. I can imagine the strain in his biceps with every stroke and wish I could look back for just a moment to witness his battle with the water as he fights to get us on top of it.

"STAND UP!" another command from Adam. "DON'T HESITATE!" His tone is firm, but not angry. He knows what needs to be done to succeed. I listen and the whole world goes silent around me as I find my center of gravity. One foot forward, one foot back. I wobble for a moment as my back foot brushes with Adam, knowing full well I am inches away from sending us into the water now rushing below our feet.

"Lean in with it." Adam places both hands on my waist and, though I know he is shouting to be heard, it comes across as a whisper. His hands push into my sides, directing me which way to lean like steering a horse with your feet in the saddle. Right, left, balance.

"WOOOHOOOO!" I can hear Zeke and the others cheering for us as they all watch from their own rides.

I am completely free at this moment. Unburdened by all that held me down before. I catch myself staring at the heavens.

Look at me, Daddy. I'm doing it.

Just like I did as a child. Wanting his validation and praise for my accomplishments.

I wish you could see this.

Wishing and praying I could hear his voice, I may have leaned my head a bit too far back. I am spatially unaware as to how close Adam is holding me from behind. All my sensations are honed in on his hands. I don't notice his head is mere inches from mine.

As I tilt back to stare into the cloudless sky, I go back a little too far and jut my head into the bottom of Adam's lip, thrusting his head back and releasing his grip on my body. Subsequently, we spiral into the base of the wave we had just dominated together.

The last thing I hear before submerging is a cacophony of "OOOOOH." A surge of sympathetic cries as I send both Adam and myself soaring into the tide.

I am able to pull myself up for air when Adam is calling out for me. I don't have an ankle strap tethering me to the board, but fortunately, we had ridden most of the wave. We are close enough to the shallow that I can find the surface without being tossed around in a tumbler.

"Jenny!"

Adam makes it back onto the board while I still expel salt water from my nostrils and mouth. His arms scoop me up from my armpits and effortlessly pull me to sit on the board, which luckily still looks in good condition. The same cannot be said for his mouth, though. Now that we are face to face, I can see the stream of blood turning pink in the mix of seawater and his now plump split lip.

"Oh my gosh, Adam, I am so, so sorry."

Out of instinct, I reach out to touch the wound. I wish that I could heal it with a touch, or if I'm being honest, if I had a wish, I would wish to go back in time and not daydream about speaking to the dead. The moment called for all my attention, and I couldn't remain present.

My thumb brushes over the cut and Adam winces slightly. I'm sure the salt on my fingers stings. I use my hands to cup my face, hiding from his line of sight. If I could evaporate into the sea mist, I would.

"I'm sorry." I sob, muffled, behind my hands.

Adam pulls my hands away, but I still refuse to look at him.

"Jenny." His voice is soft as he holds my hands in his to keep them off my face.

I pry one eye open, hoping humor might diffuse how horrible I feel. *Laughter is the best medicine. Maybe if I can make him laugh.*

My thoughts are interrupted by his torn pucker pressing

against my mouth. It is only a peck, but it stuns me into silence. The redness in my face deepens.

"My lips still work, Wanderlust, so don't worry about it too much." The shock on my face causes an outburst from Adam. A deeper laugh than I have heard from him. Just a single laugh.

I, however, don't laugh, just brush my fingers across my lips and turn around to begin paddling to shore.

"You did it. I am so proud of you." I had to make sure that was Adam speaking. It sounded like something I would hallucinate the ghost to say. "You conquered your fear and triumphed. Not a lot of people can say that they have done that."

"I wasn't afraid, I was just tired of failing," I mumble, not looking back, even though Adam is complimenting me.

"That too then," He says as he continues to paddle to shore. Now, without my assistance. "You didn't give up. It's commendable."

All I can think about now is how to get him to stop saying nice things to me, why he kissed me, and when we are going to eat because at this point I can't tell what's dizziness from hunger or dizziness from the kiss.

I say nothing else about the kiss for the duration of the float back. A brigade of people he knows and I don't welcome us. Some have faces of cheer and some are sympathetic since they watched us eat it pretty hard out there. I don't know if I feel like I accomplished anything. I accomplished making a fool of myself. I accomplished, splitting Adams's lip open. That's going to leave a pretty good bruise. And I accomplished not drowning, I guess.

I could stand on the board for a grand total of a minute before I befuddled it all with my literal colossal head. And then there's Adam, doing all the work to get us ashore and still complimenting me on my efforts. I know I have a hard time accepting things that are good for me. Telling myself I don't deserve things is a trait I know I possess, but this doesn't feel like one of those self-deprecating moments. I don't feel like I earned any of his praise and would give anything for him to just shut up.

The brigade is waiting for us when we finally come ashore. I can feel my weight grow heavier and heavier like someone pulled the drain from the bathtub and now I can feel all my muscles. All the soreness reverberates through me and I know it's only going to get worse. Quite honestly, this isn't the exciting surfing experience I had set such a high expectation for. I can hear my therapist now. *Expectations are premeditated resentments.* Adam set the bar so high yesterday, I guess I thought today would be no different. It isn't Adam's fault. The whole day has had everything needed to be perfect. The sunrise, the coffee, the sand, and the surf. All of which equates idyllic. I get in my own way. I know that.

"Who's down for some 'ono grinds'?" Zeke asks as he shoots all of us a Shaka sign. I can't be certain I know what that means, but since everyone is nodding their heads emphatically, I assume it is something good. Frankly, I am assuming it's food.

Part of me wants to beg Adam to take me back to the hotel. Another part of me wants to stick around and try to save face with how poorly I surfed.

No one cares. Everyone has been rather unbothered by

my presence here. I'm mostly just in my head about it all. I'm waiting for anyone, Adam, Zeke, or the other six people whose names I didn't get to make a snide comment and put me down, but no one does.

"Well, that was a disaster," I say with a chortle. I guess if no one is going to be the one to say it, I will.

"Nah, Sis, the waves can be mean the first time around. You are a wahine now, you know." Zeke is through and through the traditional Hawaiian I envisioned. He reminds me a lot of that cook in that *Adam Sandler* movie, *Fifty Firsts Dates*. He's just as tall and talks the same, only he is a lot more muscular in stature.

I look at Adam with my eyes bulging, begging him to help me decode what a wahine is.

"Female surfer." Adam mouths at me.

"Ah, okay. Thanks." I retort back to Zeke.

"Some say wahine, some say gurfer. The point is, you are one with the ocean now." Zeke uses his large hands to do the wave.

"Oh, I absolutely feel one with the ocean. I have sand in every single part of me. I'm also pretty sure I have swallowed enough salt water to replace the other liquids in my body completely." I use my blistered fingers to trace over my body. "I'm part mermaid at this point."

"Well, then we better get you better acquainted with the land before you pop out a few gills and start craving seaweed." Zeke is poking fun, but all it makes me think about is how much I would kill for some sushi right about now. Almost on cue, my stomach growls so loud, the fish start poking their heads out to see what on earth made that ridiculous sound.

"On that note," Zeke starts as he points to my stomach, "who's ready for Spam and eggs?"

I try so hard to hide the disgust on my face, knowing full well I should heed Adam's warning and not offend a local. Adam covers his face to hide his Cheshire Cat grin.

17

FLASHBACK

2001

After Mom died, Dad and I didn't really do a lot together anymore. I watched as he used bottle after bottle of both liquid and pills to assuage his mountain of grief. I'm sure he never planned on being a single dad and the loss of my mother wasn't something his heart prepared for. It was fairly quick and unexpected. The cancer came out of nowhere. She was bright and vibrant one day and then she got a bad headache. When it didn't go away for a week, Dad made her go to the doctor. Turns out the tumor had weaved its way into becoming inoperable. She was gone six weeks later. Withered away like sand in a dust storm.

Now, I don't believe that every addict has to have a tragedy trigger their excessive consumption, but in my dad's case, this was true. Some have an injury and just can't get off the painkillers. My dad injured his heart. It was irreparable, and Western medicine hasn't developed an opiate for a broken heart. At least not one patented, but that was how my dad used his newfound saviors, sought out in the form of a mind-numbing pill. A swig here and there was just an added bonus. After decades of altering his mind, that was how he began to understand reality. The lack of a high became more unreal to him than a sober mind.

That being said. It took some time to get to that point. In the beginning, there were only days, rather than long stretches of time, where Dad was inebriated to the point of not being able to care for me. It wasn't like a light switch turned on and off. It was more like a train on a one-way track; starting slow and then ramping up speed, all leading to a singular destination.

I remember, a few years after mom had passed, Dad told me we were going to go somewhere fun. "Get out of the house, just the two of us," is how he worded it. It was the first moment of excitement I had felt since my mom's passing. We hadn't moved and the house was still haunted with the memories of her. All I could register was the word fun. I was going to go have fun with my dad.

We hopped in the P.T. Cruiser that was custom-painted with flames on the sides. We stood out everywhere we went. It wasn't enough that Dad could have been a stunt double for his doppelgänger Hulk Hogan, but he had to stand out with his assets as well. Honestly, I think he hated being compared to anyone. He was Gideon Haynes.

We lived in a big ranch house with eighteen acres and horses on it, a pool, and about five different vehicles, including two Harley Davidsons and a classic 1968 California Special midnight blue Mustang. We had things. Mom was a big equestrian girl. We had her money, until Dad plundered it all away on his substances. He ended up losing the house and all the "stuff" after I moved out. It left him with debt and a shack he rented for way too much, since it was practically falling apart.

Since we were in the Cruiser, my mind assumed Dad was taking me to a car show. We had done that in the past and while it wasn't necessarily my idea of fun, I liked how he interacted with me while we were there. It was something he enjoyed and therefore I found pleasure in it as well. I liked being around him when he was happy, which wasn't often after Mom's passing.

"Do you want a hint?" he looked over at me from the driver's seat with an all-teeth grin.

"Sure." It was contagious. I smiled right back.

Dad simply put on *The Doobie Brothers* cassette and we proceeded to jam to the songs I had grown up listening to, like *Jesus Is Just Alright With Me* and *Takin' It to the Streets*. My eight-year-old self didn't pick up on the hint but enjoyed myself nonetheless as my dad harmonized with the music. His singing voice was always soothing to me. My heart felt lighter when he sang.

Every night, Dad would sing me a lullaby. It wasn't a typical lullaby. It wasn't Rockabye Baby or even a Disney tune. It was *The Beatles'* song "I Will" and he sang me to sleep with it every single night. Even after Mom died. He didn't stop until I was well into my teen years and stupidly told him I didn't need him to tuck me in anymore.

Singing was a great indicator of his mood in the later years and when he would call me on the phone, I always knew it was a good day when he sang to me.

We spent the entire car ride singing to each other in different harmonies until we pulled up to a small concert hall about a two-hour drive away. I almost hadn't noticed how long the drive was because we were having so much fun. That was the kind of fun I was hoping to have. It didn't matter where we were going or which direction we were driving in.

The marquee above read *Michael McDonald.* I knew that name. He was in the band *The Doobie Brothers.* Hence the choice of music for the drive here. It all finally clicked. We were going to see a concert. This meant. . . more singing.

Dad had told stories of how he and Michael were close friends, but I couldn't grasp how my dad was friends with such a celebrity. Someone whose art I enjoyed, but as soon as Michael McDonald heard we were there, he had his security team come and get us and lead us backstage.

The security guard was even bigger than my dad, which was a feat I had never seen outside of his bodybuilding magazines. It was quite the sight for a child who had been used to seeing rather large men, but then there *he* was. And he hugged my dad immediately, like they had been best friends for years. It was the story my dad told me, played out right in front of my eyes.

For the first time since Mom died, I actually saw Dad's belly laugh. He had the best laugh. Then Michael came over to me and hugged me as well and told us to "enjoy the show" before he had to go on stage and we were shown back to our seats.

I'd love to say the rest of the evening went as idyllic as I had perceived the start, but sadly, that was when the night began to crumble. Nothing good ever lasted.

As soon as we sat down in our seats, I could feel my stomach twist in knots. It had been doing that a lot as of late. With Dad's ever-changing moods and the passing of Mom, my anxiety had turned into a physical stomach condition. Or at least that is what the doctor told my dad.

It had become hard to decipher what was anxiety-driven and what was actual stomach aches. Every inch of me begged my body to stop; to will it to be anxiety and not a stomach problem, but after the first several songs passed, and I didn't feel any better, I knew I had to tell Dad and disappoint him.

"Are you sure, honey?" I couldn't bear to break his one moment of happiness and that's exactly what I was doing.

It was a fair question. I had thrown up almost once a week for the past several months. Especially in the evenings when the sun went down for some reason. All I could do was nod. I was too afraid to verbally answer him. I knew Dad thought this was all in my head. Anxiety wasn't a real ailment to him and I felt it deeply that I was ruining the only fun we had had in a long time. But Dad grabbed my hand and led me out of the crowded concert hall and back to the motel we were staying at.

When we got back to the room, I admittedly did feel a little better only furthering Dad's notion that it was my "anxiety" driving my stomach ache. It never occurred to him that a lot of his actions fueled my anxiety, but he was trying here, so even I was confused.

Maybe it is real. Nothing feels real anymore.

Dad ordered me some chicken tenders from room service and put on a movie for me before he hopped in the shower. This was everything I had been wanting to do with Dad for months now and yet my body was deliberately ruining it all. I tried to nibble a few bites of the chicken and fries, but it only made things worse. The second Dad came out of the shower, I puked all over the bed.

"Oh, honey."

I saw it on his face. He didn't blame me anymore for "faking it" or ruining the night with useless child anxiety. He saw it was real. I felt relief both in my body and in my mind. I hated throwing up. I felt nauseous when I got anxious, and then the anxiety from being nauseous only made it worse. A vicious cycle.

The next few days were filled with symptoms of the stomach flu and I let the idea of anxiety go for a little bit, knowing my dad was taking care of me, but we never went to a concert ever again.

18

MAUI

2022

Turns out Spam and eggs aren't that bad. The whole "pretend it's just chicken" trick works pretty well. I ended up also trying some Spam musubi and I think that was my favorite overall. The texture of the rice hid any textures I might dislike, and the flavor was surprising.

"How are you feeling now?" Adam turns to look back at me as we both walk into his studio apartment. Maybe a bungalow would be a more appropriate term, but regardless, we were at his place.

For being a typical bachelor pad in size and organization (meaning total lack thereof), the only mess really is a pile of shirts scattered on the ground and a few dishes in the sink.

"You're surprisingly clean for a single guy," I note out loud as I scan the room. On the wall next to his bed, a few polaroids are pinned with precision, which I only notice because his bedroom and his living room are one. The entire space can't be more than 400 square feet. I feel uneasy standing in his bedroom, but tell myself that it's the same as walking into someone's common living area, it just happens to be all in the same room.

My arms cross so tightly around my chest, it makes my breasts look like I have cleavage that I don't actually possess. Not my intention, but also not, NOT my intention.

I ditched the wetsuit when we went out to eat, but that left me with a bikini top and my sarong. I didn't plan on surfing taking up an entire day or I would have brought a change of clothes. I'm not even sure how he convinced me to come back to his place. The funny thing about Adam is that everything we do is presented in such a casual way and yet what we end up doing isn't casual at all. Taking me to his hidden spot on the island and spending all day together two days in a row are things that people do when they've known each other for more than twenty-four hours. Better yet, most of the things we have done are things that people who are dating do, which Adam has made clear we are not. What he actually said was it would be considered a date if he kissed me. He kissed me on the surfboard after our rough and tumble made his lip a little swollen. But does that count? It was more of a joke than an actual kiss. Everything to Adam is a joke. It's hard to tell when he is serious unless he calls me Jenny. He wasn't exactly talking when he pecked my mouth with his split lip. I took it as more of a show that I didn't hurt him that badly. More machismo than sensual.

There is no way in hell I am going to ask him. I am no "pick me girl" and asking him what he considers being a date just sounds desperate.

Who cares what the label is, anyway? I am in no state to be dating anyone and enjoying myself is no crime.

It's a pep talk in my head, but I can feel my arms relax a little around my upper rib cage.

"Did you think you would walk into a pigsty?" Adam looks offended.

Honestly, the more I read my dad's journal, the more I anticipate every man in their early thirties to be living on a fold out cot on the floor. Especially if they are single.

"Yeah, a little," I'm honest as I point out his full bed in the corner of the room. "I don't even make my bed on most occasions." It's the truth. Not one I am particularly ashamed to admit, either. Most people don't make their beds daily. Or so I assume. It's not like I meander into people's homes to see if they make their beds, but I don't think Adam planned to invite me over when he picked me up for surfing this morning, so I know he isn't trying to impress me with a tidy space.

"It's a studio. Do you know how chaotic the entire space looks when just one thing is out of place?" It's a question, but a rhetorical one.

"I imagine it can look pretty disheveled pretty quickly." I agree, but also throw out a compliment, "I'm just impressed is all."

My shoulders go up into my earlobes in a shrug as I say it. I am just trying to make conversation so I feel less awkward, but the reality of it is I make myself even more uncomfortable with the topic I selected. Being around Adam feels easy, but sometimes conversing feels like I say the wrong thing at the wrong time. He always just shrugs it off, but for how often I have allowed myself to be around him the last couple of days, it still feels slightly unnatural just to talk to one another. I feel drawn to him, though. The adventures I can tell he has experienced makes me green with envy. I almost wish I could siphon his free-spiritedness, take it, and run, but being around him makes me feel like I can mimic it, so I stay.

Adam has left the screen door to the patio open just a crack. Enough to let the warm air into the room and the sound of the ocean reverberating off the cream colored walls. Adams' home is completely different from my dad's. Both are small in space, but Adam's is a sanctuary. Being so small, it almost allows for the outside to flow into inside, making it feel more like being in nature than anything else. Peter Pan's secret hideout of sorts.

Dad's cabin felt more secluded. The sounds of the woods outside still made their way in, but it wasn't as welcoming as the sounds of the island. Dad would bar the door so as not to invite creatures into his home, i.e. bears, mountain lions, etc. Whereas Adam's home feels like it also belongs to the creatures outside.

"Have you ever woken up to a gecko on your face?" My question is somewhat out of the blue, but easily traced when Adam notices my line of sight on his slightly cracked sliding glass door with no screen.

"No," Adam finds the idea humorous. "I haven't experienced anything like that," He pauses as if he is combing through the recesses of his mind to recall anything similar he may have witnessed here, "but I have woken up to a couple of birds pecking at my leftovers on the counter once. Part of the reason I try to keep it tidy."

"You could just keep the door closed." My comment is logical, though not to Adam.

"And block the outside. Not a chance. I welcomed them as friends and let them have the food. They ate and then I gently urged them back outside."

"Are you that gentle with all living things?"

"You sure do ask a lot of questions for someone who hasn't told me much about herself." Adam copies my crossed arms and pinches his eyebrows together. Very obviously mocking my guarded stature and overall vibe.

"I know, I'm sorry, bad habit," I say as I uncross my arms and let them hang awkwardly at my sides. "But it's not like you have asked me very many questions in return." I point out.

"I'm not particularly in the habit of asking questions I know people don't feel inclined to answer."

The air feels thicker as I chew on his comment. I don't have a middle. I am either completely closed off and my body shows it or I am purging all my gritty details to perfect strangers. There is no in-between.

"Am I that obvious?" I know the answer. I too am being rhetorical when I ask Adam, who only answers by coming up to me and rubbing my triceps gently as if I needed warming in this sweltering heat.

"I can tell you're guarded and have a hard time letting people in, but I don't press you because I want you to know that you can trust me. You don't know me well enough to know that yet, but I'm hoping we can be comfortable enough around one another. Not to share secrets, but just to be in the moment with one another."

I can feel the heat of his breath fall on my forehead. He is still close in proximity to me after rubbing my arms, but the small touch has melted me into his chest.

"There you go," Adam says as he leans in slightly.

It has been so long since I felt the warmth of someone radiate close to me.

"I like to keep people at arm's length." I am speaking literally, though Adam doesn't take it as such. He is far from an arm's length away.

"Could you step back, just a little," I whisper into his chest, still bare from a day of surfing. My throat feels tight with how close he is to me. His towering presence makes me very aware that only a bikini top stands as a barrier between both of our bodies, being unclothed against one another.

"Do you want me to step back?" Adam's forefinger still tracing the back of my arms in a circular motion as he questions me. My words say back off, but my body is beckoning his closeness. No wonder he's confused and would question my genuine desire.

"No. Not really," I whisper, and before I can even finish the thought, his mouth covers mine, absorbing the sound. I can taste the salt still lingering on his top lip from the ocean spray collected hours before and whatever inches of space were between us, fold into nothing as he holds me. One hand is on my lower back, just under the tie of my bikini string, and the other moves slowly into my soft, sea-salted, damp hair. My hair is thick and doesn't dry easily despite it having been hours since we stepped foot in the water, but the cool dampness and his warm hands stroke my scalp, creating steam.

Our kiss deepens as his tongue brushes over my teeth. His touch scorches every place they roam. I can feel a plump spot, still swollen on his bottom lip. I pull it gently into my mouth and Adam releases a guttural rumble. I don't know him well enough to know if I am hurting him or enticing him, but it is safe to assume it's the latter when he scoops me up from my upper hamstrings and carries me to the counter. Thank God it's clean.

Our heights are more comparable now that I have the countertop underneath me. My hands easily interlock on the nape of his neck. No space lies between us, my thighs brushing against the sides of his. My mind rushes in hyper-focus from my mouth to the place on my back where his hands dance around the strings of my top. I can tell he wants to tug on them, wants to undo me completely.

I might as well be drunk with my lack of inhibitions. Without pulling our lip lock apart, I reach behind me, giving him the green flag he needs to untie me. I can feel his breath stutter as he pulls away towards my neck, but his hands are confident as he finds the one pull to unravel my bikini from my body. We both succumb as the fabric falls between us, exposing my breasts and vulnerability.

Adam steps back away from me. Undoing all touch and placing more space between us than has been since we got entangled. His eyes roam over me and I can feel it more than I did when his hands were physically touching me. Part of me wants to cover myself, feeling completely exposed to his gaze, but the part of me that devoured his "live in the moment" comment is the part of me that wins. I lean back on my arms, saying nothing, just letting him view all of me. I watch as his eyes settle on my nipples and pause. The moment feels like it lasts an eternity, frozen in his endless surveying. My B-cup breasts might be smaller, but haven't given in to the cruelty of gravity and age just yet. I don't detest my naked self and if I can read Adam's thoughts out loud, I don't think he does either.

Funny how our bodies can be so comfortable with one another when mere moments ago, our conversation made me rigid and awkward. Sometimes what isn't said is more profound than what could ever be verbalized. I felt the chemistry between us in Alaska, like a magnet drawn to one another. An instant flame was lit, but it's easily extinguished when you think you will never see someone again. I still feel that way. The likelihood of our paths continuing alongside one another is slim to none. The only difference is this time, I am giving into my indulgences. The magnets will win before I pry them apart yet again.

I let Adam look at me. Allow him to trace his fingers over my skin. To carry me to his bed. I have all the control. As much as I feel I have let go of myself completely, I still maintain all the power over self.

Adam's core tightens as he lowers me onto his bed. The sunlight streaks through his shades and bounces off his body as he flexes under the strain. There is grace in the strength of him lowering onto me slowly. There is no crash of his body into mine, like a wave on the shore, but more like our bodies are a moving current, swaying back and forth together as one.

I sense him relax into me. His upper body still levitates above mine, but our legs have tied together in a knot. We twist and tug at each other, both wondering how far is too far and how far we can take this before the other cries out "uncle." My stubbornness doesn't allow me to flinch. Even when Adam pricks the skin of my collarbone just a little too hard with his teeth, my only form of reciprocation is to bite him back just as hard. This only escalates what started so soft and tender into a match of who can unveil the most of their skin first. I become so caught up in the competition that I hardly stop to appreciate that we both have stripped completely bare in the midst of the tangles.

"How many places can I make your skin pink with my touch?" Adam growls breathlessly into my ear as his body towers on top of mine. It's not a threat. It's an invitation. One I haven't received in a long time. My cheeks pink with the words and his hands tread across my stomach with such pressure that the redness follows his trace, as if his touch were leaving behind an ink trail of everywhere he has been.

The banter that has passed between us since our meeting has stalled between my lips. Partially halted by Adams' mouth pressing into mine and partially because the rest of the time unoccupied by his kisses, my only utterance is a moan. With every movement of his body, mine follows.

"Who knew surfer boys were so good in bed?" I'm embarrassed instantly by my remark, but when Adam laughs, "everyone," and nestles his face into my neck, I am at ease. I slow the dual of who can consume who first by my silly outburst, changing the tone of our interlude to something more tender and soft. Back and forth we go.

Like inebriation, I release myself to him. Unsure of how my body can so blindly trust someone so intimately and also trying not to overwhelm myself with vulnerability. I'm not aware of how cold my body feels internally until he touches me, is on top of me, is inside of me. It feels freeing. He makes me feel warmer and free. Free to feel pleasure. Free to be in the moment. Free to just worry about me and not what anyone else needs.

A moan escapes my lips and with it, my body arches up and into his.

"Yes, please," he says, the weight of him fully in me and on me. "Let me pleasure you."

And with those words, the entirety of my being turns over to him and I am lost to it all.

19

FLASHBACK
EARLIER 2022

The night Dad died, I didn't sleep. I finally put down his belongings and went home the next night. I knew I needed to sleep in my own bed in order to get any semblance of a "good" night's sleep. I was already awake past the twenty-four hour mark by then.

I walked through my front door close to midnight, and it was strange walking into a home where nothing had changed. There was no earthquake or fire. The world did not stop spinning and yet everything felt different. My entire world had shifted and at the same time, not even a throw pillow on my couch had moved from the spot I left it. There was before this night and then after. I knew it would be like that for the rest of my life. This rift that now divided these two timelines was so definitive.

There was a hollow silence that filled my apartment. A silence I knew would be there for a long time. He was the only noise in my life. I canceled everything else out because his voice had become so big. Now forever hushed, I didn't know how to add noise back in.

The only sound was the whisper of my ragged breathing. In and out. Like it was getting caught on sandpaper in my windpipe.

"My dad is dead," I said to myself. "I am all alone."

In a rush of blood flow to my stomach, I felt my face become balmy and sweaty. A wave of nausea took over me and I ran to the bathroom, thinking I might be sick. I was hardly ever sick to my stomach, but the phrase "he's *dead, he's dead, he's dead" rang* back and forth between my ears, making me feel seasick.

I coughed roughly into the toilet bowl and could feel the chill of the porcelain on my hands.

What can I feel, what can I smell, what can I see, what can I hear?

A grounding technique I learned from therapy to stop the vicious effects of the panic attacks I have suffered since I was about ten. I didn't necessarily like what I could see, smell, hear, and feel. I could feel the cold toilet seat, I could smell the chemicals in the water I had just placed earlier in the week, I could see the ripples as I dry-heaved, and I could hear myself attempting to wretch all the emotions pulsing through me.

It wasn't pretty, but it helped me escape the panic and after a few calculated coughs, I removed myself from in front of the toilet and slid back onto the tile floor.

The tears had stalled for a bit but now flowed freely. Each one traveled down my cheeks and onto the floor as I just laid there. It was a disgusting place to collapse. My bathroom or not, I really should have picked the couch, but it was too late, I didn't feel like I could move.

My body felt heavy and my muscles ached with how I contorted myself on the tile. I didn't even bother adjusting to relieve my joints of the pain. My hip bone jutted into the hard surface of the floor as I laid on my side, but at least I could feel it. The rest of me was completely numb. I should have taken Jules up on her offer to stay with me tonight, but I turned her down, thinking I would just crawl in bed and sleep for days.

My own emotional roller coaster moved from tears to anger pretty quickly, the nausea now having left me and color returning to my face. The rage felt like an inferno. Beginning deep inside my core and working its way out of me. Heating me as it did so.

"YOU FUCKING BASTARD," I screamed at the top of my lungs to the ceiling above me. As if his soul was peering down and watching me trade through these emotions so quickly, like they were being shuffled in a deck of cards.

I don't curse. I should clarify, I don't curse often. I have on a handful of occasions. Mostly when I am afraid, and always when it has something to do with Gideon. I can count on my hands how many times in my twenty-nine years I have said the "F" word. This was just another notch in my less-than-ten.

I looked around as if maybe someone could have heard me and would be ashamed of my foul language. The part of me that was raised to respect your elders recoiled at my sudden outburst of rage directed toward one of my parents.

Dead or not, I somehow felt he could hear me. Maybe it would have upset him and yet there was not a single part of me that wanted to take the words back.

Hours passed like seconds and I watched as each one ticked on and on. A very blatant reminder that time continues, even when you feel like it should have stopped. Or at least slowed down so that you could catch up. Time has no empathy. It trudges on, plain and simple.

When I finally pried myself off the floor of the bathroom, I laughed out loud at myself and the ridiculousness of it all. I may have been dramatic, but so far I have cried, rage screamed at nothing and no one, plopped myself on the floor, immobilized, and laughed hysterically at how ridiculous it all must have looked. If I was a fly on the wall, I'd buzz off and find a less manic house. I cackled at my insanity, which only made me cackle more.

The same, *he's dead, he's dead, he's dead,* tune continued to reverberate in my mind. Only this time, it sounded more like a clown at the circus. A chant taunting me with hilarity and annoyance. My laugh followed me all the way into the shower, where I inevitably broke down and cried again.

I let the water wash over me until I couldn't tell what were my tears and what was the shower water. I liked it that way. I wanted to become completely invisible. I could not manifest it so, but I could hide my tears in a sea of other beadlets of water, rendering them nearly nonexistent.

What was it all for? What was the point of it all?

The hope was just gone. All those years of sticking by his side, through every literal opiate-induced high, the hope that one day he could clean himself up and be the daddy I had when I was young, clung to my soul like a leech. It sucked everything out of me. I always went above and beyond what was asked of me. I didn't bail years ago like everyone else in his life had. He ostracized everyone. At a certain point, no one could handle the roller coaster and wanted off. I stayed strapped in. And for what? He never got clean. He died.

The loss of that hope digs the deepest hole. An open wound in my chest.

Truth was I could convince myself that there was a small part of me that was happy he had died. It was over. The ride eventually came to an end, only I still felt upside down and taken for a loop-de-loop. Like the roller coaster ended, but not at the beginning where it began. I somehow had to unharness myself and get down. After all these years, I had somehow managed to have the stamina to stay intact, but now I was shaky without the current of chaos following me. I had to create it myself now.

The hot shower cleansed everything but my mind. I couldn't remember if I even used soap or if I just tried to steam off the effects of the day before.

When I finally made it to my bed, the comforter wrapped me in the only hug I would willingly accept right now. I buried myself in the sheets, fortunately drained from all the crying. The tears stopped and my eyes were heavy. Now at four in the morning, I was bound to drift off. I was going to try, anyway. I needed to get up soon to get back to his cabin. It wasn't going to pack itself up and I wanted it over with. If I could get two hours of sleep, I'd be happy. I did fall asleep with one very truthful thought. . .

I am going to miss him for the rest of my life.

I HAVE ALWAYS BELIEVED THAT THE SOUL GOES ON. THERE are no exact depictions of what the afterlife is like step by step, but I prefer the streets of gold, Heavenly Father idea. A loving God. After this night, I know it to be true without a doubt. The veil between worlds turned into more of a mist and allowed me to partake on both sides simultaneously.

Sleep did indeed finally find me, but when the sun just began to crest over the foothills, I heard a noise. It was a sound I would recognize anywhere, but this time it was just a little bit different.

"Jenny"

"Jenny"

"JENNY"

The voice got progressively louder, but not more shrill. It was effortless, happy, whole, and clear. Dad was calling my name as if to wake me from my slumber. Much like he did when I was young, though I hadn't heard his voice that free in decades. If ever. I honestly don't recall a time when he sounded so carefree, though it was distinctly him. Possibly a younger version.

I awoke fully when my name was loud enough to jostle me. Shot straight up in bed, staring at the door as if he would be standing there in it. Yet, I was met with no one and nothing but the reality that he indeed no longer existed. Not just in this room, but on this earth.

I shattered instantly upon waking. There was no build-up, just streams falling into pools from my eyes. My shoulders shook as I pleaded between the dream world and the real one, and begged them to combine into a mutual reality. Of course, that would then have altered the definition of dream and reality, making them both something they are not.

I turned to my phone that I forgot to plug in on my nightstand. The battery was about to die, but I snagged the time before any notifications.

7 a.m.

It read brightly, causing my eyes to squinch and I noticed how raw my face felt. My body ached with the need to get up and drink some water. Maybe with a little lemon in it.

When was the last time I consumed any fluids?

I knew that if I had to think about it then it had been too long. It was still hard to move, but I could do it. I just knew that somehow Dad had been here. His calling to me was his way of saying goodbye. I was instantly reminded of the quote we used to say to each other from Peter Pan. *"You know that place between sleep and awake, that place where you still remember dreaming? That's where I'll always love you, Peter Pan. That's where I'll be waiting."*

The tears coming from me choked me and I decided to lay back down and try to reclaim the dreamworld he was in again. I didn't bother to glance back at my phone and the many notifications Jules had sent me through the night and I definitely didn't bother to slice a lemon in my water.

20

MAUI

2022

"This was a mistake," I say as I scurry out of Adam's arms and out of his bed.

When Adam and I finished in our horizontal positions, the reality of it all fell back on me. The pleasure is over and giving myself so freely to someone I hardly know and who hardly knows me feels foolish and completely immature. In a rush of embarrassment and insecurity, I clammer across the floor to my clothes. My bikini top gets stuck on my limbs as I hurriedly try to pull it over my exposed breasts. It never works to put bikini strings on in a hurry and I probably can cover up faster if I actually slow down and do it methodically, but all I want is to be anywhere else.

"What do you mean?" Adam, still in bed, looks like I bruised his ego. His sheets drape around his middle as he sits up and just stares at me. If he feels my vulnerability and desire to cover, he doesn't look away to give me any privacy.

He wants me to tell him why what we have just done is wrong.

"I just shouldn't have done that." I reiterate, not looking to divulge any further.

"I disagree."

"What else is new, Adam?" I spin around, finally covered up enough with what I had brought with me, though I am tempted to snag one of the several shirts that are folded up on his chair. "We haven't agreed on anything since we met. All we do is banter and chide at one another. I can hardly tell if you even like me and yet thirty minutes into knowing one another, I sleep with you!"

"Okay, first of all, we have known each other for more than thirty minutes." He says, holding up his fingers as he counts his reasons off one by one. "And second of all, are you familiar with the concept of flirting?"

"See!" I shout, pointing my fingers at him.

"See what?"

"You approach everything with sarcasm. Of course, I am familiar with flirting, but how am I to decipher that's what *this* has been?" I gesture between the both of us when I emphasize the word *this*.

"Come on now," his tone changes to mellow. I can see him choosing not to match my energy and escalate the conversation.

He doesn't finish his thought. *Come on, now what?* I want him to convince me I didn't just make a huge fool of myself. A silence echoes between us. Nothing but stares as one of us waits to break. Adam inches out of his bed, slides his boxers on, and starts over towards me. I look away to give him the privacy I wanted for myself. His body is still glowing in what is now the golden hour. Sunset is approaching.

"Come with me." Adam reaches for my hand, barely clothed, but I guess the same goes for me. Once again, I cross my arms over my chest and Adam hands me one of his folded tee's. Like he can read my mind. I crave to be less exposed.

"Here." he hands me the shirt.

"I'm fine."

"No. You aren't. Take the shirt, Jenny."

I listen and slide my arms through the graphic band tee that feels like it has been worn into its softness.

"Thanks." My line of sight doesn't leave the ground.

"You can't even look at me?" Adam comes closer. "Please Jenny," he whispers, pleading as he tests the waters by coming even closer. "Let me fix this."

I feel better with his shirt on. Like it's the armor I need to protect my heart. The walls are back in place where I had stupidly let them fall.

"Fix this?" My throat grows tight, trying not to cry. I can't let him see me cry. "You can't fix this." I manage to choke out and shake out the lump that shows up when I swallow.

"Let me try. Come with me." when he reaches his hand to mine, I pull away.

"Where are you taking me now? Some magical place on the island that somehow reminds me of my childhood. Simultaneously the one I had and the one I missed out on? No," I turn to the door, "No, I need to go."

I don't even wait for a response. Don't look at his face

when I close the door. I just run with my flip-flops in my hands and not on my feet, leaving us both blindsided.

BY THE TIME I GET BACK TO THE HOTEL ROOM, I AM already bombarded with texts from Adam. I knew I shouldn't have exchanged numbers with him, but in the heat of the moment, I thought I wanted to be with him and it felt wrong to have sex with someone who wasn't even a contact in my phone. Like that was some barometer of making sex with a stranger okay? At the time, my logic seemed sound, but now I don't feel okay.

I couldn't hide it either. Adam could read every uncomfortable sensation that came over me. I didn't want him to read me and help me. I just wanted to get the hell out of his beach bungalow. There was no chance I was going to snuggle, but I kind of hoped that I could at least pretend to be cool when all was said and done.

I've never been able to hide any emotion from tattooing itself across my face. You don't have to know me to know what I am feeling, though it helps to have context. All Adam knows is I am upset and got out of there like a bat out of hell. My body, first welcoming his touches, then recoiling at his nearness. I don't even want the shirt still loose on my body. It smells like him and I don't want his essence to permeate me any longer.

I need to get back to the task at hand. *Why am I here?* I

need to remember my purpose. Need to retrace the steps of my father and find him, not run into the arms of someone else, but again, context, and Adam didn't have any of that.

*Knock Knock

A gentle beat on my door pulls me from the edge of my bed. Must be the hotel cleaning staff to come and change the sheets. I requested it earlier because of all the sand that managed to find its way into my bed. Not sure how I can avoid that. I should have put the do not disturb sign on when I got in. I just want to be alone. I want to hold up in this room forever and never leave. Forever sounds nice.

"Can you come back later?. . ." I blurt out as I open the door without looking. I never seem to learn. "What do you want, Adam?"

"I came to make sure you're alright." He isn't looking me in the eye. "I'm sorry if I overstepped or if I hurt you." It comes out as a mumble. A sincere mumble, but a slightly pathetic sight to see.

"You can't hurt me." I laugh and bring his direct eye-line to my face. I didn't say he didn't hurt me. I said he can't hurt me. Nothing can hurt me anymore. I'm numb, but Adam doesn't catch my subtlety.

"Okay, it's just. . . you tore out of my house like you were on fire and you didn't give me a chance to make it right."

He's right. I did leave him clueless and half-naked.

"Look, Adam, we don't have to do this. You did nothing wrong. You didn't break me or hurt me. I gave you full consent. I said yes. Heck, I think I even initiated. I just, I am not capable of feeling anything right now and it has nothing to do with you. I don't want that kind of relationship. Physical or emotional. If anybody should be apologizing, it's me. I shouldn't have done that with you. Like I said. It was a mistake, but really, I am fine."

"Okay. . . well, what about me?"

"What about you?" *I hear myself. So selfish.*

"What if I'm not fine? What if I feel something here?" His hand moves in a gesture between our chests. "What if I don't think it was a mistake and want to continue to be around you because I like being around you?"

"We just met."

"You can't tell me that our meeting feels like a coincidence."

"I don't believe in coincidences." It comes out before I can stop it and, of course, Adam takes it as an admission that our meeting over two different states does feel more like divine intervention than just pure happenstance.

"What I mean is, I don't believe in any of it. Coincidences, fate, dumb luck, etc." It is my best attempt at a recovery, but he still smiles. "We can just walk away and chalk it up to a strange experience where two people were in the same place at the same time. . . twice."

"Yeah, we could, Wanderlust, but I don't want to." I have never noticed how puppy dog his expression can be.

"Yeah well, I do." It doesn't come out as strong as I hope and Adam is increasingly getting closer as he hangs on the doorframe of my hotel room.

"That wasn't very convincing."

There's that smirk again. Whatever emotion burdened him on his way over here has been relieved. I don't invite him in, but I am still in just his tee shirt and my bikini bottoms, giving the illusion that I am not wearing pants. He has seen me with no pants, just a few hours ago, in fact, but the thought of him looking makes me blush.

"So what now?" I ask, definitely staring at his mouth. The tiny scar under his left nostril that meets the tip of his upper lip. It's so faint I almost wouldn't have noticed it if he wasn't leaning in so close.

Is he going to kiss me? Am I going to kiss him back?

"Let's be friends." He says as he pulls back from the frame and offers me his hand to shake.

"Really?"

"Yes, really. And we shake on it to make it official. You know what a friend is, right?"

He jokes, but other than Jules, I haven't had many friends in my life. Especially not friends who are boys.

"Yes, I know what a friend is. I'm just not sure one can be just friends with the opposite sex." I haven't taken his hand yet. "Especially those of whom I have already had sex with," I mumble out of the side of my mouth.

"Is that a challenge?"

No. No, it wasn't a challenge; I was being pensive, but from the few interactions with Adam, I can tell he is always up for a good bet.

"Do I need to prove it to you?" There it is. There is the challenge.

"You want to prove that you can just be my friend? Even after we have had sex and you just admitted to me that you feel something more for me; something between us." I emphatically mimic the same in-between gesture with my hands that Adam used. I sort of am mocking him and he knows it. His eyebrows pinch in and his eyes narrow.

"You don't think I can do it?"

"It's not that. . . well. . . yeah. I don't think you can do it." The more I think about it, the more I think maybe he could prove me wrong. Part of me wants to see him try.

"Why don't we make it interesting, then?"

"What do you mean?" My face twists inquisitively.

"I will prove to you that I can just be your friend, but if one of us does end up falling in love with the other, they lose the bet."

"What bet?"

"Pay attention, Wanderlust, the bet we are about to make a deal on. The first person to fall madly and truly in love with the other loses."

"What do we lose?" I ask, intrigued. "Besides the fact that you would have to eat crow and admit that you can't just be friends with the opposite sex?"

"We can figure out the parameters later. What do you say? Wanna be *just* friends? It might be harder than you think."

"I bet I can handle it just fine and you're on!" Adam takes my hand like we have just struck some accord. "The first one to fall in love has to not only admit it to the other, but has to give a map to the secret hiding place you took me to."

"How will that work if you lose? You don't know where it is."

"I don't care. That is what I want. And I am not going to lose, so there's that."

"So you say, but what if you do lose?"

"Well. . . what do you want?"

I can see the fire light up in his eyes like the mischievous boy I know resides inside the masculine frame.

"Hmmmm. I don't know, *Wanderlust*, I am going to have to think about it."

The way the nickname rumbles from his throat makes me feel like I've taken a bath in warm honey. It's sensual, and he knows it.

"Now that's not fair. How can I agree to the terms if I don't know what it is I am agreeing to? You could ask for my firstborn child or a vital organ or something."

"Oh, I most definitely will be asking for your firstborn child." We both laugh. "You're just going to have to gamble on it. I mean, you said it yourself. You aren't going to lose."

"You're right. I have nothing to worry about. It's a deal."

"Good." I love how his smile is wide and shows his teeth. "A bunch of us are going hiking tomorrow morning. A volcano here on the island. Don't wear that." He points to my attire. "In fact, *friend*, can I have my shirt back?"

Without hesitation, I pull the graphic tee over my head, leaving me exposed in just my bikini. I relish in the fact that I know his eyes will roam over my bare abdomen and linger on my breasts that threaten to spill out of the tiny string top that one second before felt secure under the veil of his shirt.

"Sure thing, *friend.*" It comes out of both of our mouths far more sarcastic than it should.

Not sure if the droplet of sweat perched in his hairline is

from the humidity or my now mostly exposed self, but I am right that his eyes linger over the peaks of my breasts.

His full body leans in to press up against me, stopping just before my naked skin touches him. One hand hangs on the doorframe still, supporting his downward angle. His breath feels hot against my ear as he whispers into it.

"Thank you."

Then promptly pulls himself upright. Just in time to witness my hard swallow.

"See you tomorrow then. Bright and early." He says as he spins away from me. "Meet me in the lobby at 4:30 a.m."

"Seriously, do you guys do anything that isn't at the crack of dawn?"

"This isn't the crack of dawn. It's before then. We want to be at the top of the volcano by the crack of dawn."

"UGH!" I screech into my hands but know full well I am going to be up and ready with bells on.

He completely ignores my cry of angst at the earliness of the hour and just waves a hand back at me with a chuckle.

"Wear boots!"

He will torment me until I cave. . . but I won't.

21

MAUI

2022

The ungodly hour of four in the morning comes way sooner than I hoped it would. There is no expectation for me to go and yet sitting around in a hotel room all day sounds far worse than being awake at the butt-crack of dawn for a hiking trip up a volcano. It sounds like an adventure. One that Dad would probably jump on if I was in a different place in time. The diving trip from his journal came to mind and a little voice in my head says, *don't miss out on any opportunity that is presented to you.*

It wasn't a little voice. It was Dad's voice, and I know that the only real legacy he is going to leave me is to experience as much of this world as I can. So I do it. Plus, I want to prove to Adam that no matter how much he teases me, I will not fall in love with him. Chemistry differs from love. I don't have to not find him attractive because he is. Love is more. The best way to show him I am not in love is to be around him as much as possible. I don't want him to think I forfeit our arrangement, due to avoiding him.

I haul myself out of bed and grab a latte in the lobby before Adam rolls in at precisely four-thirty. For someone who is so laid back, he is more punctual than laissez-faire.

"You're here?" He points to my latte in hand. "And awake."

"Did you doubt it? I said I was coming."

"No, you didn't. I thought I would have to come up and drag your tiny hiney out of bed."

"My what?" He looks unfazed. I kind of liked it. "I didn't say I was NOT coming." The double negative sits on my tongue before my brain catches up, but I am right. Even he looks a little confused.

"It's too early for games." Ironic since he always insti-gates sarcastic playfulness.

"I agree. Let's go."

Waiting for us in a van is everyone from surfing yesterday and maybe a few others. I'm hoping Adam intro-duces me again, so it doesn't look like I am terrible with names, (which I absolutely am).

I do notice a stunning blonde in the front seat who wasn't there yesterday. She doesn't say anything as I roll back the van door to sit in the backseat. I send a small wave her way before sliding in and she adjusts herself to sit straighter in the front seat. It's early enough that she could just not be a morning person. It's dark enough that maybe she didn't see my wave. But I can't shake the feeling that she and I are not going to be friends.

Her bouncy hair, pulled back tight into a ponytail, is stark straight and bobs up and down as she turns her head to face Adam plopping into the front driver's seat. The smile she gives his direction is warm and her bright white teeth shine against the glow of the car's lights and her perfect island tan.

She's really beautiful even when she scowls, but I get the feeling that as long as I am around Adam, I will not be getting a smile from her. It makes me wonder why Adam isn't dating her. Or maybe he is, which is why she seems pissed he befriended me, a female. I'd be pissed if my boyfriend picked up stray travelers who were girls too. I don't know the entire story and until I do, I plan to stay out of it.

The five of us in the van are pretty quiet on the drive to the base of Haleakalā Crater and it lasts a lot longer than I hoped. About thirty minutes into the drive of twists and turns in the back of this van, I can feel the coffee sloshing around in my stomach. I don't throw up anymore. Never. Not since I was super young and would throw up consistently out of anxiety.

"Mind over matter" became my mantra into my teen years and I stopped. What didn't stop is my crippling emetophobia - fear of throwing up or other people throwing up around me. It makes traveling a little difficult.

On airplanes, I can put on my noise-canceling headphones and make sure I have rubbing alcohol and peppermint essential oil just in case, but I don't like feeling like I am trapped in a place where someone could throw up at any moment.

I know I can control myself in the backseat, but I don't know these people next to me well enough to know that they can. Zeke looks like a tank, so I am confident he has an iron stomach. I've seen him eat. So I sit closest to him in the back row.

I think back to the fact that a lot of them surf waves all the time and their bodies are accustomed to movement. Not to mention, this doesn't seem like the first time they have done this hike.

I try to breathe in through my nose and out through my mouth. Discreetly though, I also don't like to draw attention to it. I don't want anyone to know I feel queasy. I always travel with a sick bag in my purse, just in case. Part of the phobia that keeps me prepared for any situation. I probably shouldn't agree to any adventures that aren't close to the shore. Sea levels are always my friend.

"You okay back there?"

I know Adam is talking to me. I just give him a nod and a thumbs up.

"You look a little green there, Wanderlust." At the mention of my nickname, I can see the girl in the front seat twitch. It's too familiar to call someone by a nickname and everyone in here knows we haven't known each other long at all. Paying attention to her emotions distracts me from mine, which is trying so hard not to hurl.

Mind over matter. I think again over and over.

"We are almost there. About five minutes out." The guy next to me (not Zeke; Can't remember his name) taps me on the leg. "It'll be okay, but just in case. . . " He hands me a small grocery bag from the floor of the van. He has no idea that. . .

1. I can will myself not to throw up and. . .

2. I already come prepared in every single situation.

I didn't tell him any of this and set the bag between us. I hope this reassures him that I am indeed going to make it. No one likes to sit by someone who is puking. Phobia or not.

Sure enough, we pull into a dirt lot with a small hiking path to the side and Adam wastes no time in opening the doors for us so I can get out.

"You alright there?" He rubs my back in circles as I take deep inhales of the humid air and instantly feel better. "I didn't think to mention the windy road. I'm sorry."

"Don't worry about me. I'm fine." It's not as convincing a sound coming out of my mouth because I am trying to keep other things from coming out of my mouth.

We have a whole hike in the dark before us, but I can see how concerned Adam is and how bad he feels for putting me in the backseat. "We will put you in the front on the way home."

Again the girl flinches. I've just booted her out of her seat. The one next to Adam. I don't want to make waves, but I want to sit up front on the way back and hope she can at least be understanding.

Doubtful. She'd probably rather see me puke my guts up.

Adam hands me a headlamp and the five of us begin our ascent. We all walk in silence for a while, watching the terrain so we don't lose our footing in the dark. I like it out here and pretend for a moment that I am alone with nothing but the nature of the island around me.

"I'm Natalie." The girl with the blonde ponytail interrupts my trance. I hadn't thought to introduce myself and Adam only had briefly when I got in the car. Wanderlust isn't a name others call me. There were no other introductions made.

"I'm Jenesis." I put my hand out to shake hers, but she doesn't reciprocate. Adam is a ways ahead of us, a beacon for us to follow.

"What's your deal? I mean, I know that Adam likes to pick up a new charity project every once in a while, but why are you here?"

Oof

"I'm sorry. How have I offended you?" I say with a bit of snark. I thought I might play nice, but Natalie sure isn't, and I am very good at matching people's energies. If she is going to be a bitch, then I can be an even bigger one. It's not healthy, but sometimes it's fun.

"Did you expect me to stutter after you called me a *'charity case'*? I have enough headaches of my own to add whatever drama you are trying to stir up into the mix." I am on the offense. There is no defense. I don't feel the need to defend myself against her.

"Wow, I was introducing myself to see if we could be friends. Clearly, you aren't interested." I can see the shock on Natalie's face. She didn't expect me to hold my own.

"You're right, my bad. When I want to make new friends, I usually accost them verbally and am affrontive, stand-offish." The sarcasm is dripping from me. I have no desire to talk to her anymore and have nothing else to say about this pointless introduction.

"Just stay away from Adam. . . okay?" Natalie's lip pinches into a straight line and she picks up her pace to walk ahead of me.

I won that round, but at what cost? She is (for some reason) Adam's friend and I just made sure that there is no chance of a reciprocating friendship. I could have been nicer even though she started it. And now I have no idea what she will tell Adam about me.

I watch as her curvy and athletic frame stomps in front of me. "Adam, wait up." She yells before catching his hand and whispering something in his ear. I'm not close enough to see his face, but his body language says a lot when he doesn't let go of her hand.

Maybe they are together?

It doesn't matter to me. I don't want Adam, but we did sleep together, and he does flirt with me often. If he is in a relationship with Natalie, I can understand why she is so confrontational, and maybe I should have been more empathetic to that. A girls girl if you will.

Her question runs through my head. . . *why am I here?*

I know she meant here at this volcano; On this hike with people I don't know very well or just met, but in my mind, it's a lot bigger than that. I am trying to retrace my steps to find something, or rather someone, I lost. Except they aren't my steps, they are Gideon's and here I am, following in the literal footsteps of someone else. Behind Adam. This isn't what I came here to do. I've lost focus on my task at hand and have honestly spent too much time in Hawaii as it is.

I cross my arms over my chest. My typical move to show I am uncomfortable in my surroundings. I don't want to be here anymore. Maybe some opportunities we are meant to miss out on.

"Hey, you look almost as green now as you did in the

car." A hard thump on my shoulder lurches me forward and I realize it's Zeke. At least a familiar face. "Don't pay attention to Natalie. She thinks she is the queen of the group and feels threatened whenever there's additional estrogen around us. Around Adam especially."

Zeke is a lot bulkier than Adam is. Not heavy set, but very muscular. He towers over me and yet I feel very comfortable around him. He reminds me of the friends my dad used to hang out with.

"I'm Zeke, by the way." This time, when I outstretch my hand, it is accepted.

"I know. I remember you at the restaurant on my first day here."

"Oh, yeah?" He bops his head like he is silly to have forgotten.

"And we went surfing yesterday."

"Oh, I remember that. You just took so much water to the head. I thought maybe you didn't remember my name."

"You're hard to forget." I point up and down, making a dramatic inclination of his stature over me.

"I'm Jenesis." I reintroduce myself because he is courteous enough to do the same. Even though his is the only name of Adam's friends, my brain decided to retain.

"I know. Adam talks about you a lot. Though he calls you Wanderlust often."

My cheeks flush even more than the hike's exertion would warrant.

"Ah, well, I'm just Jenesis. His 'girlfriend' is quite a treat." I nudge my head to where Adam is still holding Natalie's hand as she trails behind him.

"What, that?" Zeke points in the same direction. "No. That's not what you think. Natalie has been pining after Adam for years now, but he's made it very clear he isn't interested in her more than just being friends. She refuses to take the hint. Feels she has some sort of claim to him and likes to make others feel like he belongs to her."

"Ah." *At least I didn't make Adam a cheater.*

"Yeah. I guess she thinks if she can keep other girls away from him, he will have no choice but to fall in love with her. We all just kind of ignore it at this point, but I can tell she gets under your skin."

"No, she doesn't," I say, rather unconvincingly. I'd like to believe our interaction does not affect me. Zeke doesn't buy it.

"Well, good then. She means nothing by it. Natalie is harmless. She's just smitten with a man who refuses to love her the same way back."

"They never. . . " I make a vulgar gesture to articulate my thoughts.

"NO! Adam would never. I think he would have told me. I've known Adam for years and he only is physical with people he tattoos on his heart. I haven't ever seen him even exchange a simple kiss with someone he didn't have deep affection for." Zeke knows him better than I do, but I have to note. "Really? Adam comes across as such a player."

I also didn't mention that we had already slept together. It seems like maybe Adam does get physical before feelings are there, but I keep my mouth shut. I don't want people to know. I'd like to pretend it never happened.

Each step feels like it is harder than the last. Not sure if it's because we are gaining altitude or if the conversation is making it harder to press on.

"I'm not going to be around here long enough to see what kind of person Adam is, player or not."

Zeke just blinks at me.

"That's a real shame, then. I know Adam must like you. He is kind of the ringleader of our friend group and doesn't allow anyone in just willy-nilly."

I try not to laugh at the word willy-nilly and also try not to fixate on the fact that even his friends think he cares for me. Though Natalie alluded he likes to pick up strays.

"We have a deal. Neither one of us will fall in love with the other. We are just passing acquaintances. *Maybe* friends." I emphasize the maybe and elongate every syllable.

"That seems like a good idea." I know he is kidding. "You guys seem to get along a lot better than maybe just friends. Why not see where it goes?"

"What are you, his wingman?" I swiftly giggle. Trying to change the subject.

"He's my best friend. I will always have his back." My attempt to lighten the subject backfires. Zeke is so sincere. I can tell he deeply cares for Adam.

"That's nice." I make sure all the sarcasm is gone from my tone. I really do think it is nice, "but I still can't stay. I'm leaving soon." And I just decided I'd be leaving tomorrow. Every inch of me wants to retreat and is screaming that I have overstayed my welcome. The island feels like it is rejecting me now. I hurt one of its own.

"Maybe Natalie is the right person for him. If she loves him, maybe he just needs a nudge in her direction."

Zeke sputters a swig out of his Camelback. It's a mix between a laugh and a shriek.

"You don't know Natalie." And we leave it at that.

We must be getting close to the top because I can see the color in the sky start to go from charcoal to a softer gray. The stars are beginning to disappear one by one like some expert hand is blotting them out of the sky. And Adam has let go of Natalie's hand. Now that I think about that interaction, he never looked back at her and never pulled her any closer to him. It was like he was guiding her on a leash up the trail. Empathetic, but not affectionate with her.

Natalie has the same arms-crossed posture I have. It is so discouraging to love someone - romantic or not - who won't love you back in the way you want. I should know. Maybe we could be friends. If anyone can relate to that feeling, I do. Now I kind of wish I hadn't been so catty towards her. I won't ever see her again, so it doesn't matter, but part of me wants to make amends.

We reach the peak of the volcano finally, or at least the part where we can safely stop. Zeke pats me on the shoulder again, gentler this time as Adam comes up to my side.

"What do you think, Wanderlust?" I can feel his body heat next to mine. "You and Zeke were holding up the back there for a while. I thought maybe you still weren't feeling well."

Oh, I definitely am still not feeling well.

"I was just getting to know your friend more. He's pretty cool."

"He's the best. Zeke and I are like brothers." Adam runs

a hand through his unkempt blond hair and removes his headlamp.

"I can tell."

"Check it out. We're going to miss it. It's the best view on the island. Or so people say." Adam turns my body towards the view and the ocean below us.

All at once, the sky lights up in a flash of pink and orange hues. The ocean goes from a dark void into a crystal blue beacon. One where it melds perfectly with the sky above it, blurring the line where the sky and water meet. It's breathtaking. It's one thing to see this view from my hotel balcony. It's another to see it from the top of one of nature's most volatile structures. I feel empowered and minuscule all at once.

"I will never be able to forget this moment."

Adam doesn't say anything, but grabs my hand and pulls me closer to his side. It's not the same way he held Natalie. Her hand limped in his. Adam interlocks our fingers and rubs my index with his thumb.

"In all my travels, I have yet to see anything that tops the majesty that is Hawaii."

His love for this island is palpable. An ache inside me wishes that I too could be welcomed into this oasis, but I know that my being here is like trying to squeeze into a pair of shoes that are a size too small. You can fake it for a while, but after a bit, it starts to hurt enough that you eventually remove the shoes and admit it was never really a good fit to begin with.

22

MAUI

2022

I slam the door of my hotel room closed. It is so aggressive that the walls of the bathroom shake and the locks rattle.

"Ahhhhh!" I scream into the void like I have done several times since Dad's passing, but this time I am sure the thin walls are giving away all of my angst to any neighbors who aren't currently out enjoying the island. I don't want any concerned hotel staff coming to knock on my door from all the shouting. So in one fell swoop, I manage to throw all my clothes across the room, creating a silent torrent of frustration. One that won't elicit any unwelcome visitors.

You are such an idiot! What were you thinking?

My inner voice is thrashing and hurling all the insults it possibly can at me. All the things I hate about myself, all the stupid decisions I have made in the past all culminating into this one moment. This whole trip. This stupid decision to follow my dad's journal around the world. It all felt like a Julia Roberts movie in my mind, my own version of *Eat,*

Pray, Love. But the horrible reality of it is I am alone and even worse are the thoughts in my head that say *you deserve to be alone.*

Adam doesn't deserve the bailout I pulled at his bunga-low. He doesn't deserve someone so selfish. I wasn't seeking to pleasure him. Only myself. I didn't care about anyone but myself. Just like *him.* I should never have slept with Adam and then to perpetuate the charade by gallivanting around the island with him and his friends like I somehow *belong* within his circle is just a joke.

Gideon was a narcissist. Undiagnosed bipolar probably or multiple personality disorder that was never treated. It was hard to tell what were the pills taking form and what was maybe another issue. The two fed each other like the monster it was, and yet when I stare at myself in the mirror of this luxury hotel room in Hawaii, all I can see now is that same monster with a new face. Mine.

In my last outburst, I grab the journal sitting on the bedside table. The journal that gave me delusions of fixing my shattered life. The journal that keeps a piece of my dad that I want so badly to get back.

The maids had come in and made my room spotless, but now my entire existence, everything I brought with me on this fruitless adventure, is scattered everywhere. I am chasing a dead man. This journal isn't going to bring me any satis-factory answers. And in one fluid motion, I hurl it at the wall with all my rage and dashed expectations.

"I hate you!" I bellow.

If I keep this up, a knock on my door is inevitable. I also don't know who my comment is directed at. Is it Gideon? Is it the journal? Is it my days spent with Adam? Is it me? The answer is yes. Yes, to all of it.

And just as quickly as the anger boiled inside me, it dissipates. Leaving my face flushed with a runny nose. I go to wipe my face with my clothes and I remember it isn't mine. Once again, I have borrowed a piece of Adam's clothing. There was a slight chill on the way down from the volcano, and Adam had lent me his sweatshirt. I don't think Adam will appreciate the return of his garment with snot on it. If I return it at all.

As it always does, the anger gets replaced with tears. So many tears. I throw it off my body and add it to the pile on the floor. What feels like a guarding of my heart now feels like it is trying to break the barricade down. I can't allow those walls to fall. I'm not comfortable being exposed. I have too many feelings to battle as it is.

I tear out of my clothes and go to step over my mess that now covers the majority of the floor to reach the bathroom and tidy up my face. Gideon's journal just lying there. Only there is a page sticking up out of the usual binding. I figure it's a tear. I threw it with so much gusto it had to have broken down a little, but upon further inspection, it's proven not to be a tear, but a folded letter.

How I hadn't noticed it before, I don't know. There is a small pocket in the back that acts as a folder for it. Tucked perfectly away out of sight of the usual entries that were logged on each page. I sit on the floor naked, somewhat unintentionally, and read the hidden words that quite literally fell before me. I sit on a mix of hotel carpet and crumpled clothes and simply use my forearm to wipe my nose.

Sand is sprinkled around me. I am always tracking around sand with me here even though I haven't been to the beach today. My hair, still damp from the humidity, hangs on my face. Disheveled and unknowing, I digest every word. And with the last sentence, I pick up Gideon's journal and tuck the letter back in the secret compartment that is now not so secret. I toss my clothes back in my suitcase, straighten the picture that had turned slightly when I slammed the door, and get the hell off of the island of Maui.

23

LONDON

2022

From one island to another, I land in the UK, (London to be exact), after what feels like an eternity suspended in between. My mind reels from what I read. The knowledge I held in my hands. I snapped at the poor flight attendant when she asked me if I wanted anything to drink. She pulled me from my daze, and all I could bark back was an order for Dr. Pepper. No polite please or thank you. I may have even thrown in an eye roll, but she probably did it first.

The people pleaser in me knew she was going to tell her colleagues how rude the girl in seat 34A was, but I didn't care. So what if I was rude? My rudeness would not turn her world upside down like mine had multiple times in the last few weeks. All I could do was put my head in my hands and try to doze off.

"I just don't like flying." I lied to the person next to me, who very clearly was concerned I would be airsick next to her.

It was a lie. I have always loved the sensation of flying. I grew up and discovered that pixie dust doesn't make you fly, but that doesn't mean people can't. This was how I reclaimed a little of that magic. I exclusively book window seats so that when the plane ascends above the clouds, I can pretend I'm out there soaring on the cotton candy puffs myself. Just as I had through the pillowcase as a child. In a way, it was real. I made it real.

I had to find answers. Uncle Max would know what I didn't. He had to. He was the closest thing Gideon had to a brother. He was the closest thing to family when it was just me and Gideon. Hell, I still call him *uncle* for crying out loud despite no actual blood relation. One little snafu; He doesn't know I am coming. After packing, I went straight to the airport and waited for the next flight out. It was the first time I didn't watch the clouds out the window. I did not see the island grow smaller behind me. I closed the shade and put up yet another barricade in my heart.

London is colder than Hawaii. The shock of it is more than the chill in the air of Alaska. I always expected Alaska to be cold with snow. London is snow free, but gray and it bites you. Goosebumps prickle every inch of my skin. I didn't pack methodically when I just threw my stuff from the floor wherever it would fit into my suitcase. I was smart enough to not wear my swimsuit on the plane, but the shorts and tank I grabbed in my hurry weren't exactly weather-appropriate.

I shouldn't have had caffeine today. No matter what I eat, I can't seem to soak up the jitters pulsing through me and it's making my hands shake. I am not a confrontational person, but I have to find answers and if anyone is going to help me, it's Uncle Max. I don't know if I trust myself not to be angry at him.

He isn't who I am mad at. I try to remind myself.

My heart is pounding in my chest as I grab my luggage off the carousel. More like fumbling with it, but I'm so shaky I can't seem to do anything gracefully. One hand holds my almost empty to-go coffee cup, the remainder of its contents dribble onto my pants, and the other hand reaches down to grab my luggage. Hair has fallen into my face and I like to think no one is watching the sad, pathetic girl alone at Heathrow Airport in tropical garb during an English fall. The logical side of me knows that no one is paying me any mind, but the other, less logical side is mortified with the delusion that every eye is upon me, mocking me as if I were on display with my absurdity.

Bags in hand, there is only one more thing to do. I hopped on a plane with nowhere to go and no plans settled. England wasn't on my original list of locations, considering it's the only spot in Dad's journal that's outside of the United States, but I have to find the answers I need. Isn't that why I embarked on this ridiculous journey, to begin with?

I reach into my bag where I most often keep my cell phone and come up empty. *Maybe I put it in a different pocket? I had it on the plane, right?*

No. No, I didn't have it on the plane. I sat in silence in my window seat, actively not staring out into the clouds, remembering when I used to dream I was flying to Neverland and none of this nightmare was real. I held my dad's journal in my hand with the letter safely stored in its secret pocket. I sat doe-eyed, wishing it had stayed hidden, and that I had never met Adam to begin with. I wished I had cleaned up Gideon's things and tried to find myself in my own life. . . not his.

Alas, I had no magic genie to make all this go away, so wishing was futile and I am in actuality, haphazardly going through my bags in the middle of an airport in desperate search of my phone. My only resource to the world outside these doors. I am completely lost without it.

How had I not noticed sooner? You know, before I was out of the country for the first time in my life. If I wasn't zoned out on the flight or glued to that accursed letter, I succumbed to exhaustion and slept for a few hours. My subconscious nightmares are a much easier reality to stomach than the one I am awake in. For once, it was just darkness.

All of my belongings are either draped over my body or narrowly hovering over the well-tread international ground. I have to accept that my phone is indeed not on my person.

"Well, isn't that just great?" I shout to myself. If I didn't have all eyes on me when I stumbled over my suitcase, I definitely have attracted several wandering eyes of the passersby with my recent outburst. The difference is now I feel no embarrassment. I am alone in the world, especially without my phone. It's not just a contact issue. I have no maps, no guide, no way to call an Uber, no way to look up the nearest cheap hotel, and most importantly, no way to contact Uncle Max. It's been almost two decades since we've seen one another in person. Like a child is going to memorize an international number that may or may not still be in use. I am a sitting duck.

Fortunately for me, England still believes in the importance of a payphone. I can at least attempt a call to my phone and see if someone has found it before I head to the closest *Apple* store. My very first tourist attraction, after repacking all my belongings, is one of those adorable red booths. They feel timeless, but I never thought I would use one.

A few rings later and a faint, "hello," makes me rigid.

"Um. . . yes. . . hi. . ." I ramble, "This is my phone. Who is this?"

"Hey Wanderlust. . ."

The chill of the airport is nothing compared to the chill that swirls in my blood when I hear that ridiculous nickname crackle through the phone transcontinentally.

"I was wondering when you would reach out."

"Oh, yeah. . . were you waiting by the phone?" I smirk sarcastically.

"There's nothing quite like the rush of waiting for the girl who left without saying goodbye. Usually, I would have no hope in that situation, but it seems fate isn't finished with us just yet."

I abhor how cocky he sounds. It's all a game to him. A bet he doesn't want to win just by the default of my fleeing. It's a game where I have jumped into the ring voluntarily, but it is much easier to keep him at arm's length with witty banter and snarky comments.

"Well, I need my phone." I switch gears.

"Great, where are you and I'll bring it to you?"

"I am not on the island anymore."

"Yeah, I know, but that wasn't my question." He bubbles out like it is a challenge. "I asked where you are."

"You can't bring it to me," I reply emphatically. "I am not close by. I'll just go to the store and buy a new one." I lie. I cannot afford a new phone right now.

"I can chase you a bit."

There is a lump in my throat.

"You would have to cross oceans."

"Sounds great. I love adventure. So I'll ask again, where are you so I can bring you what you want? Otherwise, I am Googling the phone number."

I know he is talking about bringing me my phone, but there is a slight undertone to his voice that makes me wonder if "what I want" is him.

"I just want my phone back." I clarify as if in answer to a question that wasn't asked. "You could just mail it to me. That would be easier."

"Oh, yeah. . . where are you staying?"

It's like he knows I am stranded without a place or a plan.

"I have someone I am meeting here." I don't specify that it's my dad's best friend who's practically a second father figure in my life. Even though I have only seen him on Face-Time in recent years.

The phone beeps on my end and I know I am almost out of time. I have to decide if I argue with Adam more or if I ask for what I need.

"Listen, I am running out of time here. I need a number

on my phone and then I will tell you where I am and you can *mail* me my phone."

"Sounds like a bargain." There is a different tone in his voice. I know he thinks I am meeting another guy and I don't dissuade him of that notion.

"I need the number for a contact. It's under Uncle Max."

And with that, he knows I am not meeting anyone romantic. Adam rambles off the digits and I scribble it down on a gum wrapper I had from the plane. Thank goodness I always carry a pen with me. A symptom of having memory loss issues because of trauma, according to my therapist. She recommended I always carry one. If not to remember things, then to at least write my thoughts down to still my mind.

"I held up my end of the bargain. Where are you, Wanderlust?"

I inhale deeply and on the exhale say, "Heathrow Airport."

"Never been to London. Meet me at the London Eye in two days at noon. See you soon, Wanderlust."

And before I can protest how mental it is to bring my phone in person, the line disconnects. Not sure if he hangs up or if I run out of time at that very inopportune moment, but I only have enough change for one more phone call and I cannot waste it on Adam when I have Uncle Max to ambush with my unexpected arrival.

My hands shake as I enter the digits into the pad. We haven't spoken over the phone in a long time, other than the occasional comment on Facebook for birthdays or significant events, but that doesn't exactly equate to nerves. I'm not even sure this is still his number. If not, I guess I'll just wait until Adam comes down the escalator to meet me. *Tom Hanks* lived in an airport for months. I could do a couple of days.

The chill of the phone is cool on my burning and flushed face. It feels like I placed an ice cube on my cheeks and I secretly beg it to ring and ring incessantly. To be left in this kind of limbo wouldn't be so bad for a while, but after two rings, I hear a plucky answer rumble through the other side of the phone.

"Ello?"

The warmth of his voice softens every bit of ice, encasing my heart. The melted ice turns to tears that brim on my eyelashes; pooling and making the airport atmosphere look like a watercolor painting.

"Hi Uncle Max." It comes out weak and garbled, but he hears me.

"Darling, is everything alright?" his thick Liverpool accent melts like jam on warm toast on the other end.

"Dad's gone." I muffle through the tears. It all feels so heavy right now. I am surrounded by people moving around me and yet I feel so alone. Everyone has a journey ahead of them, a place they are going to in earnest, and yet I feel so lost. There is no map to navigate this journey of grief.

"Oh love," I can hear the choke in his voice. "I think part of me knew. I thought I saw him in my queue the other day. It looked just like him. White long hair and a cowboy hat. It made me double-take. The smile he gave me was like peering at his soul, though I knew it wasn't him. . . not enough muscles."

We both chuckle at the lack of muscles this doppelgänger had. Uncle Max always said that Dad had a "heart as big as his biceps," which were twenty-two inches around at their peak. Big, to say the least.

I can hear his soft sobs through the static on the phone. It's not the clearest connection, but the important stuff is being conveyed.

Dad and Max hadn't spoken in years. There was no large falling out. There were a few miscommunications, but I think the biggest instigator of the relational distance was the physical one. An entire ocean away and then some is "geographically undesirable," as Dad would always say. That doesn't mean that the closeness died, just the frequency at which they shared it. Max was always like Dad's brother. Maybe not by blood, but that sort of thing didn't matter with these two.

Not much is spoken between us in the last few minutes, just a few tears and "I'm so sorry." That is until someone else needs to use the booth and with a very clear British accent, asks how much longer until I'm done.

"Where are you, darling?"

My location has been given away for me.

"Heathrow." I squeak out.

"I'm on my way."

Click

It ends abruptly, but the relief that washes over me is palpable. The flush in my cheeks cools, only leaving behind a revived shade of pink and I exhale out all the tension that was building in my shoulders from fear. Fear of being in a strange city with no plan, fear of the unknown, fear of what that letter said and who knew about it. And the betrayal that might follow.

I don't get a chance to tell Uncle Max where at the airport I am waiting, but I just know he will find me. He hung up so quickly that it was like he knew my exact location and was honed in on it. He always could make me feel at ease, like if it came down to it, he would jump in front of these insane double-decker buses, just to save me. Some things never change and about an hour later, I hear that familiar voice again. Only this time it comes out crystal clear.

"Need a ride, love?" The words string together with a heavy British hum.

His eyes look red, like the after-effects of heavy weeping, but his voice is cheery. "It sure is a long way to Neverland."

"Uncle Max!"

I lose a long breath as we embrace, like none of the time lost between us has passed. Even though it wasn't true, it was.

24

FLASHBACK

2015

"Hold your elbows tight against your body as you curl." Gideon demonstrated with forty-five-pound dumbbells to my fifteen with very little effort, but the motion was what he wanted me to mimic and not the weight, thank goodness.

"Like this?" I did my best to copy his technique, with just the fifteens causing strain on my biceps. Even in a workout, I sought to gain his approval.

Gideon nodded his head and I felt that rush of validation from my father I so ardently wanted in every moment we were together. Getting it felt few and far between, but when my dad was clear-headed, it was like his admiration for me as his daughter out-poured from him like a fountain.

It was hard not to be in awe of him when he was in the gym. There were always those who stopped and stared, mouths agape, waiting to see what the hunk of muscle that just walked past would do next. His arms were bigger than most of the heads that turned to observe his mass and strength. Gideon picked up bodybuilding shortly before he moved to London for a beat.

Most people didn't know who he was because he was such a nomadic traveler, but when he made himself known, he made sure it was in the papers.

MAX AND GIDEON WERE IN CHARGE OF DRIVING ONE OF those big red double-decker buses. It paid the bills back in the 80s. Anything they could do to make an extra dollar here and there as literal starving travelers. It hardly paid enough for them to stop at the wharf for a newspaper wrapped dinner of fish and chips, but it was fun and guaranteed another night of shelter and food, no matter how meager.

When the engine sputtered and stalled a couple of miles from their destination, it looked like they weren't going to be getting that paycheck after all. Max threw in the towel, but Gideon refused to call it quits.

"What's a mile or two, anyway?" Gideon smirked, his green eyes flickering with mischief.

"What are you going to do, Gideon?" Max asked in accusation. "You can't push it alone."

Oh, what a challenge. Gideon was never one to turn down an impossible feat. Max might as well have said, "I dare you to push a double-decker bus all by your lonesome."

"Yes I can." Was all Gideon had to say before he swung

himself down the steps of the bus and stretched his arms out on the rear of it.

"Put it in neutral!" Gideon yelled before holding his breath to push. The bus lurched and for a moment Gideon anticipated becoming the next London spectacle. He could just picture it. . .

A Crazy American Turns Into Roadkill Upon London's Cobblestone Streets.

At least he would die with a chuckle, which is the only way to leave this world.

I don't think Gideon was laughing when he died.

A twist of fate and the bus began to move. One man pushed a double-decker bus two miles to its destination, with his best friend steering the way there. Never again would Gideon see such accolades for his raw strength, but that moment sparked the rest of his life where he was known as the man with enough muscle to push the double-decker iconic vehicle through the streets of London.

"YOU'RE LOSING YOUR FORM, JENESIS." GIDEON GRABBED my elbows under the dumbbells and snapped me out of the memory he shared with me.

"What were you thinking about, baby girl?" I could see the concern in his eyes.

"I was just recalling the story you told me about pushing the double-decker bus down the streets of London, wondering if I will ever venture to see the roads you were talking about. I can hardly believe that you pushed it single-handedly."

"Uphill." He interjected.

"Yeah, uphill. Right. It all seems too impossible." I knew that this would spark his need to be believed. He would need to prove it to me. Yet again. Even though I, of course, believed every word he ever told me. Even the blatant lies.

"Do I need to get the paper clippings out again?"

"No Daddy, I know it's true." Even if I didn't, this one was irrefutable.

25

LONDON
2022

Uncle Max picked me up from the airport and even though the last time he saw me I believed in Santa Claus, he recognized me instantly. I was worried that womanhood might have changed me enough to alter his memory of me, but he just got out of his cab - that he drove - and enveloped me in the hug I had been missing for the last nineteen years.

"Ello darling," he drawled in that perfect British accent, and I melted into a sob of tears.

"You knew it was me." I didn't come out as a question because it felt like he not only recognized my now-grown body, rather than the scraggly pre-teen he saw last, but he saw me. All my hurt, all my grief, and all I was feeling in that moment. For the first time in a while, it feels like my feelings matter and are matched by someone who isn't trying to trump my emotions, but rather join me in them.

"He's gone." I cry into his green knitted sweater. October in England is cold, and I am still not dressed appropriately. Though I did throw on a hoodie when I dumped my bag out.

"I know darling, I can't believe it."

It had been almost just as much time since I saw Uncle Max, since Dad saw Uncle Max. And yet it was one of those friendships where it feels like nothing has changed at all. Uncle Max has a few more wrinkles and gray hair. His middle is a little larger as well, but what matters the most has not changed. His eyes still squint when he smiles, his hug is still warm and welcoming, and I still feel like a safe child when I am around him even though we have both grown up, just a little.

His home is just as cozy as he is. A little abode just outside of London proper and it smells of ale and cinnamon sticks. A small fire roars in the hearth, that is surrounded by a weathered brick fireplace and a mantle filled with photos. Some I even recognize.

"You have this?" I ask as I pick up a picture of me dressed up as a lost girl for Halloween so many years ago.

"Darling, have you been to Neverland lately?"

I love how he calls me darling. Reminds me of how Dad would call me baby girl and it just feels familiar. "What do you mean?" I want to ask him more why he would ask me that. I hadn't told him about Hawaii and how Neverland felt so real, and at the same time, not at all. "I haven't had a lot whole lot of magic in my life lately."

At this he just hemmed.

The conversation has lagged between us, but there is no discomfort. I just watch from the simple plaid couch as Uncle

Max roams around his home, straightening things up here and there. The sound lulls. I think I hear him say that love is the most profound sort of magic our world has to offer us, but my head has grown heavy from my lack of sleep. With the warmth of his home and the ease, I finally feel so welcome. I didn't even realize that I had let sleep wash over me.

"DARLING, DARLING."

I wake up to gentle pressure on my shoulder and a friendly face looking down at me.

"Darling, would you like some food?"

I must have dozed off long enough for the sun to set, though in October that is pretty early in the day still. My stomach growls with want to be filled and the small home fills with the smells from the kitchen.

"It smells amazing." I stir and rub my eyes with the palms of my hands to erase some of the sleep away and the grime I still feel from flying so far. I hadn't noticed he had covered me with a blanket. Also in a plaid. It felt like a less mentally unstable version of *Sherlock Holmes* in here.

"Cottage Pie?" he reaches out for my hand, urging me to sit up and join him at the table. The entire room is enveloped in the smell of seared beef and creamy potatoes. I have never heard of cottage pie, but for some reason, I know it will be my favorite meal, regardless of knowing what ingredients make up the dish. I could guess based on how many spices fill my senses.

Uncle Max led me to his small wooden table placed in a corner of his also small kitchen, and yet it didn't feel cramped or congested. The feeling is akin to being curled up in a blanket by the fire, which I was only a few moments earlier. You know that feeling where you are so cozy and warm that getting up feels like it might destroy you? It's so hard to move. . . well, I had the opposite reaction in Uncle Max's cozy English home. It was like I never left the comfort of his couch, but instead traded one comfort for another.

I could have slept a lot longer than I had. Jet lag was settling in and I could feel the redness in and under my eyes encircling me, enticing me to return to a state of rem, but its emptiness angered my stomach. I ate the warm and simple dish in heaping spoonfuls, hardly pausing to chew and not stopping to engage in polite conversation.

I do notice Uncle Max picking at his potatoes a little bit with his fork before speaking. Not sure if he isn't as hungry as I am or if he is giving me time to consume the food before breaking the silence and is more polite than to speak with his mouth full.

"What brings you here, love?" His tone is still the same, but there is an understated whisper of concern in his voice. Maybe guilt.

"What do you mean?" I do not bother swallowing before talking. My manners have been banished.

"I am so happy to see you, darling, but you just showed up. No text, call, or email? It just seems sudden and I want to make sure you are alright."

"I'm alright." I smile with a mouthful of mashed potatoes, peas, and carrots brimming in my teeth.

"Darling, I know you aren't alright. Your dear dad is gone and despite the time that has been lost between us, I never stopped missing him." His eyes fall back down to his fork. "I'm not alright. How could you be?"

"You asked me why I'm here."

He does ask me if I'm alright; he wants to be there for me if I am not alright, but I feel a little confrontational suddenly. Remembering his original question, why are you here? Reminds me why I am here. I am here for answers. I am here to see if he knew about what was in the journal.

"Did you know?" I ask, finally consuming the massive bite of cottage pie that has been in my mouth for the last few moments.

"Yes."

"All of it?"

This question confuses him.

"To what are you referring?"

This is the most proper "non-argument" argument that I have ever had.

"You know, all of it. Did you know about his addictions and how he would swing his fist at me, but intentionally miss and hit the dashboard of my car or the wall just so he could claim he never hit me? Did you know that I couldn't go anywhere or have friends, let alone a boyfriend, because I was afraid of what he would say or do around them? He hit on every single one of my girl friends. Only one was strong enough not to take offense to it. Did you know that I had no one? No one to help me. Not even his estranged aunts and uncles sent an email when he died." The tears are choking me, but I need to get through this. "And did you know that in all of that, I have an older brother? Family. I have a blood family relative who I didn't know about. A sibling. Someone I maybe could have leaned on during all the times Dad was out of control."

I've cried sufficiently into my cottage pie now. It's a little soggy, but mostly eaten. Max is just staring at me. His tears catch the light coming off of a candle between us.

"I didn't come here to interrogate you," I say, wiping away a tear of my own and gaining more composure. "I didn't even come here to blame you. I just wanted to know if you knew."

There's peace all around us. It really is the best place to have such an uncomfortable conversation. Max is choking back soft sobs. I don't blame him for any of it. He lives on another continent. I only saw him a handful of times in my life. Those moments were meaningful, but he couldn't exactly help me pick up Dad and his car when he was told by police officers that he couldn't drive home. He couldn't come over and dump out the extra bottle of Oxy he somehow managed to get from the doctors. After a while, even I stopped doing those things, which Gideon started to resent me for. If he was going to be reckless and take the pills, nothing external would change that trajectory.

"I just want to know if you knew," I whisper, my hands folded and head down.

Max inhales sharply, like he needs to catch his breath.

"I didn't know all of it, darling. Had no idea it had gotten that bad."

So he did know some.

"I didn't know he ever got violent with you or even near you. He was always such a happy drunk, but I didn't know about the pills." Another deep breath.

"I did know about your brother."

There it is. That was the real reason I came. I wanted to know if he knew about the letter.

"You knew about this. . ." I throw the letter across the table. The edge of it landing in the butter. "It was a phone call." I'm a little mad now.

"He made me promise. He never wanted you to know." There's shame on his face. His brows scrunch.

"He never wanted me to have anyone but him."

"No!" Max shouts, rather surprised.

"That wasn't his mindset at all. At least not when he asked me never to share with you. He never wanted you to think less of him. He didn't handle the situation well. He didn't handle it at all and he never wanted you to know that he didn't do right by them."

"Them?" I ask curiously, like maybe there's more than one.

"I just mean your brother and his mother." Max winces with his correction. "He was going to marry her. He didn't know about the child, but something went awry and your dad left. It wasn't until he was here that he discovered the pregnancy. She sent that letter to him here in London. I was with him when he opened it. That's the only reason I was privy to that information. I watched as he wept while reading its contents. Then he closed it and looked at me, pleading that I never bring the subject up ever again. I've never seen a man so broken. He was my brother, and I never wanted to see him like that again. I chose to honor his wishes."

Now it is my turn to sit and listen.

"Looking back, it probably wasn't the right decision, but we were fairly young and I wasn't involved enough to have an opinion. Then you came around and he only brought it up once to ask me to never tell you about your brother. It was the night we set up Neverland for you. I saw how much he loved you and had no doubt that if he had the honor of knowing his son, he would love him just as much.

"I asked him after we put you to bed, if he was certain. His response was so calloused. He said he was better off keeping away. He was certain that it would change your relationship and you had already lost one parent. He didn't want you to lose him in a way as well."

"What changed our relationship was not him having a past. I would have loved a brother. What changed my relationship with my dad were the pills."

I chuckle a little at a very inappropriate time.

"If you don't laugh, you'll cry." I continue to laugh. Now it's growing into a belly laugh. I can't catch my breath. "What a ridiculous place reality is sometimes."

Max looks relieved. I would bet money he didn't envision this conversation taking this kind of turn.

"It isn't your fault." I reach over the small wooden table with many years of scratches and character to take his hand. Max's tattoos are worn from being in the sun and years since their original ink. He has them speckled across all of his arms up to his shoulder and a few on the top of his hands. I rub my thumb over the top of it as if the blurred lines would smudge more by the friction of my fingers. "Do you think they know about me?"

"There's only one way to find out, darling."

I reach for my phone and remember that Adam is probably on a flight right now, acting like my personal courier service, and I find myself excited to see him.

26

FLASHBACK

2011

We had tried. And I think it's safe to say we failed. I failed. I wasn't good enough. I wasn't clever enough. I had crushed the eggshells I was so delicately balancing on, but really, what else was going to happen?

Dad and I had attempted a trip. Just the two of us. Well, us and a whole bus full of other people touring Colorado at the time. It was a failed attempt at a "family reunion." Dad was on a high, metaphorically speaking, and wanted to show me where his dad grew up. As a recent high school graduate and headed for college in the foggy city of San Francisco, I was more than willing to oblige. It felt like a last-ditch effort to do something together before I had my first real taste of freedom. Ironically, I chose SFSU because it was far enough away to breathe a little, yet close enough to be back home in an emergency. I knew there would always be an emergency. I was a small bird stretching her wings for the first time, but in order not to fall to my doom below, I prepared to fall back into the nest if need be.

I had no one with me when Dad had his "episodes." It would be nice to learn of my family history even if my grandparents were long gone. Dad grew up in Alameda, California, but Grandpa was one of twelve brothers and sisters who, after emigrating from Ireland, grew up in an adobe hut in the 1920s. It was a little more fascinating of a trip than a jaunt around the island of Alameda. It was a hare-brained idea, but Gideon wanted to make it work. The fantasy of it was nice, but that's what it was. . . a fantasy.

I was not willing to drive the two days to Gunnison, Colorado, and be trapped in the car with him, so we opted to be trapped on a plane instead. It was still an entrapment, but at least it was faster than two days. Then we would take a bus to the neighboring cities, ultimately seeing the dilapidated mud structure my grandfather was raised in. It's now overrun by wild horses, which, spoilers, seeing those amazing wild creatures was the best part of the entire trip.

I don't know what went through my mind and why I agreed to do this, except I wanted to believe in the idea of family so much. Our family. The family we used to be that I never stopped believing would one day come back around to me.

The flight there was fine. I think the excitement for him was keeping him feeling better than he usually did, but when we got there, it all went downhill fast. He immediately retreated into his motel room and kicked me out. It was a bad idea to share a room for a week, anyway. It was a relief to have my own space, at least. The small motel room next

to his smelled of cigarette smoke and old cherry wood, but
the TV was a nice noise diffuser with thin walls. I could hear
Dad's and he could hear mine I am sure. I listened intently
to see if I could decipher what he was watching. I deduced it
was some sort of *Marvel* movie and mine was a rerun of
FRIENDS. I could always get lost in that fictional circle of
people. I always felt I related most to Monica.

The motel was packed with people ready to take on
Colorado. Mostly older couples with binoculars and folded
paper maps instead of an app, but they all seemed nice
enough. The stop in Saguache showcased the burial place
of my great-grandparents and there was even a picture of
all of them in the smallest museum of all time. I was even in
the photo. A tiny baby standing with such a large family of
people I never knew. The realization that I had been here
before and was never told sent a chill up my spine. You
would think that living with only one person your entire life
would mean that you would know that person inside and
out. It was the first time I realized that I knew nothing of
my heritage or the past of the person I claimed I was closest to.

There I was, surrounded by aunts and uncles and
cousins and grandparents. An entire tribe of people and I
had not heard of a single one. They can't all be dead, right?
I chose not to ask though because Dad was already sweating
with withdrawal symptoms. I saw him trying, but it was also
such bad timing. He told me what he was willing to share,
which was a whopping, "Look, that's you and there's me." I
didn't have the heart to even ask who was holding me in the
photo. She looked matronly and nice.

We didn't stay out long, and the bus ride back was awful. Dad started to get the shakes and immediately retreated to the small motel room that I was sure now smelled of musk and Fritos corn chips by now.

I tried to socialize with the others who set up a small bonfire on the lawn in the middle of the horseshoe-shaped motel, but after I was offered my tenth s'more, I politely excused myself back to my room. At least I wasn't trapped sleeping in a bed next to an addictive insomniac who made the small space smell like a frat house after an all-nighter.

So much for being around "family." I went to check on him a couple of times, but he was most often asleep at noon and I didn't want to disturb him. I could hear his labored breathing through the screen door, he left ajar for the slight breeze, and I knew I could probably set off fireworks near his head and he wouldn't wake, but there was no chance in hell I was going to gamble on it. This week would end eventually and then I would be off to college and away from all of this. I just had to get through this nonsense and I wasn't sure Dad was enjoying himself either. He didn't enjoy anything anymore, it seemed.

I knew he would stay boarded up in his room for the remainder of the trip. Only coming out to get another liter of coke and another bag of chips. His only request was to be included when we eventually made the excursion to Crested Butte. Or "Crusty Butt" as I had affectionately come to call it. Dad had a lot of childhood memories visiting this small town only an hour or so drive from Gunnison and it was something I knew he would pull himself out of bed for. I couldn't tell if he was indeed detoxing his meds or if he was having an adverse effect from taking a little too many of them. Both seemed to elicit the same symptoms, but he was not coherent.

Dad and I didn't rent a car, and the bus had a very specific timetable to stick to.

For some reason, that day was testy. Everybody was in a mood and either grumbled onto the bus or threatened the people around them with, "I just won't go." I went to grab Dad but was told by the driver that the bus was now too full and we really couldn't wait another minute. It was the only thing he asked me to do. Wake him for this and only this. Maybe I just wouldn't go.

Oh, what a shame that would be. I thought sarcastically.

"Please take a seat miss." Everyone, now in some great hurry, yelled at me or grumbled in agreement with the driver. These people were so kind yesterday. They were either massively hungover or had one too many s'mores last night.

My intention was never to leave him behind. It was the only time this whole week he had planned to spend any time with me. Intoxicated or not, it was the entire reason for this stupid vacation.

It was anything but a vacation.

"Wait. . . uh. . . we have to. . ." I had very little articulation. Everyone else took their sweet time and now that I had a delay, it was out of the scope of any accommodation. Typical, and I just rolled over and took it.

"So you're telling me we have time to wait on everyone else's grumpy ass, but now all of a sudden it's too late?" I never exploded like that to anyone in authority, but felt rather proud that I had managed to at least speak my mind.

"We HAVE to! It's the only thing Dad asked of me." I always did what Dad asked of me.

"Take a seat now and quit arguing. The answer is no. You know, you have a real anger management problem, you know that."

I snickered under my breath. If only the driver knew how little I ever expressed my anger and how that was the actual problem.

I would have laughed out loud more at the idiocracy of that statement. I had an anger management problem. Take the speck out of your eye, am I right? Like I said, I would have laughed had it not been for what happened next. Completely powerless in the back of the bus and my voice now stifled, I watched as we drove past Dad on the gravel road headed to the freeway. My heart sank as I watched him and studied his face. I also sank into the backseat. Maybe if he didn't see me, he wouldn't know I was leaving with them. It was a crisis almost averted and I would insist it wasn't my fault later, but several people on his side of the widows opted to wave at him instead.

I watched, utterly speechless, as the driver yelled, "Better luck next time." Could he have done that on purpose? Could he have been so cruel as to try to "get me back" for calling everyone an ass? Whether intentional or not, the damage had been done.

Dad, however, went from walking tall to looking at me through the backseat window with more hurt in his eyes than I had ever seen. Not only did he grow smaller as we drove away, but I knew he shriveled inside as he watched the one thing he wanted out of this terrible experience proceed ahead, leaving him behind. He was out walking, too. I just know he was trying to rally to make this day a good one. I should have gotten off the bus.

I knew there would be consequences for it later. I just didn't know how damaging they would be until it was too late.

A SHORT PLANE RIDE LATER AND LITTLE TO NO WORDS spoken between us, it happened. I drove away under the cover of nightfall. Dad was still not feeling very well. Not well enough to drive. So with me at the wheel and the Sacramento Airport shrinking in the distance, making the large planes turn into toy ones, he swung. His fist closed, he hurled his culminated wrath at me, narrowly missing my face and hitting the dashboard instead. When that wasn't enough to scare me the way he wanted to, he threatened to jump out of the car. When that part was over, he told me he couldn't believe I was so selfish and to drive faster so he could be home and get rid of me. I never choked on tears more. He wanted me to cry, but screamed at me when he saw the tears beginning to form.

There was no such thing as time. I drove onward physically and hypnotically and unaware of how I got from point A to point B. He swung his fists into the dash a few more times. Later, when I told him how much he hurt me, he just said, "You hurt me more. Plus, I never hit you."

He never hit me. He never hit me. He never hit me. Is the mantra I would chant to myself when the fear would inevitably creep in again. Driving to the airport at night had become a trigger for me, whether he was with me in the car or not.

27

JOURNAL ENTRY
1984

P ostmarked: August 29th, 1984

Dear Gideon,
It's been some time since we last saw each
other. I know I broke your heart when the engage-
ment was broken, but you have to admit that I was
right. It was hard enough to find an address to send
this letter to since you are constantly on the go. I'm
so desperate to reach you that I resorted to calling
your mother. It was she who informed me that your
job transferred you to England, where you will most
likely be staying for a while. A while for you is still not
very long, so it is with hope that this letter reaches
you. I guess there's no surefire way of knowing if you'll
ever read this. I could call your mother again, but
then I would have to tell her the truth and you

should probably know first.

She seemed hesitant to give me your current whereabouts. Mothers don't exactly take kindly to women who hurt their sons, and I got the feeling by the tone in her voice that you told her everything.

Well. . . not everything. You don't even know everything.

I know how much you love to travel; How your only goal in life is to witness every culture and every climate and every place you can in this world with the time you have on it. It's your nature, it's your calling, it's your purpose.

Mine is different. I am meant to stay on this island. To live here with my family and continue the generational living and roots we have planted here. I am a rooted tree and you are a floating feather. Nothing is wrong with either one, but when put together, one will lose itself entirely.

When I told you I couldn't marry you, it wasn't because I didn't love you. It's because I do. So much. Even now. I can't take away your wings. And I know you told me you love me enough to stay for me, but I know in my heart that that wouldn't last us a lifetime. If it even lasted us a year. You proposed so quickly. We hardly knew each other, but I knew I loved you and for the brief amount of time I had you, it was worth it. I knew it couldn't be forever.

I think part of you knew that, too. The call of adventure will always be ringing in your ear and as much as I would have liked my voice to be enough to quiet the urge to see the world, I knew I never could completely drown it out. I didn't want to. It makes you who you are. It's why I fell in love with you.

Part of me tried to envision traipsing beside you. I could have been the Marion Ravenwood to your Indiana Jones, but even that relationship couldn't stand. I wanted to be by your side, wherever the wind whisked you away to, but the thought of leaving my home, my island, my culture. It was too much. The sadness I would carry with me as I longed for my home would be equal to the sadness you would feel by being in one place for the rest of your life. Especially an island. No matter how much you love Hawaii.

I'm not writing to rehash the past or reiterate why I broke it off. You already know this. And breaking your heart once was enough to shatter my own. Sadly, I am afraid I might be doing it again, but you have to know.

Shortly after you left, I felt awful. I thought it was just the ache in my heart from losing you. I felt weak and nauseous. I tried my hardest not to throw up daily and I couldn't eat anything. It was the saddest I've ever felt. I only imagined it physically manifested in my body. Then I skipped a period, and it clicked. I just knew. I was pregnant.

I went to the doctor just to be sure, and he confirmed what I already knew. Only I didn't know how far along I was. Learning I was carrying your child made the sadness worse and better all at the same time. I was miserable physically and didn't have you by my side, but a part of me relished the fact that I would have a piece of you with me now forever. I couldn't have you, but I could raise your child.

My parents were furious, but they have since come around. It's easier to love a child when he is here. At least, for those who aren't the mother. I loved my baby - our baby - the minute I knew he was inside me.

You have a son. His name is Keone. In Hawaiian Keone means homeland. I named him that because I gave you up for my homeland. I gave you up for Keone.

I don't expect anything from you. I just needed you to know. I'm not sure if this letter will even get to you, but if it does, could you let me know? I've lost many hours of sleep with the reality that you don't know that this beautiful boy exists. He is such a beautiful child, Gideon. I weep every time I look at him. He has healed so much of my brokenness and it would be so unfair of me to keep this all to myself. To keep him all to myself. He is as much a part of you as he is of me.

He has your green eyes and a wave in his hair that reminds me of your dark curls. I look into his face and I see so much of us. He is the perfect culmination of a relationship that had no chance of survival but didn't obliterate entirely. He is the aftermath of something beautiful, turned into something even more so.

I just can't express on paper how grateful I am to this little boy for simply existing. He was born out of love and love just radiates from him. I will love you, Gideon, til the day I die, but instead of grieving what could not be, I plan to shower Keone with all the love that was lost. I will funnel it into him.

I not only believe that you deserve to know he exists, but I believe Keone deserves to know who his father is. You are a great man, Gideon, and Keone will have those great tendencies as well. He deserves to know where that part of him comes from. I will never keep him from you.

In a twist of fate, his birthday is the day we made us official. The fourth of July. Turns out I was pregnant at Christmas and we had no clue. I don't believe any of it is a coincidence.

Whatever you want to do, Gideon. I wasn't always convinced I should tell you, but then I gave birth to him and saw his face. His features. You. And I knew that I just couldn't be that selfish. You have to know.

All my love. Forever,
Kailani

28

LONDON

2022

I obey Adam's instructions and get to the London Eye at 11:30 in the morning, two days after our call. It is amazing I retained that information since I was quite frazzled during our conversation and it was very prudent of him to set up a time and place to meet since I had no other means of getting in contact with him.

I get to our meetup thirty minutes early. Partly to prepare myself for what I am going to say to him and partly because I want to check out the environment while I am alone.

Uncle Max and I have spent the last few days hibernating in his cozy home, watching some of the VHS tapes Dad sent him over the years and drinking hot black tea and honey. Max likes his with a little cream, but I like mine so hot that any time I add the cream, it just instantly curdles.

"That's not how we drink it over here." Uncle Max informed me.

"I don't drink my tea lukewarm." He'd laugh at me and

call me out for being so "American," without actually saying it.

"Just like your Dad."

"Oh yeah?" I asked. This isn't something I noticed about Dad.

"Well, he just wouldn't touch the stuff. He was more of a coffee and cream kind of guy."

"Oh, that's right. He called it half and half, but he meant half regular half decaf." I giggled at the memory of Dad trying to order coffee half and half at shops back home and getting mad the baristas didn't understand what he meant. "I was always correcting him."

Anytime someone would say I'm a lot like Gideon, I would usually take offense to it, but lately, it has been nice to have someone who understood the good in him and noted that there are those qualities in me, too. Though drinking scalding tea and coffee might be more of a neutral trait, not good or bad, it is something completely unrelated to his addiction. Reminding me that he wasn't the sum of his mistakes.

We spent time watching the video version of Dad's journal on an ancient television set under a large blanket and crackling fire. It's hard to grasp the idea that Gideon was ever young. We usually never view our parents as ever being anything but our parents.

It has been a nice few days. And now Adam is coming and I am not sure I am ready to break that bubble just yet. It feels like I just got here.

Nevertheless, he is here. Flew across the world to bring me my phone. The least I can do is greet him nicely.

A tap on my shoulder sends me spinning.

"Sorry," He laughs, "I didn't mean to startle you." There he is. Adam. The man I hardly know and yet always greets me with the confidence and familiarity of an old friend.

"You really could have mailed me my phone," I say, taking it from his outstretched hand. It's obvious I am trying not to smile. "What fun would that have been? And besides, you're happy to see me."

"No."

"No?" His eyebrow inches up. Only one.

"You couldn't have come all this way just for me."

"You're right." Adam looks around and in a rather poor British accent continues, "I also came for the surroundings and the eel pie!" He points to the abundantly gigantic Ferris wheel next to us.

"Please don't ever make that sound again." My face is red from laughing and partly embarrassed by such a bad portrayal of the local dialect. "Someone might hear you."

"If it makes you laugh like this, I may only speak in this kind of accent." Adam just won't quit with the bad Cockney imitation.

"What can I do to make you stop?" I grab his shoulders, which are anchored well above me. My elbows are outstretched as I shake him in mock desperation.

"You can tell me why you left without saying so much as a goodbye." Adam is good at being goofy, but when he is serious, the world stands still.

"I. . . I didn't. . ." I stutter the words I am meant to say. He is right. I did leave without saying goodbye and we are friendly enough that I should have at least informed him of my departure.

"It was a last-minute decision."

What a terrible lie.

"Clearly, you left in a hurry. You left without your phone." He points to the device now nestled safely in my hands. It feels good to have it back and know that I am no longer lost. Amazing that Dad had to receive a letter telling him he had a son instead of a text. Oh, how far technology has come.

"Thank you for bringing it to me."

He smiles at me like my appreciation is more than enough thanks for all he has done for me.

"Want to ride this thing?" Adam smirks.

"That isn't how I planned to thank you." My mouth twists in confusion. It was brazen of him to think I'd sleep with him again if he flew over here.

"No, no." He shakes his shaggy hair. "No, I mean the Eye. Would you like to take a ride on the London Eye and see all the city all at once?"

"Oh." I feel rather foolish for assuming. "Yes, that sounds like fun." Adam interlocks our hands before I'm even done agreeing and leads us to where we need to be.

"The thing you suggested sounds like fun, too."

"Let's pretend I didn't misunderstand you." I look as embarrassed as I feel.

"I'll never forget what it feels like to have you under me." Now I am even more red. "You take everything so seriously, Wanderlust. Come on." We laugh, but I still don't get the feeling he was joking.

ALL OF LONDON LIES BENEATH US. OTHER THAN A FEW *000's* and *aahhh's* Adam and I have just been taking in the scenery. Adam points out the places that I can't pinpoint like the House of Parliament, St. Paul's Cathedral, and the Shard. I know the Tower Bridge and, of course, Big Ben. Mostly because of Peter Pan.

"I thought you said you've never been here before," I ask with curiosity because Adam has taken on the role of seasoned tour guide.

"I used to check out travel books at the library as a kid. I would hide under the covers with a flashlight and study all the amazing places outside of my bedroom. My world became so infinitely large and I would pretend I was at the Great Pyramid of Giza or the Great Wall of China and so on and so forth."

A part of me cherishes this piece of his history.

"So being a nomad wasn't exactly a choice for you." It's not a question or an insult.

"I guess not. I was born with an all-consuming need to explore and as soon as I graduated high school, I got out of my small hometown and set off to see as much of the world as I could." He sighs like it's been the greatest gift he's ever been given.

"I feel more at home on an airplane than I do in my own bed because I know it is taking me somewhere new and thrilling. Somewhere I can soak up everything around me. It's like gaining magic in my veins.

"I study a place before I get there, just to make sure I don't waste whatever time I have and I can see everything I want to in one go. It's never fully satisfying. If I could have a superpower, it would either be teleportation or being able to be in several places at once."

I laugh at his boyish idealism of being a superhero.

"Or maybe slow time so I can live longer and just see it all!"

"You would want to be omnipresent?" I snicker.

"Yeah, that's the word." He points to me like the word was on the tip of his tongue and I hand it over to him on a silver platter.

"You would want to be God."

"Oh, no! That's far too big of a job. I don't want all of humanity in my care, just the ability to be everywhere." He opens his arms wide like the whole world could fit in its circumference.

"I was kidding." I look down, "plus, God and I aren't on the best of terms right now."

"Oh?" Adam's ears perk up. Not sure if he even believes in the God that I do, but I keep going. "Yeah, I prayed for years that my dad would get clean, but a few months ago, I found him in his home. . . overdose." I cross my hands together and rub them between my thighs like I'm cold. I'm not. Max gave me a scarf that doubles as a blanket and is as long as I am tall, but I am uncomfortable.

"That's terrible. I'm so sorry."

It's what most people say when they too feel like they

are in an awkward situation and don't know exactly what to say, but when I look at Adam, that isn't his posture at all.

"I can't imagine how hard that must be for you." He takes my hands and strokes his thumb over the top.

"Let's change the subject. I don't want to cry in front of you." I pull my hands away softly to wipe a tear away. "I'm not a very attractive crier." It's true. I get all red and splotchy, and my face tightens in a way that looks like I am constipated.

"We can change the subject, but you can most definitely cry in front of me."

My eyes grow wide and he knows exactly what I am thinking. *Why?*

"I am your friend, Wanderlust, and friends always offer their shoulders to cry on." He pats his shoulder in a staccato with enticement. I just laugh. "Good to know."

"I know we are going to change the subject, but I just want you to know that I understand, on some level, how you feel. The hope and constant prayer that an addict gets clean. It can be discouraging." He pauses for just a moment, like maybe he doesn't want to tell me, but he already opened the door.

"My brother's an addict."

"Oh?" Now it's my turn to query the conversation.

"Yeah. Alcohol, prescriptions, heroine."

"Oh wow. That drug is no joke. Not that any of them are really, but I've heard that last one is hard to detox from and stay clean. How is he now?"

"Clean for three years." A smile curls in the corner of

his mouth. I can tell he is so proud of his brother but is being sensitive because my experience wasn't so lucky.

"That's amazing." And I mean it. Anyone who can find recovery is worth celebrating.

"Now we can change the subject." Adam rubs his hands together like he is about to indulge in a delicious feast. "What should we do today?"

"You mean besides this?"

"Yeah, we have all day, and I don't think this ride takes that long."

It might be slow going round and round, but he's right that it won't take all day. What I didn't anticipate was that he would want to spend the entire day with me.

Do I want to spend the entire day with him?

"I'm staying with my 'uncle' while I am here and we were going to go to the Peter Pan statue in front of the Great Ormond Street Hospital. It has some significance to us." I use air quotes around the word uncle.

Adam just stares at me with the deepest cerulean eyes. Every shade of blue exists in them. I count his blinks. "You could come if you'd like."

The subtlety of his wanting to come is not well, subtle, but he just responds with a full teeth smile that makes my heart beat a little faster and says, "Sounds great."

I know Uncle Max won't mind me bringing Adam along. I'm just not sure how I will explain to him how Adam and I met.

Um, we met at a bar in Alaska where Dad used to hang out. Then we ran into each other again in Maui, again where Dad used to hang out and we have a kind of bumped into each other often and in a lot of different places. All centered around where Dad has been. What's the worst that could happen?

I text Max to meet us at the hospital.

THERE IT IS. IN ALL ITS GLORY. THE PETER PAN STATUE that still stands as it had over thirty years ago when my dad stood in this very spot. Throughout my travels, it hasn't gotten easier to stand where he stood.

"It's smaller than I anticipated," is all I can say. Unblinking, I look upon the bronze art piece that holds so much meaning to me, and yet I have never been in its presence until now.

"Oh, yeah?" Adam reaches his arm around me and brushes the back of my shoulder.

"It's just a thing." I don't know what to expect. Maybe pixie dust will fall out of its center and whisk me away to Neverland.

Though I have already been to Neverland. Haven't I? And I still feel so hollow.

"Did you know Peter Pan's character first appeared in a novel called 'Little White Bird?'"

"I didn't."

Adam surprises me with his little fun fact. He, too, looks like he is in awe of the metallic monument perched before us.

"My mom used to read Peter Pan to me and my siblings

when we were children. I remember thinking what a foul mouth Tinker Bell has in the novel. I always giggled when she called Peter an ass."

"She does not!" I shout, flabbergasted that a children's book would contain such obscenities.

"Not only that. She has orgies."

"Now you are just making stuff up! I don't remember any of that! I refuse to believe it." Dad must have censored his reading to me.

I wipe a tear away from laughing so hard and I realize it's the first genuine smile I have had since the last time I was with Adam. I feel lighter. He tends to make me feel this way.

Maybe this is my pixie dust. Happy thoughts and all.

There's a moment between us. Adam and I. Before Max comes, where I forget how ridiculous it is that he followed me to England. How bizarre it is that he reminds me so much of Gideon. And how much I sometimes ache to feel Adam against me again. Part of me wants to lose this stupid bet and kiss him so intently that I forget I have walls up in the first place. But the same instant I think about it, is the same instant where I am pulled out by a phone buzzing.

"Do you need to get that?" It's Adam's phone. "Your pants are vibrating."

I can see the screen as he removes the phone from his front pants pocket and my fluttering heart dampens when I see who it is.

"I should probably see what's up." Adam turns away from me as he accepts a call from Natalie. It breaks the blissful moment between us and mentally reminds me that nothing can ever happen again between us. The person on the other end of that phone call is one reason of many.

I still am not assured he didn't cheat on her with me in the indecent moment in his bungalow, but regardless of technicalities, I know there is an emotional bond with her. Zeke is confident that he was in no way attached, but based on what I saw, it's hard to say I agree. She is in love with him, that much has been made clear, but Adam runs to her easily too. I fear he loves her also. He just doesn't know it yet. I can't get in the way and yet here I am with him, half a world away. That doesn't mean nothing.

"Do you think if we stare at it long enough, Peter will move?"

Uncle Max has come up behind us and places his hands on my shoulders, eliciting such a squeal from me that even Adam snickers.

"You scared me half to death," I shutter breathlessly, like he frightened all the oxygen from my lungs.

"Were you not expecting me?" His face twists quizzically.

"Of course, you just snuck up behind us so suddenly."

"I think it's more likely that you were deep into contemplation, darling. I called your name from a ways back and you must not have heard me." He pats my shoulder where his hands still rest. "Don't fret love, he sure has a way of captivating one's attention."

"Who? Adam? No, we are just friends." Even Adam looks confused by my defensiveness. His eyebrows raise to almost his hairline.

"Darling no," Max laughs. "Peter." He gestures to the

art piece brazenly before us and I too stop to stare at it yet again. It feels almost like the facial expression has changed. The boyish charm radiates from the metal and now he looks a little more mischievous than before.

Adam, who has conveniently said nothing with his words - though loads full with his eyes - now finally extends his hand to introduce himself. Of course, I had already done that when I swore up and down that Adam was only a friend.

"How long do you want to stare at this?" Adam does not say this with any sort of boredom or to hasten me away. "Just curious."

Until I feel him. Until I can travel back in time and witness him here for the first time. I want to feel what he felt, to see what he saw. Did he see the face change? Did Tinker Bell glisten around him? I feel all of this and yet not him. Not yet. How can I possibly tell Adam that I am waiting for a dead man to appear before me? How do I tell him he has before?

Max could feel my hesitation to answer - all of the above. "Come, Adam, let us get to know one another better. Have you been to London before?" I can hear their voices trailing behind me. Adam is not shy about conversation. He matches my uncle in chattiness. Both trying to out talk one another and I just know that Max loves it. Dad was like that, too.

Now, with a smidge of privacy, I stare at the patina of Peter Pan's leaf-laden pants and pull out the picture I carry in my pocket. I had folded it, and honestly hate that I did that. I am not too keen on the crease, but in a moment of urgency, I shoved this photo in my pocket to pull out at just this moment.

Dad, in his thirties, standing where I am now.

If you're here. Please show me a sign. Anything.

I just continue to fixate on the picture, then on the bronze boy who will be forever young. I see so much of my dad in this statue. The way his eyes squint, the way his curls fall, the way his muscles ripple on his arms indicative of an active youth. He looks so much like who my father was as a boy.

Maybe I wasn't blinking. Maybe my constant gaze blurred my vision, but I swear, I swear, I saw Peter Pan give me a little wink.

29

JOURNAL ENTRY

1993

November 25, 1993

Dear Jenesis,

It is your first birthday. I have never felt more alive than I do right now. You are constantly babbling and I love that I can only see certain parts of me in you. You don't have my hair. Praise God. I prayed every single night you were in your mother's womb that you wouldn't be born with my ridiculously curly hair. I can't stand my curls. God granted my wish, as vain as it was, and you have the most perfect brunette straight hair.

I find myself in awe of it. Of you. I love it when you let me brush it. You wiggle so much I hardly can ever get you to sit still for me to do anything to your hair. I have yet to cut it. The hairdresser in me is so ready to style your adorable wispy bob, but the other part of me can't bear to even go near it with scissors. I have time.

Mostly, I am just in awe of you. I love being your daddy. I love singing to you, the Beatles, until you fall asleep. I love babbling back along with you. I love that you can already walk and I can always be by your side in case you topple over.

I will never let anything bad happen to you. I swear.

I didn't know I would ever be a daddy. Almost forty is kind of pushing it to be a parent, but God had other plans for me. Who knew what would get me to stop living on the road, was you? A perfect bundle of pink and kisses. My heart has never been so full.

Your mom and I couldn't think of a birthday gift that would encapsulate what an adventure life has been since you entered the world. We decided that things come and go, but experiences last a lifetime. So, here we are, celebrating you in Palm Springs! Well, Palm Desert, if you want to get technical. And guess what, baby girl? We have been having such a good time that we bought the condo! Again, technically we bought the timeshare, but we did it! I honestly can't believe we were so impulsive, but we love it and plan on coming back every year until you are old enough one day to take it over. So happy first birthday baby, we bought you a condo in the desert. I bet many of your friends when you get older won't be able to say that.

This place is great. The J.W. Marriott has every-thing. Pools and palm trees and talking parrots and even flamingos. Yes, flamingos! You love them. You even tried to yell "bird" and "pink"! But it came out "blurf" and "plint." You are more precious to me than gold and I love listening to you learn how to speak. Your activity did not bother the birds. We kept our distance, but the parrots inside were a hoot. They spoke back to you and everything. "Pretty girl," is all they crooned. I have to agree with them. You are the prettiest girl alive.

The lobby is a harbor for these tiny boats that will take you around the property. It's such an oasis. We took a ride last night, and I watched you as you watched the water sparkle and splash under the light of the moon. I watched you as you watched in wonder of the world around you. A feeling I know all too well and it warms my soul to see that passion in you.

So cheers to you and your life. I cannot wait to see what the years bring us here and the memories we will get to make. You are my entire world. My angel. Happy birthday, now let's go to the pool!

Love, Daddy.

30

PALM DESERT
2022

"Well, I have officially taken six to ten years off my life." I run my fingers through my tangled hair. I didn't sleep a wink during the double-digit hour flight. Even though the flight from Hawaii was longer, it placed me in such a daze it was hard to realize how many hours my butt was sitting in that uncomfortable space.

Not to mention we flew into LAX and then hit a puddle jumper to Palm Springs, which was bumpy as hell. "I could kiss the ground. I am so excited to not be in an airborne tube!" If it were Halloween, I could cosplay as a Zombie in the apocalypse. I look like I died.

"You look as disheveled as you feel." Adam snickers and pulls what might be a cheese puff out of my messy bun - if I can even call it that. At this point, the bun is hanging off the back of my neck, and eighty percent of my hair is loose from the scrunchie. He flicks the chip on the ground and pulls some hair out of my flushed and sheened face.

"I am not one of those girls who travels pretty," I say as I shove my hip into his side in a teasing bump. "I have combination skin and the air pressure makes my face look like I dipped it in olive oil, all while simultaneously sucking all the moisture out of me like a prune. It's a lose-lose." *I bet Natalie travels pretty.* The intrusive thoughts of Natalie tend to surface when I am insecure.

"You travel adorably." Adam sniffs the air around me. "Though maybe a shower wouldn't be a bad thing." He scrunches his nose at the smell. My smell. "I stress sweat too, okay!" My embarrassment is showing defensively. "Not all of us can smell like the ocean all the time," I add.

"The ocean just smells like salt. Sweat is salt."

"It's different and you know it."

"I do. I'm just trying to make you realize it isn't a big deal to have a normal bodily function."

"I know." Again, I am defensive and ready to talk about anything other than my body odor. Normal or not.

"Let's change the subject. I need to go rent a car." I make no assumptions that Adam is going to spend all his time here with me. Yes, he followed me to Palm Springs, but I don't know what that means. When I learned of the condo/timeshare, or whatever it was that my parents bought into in the early 90s, I immediately booked it. Max wanted to come, but couldn't get away from his family. I told him he was welcome in the States anytime and he reciprocated the sentiment. We left one another on good terms. I even cried in front of Adam when we left him at the airport, though I denied it.

Unfortunately, we landed later at night and all the car

rentals are either closed for the day or empty of inventory. "I guess this is why it is advised to plan ahead instead of traveling on a whim." I jest towards Adam before realizing he does this kind of traveling all the time.

"I've already booked us an Uber. It will be here in fifteen minutes." I should have known he would have a plan. I have to admit to myself that I like traveling when it's with him. He knows what he's doing, and it takes a lot of pressure off from how novice I feel at it. Sure enough, in no time I am sitting next to Adam in the backseat of some guy's brand-new Tesla fully stocked with water bottles and even complimentary sick bags I know I will not be using, but am relieved to know that they are here just in case. Adam indeed does slide into the backseat with me and, for the first time around him, I feel uneasy. Panicky even. In an instant, my heart rate elevates and my breathing labors. *I haven't had a panic attack in years. Why now? What can I see, hear, smell? Oh my gosh, it's not working.*

"Hey, are you alright?" Adam takes my hand in his and I instantly pull it away. Partly because I just wasn't expecting his touch, and the other is because my palm is so clammy.

"Yeah fine." I cross my arms over my knees and breathe deeply into my abdomen. *One, two, three, four, five, four, three, two, one.* I count down and back, trying to stabilize my breathing.

"No, you aren't." Adam unbuckles and scoots over to the middle seat to be closer to me. One hand perches firmly on my knees and the other draws circles over my back. "You're panicking." It unnerves me that he notices the signs.

"It'll pass." I'm hyperventilating despite my best efforts.

"I can make it pass." I try to convince myself more than him.

"Yes, you can." His hand still trails the ridges of my spine. "Let me assist. What can you see?" I like how he doesn't ask why I am freaking out. I don't have to elaborate that airports at night remind me of a horrible memory. At least for now, Adam's not concerned with the why, but rather the how of getting me to calm myself down.

"Your feelings are valid, but remember, not rooted in reality. I want you to look around you. Where are you right now? What are we doing? Who is here with you? What can you see? Is there anything threatening you right now? And if the answer is nothing, then I want you to breathe and tell yourself you are safe." Adam whispers into my ear, knowing full well I don't want to make a scene with the driver.

I am in a car in Palm Springs. I am headed to my condo. Adam is here. Adam is touching me. The driver is driving. I can see the lights on the dash and the shadow of palm trees. Nothing is threatening me except the unknown. My lack of control. I am ok.

I don't tell Adam that my anxiety both settles and amplifies with his touch. The reason for my panic attack has to do with my father almost hitting me while I was driving us home from the airport. I don't tell him that he makes me nervous because he helps with my anxiety disorder in a way no one has ever been able to. Not even my therapist. The only legitimate threat to my sanity is Adam, but I will never tell him that.

"There you go," Adam says as I slow my breathing. "I can't feel your heart pounding against your spine anymore."

"We are here." The driver announces, like he wasn't privy to my whole production in the back seat.

"Thank you," I utter as I exit the car and into the parking lot of about a hundred apartment structures. "You coming?" I ask Adam, who hasn't moved yet.

"I think you need a minute to discover this next part on your own, and I want to give you space to do that." Always the courteous Adam.

"I think you're right. Well, it was nice to see you. Thanks for keeping me company and for bringing me my phone, I guess." My hand goes to close the door with Adam still in the backseat.

"You'll see me around. We haven't been able to shake each other yet. I highly doubt this is where we part ways."

All I can do is laugh and close the door. He's right, and he knows that I am okay. He also knows where to find me.

So with panic leaving my body and the blissfulness of an introverted isolation, I grab my luggage handle and set off to find condo 747.

31

FLASHBACK

2021

Sleep. I was sleeping a lot more. Naps specifically. Hours in the night stretched on and on. I ached with fatigue. So when I saw my phone light up with a voicemail on it, I didn't think much about the fact that it was from two hours ago. I laid down at noon and it's already 2:30 in the afternoon. Saturdays afford me more sleep than I even needed, but what else was there to do other than sleep? I could rest in a dreamless snooze, knowing full well the nightmare was when I awoke and not while I asleep. I never woke up feeling refreshed.

I responded to an email from work quickly, even though it was a weekend. My editor just needed my column for the Sunday paper. I forgot to submit it before clocking off. I was forgetting to do a lot of things lately. Felt like I was always operating at half-speed. No matter how much I attempted to recharge, I just never felt fully rebooted.

I responded to a text from Jules. Defensively, I was trying to delay listening to the voice message from Gideon. Sometimes it was ok. Sometimes it was not. The gamble was just something I wasn't awake for yet. I needed to shake off the lingering nap from me first. Waking up enough to deal with whatever mood Gideon was in when he left that message was never likely. The cortisol spike from the anxiety of hitting play was more invigorating than a cup of coffee, though.

> Jules 1:30 PM: Hey you awake.

> Jules 1:45 PM: Since you haven't responded, I am going to say no. 🙄

She knew.

> Jenesis 2:32 PM: I'm up now. Sorry. I put my phone on Do Not Disturb.

> Jules 2:33 PM: Don't apologize to me, girl. I know you're going through it right now.

> Jules 2:33 PM: I am a little worried about how often you have to sleep though, have you thought about seeing a doctor?

> Jenesis 2:34 PM: There's nothing wrong with me. At least, not that a doctor could fix with a pill and a new fitness regime. Unless there is an antidote for the crap Gideon has put me through, then I'm pretty sure it's a lost cause. 😔

> Jules 2:35 PM: I know, I just hate to see you this low. If there is anything I can do, let me know. Promise? 🩶

I paused there and figured then was as good a time as

any to listen to the voicemail. A message from my boss came through, letting me know that she got my column and we would need to have a chat about deadlines come Monday morning. That wasn't ideal, but here we go.

"Guess I am just going to have to leave this message instead of talking to you in person, since you never seem to answer your phone. Oh well, I guess you don't care about me enough to pick up. Doesn't matter since I am going to die soon anyway. Sooner than you think. In fact, I think I'll just die today.

"I have nothing to live for. Your mother is dead. I have no one who loves me. Even my own daughter can't take the time to answer a call from her dear old dad. What do I have except for my pain? You tell me? What do I have to live for? I may as well just end it all. That's why I am calling. Just to say goodbye, I guess, and tell you I love you. You are the only person I have ever truly loved, and I still didn't even do that well enough. So I will probably be dead when you get this, so. . . anyway. . . I love you Jenesis. I'll love you forever and forever. I'll love you with all my heart. This time I will say goodbye instead of 'see you later.' Even though I may see you in whatever life comes after this. Take care of yourself. You've been doing that apparently without my help for years. It will probably be easier to do that once I am gone, anyway. The burden of me will leave you. You might even be relieved by my death. So I will just do you a favor and off myself. It wouldn't be the first time I've thought about it or even tried. Hell, it's not even the first time someone told me I should. I'll just do the world a favor and go. Bye baby girl."

With that, the message ended. It was almost like the line went dead, but his message took three minutes to get through with all his slurring and that's all the time allotted in voicemails, anyway.

Holy Crap!

The first thing I thought to do was call Jules. It probably wasn't the best first move, but this kind of things had happened before and I was still groggy from my nap. I needed advice. She answered on the first ring.

"Hey girl, you okay?" I heard her concern through the cell phone.

"Um, not really. Dad called and said he was going to kill himself. I don't know what to do." The hysterics were crawling up my throat, making me sound like I had a rubber duck stuck in my esophagus. No matter how many times I went through this carnival act, I still always wondered if this time he would actually do it.

"Okay, when did he call?" Jules was my voice of reason. My grounder.

"He called two hours ago." He called at noon. It was now 2:30 p.m., but that's close enough.

"Are you worried?"

"I am always worried when he calls me in this state." True. No matter how many times he bluffed, I still took it seriously every single time. He was the boy who cried wolf and I was the villager who never got the memo out of fear that the wolf would one day rip my life apart.

"Alright, then I would call for a wellness check. I can do it for you if you'd like."

"No, that's okay. I will do it. I just needed someone else to tell me that that's the right next move." My fingers fidgeted with anxiousness to hang up and dial 911. My whole body was tingling with fear, stress, and sleep.

"I'll let you go, girl." Jules could tell. "Call me back, okay?"

I didn't even need to reply to her before I hung up and dialed for emergency.

32

PALM DESERT

2022

"What are you doing here?"

I am genuinely shocked and pleased and overwhelmed at the sight of Jules. She did not tell me she was planning to meet me in Palm Desert when I texted her an update from England.

"I would have picked you up from the airport had I known. . ." I can't help but feel guilty that she paid for an Uber when I finally got around to booking a perfectly good rental car I've been using to shuttle my depressing self all over this beautiful oasis. I'll admit, with Jules here, I feel a little less depressed. And I haven't heard from Adam again.

"I've never been so relieved to see you." I exhale into her embrace.

"Wow, it's that bad, huh?" Her response doesn't come across as a question, but more of an "I told ya so." She knew this trip was an emotionally fueled bomb that would end in disaster, but it's not over yet.

"You are always coming to my rescue," I say. I am resistant to letting her go.

"Why do I have to always remind you of how much I love you?" She strokes the tangles in my hair between her fingers.

"Because." It's not an answer, but it's enough for her.

"I will always be here for you." Some of her fingers get caught. "Starting with making you brush your hair. When was the last time you showered?" She sniffs the air between us like she might detect my odor.

I haven't noticed how crusty I've become in the last few days. Since getting here and realizing Dad left me a condo I didn't know we had, I haven't left the comfort of the bed unless I was taking the inventory of the space.

"When was the last time you ate?"

"Jeez Mom, so many questions," I say sarcastically. "I'm fine."

"Oh, yeah." Jules looks me up and down as if to take it all in. It's over a hundred degrees outside and I am in dark, bleach-stained sweatpants and an old Dad shirt I found in the bottom of my suitcase. It smells like dust and yet the thought that he wore this at one point is enough for me to have lived in it for the past three days straight.

"I had *In n Out* yesterday." And the leftover animal fries and flat *Dr. Pepper* this morning, but I am calculated in leaving out that detail. Though I am sure my breath smells like it.

"I'm wearing deodorant, I swear." I lift my underarms to my nose just to corroborate my story.

"Well, then fast food is seeping out of your pours. You

don't smell the best, and I say this with love. You need a shower."

"Adam said the same thing. I've been a little preoccupied." I'm not offended by her honesty. She is like a sister to me. If she told me I look great, then that would upset me because I know it's a lie. Jules is just looking out for me.

"Oh, that's right. You have a boyfriend now. How is he? When do I get to meet him? And also one should never be too busy to enact basic hygiene and self-care. You have someone to impress now."

"First of all, I do not have a boyfriend. Adam is just a friend. And second of all, he isn't even here."

Jules is the type of girl to wear a full face of makeup at the gym. Five foot one in a pink matching Lululemon set and hair in a high pony. She wouldn't be caught dead looking anything less than perfect. Perfect nails, perfect eyelashes, and perfectly plumped lips. Yet she makes it all look effortless. Even now she looks like a ten. When I get off of an airplane, I look greasy and red and undone. She looks like she just emerged from a spa. Slightly dewy and refreshed. My opposite in almost every way, which is one of the many reasons I love her.

I've known her since first grade and we have been friends ever since. Making her the oldest and longest relationship I've sustained. Mostly on her end. She is so good at coordinating coffee dates and making sure I don't retreat into myself too much.

I like to think I am just as good of a friend to her as she is to me, but let's be real. I'm not right now. What's even better is I know it won't affect our friendship.

"I thought you said Adam helped you at the airport? Where is he?" I've been keeping Jules up to date about everything that has happened with Adam this whole time. She is all caught up.

"Not sure." I shrug.

I have only been concerned with sleep. I left Adam in the Uber, assuming he hopped on another flight to Maui or wherever he was jetting off to next, but I haven't seen him in a few days and never actually said goodbye to him either, which after getting to know him a bit more really doesn't seem like him. He did leave me hanging with his comment about not being able to shake him. So where is he?

"Well, then my timing couldn't be more perfect." A cheeky grin creeps across her face, stretching her pouty lips. "Girl's trip."

Like the one we had been planning for years, but could never take because I couldn't leave Gideon alone for fear of him killing himself while I was gone. I couldn't breathe around him and now I have so much air I am light-headed.

"Girl's trip!" I screech as I bring her back in for a hug.

"Jen. I am so excited, but it is imperative we get you bathed."

I laugh as we pull away from one another.

"I'll go get us both some food and you take a long, hot shower."

"I'm so glad you're here," I say, with tears brimming.

"Me too Jen. Me too."

THAT SHOWER MIGHT HAVE BEEN THE BEST I HAVE EVER HAD. The steam seemed to draw out all the lingering fast food smell and the grime off my body and my heart. For the time being, I feel overall better.

Jules shoved some of her beauty products at me before she left to grab us some food that wasn't a burger and fries. Determined to feed me a vegetable, she wouldn't even let me have input. "I have an app for that," is all she said.

Demanding that I clean myself up, she handed me her shampoo that smelled of lavender and bergamot, a matching body wash she brought, and a new loofah. Always prepared when it comes to pampering.

She comes with an entire Sephora when she travels, and I adore it.

Then she scolded me and told me to wash behind my ears before skipping off with my keys. As if I didn't know how to shower. Like I haven't been doing it for the past almost thirty years. Jules isn't here for no reason. Unprovoked. My thirtieth birthday is this week and even though I have done everything I can to forget about it. . . she, like the good friend she is, hasn't.

I don't have any clean clothes from my lack of laundry and everything in my suitcase is still covered in sand. It's a perfect evening, however, and I wrap the towel around myself before I head over to the double doors leading onto the second-floor balcony. I feel a little exposed since the condo is not secluded, but rather a cluster of them in line. I guess Dad was keeping up on payments. Auto withdrawal I guess. Glad I didn't have to manage it, even though knowing would have been nice.

I feel a pang in my chest at the thought of managing yet another aspect of Gideon's life. One more thing probably would have broken me and on the opposite side of that coin, I might have used this place as a brief escape. Maybe it could have been a place where I could forget and be someone else for a week or two out of the year.

As quickly as that daydream comes, it passes into the reality of what it would have been. Gideon would have used his manipulation over me to make me feel bad for leaving him. He would have gaslit me into believing that it was unfair to him, that I was unworthy of such an escape, and let's be real, he would have texted and called every minute of every day while here. Probably leaving his signature suicidal phone call, which would inevitably spin me out and result in either my immediate return or a wellness check that he would blame me for later on.

I have my escape now. He's gone, and as much as I craved it. I resent it now.

Even as the sun begins to set, the heat from the day still lingers - even in November, which is a first for me. The mountains are colored pink and I feel immediately dry from my steamy shower as I loiter in the doorway of the balcony. I can hear the busyness of the pool a few units down as a couple of people soak in the hot tub and a few rowdy kids start to exit the pool. Swimming in November seems like it doesn't make any sense, but nothing makes sense here and that's kind of what makes it work.

I watch as the sun just dips over the mountains that surround us, which makes the golf course below us turn from a vibrant shade of green to more of a deep emerald. Shadows begin to grow, and I can start to feel a chill in my bones. I take this as my queue to go inside and use the in-house washer and dryer.

I throw in my light green sundress, that Dad said brought out the gold in my eyes and a tee-shirt and jeans. Something nice and something casual, just in case Jules decides to make plans. I'll be prepared for upscale or low-key. Until they are clean, though, I am prepared for literally nothing, unless I want to pull a *Mary-Kate* and *Ashley* in *New York Minute* and run down the streets wrapped in a towel. They made it seem sensual and chic, whereas I look like a homeless drowned rat. It would not carry the same allure if I were to do it.

Struck with the sudden urge to watch an *Olsen Twins* film, I plop my toweled butt on the couch and start flipping through whatever streaming services I can log into on the TV. The two-bedroom villa has a TV in every room, including both bedrooms and the living room, but it comes down to a matter of where Jules and I want to burrow for the night and inevitably pass out.

I cross my fingers that she brings back a large meat lover's pizza and a full liter of Dr. Pepper, but I know she instead ran to Trader Joe's down the street to get us groceries for practicality. She will whip up something incredible like the healthy girl she is, but my stomach is starting to growl. I'm not so slovenly to dig through the trash for a long-lost french fry. I think.

Just as I contemplate how intense my hunger is growing, there is a knock at the door.

"Just in time!" I shout at the locked door. "I just found us a movie to watch and I am literally starv-ing!" I finish the sentence as I open the door not to find Jules with bags full of food, but Adam with a case of coconut water and a bold smile. *It would be coconut water, island boy.*

"I don't have food, but want to have a drink with me?" He eyes me up and down, making me acutely aware that I am still in a towel. Not the most naked I have been in front of him, but taken by surprise, it sure feels that way.

"I wasn't expecting you." I grip my towel closer to me in case it slips.

"Clearly." Adam takes his pointer finger and wiggles it up and down, pointing to my towel wrapped around my body and in my hair.

"I thought you left." I indeed thought he disappeared into his gypsy lifestyle after my panic attack scared him away. I'm partly relieved to see him knowing that isn't the case, but still shocked he came back after three days of no contact.

"What have you been doing for the past three days?" It comes out more accusatory than I desire.

"It seemed like you could use a few days to sort through all this. I didn't want to distract you from that. Plus, I said I'd be back." He has such a boyish charm in his consideration towards me. I didn't scare him off. He wanted to respect my boundaries.

"You said I couldn't shake you. That wasn't exactly descriptive. Well, where did you go?" I'm curious.

"I haven't been here before and as a habit, I try to see as much as I can of a place before I have to leave it. There's too much in this world to see. Like I said in London, I want to see it all." Adam opens his arms wide.

"Yeah, but you spend so much time in Hawaii and Alaska. You go to those places multiple times. What about everywhere else? Don't you need to move on?" It feels more like asking him if he is ready to move on from me and whatever this is.

"There are some places worth staying longer than a few days."

I can see the lust in his eyes, but it isn't for me - it's for the world around him. A lust for travel. Just to wander. Wanderlust.

"So. . . are you going to invite me in or keep me out in the cold?"

He's so dramatic and he's trying to be. It's maybe seventy-two degrees outside now. With a light breeze, it chills, but it's a far cry from the cold.

I don't say anything, but I turn my body to the side, making a clear path for him to come in.

"Nice place," Adams says as he draws his eyes over the small space. I want to say thanks, but it still doesn't feel like mine, so I just let the comment hang between us.

I'm still dumbfounded. He is here and just awkwardly stares around me until he breaks my stiff-necked posture with, "You wanna go get dressed?"

"Yes." I leave to go dig through my sandy suitcase for something, anything, to put on that doesn't smell like hamburger or salt water. When I come up short, I resort to pulling an outfit out of Jules's suitcase.

She won't care. I think to myself.

I pull out a white tank top and a maxi skirt from the top of her luggage. I can always wash the clothes again. I just need something now. Jules is a short queen. I stand at five foot three. She is a solid five feet tall. So we both are below average, but what Jules lacks in stature she makes up for in personality. All that to say, the three-inch difference between us makes it so her jeans don't fit me.

I don't bother grabbing a bra. She is much more blessed in that area than I am, and I wouldn't even come close to filling one of hers out. I try not to focus on the fact that you can pretty much see my nipples through the white tank. If I don't seem to be bothered by it, maybe no one else will notice.

Five minutes later, I emerge back into the living space of the condo. Adam has grabbed a few glasses and poured the coconut water out of their cans for us. I take the offering and wait for when Jules will inevitably walk through the door. I'll just sip slowly.

Jules will have so many questions. I lead us out to the balcony. Partly because it is a pleasant night and partly because it will give me a minute to interject Jules' arrival before she assaults Adam with her interrogation. She will do so out of love, but in the meantime, I will conduct my own survey of the situation.

"Where are you staying?" I ask as I take my first sip.

"A motel in downtown Palm Springs."

"That's thirty minutes from here." It comes out like a

shock. It isn't that far, but there are lots of places in Palm Desert that would accommodate just as well.

"I had to see the heart of it all." He says it so nonchalantly, like it was a duh statement.

"And did you?" another sip.

"Three days is hardly enough, but I saw what I needed to."

Even in the shaded hues of the night's arrival, I can see Adam's face lit up by the moonlight and the neighboring porch lights. They, of course, linger over my chest and my nipples that are poking through the ribbed fabric in the slight chill of the air.

"I have an extra room here," I say it before I even ask him if he plans to stay here. "Unless you need to get back to. . . wherever you go next."

"You want me to stay here with you?" I can see delight in his eyes.

"I mean, you can have your own room or the pullout in the living room. I kind of forgot that I already offered the guest room to Jules."

"Who's Jules?"

As if almost on cue, Jules throws open the front door with bags and bags of groceries in her arms. I was right. She went to Trader Joe's.

"A little assistance Jenesis. It doesn't help that you are on the second floor."

I can't see her face buried behind a couple of bags, which also means that she hasn't seen Adam yet.

"Stay here, please." I plead with Adam, though he doesn't fight me back into the villa. "Just wait here."

"As opposed to jumping off?" he laughs. When I don't, he follows up his joke with, "I'll stay put."

I run back inside and set down my drink on the counter before grabbing a bag from Jules right before it slips out of her hands.

"You know there is nothing wrong with taking two trips."

"*You* take those stairs twice," she brushes her hands off on her pants, "Nice outfit." She looks me up and down.

"Sorry, but it was this or the towel I was in and Adam kinda showed up."

"Adam showed up?" Her eyes go wide. She has completely halted putting the groceries away. She's waiting for me to elaborate.

"He's here." I point to the balcony.

"HEY ADAM!" Jules wastes no time. "Get in here."

I slink into my skin.

"Do you like lemon ricotta pasta with arugula tomato salad?"

I looked shocked. Not only because that sounds delicious, but also because it is very unlikely for Jules to not feel someone out first before asking them to join in a meal. She didn't even introduce herself. She's a hugger too, so I thought she might just start with that.

Adam looks directly at her. "Yes." Short, sweet, and to the point. I can see a smirk creep on Jules' full lips.

"Great, have a seat you two. I'm cooking and if there is another one of those coconut waters, I'd like one, please."

And just like that, everything feels like it is falling into a symbiotic rhythm. One I could get used to, I think.

33

PALM DESERT

2022

Adam insisted that Jules take the second bedroom and he'd sleep on the pullout in the living room. Jules didn't pitch much of a fit. She wanted her own bed, even though we have cuddled in the same bed many times before. The back and forth was brief, and she even threw in an inappropriate comment about us sleeping together, but ultimately Adam landed on the couch. Probably since Jules had already unpacked into the room. She didn't anticipate Adam joining us. Hell, I didn't know.

However, that means that a sleeping Adam is between me and the pot of coffee I so desperately want. I feel rejuvenated, but that doesn't mean that I am not jonesing for my morning caffeine boost. It's still early though. Earlier than Jules would ever be awake, so her waking up first and entering the living area is out of the question. She will probably be asleep until noon.

The sun is about to crest over the mountains and I want so badly to sit out on the back patio and enjoy a latte with the sunrise. While the desert is a very warm place still this time of year, it's November and the mornings are brisk, even with a sweatshirt on. I don't like iced coffee even in the summer and will forever choose something warm to drink. Plus, it's my routine and I have always had a hard time straying from the only constants in my life. Even something as basic as coffee in the morning. It is one reason I wanted to travel this year; hoping it would break me from my need to have everything go a certain way. It hasn't happened yet. I have control issues. Having a routine that I stick to is one sure-fire way to have as much control over my day as possible.

I slink out of the cloud of a bed and bring the duvet with me. Just to the door. I press my ear against its solid frame, hoping that maybe I can hear stirring on the other side.

I deduce that I have two options. . .

1. I can sneak out there and hope that pouring myself a cup of coffee won't wake a possibly slumbering Adam or. . .
2. I can chance that maybe he is already awake and brave whatever lies behind that door.

I crack the door open with an obnoxious *SQUEEEAAAK*. So much for trying to be quiet. Why is it always the case that noises are the loudest when one is trying to be silent? I pause, with the door just open enough to slip through. I hear nothing. There are no lights on. Adam is most definitely still asleep.

I ditch the duvet and slink through the opening that isn't big enough for a California King comforter to come along with me. I am going with plan A.

I can do this. I think. Even my thoughts, I am afraid, are too loud.

Sure enough, there Adam is, sprawled out on the pull out, a sheet wrapped between his legs like he had been wrestling with it all night, and finally they both succumbed to defeat. The blackout curtains are all closed, but I can tell he is shirtless. The small glow from where I left the lamp on in my room highlights every ridge of the muscles that ripple on his back. His arm acts as a pillow for his head as he lies on his stomach. I just stare. I keep moving, but fixate my gaze upon him. He looks so peaceful. His tousled dark blond hair splays over his face in different directions. It's the only part of him that looks soft. For a moment, I almost want to see for myself. To see if his body heat is as warm as his island skin looks. To see if his hair feels like the down pillows I left smashed in piles on my bed.

Then I remember my mission. The Mission Impossible theme song rumbles in my head and it takes everything not to hum it out loud. I'd lost sight of my goal for a silent cup of coffee the minute I saw him there. I've never seen anyone sleep with a smile on their face, but Adam's mouth is almost curved up like so. . .

"OUCH!" I yelp as my hip juts into the side of the bartop. Crap I am going to bruise. Instantly, I start to rub my hip with one hand and cover my mouth with the other. So much for quiet.

"Morning Wanderlust." A deep gravelly voice reverberates towards me. I fail. "Morning." I say back, "I didn't mean to wake you, I just-" I am cut off.

"You just thought that yelping in my ear would be an effective way to sneak by me and not wake me up?" Adam laughs while rubbing his eyes with the palms of his hands.

"Nooooo," I drawl. "I didn't mean to impale myself on a stupid sharp corner in my pjs just to wake you up. Duh." The "duh," comes out kinda breathy. "I just need a cup of coffee."

"Well, I am up now, and since you *need* it, let me make that for you. I make better coffee anyway."

"You have never had my coffee before, so how would you know?" I point out.

"No, but I have had your English tea and if you make coffee how you make tea, then I think it's best for both of our internal organs if I make it this morning." Adam stands up from the bed as it groans underneath him. All parts of him up. I try not to look at his short sweats as he comes toward me. I beg myself not to look down at the other part of him I know is hard and awake.

"I like my coffee strong, okay?"

"I can get down with that, but there is a difference between strong and lethal. We can't have noxious fumes pour into the condo before Jules wakes up."

Jules. I almost forget she sleeps in the next room. I know my outcry didn't wake her and even if it had, she is not coming to my rescue from a shirtless man willing to make me coffee. She will hate herself if she disturbs whatever this moment is. Whatever she would perceive this to be. For all I know, she somehow orchestrated the whole thing. She told

Adam to sleep shirtless; she told the counter to jump out and hit me, and she put the coffeepot in the living room even though I have a kitchenette in my bedroom. That last one is actually very likely.

The heat from his body is exactly how I thought it would be. Even without touching him, I can feel it radiate to me, instantly warming my chilled skin. To touch him would be to burn. He still carries that cozy in-bed warmth and the heat of it flushes my face. In addition to other places.

It takes him no time at all to scoop the ground coffee beans into the machine and have it start humming and sputtering with bubbling water.

"You know you really should eat something before drinking coffee. Especially for women, it's so important for hormone health. You know, protein." He says this so casually as he reaches for his glasses on the table next to the couch.

"Where did you learn that from?" I ask, but also know full well he is right. "Do you read women's health magazines in your spare time or something?"

"Something like that," he says, still shirtless and now with glasses that I swear only add to his hunk factor. You know the cliche. Except, Adam standing before me with his hair still tossed from his restless night's sleep and his sleep pants just hanging right below his hip bones is almost sending me into a place I cannot come back from. I have to check my actions as it is. Then he throws on the glasses and a part of me wants to admit that I am completely done for. My only defense is to tease.

"Reading girly magazines isn't a credible source for

women's health. Pretty sure those give a false representation of what women *need*."

"I don't read 'girly' magazines or whatever you are trying to imply," Adams's eyebrows raise as he hands me a cup of coffee. "My younger sister is a functional nutritionist. She tells me things. A lot of things I don't need to know." He mumbles that last part like she has told him some horror stories. My guess is period stuff.

"I just know that she steered me clear of consuming caffeine before eating a sustainable amount of protein beforehand."

"Thanks for the lesson at six in the morning." I sarcastically speak into my coffee mug as I take another drawn-out sip. He may have shared this tidbit with me for my benefit, but he still handed me the cup of freshly brewed liquid energy. No part of him itching to control me or my habits; just sharing his opinions on things he has picked up in his life.

"How many sibling do you have?" I say it like I am supposed to know this about him by now, even though I know there is so much about the creature in the kitchen before me that will remain a mystery to me. It's also a nice subject change from whatever territory we were headed into.

"Just the two." He pulls his lips in and smacks them, licking his lips in between. "I'm the middle kid. It was just the three of us and my mom growing up."

"Did you grow up on the island?" Suddenly I want to know so much about him that I can't ask questions fast enough. It doesn't help that I am already starting to feel the jitters from the coffee.

I detest that he seems to be always right.

"No, I was born here in Cali. My mom is part Hawaiian, but I grew up in Southern California. She's still in SoCal. I just felt like the island was a part of my heritage. I booked a one-way ticket. Part of me knew that I wouldn't be coming back. I found the job at the snorkel shack, which miraculously came with rent for the bungalow as part of my compensation. Then a customer told me about working seasonally for the Alaskan cruise lines to supplement the rest of the year's lack of income. Everything just fell into place and it felt like the spirit of the island welcoming me."

"You are part Hawaiian? That's hard to believe." He's tan, but his coloring doesn't exactly showcase his nationality. I want to run my fingers through his sandy blond hair, but instead, I just point to his blue eyes and light hair.

"My dad's DNA was stronger, I guess." He shrugs his shoulders in disinterest. If I squint I can see maybe a hint of island features, but it's hard to tell what is genetic and what is simply a result of island living. His bronzed skin could be what he looks like year-round, but it could also be a hint of his mother's caramel coloring.

"So your dad must be a very blond, very blue-eyed, white male."

"Not sure, really. I assume as much, considering I look nothing like my mother, but I never met the man. He left before I was born and mom wasn't too keen on talking about him or keeping pictures around. She met her now husband a few years later and got pregnant with my sister. I call him Dad."

My heart sinks a bit in my chest as the pieces seem to come together. My dad. . .

1. Fathered a son. . .
2. To a woman who was a native Hawaiian. . .
3. Before I was born, Adam is older than me. . .
4. Adam does remind me of my dad when we met in Alaska (Though that was more personality than looks).
5. Could Adam be my **BROTHER**?!

I start to sweat at the thought of it. The coincidence would be too bizarre. We have been intimate once before. I feel sick. Could he be the brother I just learned existed? Can I give myself grace for having slept with him because at the time I had no idea?

I am jumping ten steps ahead. Adam knows about the letter from my dad. He would have said something. Plus, Kailani said she would never leave the island and her son was to be named Keone. Not Adam.

"What's your mother's name?" I try to sound casual, though I am anything but. My anxiety is high.

"Alana. Why?" Adam takes my shaking hands when the lightbulb goes off. "Oh no! I am not your brother, Jenesis."

He knows enough of my background now to have gotten there without me having to tell him what horrible thought crept into my mind. Even for a second.

"You can see how I might have thought. . ." I start to say out loud, then realize how ridiculous it sounds. "My intrusive thoughts got the best of me. Sorry."

We both laugh a little too audibly that we flinch at the thought of waking up Jules. I know all too well the grump that will emerge from that room if we awaken her suddenly, and I fear it. Adam is just being considerate.

I take my coffee to the balcony as Adam turns to finish making the bowl of scrambled eggs that's been sitting there for a few minutes now.

"I'll meet you outside." He turns to the stove and I can see his back muscles work as he begins to cook. The statement resonates as a promise and as much as I look forward to watching the sunrise over the green of the golf course, my stomach now flutters with the promise of Adam joining me.

It's everything I wanted and more. The sunrise, that is. The coffee is a little lackluster, but that is coming from a woman who likes to double the grounds and make it like tar, then add cream to cool it down, and sugar to make it tolerable. And Adam keeps his promise to meet me outside. It feels weird to be around someone who is true to their word.

34

PALM DESERT
2022

appy birthday, Jenesis.

H   I speak my name into the wind in the space that I know we were once a family. Even if I do not remember it. I watch the pink of the sunrise speckle the sky in long strips and meditate on it as the color is absorbed into the clouds. A new day. A new dawn. A new me, that I am tearing through pages of a journal trying to discover. I thought I set out on this journey to try to ascertain who Gideon was. All those years ago when I wasn't even a concept yet. I wanted to know who he was in the cycle of life I am in right now. However, I think I am finding less of him and more of me as I continue on.

Some people say thirty never looked so good. I say thirty never felt so lonely. So I came to the place gifted to me. It's the only place I could think of to feel remotely celebratory.

I think I like the desert. The dry air, the heat, the sweat that feels like it cleanses from the inside out as each bead comes to the surface. I like to feel warm. Enveloped by its essence. I don't mind the sweltering. At least I don't when I know I can find an AC unit and a pool when I am done with my fun in the sun.

My dad didn't make it to my thirtieth birthday, but he did leave me a present I don't think he had any recollection of giving. Our condo in Palm Desert is bequeathed to Miss Jenesis Haynes in a black-type font. I still have the papers. So many secrets tucked away in that little leather-bound journal.

"You spacing out?" Adam pulls the screen door back and brings out a plate of eggs, bacon, and fruit. All of which Jules picked up last night like the caretaker she is. *Thank you, Jules.*

"It's my birthday." My arms cross over my body. Yes, I am cold. Even Adam threw on a hoodie, but that's not why I feel closed off.

"Happy Birthday Wanderlust!" His enthusiasm is a bit too much for me. "You don't seem too thrilled about it?"

"I'm entering a new decade and I have no idea who I am anymore. Aren't we supposed to discover ourselves in our twenties? I just feel alone. I have no family anymore. I am lost. Wanderlust is more like wanderLOST." I laugh half-heartedly at my sad joke.

"I can't imagine how hard it is for you to lose your dad, but there is always time to discover who we are. We are beings that change all the time, but I think I know you pretty well by now and I can tell you all the wonderful things about you. As for no family, we can go find your brother whenever you are ready and even if you are never ready, sometimes family are the people we choose to be around. I know for a fact that Jules will never leave you. I don't plan on going anywhere either, for that matter." Adam sets down the food on the patio table and comes to rub the back of my arms.

"I'm not ready." I whisper it between us. *I'm not ready for any of it.*

"And that's ok."

I sigh with relief.

"Ahem?" Jules clears her throat in the doorway. "Am I interrupting something?"

"Yes," Adam says, "and it's a good thing too. We were just about to discuss what we should do today to celebrate."

"I don't want to do anything today." My arms are still tight to me, but I quickly unclench to pop a raspberry in my mouth.

"Too bad," Jules interjects. "It's your birthday and I have a great idea."

"THIS LOOKS SO STUPID." I WATCH AS PEOPLE GYRATE AND, for lack of a better word, boogie, to the groove of nothing. Well, to us it is nothing, but to the crowd out on the outdoor dance floor, there is a symphony in their ears.

"Just because it isn't our reality doesn't mean that it's not beautiful." Adam, always with the glass is half full optimism.

"We can't hear the music. It looks ridiculous." I gesture towards the group in front of us, getting their groove on.

"Just because you can't hear the music doesn't mean there isn't any."

"Do you ever not sound like a fortune cookie?"

Adam smiles with my scowl. "Let me show you the magic you cannot see."

"Again with the fortune cookie."

Adam takes my hand and leads me over to the booth that has the clunkiest looking light-up headphones I have ever seen in my life.

"Two please," Adam asks the lady behind the booth who has pink hair, a nose ring, and frown lines.

"She looks miserable. What makes you think this will be any fun if the employees are as downtrodden as she is? The brightest thing about her is her hair." I whisper in Adam's ear when we are out of earshot and safely out of the zone of any wrath.

"You are so judgmental, you know that?"

"Yes."

"Maybe she is miserable because she can't hear the music, but let's try it out, shall we?" Adam thumps the large black over-ear headphones over my messy bun and snickers. "It looks great." His voice is dripping with sarcasm.

"Well, I wasn't expecting to add any accessories to this evening. It was supposed to be a chill outing. You tricked me into this. I am wearing sweats for crying out loud!" Adam indeed lured me into this under the guise of running out to grab some more Dr.Pepper. I am assuming he told Jules that he had other plans. That sneak. My attire appalled her. I should have taken the hint.

"Let's fix this then." Adam reaches his hand up and

slowly tugs the satin scrunchie out of my hair. "I like your hair down."

Part of me wants to exclaim I will wear it down forever and the other part of me wants to ask out loud, why I should care what his preference is? I hate to admit I may never want to put it up ever again, but I know that's not likely. I also hate hair in my face.

Adam adjusts the headphones over my ears, and a deep beat instantly swells my eardrums. He looks like he says, "There. That's better," but the music thrumming in my ears renders me deaf to the outside world.

The movement of the surrounding people finally makes sense. Well. . . mostly. Some people have more rhythm than others and as Adam puts his headphones on and pulls me out onto the desert dance-floor, I get this overwhelming sensation that he is going to be better at this than I am.

I am right.

Each movement of his hips rolls rhythmically, whereas mine stutter. His muscular arms take me in his, which only make my movements more jarring and uncomfortable. It isn't a slow song, and this isn't my high school prom where I can drop it to the floor to *Flo Rida's Low* and have it make an impression. It doesn't stop the chick in the corner from doing exactly that, but I can't grab Adam and lower my face below his hips, for obvious reasons. I just can't. That leaves me with awkward swaying and a few clumsy hand motions. What part of this idea screamed, "Jenesis will love this?" I can't say I find myself enjoying this activity.

Adam breaks from dancing and pulls my headphones off gently.

"What are you doing?"

"I just needed to make sure we were listening to the same song. Your dance moves don't exactly match my melody." He laughs on the last word and I playfully push his chest from me.

"You don't have to be mean." I know he is just teasing me.

"Me? Mean? Never." Adam grabs my arms and pulls me back to him. "It just gives me an excuse to touch you. I mean, teach you." The mischievous grin implies he intended his slip of the tongue.

I twitch as his hands slide under the hem of my cropped white tank top. I can feel every callus of his scruff against my skin. I can't help but avert my look down. "Eyes on me. It will help keep your balance." My brain goes all fizzy like a shaken Dr. Pepper can. Even just one of his hands spans a good portion of the area of my torso.

However, I am so distracted by his touch that I actually find symbiosis with Adam's movements. "There you go." Adam mouths at me in a silent over-articulation. I do like this song. *Somebody To Love*, by *Queen*, makes me giggle and I love that the disco ball hanging from a palm tree above us mirrors the magic of this song. For a moment, I am alone on the dance floor. So many people surround us in all kinds of attire. Older folks look like they saved some outfits from the disco age, and others look like this is one stop before Coachella. I am here in sweats and a white tank and have never felt more comfortable in my skin. A few of the retirement-aged couples stare at me with distaste, but not as much as my people-pleasing anxiety leads me to believe. The young lady in the middle with her mesh shirt and nothing but skin underneath is drawing more attention than my lazy look. I'm not starstruck by nipples, so it doesn't draw my stare for more than a second. To my pleasure, it doesn't seem to faze Adam either. His eye contact is intentional for one of three reasons.

1. He does believe it helps with balance.

2. He doesn't want to get caught staring at the literal exposed breasts bouncing next to us. Or. . .

3. (This is the worst one) He's falling for me.

I can see Adam's mouth moving along with his swaying. *"Can anybody find me somebody to love."* And he points to me. As Freddie Mercury sings, Adam throws his arms over his head like a sprinkle of faux glitter just rained down on us. I can't help but laugh. A quick flick at my ear to pull the music away proves that Adam is indeed singing loudly and off-key. For some reason, the fact that he can't sing on pitch is a flaw that just makes Adam more likable. Even the girl who checked us in is sporting a small grin. Her one and only smile of the night, and Adam is the reason. He is universally unable to be disliked. It makes it easier for me to justify my emotions when I am around him. I am not falling in love with him. I just am unable to withstand his charms. There is a difference, or so I will reiterate to myself until I believe it.

"You know, this isn't something I would have chosen to do on my birthday," I shout all too loudly, and yet no one can hear me.

"Huh?" Adam drops his clunky headphones around his neck.

"I said I wouldn't have picked this to do on my birthday. Not in a million years."

"Oh yeah, and. . ." Adam is waiting for the "but" that he knows is coming.

"And. . . had you told me this is what we were doing, I would have bailed."

"And. . ." he drawls some more.

"And. . . I don't know why Jules didn't come."

"Yes, you do. And. . ."

I do know why. Jules wanted this to be a date, and that's what it feels like.

"And. . . this isn't a date." I just want to clarify.

"Sure, Wanderlust. And. . ." He won't stop until he hears what he wants to.

"And. . . It's one of the best birthdays I've had."

I see his shoulders relax like he wasn't entirely sure I would admit it, but since I did, a weight has been removed from him. The first slow song comes on and even with his headphones off, Adam picks up on the rhythm change. In a swoop of his hands, our hips bump into one another as he begins to sway. Neither one of us bothers to put our headphones back on.

"Dance with me." Adam continues to swirl our hips to the music like the combination of chocolate and vanilla froyo. A perfect melding of two flavors and yet still completely separate.

"Isn't that what we have been doing?" My skin sizzles where he touches me. His cheek presses into mine and I can smell his recently shampooed hair. It smells like melaleuca and lemon balm, and I am certain it is the one Jules picked up from the store because he doesn't smell like how he usually does. It's hard to look away from Adam, who could pierce me with his blue-eyed fixation.

"Don't kiss me," I whisper. Not like anyone will hear me. Part of me hopes Adam doesn't.

"Why?" His breathy reply sends tingles between my legs.

"We have a deal, Adam. You can't fall in love with me. We are just friends." I don't pull away from his embrace.

"Who says a kiss would break our deal? Friends can kiss. Friends kiss all the time." Adam bites his lower lip and it sends me into a galaxy of stars. Oh boy, do I want to bite his lower lip?

"Do you kiss all of your friends? I am sure Zeke appreciates that." I say Zeke, but my body language, thinks Natalie.

"I don't make a habit of it normally, but is it wrong to admit that I want to kiss you now?"

I want to say no. "Yes, it would blur the lines of our friendship and this isn't a date, remember?" Even if Jules set it up as such.

Adam exhales loudly and drops his face into my neck. "This deal might be the death of me, Wanderlust." I grab the back of his neck and stroke the base of his hairline. It's too intimate, but feels natural. *Me too,* is what I want to say.

"You know how much I respect you, right?" Adam asks.

"Sure. You're a good guy. We are friends." It comes out staccato.

"Why do you have to make it so hard?"

"What's so hard?" I want to hear him say it.

"You make it hard to be a good guy. You make it hard to just be friends."

A moment hangs between us where nothing else is spoken. I can't give in to him. The stars seem to have dimmed in the desert night and a little bit of the magic is lost. Like Adam is Peter Pan and his emotions can control our surroundings. The palm trees shutter in the brisk wind and I instantly go into fix-it mode.

"Hey, buck up soldier, it's my birthday. You're just horny. It will pass."

"Did you just say horny?" Adam laughs, and the sky brightens again.

I blush.

"I want to do something a little unhinged," I say in an attempt to change the subject.

"More unhinged than a silent disco in the desert with people half naked and people half in the grave." He has a point. This alone is one of the more outlandish nights I have had in my life.

"Yes, I have an idea. I just don't want to overthink it."

"You have me intrigued, Wanderlust. Lead the way."

"We need to call Jules first."

35

PALM DESERT

2022

"Are you sure you want to do this?" Adam asks hesitantly.

"I'm sure," I say with my full chest.

"Totally." Jules chimes in. "This is a great idea. I wish I had thought of it first."

"It might hurt, though." Adam's eyebrows pull in tight.

"It's not like this is my first time." Jules chimes in.

"Mine either," I admit as well, knowing Adam is growing in curiosity. "You know, for someone who is so laid back and free-spirited, I am surprised you haven't done this yet. Especially on all your travels."

"It just feels dirty. You can never go back from it." Adam winces.

"It's just a tattoo." Jules and I say in tandem.

"I don't do needles." Adam steps away from the tray of tools and ink as the artist starts up the gun. The vibration tickles my ears.

Jules goes first. One small palm tree tattoo on the back

of her right ankle. I go next and place mine on the left. When we stand next to each other, it's like a small oasis of palm trees.

"It tickled me more than anything. You are such a wimp." I jest at Adam.

"I swam with sharks in Australia and hiked half dome in Yellowstone. I have narrowly avoided malaria in Tanzania and rode an elephant in India. I have gotten no white girl sticker tattoos, but I am not a wimp." Adam harrumphs as he crosses his arms. I had no idea he had done all of that. Adam has lived more lifetimes than I could imagine and there is so much more I have yet to learn about him.

"I just like the idea of a permanent memento of how much tonight has meant to me."

Jules was more than down on the idea. We have talked about getting matching tattoos since we were eighteen, but haven't yet. When I suggested a simple palm tree to document this bizarre trip, Jules had no qualms, but most of the time I am going along with her crazy schemes, so she was overdue to follow my lead.

It was a feat to find an artist who would come in to tattoo us this late at night, but Jules messaged this popular one on Instagram and he responded to her $100 additional tip. He may have had a lazy eye, which Adam whispered to me wasn't exactly a good sign, but his portfolio spoke for itself and I may have put too much faith in some Instagram pictures, but it didn't stress me out. Go figure. Even if it had turned out horribly, it is a reminder of how I feel right now.

"I love it!" I chirp and hop with glee. I have to twist sideways and bend over like a gymnast to see it, but I just can't stop staring. Jules comes up and hugs me.

"I love you, girl." I say.

"Well, we are marked sisters for life, so you better."

I love it when she calls me her sister. If I have learned any lesson this year, it's that I can choose my family. I always thought it was just me and Dad and when the drugs made him distant, I felt so alone. When I look back on it, I had Jules the whole time. I was never really alone.

"I want another one." I break our hug.

"You can't be serious." Adam is not having a good time for probably the first time in his life and I am honestly living for it.

"Excuse me, do you have time for one more small one?" I ask the artist who hasn't yet cleaned up the station. "I apparently have all night." I can't help but notice the subtle glance towards Jules. Like she is a cash cow who will fork out more funds. She nods to me, almost in agreement.

"I can't watch." Adam throws his hands over his eyes and turns away. I know he is masking his dislike with humor, but I don't really care what he thinks right now. I want this for me. When the night is over, I walk out of the random tattoo parlor in Cathedral City with two tattoos. One matching my best friend and sister, and the other is the *Beatles'* song "I Will" on the front of my foot.

36

JOURNAL ENTRY
1984-1998

The letters that were written as journal entries and never sent.

SEPTEMBER 7, 1984

Dear Kailani,

What the hell do you mean that you are pregnant? What am I supposed to do with that information? What do you want from me? Am I just supposed to come back and marry you and settle into our life on the island? That was exactly why we ended our relationship. You and I both knew I would be miserable in that life, and you would be miserable along with me. What am I supposed to do here? I haven't responded to you yet. I don't know how I even can. I'm not sending this. Forget it, this is so stupid. . .

Gideon.

NOVEMBER 26, 1987

Dear Kailani,

It's Thanksgiving. The crew and I made a meal on board the ship in Alaska and sat down together in celebration. I came back to the cruise line after Maui. Thought that maybe it would feel more like home. Truth is, nothing has felt like home in a long while. You were the last thing that felt remotely close to it. It's been three years now. Is Keone growing big and strong? He is, if he's anything like his island heritage. Maybe he is even a little like me? I've put on a lot more muscle since I last saw you. I even did a bodybuilding competition.

That's not the point of this letter. (I don't know why I am writing it.) Except that when the crew and I all went around the table to say what we were most thankful for, I came up blank. I always thought that I was most grateful for my travels. How I never have to be tied down and can go anywhere I choose whenever I choose. I don't know. Lately, that just isn't as fulfilling as it used to be. I thought of you. I thought of Keone and how I am very thankful you have him in your life, even though I have never met him. I think I made a mistake. I swore I could live off the sustenance of adventure alone for as long as my body would hold out for. I swore up and down that I would never stop. I'm not certain anymore that it's what I want. It's just not as fulfilling. I'm having a weird holiday and you have been on my mind more and more lately. I just. . . Maybe I. . . I don't know. Maybe it will pass.

    Love always, Gideon.

JULY 4, 1990

    Dear Kailani,

    You and Keone are like a plague in my mind. The moment I slow down enough to hear my thoughts, you both come flooding in. It makes me ache inside. I don't like that feeling. I think maybe I'm going to come and see you. I bought a plane ticket last night. My mom is letting me stay in my old room for a while. My dad is a little disappointed. If he only knew what he really should be disappointed in me for. I never told him.

    I hope you both are well. Can I come to see you?

Would that be okay? I can't imagine your family would like to see me. How late is too late? It's probably now, right? I shouldn't even be bothering you. It's just that I can't sleep, and when my mind races, I think of you. I dream of you. I dream of Keone and imagine who he is now. Six years old. I remember every birthday not just because it is the fourth of July, but because it's the day you agreed to be mine. The day my son came into the world. The day my heart started beating when I looked at you.

The more time that passes, the more I regret not being there for his birth. Not that I knew he was even in existence until you wrote to me. Maybe a part of me wondered. Maybe not.

I can't get onto this flight tomorrow. I can't screw up your life more than I already have. For what it's worth, I'm sorry to the both of you. Maybe I'll just stay put for a little while and see what happens.

Love always, Gideon.

JUNE 28, 1992

Dear Kailani,
Today is my wedding day. I am marrying a

wonder of a woman. We met at the gym I work at here in Oakland, California. I haven't left home in a while. I call this place home. She makes it feel like home. I saw her one day, and I just knew that she was going to be someone really special in my life. It reminded me of the love I had for you instantly upon meeting you. It felt like a bolt of electricity running through my nervous system. I hadn't felt that with anyone since you.

It may seem odd to write to you after all this time just to tell you I am getting married, but you popped into my head again today. If I have found another love, it makes me wonder if you have too. I've thought about you every day since we parted. I don't think I ever stopped loving you. Don't know if I ever will not love you in some way. I am hoping that in finding love again, even a different love, maybe I can let you go a little bit. I know I will always think of you fondly. I know I will always wonder about Keone, but maybe I can be rid of the ghost that haunts me daily. Reminding me that I lost you both, and it was all my fault. I just want to start over. My wife and I are opening up our gym in Portland. We both are ready to get out of the Bay Area and since we met at the gym, I think this business endeavor might just work out. Am I putting down roots? I don't know, but I do know that I would love to think about you less. I'm happy. Can I let myself be happy? I don't know if I will ever be truly happy until I know you are, too.

Still with love always, Gideon.

NOVEMBER 25, 1992

Dear Kailani,
I have a daughter. She was born at 6:14 this
morning. She is the most beautiful thing I have ever
seen. Was Keone this beautiful? Seems like it would be
impossible, considering she is immaculate. I have
never seen anything so pure and innocent. She
carries no blemishes. I know the world will have its
mark on her eventually, but for the few hours she
has been on this earth, she is perfect. She probably
will remain perfect in my eyes forever. There is
nothing this little creature could ever do to make me
stop loving her. It is a love like I have never experienced before. This is what it means to be in love and
I can't believe I deprived myself of this feeling with
Keone. Can I be a good parent now since being a
father to Keone is something I have never been? Will
I ever be? I sing to my daughter the Beatles' song I
used to sing to you. Do you sing it to Keone?
    "Who knows how long I've loved you
    You know I love you still
    Will I wait a lonely lifetime?

If you want me to, I will
For if I ever saw you,
I didn't catch your name
But it never really mattered
I will always feel the same
Love you forever and forever
Love you with all my heart
Love you whenever we're together
Love you when we're apart
And when at last I find you,
Your song will fill the air
Sing it loud so I can hear you
Make it easy to be near you
For the things you do endear you to me
You know I will
I will"

I still think of you when I sing this song. I think of my children. I think of my wife, who has no idea I have a son. I never could tell her. I will wait a lonely lifetime and I will love you and Keone and my daughter forever and ever. I may never be able to heal my heart completely. My wife and my baby girl are like patches on my wounds. But even though we are apart and I am not the man I want to be, I will love you.

Be well, Love Gideon.

SEPTEMBER 7, 1998

> Dear Kailani,
> My wife has died. Cancer. She's just gone. It feels like another great love lost to me. I love her. I miss her. I miss you. . . Maybe I had this coming all along. Maybe I don't deserve love after what I did to you. I never got rid of the ghost of you. How could I love two women and not have either one? How can I possibly screw my life up more? I let you down, Keone, my wife. It feels inevitable that my daughter is next. It feels like a curse and maybe I am doomed to hurt her the most, since all I know is how to lose people. I've never ached like this. My soul feels like it's internally bleeding, like I might drown in my grief. Walking away from you was hard; burying my wife is impossible. How do I do this alone? Why does love always leave?
> Gideon.

37

JOURNAL ENTRY
1999

ugust 4, 1999 (return to sender)

I'm coming, Kailani. Actually, I am here. I know it's been a long time. Over a decade too late. Feels even longer with what has transpired in my life since you wrote to me all those years ago.

How do I begin to apologize for not reaching out sooner? I have no right to get to know my son now. It feels wrong even calling him that. He isn't mine. He is all yours. But that being said, there is a part of me who wants to know him. If you will let me.

I have a daughter. Her name is Jenesis. We call her Jen. I know you would hate that name. She isn't an islander and as much as I wanted to give her an island name because Hawaii has always been the most like home, I felt it was unfair to claim any part of the island that wasn't given to me. I have come back to make amends to you.

Jenesis is almost seven years old. She has never seen the island and I keep telling her we are going to Neverland. She is so enthralled with everything. Especially magic. Hawaii is the closest thing to magic I have experienced.

Jenny's mom passed away almost a year ago. We have become broken people walking around seemingly fine. I need to be fine for her, but it made me realize that life is short and family is important. My son is my family and I hope I haven't ruined my chances of getting to know him.

To be honest, a day hasn't gone by where I haven't thought about you both. I was faithful in my marriage, except I thought of you fondly every day. The love of my life that ended far too soon. I should have run to you the minute you told me you were pregnant. I should have come back and stayed with you on the island, married you like I said I would, and raised our son together.

It is my greatest shame that I left you to do it all alone and whether or not you respond to this letter at all, it will forever be my biggest regret. I don't expect the courtesy of a response.

My one justifier is that I wouldn't have Jen if my life had played out any differently. She is my life, my angel, and if all my mistakes somehow gave me her, then maybe some good came out of those decisions.

I picked up my pen about a dozen times and tried to write to you. I even bought a plane ticket once, but I couldn't muster the courage to get on the flight. I hate to admit that because I know you will think of me as a coward.

Every letter started with "Dear Kailani" and I just felt like I had no right to invade your life. So many times over the years, I tried. Jen's mom never knew of you either. You and Keone are my greatest kept secret. A gemstone I have buried inside my darkened heart. I sought redemption by being a good man; a good father; a good husband. I even convinced myself that I did you a favor by not coming back. That my absence was the best gift I could have given you and Keone.

Life can be cruel sometimes and now I am raising a six-year-old little girl and I am completely and totally on my own. Karma feels like a real thing and what goes around comes around. I left you alone to raise Keone, and the universe knew it needed to right this injustice. I guess. That's sure what it feels like. Tit for Tat.

For a few years there I could silence the shame I felt. I told myself that if things got really bad to where you needed help or money, you would reach out to me again. I thought maybe if I got another letter from you, that maybe I could do the right thing with my second chance. It was unfair of me to wait for

you to give that to me. I remember your fire. How
stubborn you are. There was no way you would write
to me again, only for me to reject you once more. You
have too much pride. Not to mention, where would you
even begin your search for me? My nomadic existence
could have placed me in Timbuktu for all you knew.

Tiff reminded me a lot of you. That was her
name. Tiff or Tiffany, really. She had dark hair like
you and eyes. I swear I saw the ocean in them. For
the time we had together, I was happy. I don't know
if that makes you feel relieved or angry to find out
that I, at a time, found happiness. We went our
separate ways on mutual terms, both brokenhearted,
but in agreement. What wasn't foreseen was Keone?
He changed the entire trajectory, and I wasn't
willing to let anything alter my status quo. Especially
if that change was a child. I fled from the responsibility. I was afraid. That was until Jenesis came into
my life.

I'd love for you to meet her. It's partly why I
brought her. She has no other family aside from me
and part of me would like to know that if something
were to happen to me, that she would have someone
in her corner. Someone who shares her blood and will
watch over her. It is an incredibly selfish request to
ask that Jen and I be a part of your lives. I know
this.

I'm not even sure this will reach you. The only
address I have is the one you used to send me the

letter from all those years ago. I hope that you were true to your ambition and have never left. I know you are still here in Maui. I know you could never leave your home. If you ever did, then part of me hopes that you would have come to find me.

I know I hurt you more than I've ever thought myself capable of hurting anyone. I can't believe I allowed something so stupid to end our relationship. Seeing the world was not more important than being with you. I see the world in Jen's eyes every day and I know it will be the same with my son.

I don't want anything from you. I don't want to impose on your life in any negative way. I know I don't deserve your heart after I had it and broke it. All I ask is for Jen to meet and know she has a brother. I'm sure he is just as beautiful as you were. . . as I'm sure you still are.

You may hate me and no part of me would fault you for that. Please don't take it out on Jen by depriving her of a sibling. She should know Keone.

Should you get this letter and decide to meet me, Jen and I are staying at "the resort." I thought maybe you still worked here in the hotel services. I even asked if you were promoted to management and they said they weren't aware of you as an employee, which makes me think you may have stopped working here a long time ago. I know how much this hotel meant to you back then and I can still feel your presence here, like I am being transported back in time to 1983. We were so young and yet I was old enough to change my life's course completely.

There were so many moments where I could have changed my fate. I could have stayed. I could have responded. I could have come back. To you. To Keone. I am a coward.

I married a woman I loved until her dying breath. I still love her. Cancer is a demon that takes root and very rarely yields its grip. In this case, the cancer won. She was beautiful. Jen is the spitting image of her, which both thrills me and wrecks me at the same time.

Tiff was the one to get me to finally settle down. Looking back, I don't know if it was her influence or if I was just ready for that next chapter in my life, but not even a year after our wedding, we welcomed Jenesis into the world. I could not be more in love. It made me realize that I had never felt love like that. The love a father has for a child and I realized in that moment that I deprived myself of that love. I deprived Keone of the unconditional love I now know I can give.

I didn't think I would be any good as a father figure. That was one of the reasons I never sought you out. My parents never knew I fathered a son. They would have forced me back to you, and I knew that. I couldn't come back unless I could guarantee I wouldn't screw it up. I guess in not even trying, I just automatically failed.

Please meet me. Please come. Meet me on Sunday at the chapel on the resort property. You don't need to bring Keone yet. Just let me know you got my letter. We can talk about it together.

I want to hear about your life. In my dreams, you found a man to father Keone with. You had more children and remain blissfully in love to this day. Maybe he's teaching Keone to drive. Maybe he is the love of your life and has healed the pieces of your heart I broke. You used to call me your Peter Pan and I would call you my Wendy. I hope you grew up well. Part of me feels like I never did and that maybe you were right to call me that. I acted like a foolish child. Please allow me the opportunity to try to make it right. It's coming across in this letter like I am begging. I am begging. In all of my dreams of you, I have always found you happy in life. I want to see you happy. Please don't throw my stupidity back at me. Please respond. Please come.

I will always love you,
Love Gideon.

38

PALM DESERT
2022

I t all feels like a dream. I know it does because I have had this exact dream before. I follow Gideon's letter. He's taken me there. Both now and twenty-four years ago. I know I was just a child, but why wouldn't that memory have stuck with me? My therapist told me that memory loss can be a sign of a trauma response. I kind of laughed at the concept of not remembering things in my past because of age and time, but now I question the validity of my own opinions.

Shit didn't really start to hit the fan until I was about ten years old, or so I thought, but maybe that's just because that's as far back as I can clearly remember. And even then, it's only in spurts and random memories. Ask me what I ate for dinner regularly, or where, and I come up blank. Ask me how much Vicodin Gideon required in addition to his prescribed amount, and I can rattle that off in an instant. I lost this memory for a reason.

The realization that this faded fantasy came from an

experience, knocks the wind out of me. The fact that this letter was returned to my dad also means that maybe Kailani never got word we were there.

I remember a boy, though. If I sit still and meditate deep into my brain, I can almost remember the details. Only my mind is giving me images of me as a mermaid, and I know that didn't happen.

"What is it?" Jules asks from the couch next to me. She pulls me out of my vision or delusion. I'm not sure what to call this experience. Jules and I were reading the letters in the journal. The few I have read and the others I haven't. We are hunched on the couch, yes Adam is still sleeping on it, and we pored over the pages while our new tattoos start to heal. Adam is in the hot tub and he says it was, "because he could." Then he laughed all the way to the pool down the street.

It's all hitting me now. And as fortune would have it, Adam parades back into the condo with a blue striped beach towel wrapped around his middle. Shirtless Adam tends to distract me, so I make a point not to fixate on the moisture beads dribbling down his pecks.

"I remember a boy. We played mermaids together in Hawaii. Dad towered over me, and I remember feeling safe and alive. It was right after mom died, or close to it. I don't remember a woman, though."

"There's no way you could remember everything." Adam chimes in. "Don't beat yourself up." He can tell that I have my butt-kicker on. I feel I should remember traveling with Gideon since we never did.

"Do you think that boy was your brother?" Jules is invested, but she always is.

"If it's not just my imagination, then yeah. . . maybe? He seemed old enough, I think. He would be, what, eight-ish years older than me based on the date of the letters. That would have made him fifteen-ish. The boy in my dream seemed a little younger than that, but I don't think I can trust whatever it is I claim to remember." I pause for a minute. Taking in the truth that there was a crossroads moment in my life that may or may not have altered the trajectory of my childhood. Even into adulthood.

Did that meeting go well? It must not have, since I never knew they existed.

I thought Mom's death drove Dad to seek relief at the bottom of a pill bottle, but now I am not sure that is what set that course of events. At least not solely.

"I HATE that there are things I don't know." I grab my temples in angst, like I am trying to pressure the memories to the surface. "Puzzle pieces I have to put together, and all I have is this stupid diary to try to figure it out. He was kind of an asshole to die before telling me the whole truth!" I once again throw the journal across the room. Battering it just a little more than time has done to it already. "Maybe if I throw it enough, the answers will fall out like that one letter did." I laugh. It's the kind of laugh that comes from pain. I'm in so much pain, but can always mask it with a laugh. Jules and Adam are not swayed.

"Honey, you knew he was an asshole," Jules remarks. Now the laugh is genuine.

"So true!"

The addict in him was an asshole. Not Gideon himself, but at the end of his life, I lost the distinction. The addict was more often present than not. Hence dying of an overdose, I guess.

"What do you want to do now?" Adam asks, and there is no unwillingness in his tone. Whatever I choose to do next is what the two people sitting next to me will do too. It's a lot of power to hold. On one side of me, I have my friend of over two decades who is my rock and has been by my side through so much. I almost expect this of her only because she has proven to do so time and time again. Adam, on the other hand, is a wild card. He has already followed me all over the world and I have only known him for a few months. How can I be so comfortable with his presence in my decision-making when there is still so much to learn about him? Jules and I are woven together like lines on the palms of our hands. Rooted like a palm tree. We are platonic soulmates if soulmates exist. She is mine, but where and what does that leave Adam? He is a coincidence that just keeps occurring. He is like déjà vu.

"I need to know everything," I say the words into my hands as I rub them over my face. "Can we go back to Maui?" I ask it like it isn't Adam's home for most of the year. I say it like I want him to take me back there and not go alone.

"I've already pulled up flights."

39

GIDEON

1999

I did the hard part and got on the plane. Jen did amazingly well on her first flight and quite a long one at that. She colored the whole time while I felt like I was going to throw up from nerves.

I forgot how much the air here makes my heart swell with relief. I'm in my thirties again. A lei is wrapped around me and Jen and she is enthralled with the fact that hers is a mixture of plumeria's that are pink and orange. Her favorite colors. It's the first moment of pure joy I have seen on her face since Tiff died. Watching my wife slip into death from her body's war against her was hard. Telling Jen about how her mom was gone made me physically ill. So much loss and here I am gambling more.

I haven't told Jen she has a brother. If Kailani refuses to meet me, (which is very likely and justifiable,) I don't want Jen to get her hopes up. I can lose more and take it. My heart is nothing but splinters now. There is no chance of revival, but Jen's heart is still pure and I will protect her from any more heartache if I have any say in it.

We check into the resort and while the water pools in the lobby distract Jen and the statue of a mermaid, I ask the concierge to mail my letter. My stomach is in my throat. I guess all I can do now is wait.

- Day 1: I take Jen to the beach and we build sand castles. It's only Thursday. Four days before, I asked Kailani to meet me. I don't get my hopes up for correspondence back, but when the sun sets on day one, I can feel my disappointment and urgency settle in.

- Day 2: Friday and the resort is full to its capacity. Jen and I wander around the property. I don't want to leave just in case she stops by early or I get a letter back. I still don't know if she even got my letter. I can feel the jitters get even more intense and I want so badly to go knock on her door. If anything, I can see if she got my letter, but I check my resolve and continue to wait. Jen and I have a lot to explore here and she is the best distraction I could ever hope for.

- Day 3: My heart feels like it is going to beat out of my chest. I even thought I was having a heart attack. Then I had a panic attack because the thought of leaving Jenesis alone on this earth is my nightmare. I can't think, I can't eat wondering if she will show up tomorrow. Jen has

been eating ice cream after ice cream at the pool
and I can't even tell you what color my swimsuit
is. I am so nervous. One breath at a time.

- Day 4. Today came. Today went. She never
  showed.

40

GIDEON

1999

I refuse to accept that she didn't come because of her anger towards me. I just said that as a courtesy. I know her, and I know me, and if given the opportunity, I know we are both too curious not to at least show up. She'd never pass up an opportunity to chew me out. I left Jenesis at the kids' club. She was checked in for a two-hour program and I take the opportunity to go and see for myself.

A short taxi ride later and I am here at her door. I haven't stood here in over a decade, but there is something still so constant. I just know this remains Kailani's family home. As if there is a force field around the home, as if it's some invisible fence, I am pushed back. My feet feel like lead. I can't move, but I can't turn around. My cab left.

Only one way and it is forward. With all of my courage, which lately doesn't feel like a lot, I trudge on and knock on the door. As if someone else is making the motions for me.

For a long while there is no answer. I don't hear rustling on the inside. I have to get back to pick up Jenesis in a little over an hour. No signs of life are detected. Then a small crack.

"Who are you?"

It is a youthful voice just beginning to deepen several octaves.

"I'm Gideon. Um, Gideon Haynes. Is Kailani still living here, by any chance?" I ask this voice through a slit in the door.

He opens it fully.

"No, but did you say Gideon?" He looks at me almost like I am someone he has been expecting for a while now. There is elation and dismay written all over his face.

"You're really him?"

It's the tears in his eyes that make me realize. "And You're Keone. And you're. . ." I can't seem to get the words out past the tears choking my throat. "And you're my son." I want so badly to wrap him in my arms and pour out all the love I have staved away for him. I inch closer when a shadow appears and darkens Keone's already island features. He is so like his mother. Then the shadow speaks.

"Get back inside the house, Keone."

Without question, Keone backs away.

"Wait." I reach out to him as if to pull him back to me. So much already a man. So much of his life I missed.

"Keone has nothing to say to you." I recognize this man. Kailani had a cousin, Leo, Kyle, L. L. L. "Loto!" I exclaim.

"It's Lito."

"Yes. Sorry about that. Lito. Have you been, brother?"

"You of all people do not get to call me brother." Lito interrupts me.

"No, I mean, of course. I. . . I have come to make amends and, with Kailani's permission, get to know my son. Is she here? How can I see her? I wrote her a letter."

"Oh, we got your letter." Lito crosses his arms. "It's about fifteen years too late."

There is no convincing Lito otherwise. Nor do I want to. "I agree. I should have been here the minute I read that Kailani had the baby. My baby. He clearly isn't a baby anymore. If she got my letter and she didn't come, then I am sorry and I will leave and never come back." I can't bear to be on this porch any longer. I might be sick on their welcome mat. She didn't come because she never wanted to see me again. She didn't come even though I begged. She didn't. . .

"Wait. You said we read your letter. You didn't say, 'She read your letter.' Did she read my letter? Keone didn't know I was here. Does she?"

"She can't, bro-th-er." He separates every part of the word. "She's dead."

I think what's left of my heart just fell through the dirt beneath me and straight into the center of the earth. "No, she isn't. She can't be." I refuse to believe this.

"Oh yeah. Do you want the complete story or just the highlights? You see, she wrote you this letter. You might remember it. About fifteen years ago. She didn't know if you would ever receive it, but since you just confessed, I guess now we know our answer. She detailed in this letter, to my recollection, that she had just given birth to a little boy who was fathered by a said Gideon Haynes. Is this correct?"

"Yes," I whisper. So much shame weighs me down.

"You have to fill in some dots, you see. We never saw the end result of this quest."

"This quest?" I ask, genuinely confused. "You've lost me."

"Oh, well, you see. My cousin refused to believe that you would have been able to receive her letter and not come to see them; To come back home, she would always say. So she left Keone with me and my wife before she bought a plane ticket to Oakland, CA. A plane ticket to come and see you. Only she never made it to the plane. Some tourists got drunk and were driving on the wrong side of the highway. Her cab driver didn't see them in time. She was dead instantly. As were the cab driver and two of the tourists."

I can feel the blood leave my face. I might pass out. I go to stick my head between my knees, but Lito isn't quite finished.

His tone has dropped and has gone from caustic to subdued. "My cousin left behind a beautiful baby boy, to gallivant off the island in search of his father. The person she swore if he knew of his son's existence would come home to Hawaii and be a family. She knew she never wanted to leave this island and the island wouldn't let her. If you never left her, she would have had Keone and never have had to leave her home chasing a man who couldn't care less."

That burns my soul. "I do care. I do care. So much." The tears are falling hard now. I can't breathe. "I'm so sorry. I'm. . ." My watch beeps at me, alerting me that I have to get back to Jenesis. "I'm sorry, I have to go."

"What, running away again Haynes?" Lito calls after me. "Don't want to meet your son now?"

"I do. I do. I just have to be somewhere. I'll come back." I'm pleading. I know I'm stuck between a rock and a hard place.

"I wasn't going to give you the satisfaction, but I'm glad to see where your priorities still lie. Anyone and anywhere but here. Isn't that right Gideon?"

It isn't. I don't want it to be, but I can't disappoint Jenesis. Not when I already don't have good news to share with her. I don't say anything back. What is there to say? Kailani is gone. My wife is gone. My son wants nothing to do with me. He knew who I was or he wouldn't have asked. Jenesis is all I have to live for now.

"If it's worth anything, tell Keone I'm sorry." I plead with Lito, then never look back.

41

MAUI
2022

"Nothing clears the mind like the open horizon."

Or so Adam says, but it's easy to believe him. As I stare into where the ocean meets the sky and try to find where they seem to mix, I again feel like the elephant on my chest is taking a break from crushing me. I have had many moments of reprieve. All Adam induced now that I think of it.

Jules didn't follow us to Hawaii. She couldn't take any more time off of work after Palm Desert. I understood, but we both were bummed.

"You know you hold a lot of tension in your shoulders?"

For a brief moment, I can feel myself melt into his touch. It's light as he grazes over the nape of my neck; pulling a strand of damp hair away from my skin. A very real part of me knows that his touch means more than just a friend loosening up a sore muscle, and that same part of me knows that I cannot pull away from it. No matter how much my brain is screaming it's a bad idea. My heart is currently more influential.

"Ouch!" I yelp when his thumbs brush over a tender spot. "Can you be gentler?" I smack his hand away, and he barely flinches before putting it right back.

"I'm barely touching you." he laughs a low and breathy chuckle but continues kneading my neck. Now with both hands. "How long have you had this knot? It feels like solid stone."

If only he knew.

"It. . . can't. . . be. . . that. . . bad. . . Oh my gosh! Stop!" Adam pulls his hands away in a dramatic pull, keeping his hands up by his face like he is under arrest.

"Sorry." He says, still smiling.

"You are so not sorry. I might have a bruise tomorrow."

"Oh, you will have a bruise, but can you honestly say a bruise is worse than carrying that stress around? Look where you are. Be here. With me."

I can see the longing in his eyes. The want that has been there since I walked out of his bedroom. It's been like a dull fire behind his eyes and I know that it is just growing the more time we spend alone.

"Don't look at me like that," I say, trying to stomp that fire out.

"Like what?" I see the embers flicker. He's always playful; always teasing and yet not now. He is all anguish and sincerity. "How do you want me to look at you?"

It's a fair question. I don't have an answer that will suffice. Because the truth is, I do want him to look at me like he is. Like the world begins and ends in the small space between us. Like the world might implode if we fill that gap and neither one of us will mind.

I cover my face with my hands and laugh. It's an uncomfortable laugh. "I don't know. Just not like that."

Both of our bodies sit in the sand. The day is coming to its end, but not for us. The adventure ahead spans well into the night. I have to settle my emotions around this man before I come completely undone by him in the span of what will indubitably be a sleepless night.

"Stop looking at me like you want me," I said it.

"You think this is how I look at you when I want you?" For a flash, it looks like Adam feels called out, but then he leans in even closer. "Oh Wanderlust, the way I would look at you if I wanted you would be much deeper than how I am looking at you now."

"Oh, yeah?" I know I'm asking for it, swallowing my words as if they are stones.

"Oh yes. Not only would I gaze into your intricate eyes, but you would feel my stare roam over your entire body. I would merely begin my gaze at your eyes, then I would angle down towards your breasts, begging to lay eyes upon the perfect peaks that I was only privileged enough to lay eyes upon once before. The part of you that lays torturously hidden by that tiny bikini you wear. The most perfect breasts." He lets out a low huff as he stares at my bikini top. The hunger growing inside him. "Then I would roam lower."

My face grows flush.

"Are you blushing?" Adam scoots closer and wraps his arms around my middle in the sand.

"No! It's the sunset reflecting on my pale skin. I have been out of the sun for too long. London paled me and I desperately need a tan."

Adam doesn't believe me for a second. I probably should have said it was a sunburn rather than try to convince him my skin is so translucent it's like a mirror. Too late now.

"Then, when my eyes don't satisfy my desire for you. I will have to take you."

"Take me where?" My throat bobs up and down and mimics his. I don't dare look any lower than his face for fear of what I know I will find thick against the hem of his swimsuit. There is no disguising it. Even I feel a rush of heat as he burns for me. I play dumb, but I know better. I can't let my arousal show. I can't let him win.

"No Wanderlust, I would TAKE you. With my arms, my mouth, my body, and if I were ever so lucky again to be inside you. . . the barbarian inside me wouldn't be able to stop until satisfied. My only satisfaction witnessing you writhe in pleasure, scream my name on your perfect lips, and come around me so hard while I watch you shatter before me. I want to feel the pride of making you unhinge with pleasure."

Holy crap.

I'm sweating, trying to ignore the desire he has now churned inside me. The fire in his eyes has gone from a dull flame to a full-on roar. I don't know how the distance between us has closed, but I still don't dare look down. I don't need to look. He's close enough I can feel the strength of what lies in his shorts. Pure steel pressed now against my thigh. It's not foreign to me. I've known Adam's body in mine once before, but it was rushed and I wasn't in the right headspace. The scenario he is describing is not the same one we engaged in before. And it makes me squirm thinking about how different our entanglement could be.

"I will forever despise myself for how I had you the first time. I was selfish and hurried and I promise you I will never give you less than what you deserve ever again. I will only ever take my time making sure every inch of your body experiences pleasure before I fixate on the one place I know makes you release with such intensity. You'll see stars." It all comes out just above a whisper and his finger teases the waistline of my swimsuit bottoms. I don't move. I hardly breathe. That passion he has, he's transferred to me. I want him. I want him so badly.

"I guess we will never know. One of us is too stubborn to admit defeat."

I know he is referring to the bet, and I know he is referring to me. Although, he is just as stubborn as I am and the worst kind of tease.

"A guy can dream, though." He pushes a stray strand of my darkened hair away from my face. I want to close the remaining gap between us. I want to press my lips to his. I want to yell into the sea that the bet is stupid and that I don't care what I said. I almost lower my guard. A part of me wants to prove him wrong so that I can prove me right. I might not be as stubborn as he thinks, but that spot sitting at the apex of my thighs is begging for his touch. Aching for any sort of friction it can get. Part of me doesn't mind having to beg.

"ADAM! Hey!" That voice. Her voice. I knew Natalie

was coming. All of his friends are, but of course, she is the first to arrive. Adam inches away from me and adjusts his shorts. I know why.

Thank goodness.

Natalie has made it clear that we are not about to be friendly any time soon. She wants Adam, but she did just save us from making a huge mistake. Again. So I guess I am grateful to her.

She struts toward us with a sleeping bag, a mat, and a lantern under her arm. I swear I also see a bottle of something tucked up in her other arm. Something I don't plan on partaking in tonight. My inhibitions are already lowered. When she makes it to us, she sets her stuff down next to ours and plops her butt in the sand so close to Adam she may as well have sat in his lap. Thank goodness she didn't or she would be privy to the evidence of what was transpiring between us just a few moments ago.

"Ready to camp on the beach?" She throws her arms around Adam and places one in his sandy hair. Tossing it back and forth just a bit. It's the female version of pissing on your territory and she's acutely aware that I know exactly what she is doing.

"I didn't know you would be joining us tonight, Jenesis." She says my name like it's a curse word. Like it hangs on her tongue in disgust. She may as well have gagged afterward.

"Adam convinced me to come back to Hawaii for a bit before my travels end." I do not say that I came here to find my estranged brother and am staying with Adam because he insisted I not spend money on a hotel. "I've never camped before. At least not without a tent and heavy gear. Sleeping on the beach and under the stars sounded like a bucket list item I just couldn't pass up on."

"Yeah, he can be rather convincing." She glares at me, and part of me wonders if she heard our hushed conversation before appearing on the shoreline. As subtle as she expresses her displeasure that I am here, she pulls Adam to her and begs for his attention. "Come on, Adam, let's go for a dip in the ocean before it gets dark. Let's bathe in the colors of the sunset." She whines as she tugs him up from his seated position. She's effective. I'll give her that. She knows how to get what she wants. I don't plan to stand in her way.

Her voice and actions towards Adam are like plunging myself into cold water. It is a blatant reminder that not only do we have an agreement not to fall in love, but I am leaving in a few days and Natalie is here and in love with him. I am a factor in this scenario that shouldn't be included. I am an observer of their inevitable love story and it is a good reminder.

Natalie wastes no time throwing herself into the waves. Of course, she is feigning difficulty. There are very few actual waves.

I simply sit where I have been this whole time. I can see the imprint Adam left in the sand, and here I remain. Immobile really, except for the sand I rub between my fingers; fidgeting with the earth as I observe the spectacle before me.

Natalie playfully falls into Adam repeatedly. The perfect damsel in distress with tanned boobs she is purposefully crashing into him, chest first. I know this is all an act, but part of it is nice to see. You don't have to be a moron to see that Natalie and Adam would be really good together. She knows it; I know it. Adam hasn't gotten the memo, though. Maybe I should be the one to paint the picture for him. As little as we know each other, we have spent a lot of time together lately. Maybe I would have some sway in leading him in her direction.

She's beautiful, albeit headstrong, but maybe that fire inside her is exactly what Adam needs. All our flaws can be assets when used appropriately. Adam doesn't need a docile doe-eyed dame. He needs someone who can keep up with him. Natalie knows how to match his pace.

As soon as my mind decides to forcefully enforce their union, I feel a twinge in my chest.

It can't be jealousy. Can it?

Adam doesn't seem to mind her advances, even though I can tell with his body language that he knows she's playing a game. My guess is she is probably one of the best swimmers in the group. To be ignorant of that fact would indeed make him blind. Especially when there are no swells to carry her slender frame further out to sea.

Would that be so bad? Bye-bye Natalie. Have a pleasant swim.

I flinch a little. Appalled by my thoughts, but if the deep wells in the sand where my hands dig are any indication of the emotions churning inside, and I mean deep inside, then maybe watching the two of them play the happy honeymoon couple is kind of wearing on me a little bit.

Adam glances back at me, throws his arm in the air, and yells for me to join them. Natalie's plucky face immediately turns sour.

"No, no. I'm good just watching the sunset from the shore. No need to bathe in the colors." I make fun of Natalie's words from before.

They both swim out a decent way. The tide providing the perfect avenue for their escape into the crystal clear teal waters, so unless they decide to yell at me, I can't hear them. I've never been very good at reading lips, but I can read energies and as Adam speaks to Natalie, I can tell she is disappointed in the conversation.

Natalie, still with her arms wrapped around Adam's neck, bobs with the lull of the ocean as Adam leans in closer to whisper something in her ear. I can see her smirk wash away and with it, Adam begins to swim ashore. Natalie close behind.

Watching him swim freestyle back to the beach is something else. Each pull of the water, as it draws his body closer to the sand, ripples his muscles in its tension.

Natalie, very gracefully, swims the same stroke behind.

I knew it was all an act. She could out-swim a shark.

I feel proud that I can tell when someone is being genuine and when someone is being bogus. The realization that Adam has only ever given me that feeling of being honest is probably why I find it difficult to retreat from him. My past also makes it hard to trust him, but I want to.

"You didn't have to come back on my account," I say as I watch him emerge from the water like some sort of mythological god. Poseidon himself could never.

"That's ok. We are done. The sun is going down, anyway."

Natalie harrumphs at his comment. Her arms cross

across her chest to accentuate her cleavage more, but I can tell by her pursed lips that whatever she was trying to prove out there - well, it didn't go as planned.

The corners of my mouth curve into the smallest of grins and I catch myself before I let it show too much. Natalie just winces. She saw. Girls know when they compete with one another, but how do I tell her that my brain is a cheerleader for her and Adam to be together? My heart might be saying something different, but there is no way I am going to admit that to her. I can't even justify my emotions to myself.

THE SUN BEGINS TO DIP INTO THE OCEAN FOR A GOOD NIGHT of resting and Adam, Natalie, and I have been setting up our small outdoor campsite. Adam's bungalow is a mere feet away, but we all decided to camp on the beach tonight, which means Adam opted out of his bed for a sleeping bag on the sand. Insanity. As soon as Adam sets up the campfire for the night, the rest of the gang shows up with Zeke leading the charge.

Natalie is used to being the only girl in a group full of guys and I hate to classify her as a "pick me girl" because truly I think she is much more complex than that, but I get why she doesn't like to share her toys (I mean boys) with other females. Especially with someone who has taken so much attention from Adam. Me.

Zeke brought me one of his extra sleeping bags and it smells a little like saltwater, sweat, and orange juice for some reason, but I take it with gratitude and set it up in the circle we have spread out around the fire. Of course, Natalie, without hesitation, places hers right by Adam. I just hold mine under my arms until everyone settles in their spots. I am a newcomer and know the rules of the pecking order, but Zeke takes the wadded fabric out from under my arm and places it in between him and Adam.

"Thank you," I mumble.

"Sure thing. Did you think I was going to set you up next to Natalie? She snores." Zeke hurls his insult right at her.

"I do not, Zeke. You are so immature." Natalie sticks her tongue out at him in a hypocritical and equally immature gesture.

"She talks in her sleep, too." He loudly whispers at me. She doesn't engage this time. "Of course, if Adam is sleeping in between two girls, you better believe I get to sleep next to one of them, too. Fair is fair. I picked Jenesis because yeah, Nat, you do snore. Like an old gnome in a thunderstorm." Zeke flares his nostrils in a dramatic, mocking snort.

"Whatever Zeke."

"Whatever Natalie." Zeke mocks back at her.

"Look what I brought. I brought party favors!" Natalie gestures towards her bag and I am impressed that it is rather small. For such a girly girl, I thought she would travel with her own vanity light and a suitcase of mascara, but she does know how to get down and dirty with the rest of them. Out of her bag, she pulls a small ziplock of what looks like beet juice gummies made out of a crystal mold.

"I don't think that is such a good idea tonight, Nat." Adam pushes her hand back into her bag.

"What? Oh, come on, it's been ages since we all let loose and had a little fun. I made them myself. I promise they aren't as strong as last time."

"Oh, you mean the time that Adam started streaking and panicking that the volcano was beginning to erupt and would bury us all alive in molten lava?" Zeke jokes and I think I get it now.

"Is that marijuana?" I whisper to Zeke, who honestly has become a kind of confidant in these group settings we've been in.

Zeke does a low smile and just nods. I swear I hear a small rumble of a laugh building in his chest.

"I panicked okay, Natalie made them way stronger than she said she did. Paranoia is a very normal reaction." Adam turns a shade of red only associated with embarrassment.

"I never have." The words leave me before I can think about what I said. I don't know why I am so forthcoming and I kind of wish I could take it back. Not so much out of embarrassment, but I know what comes next, but like a tube of toothpaste, that crap is not going back in.

"Never?" Everyone in unison echoes in an almost melody.

"Nope. Never had the opportunity." (Not totally true).

"You mean edibles, right? Like you've smoked it before, for sure." Colby, (whose name I now remember,) gestures from across the flames, but I can see the disbelief in his eyes.

He's usually pretty quiet, but I guess my lack of recreational drug usage has rendered him not speechless for once.

I just shake my head and laugh. "Nope."

"How old are you?"

"I just turned thirty."

Another universal gasp reverberates around the fire. Adam, however, doesn't even twitch.

"I also brought booze for those too chicken." She looks at me. "But, if you're not scared then. . ." Natalie unzips the bag and hands me the first one.

She may as well have been taunting, "Neener neener neener."

I know what this is. It's the peer pressure that every parent warned about when we were kids. Every bumper sticker and flier read "Don't Do Drugs Kids." Only I am not a kid anymore. My parents are both dead and there is no poignantly placed propaganda to tell me otherwise.

I also know that I am at a crossroads. Either I take it and fall prey to basically Natalie's dare, or I deny her and get basically called out for being too chicken-shit at thirty years old. I have never felt like it was something I needed to experience, and I can smell the manipulation lingering in the air between me and Natalie. She has more power than I like someone having over me and it all stems from an outstretched gummy.

Even if I say no, I couldn't care less what sorts of jabs Natalie hurls my way. It's mostly my curiosity that takes the pink treat from her hand and pops it in my mouth. What's the worst that could happen - besides streaking and molten lava? The smile on her face proves she feels she's won, and with my acceptance of the offering, the rest of the circle takes one as well. I couldn't win. She pinned me in a lose-lose. At least now I might have a good time and a new "never have I ever" to check off my list.

"See you on the other side," I yell as the fire crackles in an almost excitable endorsement.

42

MAUI

2022

"I don't feel anything. How will I know when it kicks in?"

"Oh, you'll know." Adam stares at me from the periphery of his eye. I can't tell if he is disappointed I took the dare or is just watching me, making sure I don't start streaking. Maybe hoping I start streaking.

They have all done this before. It's a reminder that despite Natalie's bitterness toward me, I have been included in a family of sorts. She really is mostly all talk.

"How long does it usually take?"

Colby is back to his quiet, brooding self, just staring straight into the dancing flames, while Zeke can't help but make himself laugh. All signs that they both are on their way to another dimension right now.

"Do you feel it yet?" I gesture to Adam.

"No."

"I told you I made them less strong this time." Natalie scrunches closer to Adam. "I'm cold."

I watch as Adam takes his hoodie and slide it over her shoulders. Ever a considerate friend, but there is something in her eyes that screams trouble. I know she feels the effects of what she took. His jacket isn't enough to satisfy her lack of him, and she slides into his lap for more body warmth. I can sense Adam tense when she settles in between his legs. I note that he doesn't kick her off him, but he keeps his hands perched in the sand behind him.

"You know Adam," she hums in his ears as if she might just lick his neck if she so feels like it. "If I get as high as you did last time, maybe we can go streaking together? It wouldn't be the first time you've seen me naked."

I catch the hint. She will never know it phases me a little. *Wouldn't streaking make her more cold?*

I'm honestly amused by her territorial show. Adam, however, is not. In one swift motion, Natalie is forced off his lap as he stands tall and takes my hand in his. "Jenesis, want to go on a walk with me?"

"Sure."

If Natalie isn't warm now, her seething rage ought to do the trick. I can see the literal steam.

I take Adam's hand and he leads me down the beach. The rest of the group too high to notice we even leave.

"WHY DID YOU STEAL ME AWAY FROM THE GROUP?" I ASK AS we get out of earshot. I swear I can still feel Natalie burning a hole in the back of my head with her glare. She has too much pride to have included herself on our little jaunt.

"I just need some fresh air and I can't let you out of my sight in case you do something stupid, like take another homemade edible out of the hand of someone who very clearly doesn't like you."

"You *know* why Natalie is averse to me." I bait him. "You *know* that she wants you. Why don't you give her a chance? She is by no means grotesque (personality excluded) and wants in your pants so desperately she would probably be a ton of fun for you."

"What's that supposed to mean?" Adam takes offense.

"I just mean it's nice to feel desired so ardently. That's all. I think she would be good for you."

"Well, maybe I desire someone else. Have you ever thought of that?"

Once again, I don't like how Adam is looking at me. "I think that you're high if you don't want to tap that." I make a crass gesture and make light of the conversation.

"I'm not high because I don't want Natalie. She's a wonderful person and a great friend, I just don't see her that way-"

"-anymore." I cut him off.

"What?"

"I am assuming you guys have slept together. You might want to tell Zeke. He has no idea. Did you miss the part where she slipped in that you have already seen her perfect model body naked? It was only a second ago."

"How does that make you feel?" I watch as he slides his hands in his sandy beach-wave hair and asks the question a million therapists in my lifetime have asked me. I just pinch my eyebrows in confusion. "I'm not jealous, if that's what you're asking."

"Uh-huh." I can tell he doesn't believe me. I don't believe me. That conversation we had earlier still gives me tingles when I recall some words whispered to me in hushed tones.

"You look down at your feet when you lie, you know. You would never be very good at poker."

"Okay then. I felt *something*, but it wasn't jealousy. I don't know what it was. . . and if not Natalie, then who? Because I just don't get it."

We walk almost hand in hand along the shoreline. No part of me is chilled. Once again, I think Natalie may have fibbed a little. Feigned her little needy attitude to get what she wanted.

"Sometimes there are just people who can trigger you in all the wrong ways. Natalie is a great friend, but anything more just reminds me of a time in my past I'm trying to move on from. You know, like your dad. You love them, but sometimes they just aren't that person for you. Every story needs a villain, you know? She just turns me into the villain of my own story."

"What do you mean by that?" I ask. My body visibly inching away from him.

"What did I mean by what? Which part exactly?"

"When you said 'every story needs a villain'?"

Adam looks quizzical. "I didn't mean to offend you. I just meant she brings out things in me I don't like about myself. That's all."

"Yeah. . . well. . ." I scoff and step further away from him, brushing the sand from my body where it clung to from earlier.

"Jenesis, I'm sorry. Truly, I didn't mean it in a bad way"

I can tell he means it. He used my real name. No nicknames. No snickers. I know that this apology is genuine and yet something inside me can't just accept that and go back to swaying so close with someone who I am not supposed to be falling in love with. It's all getting a little too comfortable for "just friends." And yet, I just can't stop myself from adding gasoline to this fire and burning down the entire beach and whatever lingers between me and Adam with it.

"You mean you calling my dad a villain, or essentially an evil person, was not meant to hurt my feelings? Okay. . . got it." He knows I'm being sarcastic.

"What are you doing?" He pulls my hand, and we sit down on that stupid beach. The sand instantly feels gritty and not soft like before.

"Nothing. I'm not doing anything." I cross my arms over my body. Once again painfully aware that I am half naked in a swimsuit and wish I wasn't. Desperately, I use my limbs to hide my exposed skin.

"Yes, you are, and you know it. You are picking a fight with me because you feel something here and you are running away from it. Again. And you are using your dad as an excuse for it. You know that I understand the pain of addiction. You know, I didn't say he was the villain in your story to insinuate that he was a bad person. I've told you that's not what I think about that horrible disease. My brother wasn't a bad person, but until he got clean, he was the person who made poor decisions that leaked into my life. That's all. I don't lord it over him. It's just that he made bad decisions and I couldn't rely on him. I found the people who I call family. Those people around the fire. They are my family in many ways, and that includes Natalie. She's like a pesky little sister to me. She drives me nuts, but she is a part of a group of people who were there for me during a dark time. They were there for me until things got better and even after."

His tone is level. He doesn't rise to meet my temper, and it only makes mine grow.

Yell at me and get mad at me. I deserve it.

"I'm just saying. . ." He inhales deeply, like he knows the next words he says are either going to diffuse me or set me off. Like a bomb. "I'm just saying that we can't pick who our family is, but sometimes we can choose people who become our family in other ways."

I want to tell him I know. That I understand what he is saying. He is saying it well, actually. My head and my mouth are not working together. I feel like I have no control over my tongue. It's sharp and ready to bite. I want to backtrack and go back to a few minutes before. Before I got offended, or did I? Before I let it escalate to the point where he feels like he has to defend himself. I'm like a snowball running downhill; gaining speed and getting bigger with every tussle in the snow. If left unchecked, this will become a full-on avalanche.

"You couldn't choose who you had as a father, or the fact that your mom died when you were little. It left you alone, but you can find family-type people elsewhere. Family is an earned honor, not a blood-related title." He shrugs and looks down. Waiting. "That's all I'm saying."

A moment stands still between us. A crossroads. I can accept his apology and go back to this beautiful evening under the stars. I can curl up into my sleeping bag that has been politely laid out for me. I can not let some words that came across as hurtful ruin this entire experience. Or. . .

"I know I can choose who I let be close to me, Adam. That's just it! What you aren't understanding is that given the *choice*, I still would have chosen him! The him without all the pills. The him without the need to drink. The him without the pain in his heart that led to the pain in his entire body. The pain that led him to his demise. I would choose him. The him I had as a small child. I want him back. And he's just. . . gone. Without so much as an 'I love you' or a 'goodbye' even. Just dead.

"You can't possibly understand. Yeah, sure, your brother was an addict. He got clean, and you got redemption for all of his mistakes that affected your life. You get to witness what I never will. You get to experience him without his addictions ruling his life. You get to be privy to and partake in his miraculous healing. I don't get that kind of closure." I gesture to my chest and grab my skin so tightly it burns pink. Aggravating the sunburn from earlier.

"If I could rip my heart out so I don't feel like this anymore, I would. I want to cease the relentless weight on my chest that is this lack. Lack of hope. Lack of closure. Lack of him. Lack of love." My voice pitches up, choking back brimming tears.

I can't tell if I am crying because of anger or sadness,

but as I unload all of my pain out onto this beach (onto Adam), I watch as his eyes grow and wonder if his body will decide to retreat or reach for me.

I'm panting, I'm so overwhelmed and the only other sounds are the waves hitting the shore. Adam left his porch light on and, even from the distance away, it lights up his face. The concern, the want to reach over this invisible barrier I put between us and rip it down. I see the scar on his lip. I watch as it tightens, like he wants to say something, but then closes his mouth with the lack of anything he knows would be helpful or change what I have already destroyed.

"I'm sorry." Is all he can mutter out. It's all that's left to say when nothing is left and nothing really can be said. But then he follows it up with a soft, "please. . ."

"What? Please, what?" He's so soft-spoken and I am just berating him. Still on fire and wanting to singe him in the process.

His eyes meet mine and I can see the embers perk up. I've successfully lit him on fire. He is done trying to play the extinguisher and is ready to engage. I find it sadistically satisfying.

"Please, don't push me away. I know you're hurting that much is obvious, but you can't keep pushing the people who care about you away. I know you are comfortable in the loneliness, but it will slowly destroy you. It keeps the cycle going. The one you want so badly to break free from.

"I am here. I am standing right here before you. We are having a beautiful evening. Or at least we were until I went and put my foot in my mouth. You know I didn't mean anything by it. I was talking about me and my story and yet you can't or won't accept my apology and I know why."

I hate that he can see past all my bullshit.

"Oh yeah? Why?" I am so confrontational.

Adam looks me dead in the eyes. He does not waver from them. He wants to say this to my soul and isn't cowering in fear. He's not afraid of me, but he should be. My wildfire might burn him, but it won't disintegrate him. He's too pertinacious.

"Because Jen. You are starting to fall in love with me and you can't admit it. You can't admit to yourself that you feel anything for me beyond friendship. You made a promise to yourself that you wouldn't fall for me. In your mind, you feel like you're losing."

"I am losing." I interrupt him. "I'd be losing the bet."

"Is that why you are pushing me away? This isn't about some stupid bet! Who cares? I only struck that deal so I could spend more time with you. I wanted to be around you. To be in the pull of your atmosphere; be around your energy."

"So are you saying you lose?" I want to hear him say it. I want to hear that I was right. That we can't just be friends.

"Yes, Jenesis. I lose! Okay! I admit it. I lost the second we struck the deal. I knew I loved you in Alaska. Is that what you want to hear? The girl in the saloon with a dazed and lost look on her face and a drink in her hand. I knew at that moment I had to know you. That I would chase you around the world if I had to and I guess that's what fate had in store for us anyway. I hated that I thought I'd never see you again and when you showed up drunk at my doorstep, it felt like the universe was giving me a second chance. Like I was right to chase you and wouldn't get another opportunity to do so. I made a stupid bet so I wouldn't have to accept that I'd let you go again."

"Ha!"

Adam jumps back.

"You lose and have to tell me where Neverland is!"

I kind of feel silly calling it that for some reason. Like it really doesn't hold any magic without Adam in it.

"I mean the waterfall. You have to give me directions to the waterfall." I feel a little childish.

"Alright." Adam agrees. "Is there anything else?"

"Like what?"

"I don't know. How about you feel the same way? How you want me as well? How you're done playing games and want to be with me too? Is any of this striking true?"

Strike true. Like an arrow to hit a Lost Boy after striking down a Wendy Bird.

I want so badly to say this back, but I just watch as Adam inches back towards me. My arms still crossed over my chest. I stand up from sitting in the sand and wait for him to follow my lead.

"What would you have wanted if I did lose the bet?" I ask as he takes another step toward me. And another. I stay firmly planted in the sand.

"I wanted you. Your heart." He places a hand under my chin and leans in for a kiss. I can almost feel the softness in his sun-blistered lips as they hover over mine. For one second I think I might just and then I don't.

"No," I say as I pull away.

"Really Jenesis. Am I making all this up in my head?"
He's hurt.

"What about Natalie?" I add more fuel.

"What about Natalie?" He throws my question back to
me. "I explained Natalie."

"She's who you should be with. She wants you and she's
beautiful and she's here. She isn't burdened, and she clearly
has been pining after you."

"What makes you think that just because she wants me,
she can have me?" It's a fair question.

"What makes you think that just because you want me,
you can have me?" Just as he threw my question back to me,
so I do to him.

"I can't have you just because I want you. You have to
want me too."

"How did we get here?" I laugh uncomfortably and run
my fingers through my sandy, salty hair. I don't want to be
here anymore. I want out of my skin and out of my mind. I
want back in that salty, orangey-smelling sleeping bag and
drift off into oblivion. I feel at war with my mind and my
heart. I could let Adam in and it would be so easy and yet
doing so feels like what little is left of me might shatter upon
a collision. He feels too much. It scares me.

"We are here because you can't admit you have feelings
for me." It's the first time Adam hasn't made an obvious
joke.

"Really? I thought you were going to say 'We walked
over here.'"

"I don't feel in a joking mood." He doesn't. "What do
you want, Jenesis?"

You. I want you.

"You." I actually say it.

Nothing else is said. The minor break in our bodies that I put there when he tried to kiss me last has been consumed, and the world doesn't immediately implode. He doesn't inch into me like he had tried. He isn't treading lightly. His whole body pushes me back and catches me. The back of his forearms wrap around my waist and force me into him.

The warmth of his tongue slides over my teeth, and I part, letting him in. It was all the permission he needed. Like an engine revving and waiting for that green flag to fall. I waved it in front of him and he took off.

I want this. I want him. I silence my mind and allow my heart to take over. If only to see what happens next. What it will feel like to satisfy this part of me. And at this moment, it hits me. That sneaky pink treat I forgot I took earlier. I feel it. I'm high.

43

MAUI

2022

Every inch of my body screams for Adam to touch it. Even before he touches me, my body reacts to it. To his heat, to the anticipation of his hands on me. His mouth. Everything feels like it's been amplified times a hundred and I know that it has to be whatever strain of weed was in that gummy.

I don't feel like I do when I drink. Maybe my inhibitions are lowered, but not in the same way. I know I will remember every moment of what this night will hold for years to come. I am not afraid of the drug taking my memory of this away. It couldn't, even if that was a part of its process. I know this memory will forever be etched on my heart. Like a scar or a reminder of what I will never allow myself to fully keep.

What happened that permitted us to have this moment? Maybe Adam is high, and that's why we both fell into each other like this. Maybe his inhibitions are lowered, the same as mine.

A moan flees from his lips as he drags his hands up my hips and settles around my waist. I go absolutely feral for that moan, and I can't help but mimic. A few breaths more and Adam pulls me to my feet, leading me toward the water. The Ocean. This amazing mass called the Pacific invites us to shadow ourselves amongst its waves. We are far enough down the beach that I am not concerned the others will be lurking in on us. Nor am I afraid anyone has followed closely. Whatever transpires between us in the next section of time, however long that may be, will remain solely between me and Adam. The ocean, however, is inviting us to join its rhythm.

I take Adam's hand, floating alongside like a balloon he is trailing behind him, high in the sky and held together by a string. I have felt that string between us tether us together since the minute we met. I can admit it to myself when I am not myself, you see. I understand Alice and the Caterpillar now. Nothing makes sense and yet everything makes sense. Everything Adam is doing makes sense. That Caterpillar was totally smoking whatever Natalie put in this edible.

We both wade out into the warm water. The waves lapping our feet as we stride in. The sand between my toes has never felt softer. Everything feels sensual. Nature around me is more vibrant. Part of me never wants to let this feeling, this moment, end, but I also know it won't last forever, so I plan on making every moment of this count.

Adam's kiss is just as warm as the water itself. We aren't too far from the shore, just enough that the water sits just at my bikini top line. Adam's hands, which have been a conduit between us this whole time, never breaking, find purchase on my waist. Higher and higher, his arms crawl up me, into my hair, and snagging on the bikini knot I have tied in the middle of my back.

"Is it safe for us to be out here, you know, feeling like this?" The words slip out in between the softness of his kiss. "I'm afraid a wave might take me away."

"I've got you Wanderlust. But, just to clarify, how are you feeling right now?" Like my body language isn't clear enough, just what I am feeling. I tell him anyhow. "I feel like I'm falling. Falling and floating at the same time. . . you know, floating in the water and falling for you." That last bit may or may not have been said aloud, but regardless, they were finally admitted, whether in my head or not.

Adam doesn't respond with words as his finger slips between the loop of my swimsuit and begins to tug gently.

"I bet you are too uptight to skinny-dip?" His grin turns sinister as he ceases the undoing, waiting for me to permit his undressing me. He knows exactly how stubborn a dare is for me.

"I think we both know what happens when you and I make bets with one another."

"You're right. We break them." And with that, Adam pulls the last bit of my top loose and, with a swift arm, throws my swim top ashore.

Adam's eyes settle on my breasts, which by the grace of the ocean have a bit more bounce as they bob and perk up. Half in the water, half not, with each wave, my chest moves, now unclad of all shrouds of imagination. I swim, brazen before him and not at all inhibited in doing so. I feel more secure, completely naked, with Adam in this moment than I ever have been undone before.

"Do you like what you see?"

Adam cups my breasts and gently pulls one into his mouth. My nipple tingles at the flick of his tongue as he gently pecks the peak of my chest. I groan in ecstasy. His mouth teasing my senses into complete euphoria.

"I'm obsessed with what I see." It comes out guttural and deep.

It is so easy to float into one another. Our bodies are weightless in the wading. I take my hips and roll them into him, wrapping my legs around his middle. I can feel how hard he is against me. The stiffness stressing the cloth of his trunks. I take my bottoms off and mimic his motion of throwing my suit on the beach. Hopefully it won't wash away in the tide, leaving me like the emperor with new clothes.

"If I have to be naked, then so do you." I reach for his strings. I say it with a sneer. I just want to free him from himself, like I can feel he desperately wants to be.

"I have never been hard-pressed to say no to you."

"Oh, I'd say you're pretty HARD-pressed now." I laugh boisterously as he slaps his suit away.

"And I'd say you're a little high, and that is not as funny as you think it is." It isn't, but I can't help but collapse into his arms in a fit of giggles. This is not something I anticipated as a side-effect, but it is the most hilarity I have felt in a long while. A child-like snicker rolls out of me, and Adam shuts me up with a kiss.

This is not a gentle peck or a "let's take this slow" sort of kiss. This is like "I will die of dehydration" if I don't drink you up this very moment. The kind that shatters your kneecaps and sends electricity down your core. Pure seduction, pure intimacy.

It's hard not to vocalize loudly the intensity of his touch on my body. I stifle moan after moan as his hands find their way from my waist to my center.

Bravely and quickly, one finger slides inside and then two. I am breathless, caught for a moment in time as I already clench around him. Not in release, but in welcoming.

"I love it when I take your breath away," Adam whispers into my ear as I gasp into his shoulder. I bite down on it slightly, slipping my tongue over his freckles that have been born here in the sun.

Little by little, Adam begins to pick up speed. Alternating his fingers in a rhythm that is both rapid and concise. I can feel myself build around him, his erection pressing into my thigh so intently I feel it may bruise. All too quickly, I come around him.

"Don't fret Wanderlust, I will make you come for me again and again. On my fingers, on my tongue, and lastly, if I'm so lucky, around me."

An exacerbated sigh pulls out of me and my body feels like it's on a taffy pull. Completely at the mercy of the man before me, who looks like he might consume me whole with just one more minute of his body on mine.

I've forgotten completely about Natalie or the argument we had earlier. She has ceased to exist. She has ceased to be the one I want to drive Adam towards. At least for right now. I belong to him. Mind, body, and soul. Though maybe my mind is not my own presently. It still feels like a devotion to him alone.

This isn't real. This is the result of recreational substances. I can't trust anything I say or do. I can't trust anything Adam says or does. We should just enjoy the moment before it passes.

"Has it hit you yet?" I really can't tell with Adam. It's too dark out to see anything in his eyes. I just want to know if this is all because of what he consumed or. . . I think I might be kidding myself otherwise. I just need to hear it from him.

"I'm feeling all kinds of things at the moment."

Wow. Could he be more vague? Do I need to spell it out? DO YOU FEEL HIGH? IS ANY OF THIS REAL?

I'm just going to shut up. Inside my mind, too. *Be still.* I command myself.

Adam draws me out of the ocean and leads me back to his bungalow.

"The last thing I want to do is dress you, but we probably shouldn't be naked when we sneak into my home." Adam ties the wet strings around my neck and back, just loose enough that I still need to cup my breasts so they don't spill out of the sopping fabric. The bottoms are harder to slip on over my wet thighs, but I manage to cover up enough even with the hem still rolling like a Twizzler on my hips.

"I kind of hate how this feels on my skin." There is so much sand and drying salt water my body is now itchy.

"I kind of hate it too, but I promise I will take it off again soon," Adam says, very blatantly, having not lost his arousal. "There's no rush though. I want to take my time with you."

Just hearing him say that sends blood flow to my center. I could come again.

We sneak into the back door of the bungalow without anyone looking up from their campfire party. Their voices drown out the squeaking hinges of his screen door. He doesn't bother turning the lights on. He draws no attention to our whereabouts, but presses my sandy skin against his wall. Gently and without force. He hangs his head low to my ear and breathes like he is trying to rein himself in. Even the sound of his breath makes me shudder.

"I've wanted you again for so long. It was like getting a taste of something so indulgent all you crave is that same sweetness, but can't have it. I am afraid that if I taste it again, I won't be able to savor it. I won't be able to savor you or this moment like I want to, but might gorge myself on the bliss, knowing I will only want you more."

I can feel the pull in him, like a bucking bronco waiting for the gates to open. "We have all the time in the world," I say as I press a gentle kiss to his pouting bottom lip. "You can have me any which way you want me."

Adam draws his hand behind my back and spins me to the ground in a maneuver so slick it feels like I am still floating in the ocean water. "I want you here and now."

I might still be feeling less than myself, but I am grateful we aren't filling Adam's bed with sand. The floor is as good a place as any and I can hardly feel the sand underneath me as he slips my suit back off and presses inside me. We both inhale so sharply and he pauses as if he might lose control all at once.

"You feel so good. Even better than I remember." Adam pulls some of the wet hair out of my face.

"The counter over there wasn't exactly the best place to bang." I laugh into his mouth with his kiss.

"We just like to do things backwards." He doesn't quite get my meaning and looks at me like I am about to go reverse cowgirl on him. "I mean, we screwed, then we became friends, and now. . ." I don't exactly know how to finish that sentence. "And now. . ." Adam mirrors my thoughts like he wants me to finish it. "And now we are here."

Adam shifts slightly and even that small movement makes me moan, distracting him from the complicated half-answer I just gave. Slowly he builds, caressing my legs as he thrusts, kissing my bare chest, and grabbing the back of my neck.

"That's it," he says as he senses me tightening again. "I can't come until you do and Wanderlust, I am so close." His admission makes me shatter, screaming his name. The thought of him coming makes me come. He doesn't shush me; Doesn't mention that we are trying not to alert the others of our whereabouts. Instead, he says, "That's my girl. Thank you." Less than a minute later, Adam finishes and his saying "my girl," still clings in my mind more so than the grains of sand on our bodies. For the first time, I feel safe. His body warmth still draped over me, in no hurry to exit this moment in time.

PLEASURE STILL WAVES OVER ME, BUT THE EDIBLE IS SLOWLY wearing off. I'm relieved. While it helped get me out of my head and into my body, I want to come back to reality. I'm so proud of myself because I didn't panic and even as I begin to come out of the brain fog, there is no hesitation with Adam. I am not anxious about what comes next. One baby step at a time and all I have to do is finish showering and head back out to my warm sleeping bag on the beach. Adam offered up his indoor shower for a quick rinse, kissed me with all inhibitions removed, and then made his way back to the beach to fall asleep.

I happily took him up on the offer to shower to remove the salt water from my skin. It makes me itchy, though I know there will be handfuls of sand waiting in my covers, so there is no point in a deep cleaning.

I suds the last of our tryst and the sea water off of me and head back to the beach where everyone is no longer dancing in a haze around the bonfire, but instead fast asleep in a rumble of snores and an ember glow. I'm kind of sad I missed out on the festivities. I'm sure Natalie was a hoot, or maybe more of a bitch. All I want to do is curl up next to Adam and drift off to his scent and his embrace.

Something is off with Adam's sleeping bag. It looks bigger for some reason.

"Hey," I whisper from farther away than I know he can hear. I was going to make some joke about sleeping with a stuffed animal or something when a tuft of blonde pulls to the side and sits straight up. Sits up from straddling on top of him. *Is he inside her?* I don't know, but I know that Natalie has only one motivation to sit on his lap. *Did he kiss her back?* I can hear her breathy moan as she pulls from him and slides her hips against his. *There is no way she would openly have sex with him, even if everyone else is asleep. Is there?*

"What the hell!" I shout. This time it is no whisper, and it is right inside this stupid circle of people. Everyone jostles awake. I was not demure in my shock.

"So you have sex with me and five minutes later screw her. You get what you want from me and then go for more. Busy guy." I laugh, though not a hint of a smile breaks my face. Zeke looks like he stepped into a horror story. Adam looks. . . well. . . dazed.

"What is going on?" Adam asks like he wasn't just making out with the blonde bombshell he swore was "just a friend."

"I don't know Adam. You tell me." I cross my arms, utterly disgusted. I could vomit, but I won't.

"I swear Jen, I thought she was you."

"Ha." I scoff. "Nice line. Like I am supposed to believe that half-assed load of crap."

"I was mostly asleep. I didn't even open my eyes. I thought you had come back and crawled in with me. I get that it's hard to believe, but I swear it's true." He crosses his heart and I know he is overcompensating with erratic gesticulation to make me believe him.

"You didn't notice that her hair isn't wet, or that she is literally five inches taller than me. You didn't feel any difference in how we kiss." I'm getting a little personal for the group to overhear seeing how we have an audience to witness our altercation. Natalie just smirks to the side of Adam. He shoved her off in a hurry, but she didn't reciprocate the haste in leaving his bed. She's all too quiet. And enjoying what is unfolding.

"I swear Jen, I did not open my eyes. I am exhausted, and it's not a good excuse, it's just a reason. I would never hurt you like that. I was just so excited to be kissing you again." I can see the tears welling up in his eyes. He's always looked so pure it pains me to see him cry, but I do know when he is telling the truth.

"I guess I can understand, since we were both under the influence and not in our clear heads. . ."

Natalie, who has been silent this whole time, finally chirps in. "Oh, Adam wasn't high." Pride pulls across her face as she delivers the next blow. "He didn't ingest one of my treats because he's an *addict*."

"Recovering addict," Adam interjects. "I'm in recovery."

There it is. The blow that I don't know I can take. The deal breaker I didn't know was there and the rug that was pulled out from an already shoddy foundation for me to just free fall.

I confided in him. I shared all my woes about Dad. I told him what I endured with the addict in my life. He watched the lies unfold when I decided to go find Keone. He witnessed the aftershock of what Dad's absence had done to me and the chaos that I chased because of it. I didn't know Adam was a piece of that chaos. He just let me share my life's story and remained completely silent.

"You told me it was your brother?" I swallow the words and speak them like a rock is in the way of my vocal cords. I will not cry in front of Natalie. I will not give her the satisfaction.

"I didn't lie. It was both of us."

Is he kidding?

"Semantics Adam. It's still a lie by omission." The betrayal is sprawled across my face and I can't help but see the amusement on Natalie's. She wanted to break us and finally found the pressure point. And she's reveling in it all.

"I've been in recovery for over three years. I've been clean and sober for 1,295 days. Yes, I count the days because I take each one, one at a time. I am completely and utterly sober. I don't even drink Kombucha."

"Bit overkill, if you ask me." Natalie, still wanting to throw in her two cents, mumbles under her breath.

"You need to shut up! No one is asking you anything." Adam points his finger at her and I have never seen him reprimand anyone. She has crossed so many lines with him that I am honestly surprised this is the thing that snaps him.

"Yes, I am an addict and I have the disease, but it is a battle I have been winning for a while now. So no. I didn't tell you because I didn't feel it was a part of my past you needed to know. I knew it would trigger you. I heard how much your dad hurt you and what happened because he never found healing. I was listening, but I am not him and I can't stand the way you are looking at me. Like I am. Like I could ever hurt you." His words are choked out through anger and tears. Probably aggravated by exhaustion.

"You did hurt me, though." I don't say it with any more

brimming tears or malice. Just the betrayal I now add to the baggage I was hoping to leave behind on this stupid trip. I feel my shoulders drop. I knew better, and this is my fault. "I'm done."

Nothing on this beach is mine except for my coverup next to the borrowed camp gear. I grab it and turn down the beach. I can make it to any hotel from here. Even in the dark.

"Wait, Jen." Adam pulls himself up finally and runs after me. Everyone else has taken the opportunity to go back to sleep. Or try to in an attempt to give us privacy. The show is over for everyone. Except Natalie, who is still a stoic spectator.

"Where are you going?" Adam grabs my arm and tries to pull me to him.

"Home." It comes out like a robot. Depleted and devoid of emotion. "This whole trip was meant to find myself. Then to find my brother, which I still haven't done because I wrapped myself up in you. I started traveling to remind myself that Dad was a different person before I knew him and instead, I found you. Someone so similar you are cut from the same cloth. I opened my heart up to you and it broke yet again. I was supposed to find healing and instead, I discovered a brother who I never knew about and had my heart betrayed by a boy who was thrown into my path at every turn. I thought you were my fate, but now I just think it's all my fault. I choose people who hurt me and I'm just done. I failed in whatever this was supposed to be. This stupid idea of chasing a ghost has now turned me into one. I don't recognize myself and I feel even more lost than before. I would rather be an agoraphobic human alone and broken in my own home than endure any more heartache in this lifetime." I don't jerk my arm away, but I slide it away from his reach. *I won't permit him to touch me again.*

"You never opened up your heart to me." Adam doesn't move. "You think you did, but you blocked my advances every chance you got? I fought every moment to get close to you and just when I think you finally lowered your walls to me, you throw them right back up. You aren't finding the love you're looking for because when it is finally in front of you, you run away from it."

"Excuse me."

"I'm not going to convince you to stay. I am not going to tell you that I love you. That I am in love with you because those words mean nothing to you. Sorry means nothing to you and I somehow can't seem to prove my feelings to you through actions either. I shouldn't have to defend how I feel every minute I am with you. I'm done too, Jenesis." Adam's arms hang by his side.

"Yeah, Natalie dry humping you just now really proves you love me. If that's the love you have to offer, the I just don't believe in love anymore." Things are heated now.

And just like that, I throw the betrayal I feel right back at him. I want to hurt him back, but it doesn't feel in any way satisfying.

"Take care of yourself, Jenesis."

"I have been my entire life."

"Don't forget your bag." Natalie apparently went inside the bungalow to get my rollaway. I want to slap her, but I don't give her the satisfaction of a response. Just take my things.

And just so both of us have the upper hand, Adam and I turn away from each other simultaneously and walk away in opposite directions. For the first time, that pull I feel to him is no longer there. It's been severed and I have the scissors. It's over.

44

FLASHBACK
MAYBE 2004

Certain memories don't have specificity, but rather certain smells and feelings that make up an image in my mind more so than the reality of it all.

Christmas morning. . . doesn't matter which year or what age. Certain things just don't change.

The smell of bacon in the pan mixed with the smell of freshly brewed coffee - always in a novelty Christmas mug (or the Tasmanian devil mug from *Christmas Vacation.*) There's also the sweetness of eggnog and a whisper of peppermint that probably came from the hot chocolate and candy cane sticks the night before as we sat up and watched the computer to see where in the world Santa was.

Even years after I stopped believing in Santa, we would watch to see where he was in relation to us on Christmas Eve. It took years for that little bit of magic to die. Dad always made sure the magic of the holiday encircled us like the wreath on our door. It wasn't until I was about ten that I realized it was him on the roof with his steel-toed leather boots, jingle bells, and a cassette tape of reindeer sounds and sleigh bells.

He would always come up with some excuse to get outside.

"Hey Jen, I need to take the trash out. I'll be right back." or "Hey Jen, I am going to go check on the Christmas lights. You hang out here for a second. I'll be right back." No matter what his excuse was, he always promised he would be right back. As a kid, I never noticed the pattern, but I would always hear his jolly "Ho, Ho, Ho," and go sprinting for my bed to curl under the covers and pretend I was asleep.

Some Christmases had a dusting of snow, and those were the most magical of all, but we didn't live at the right elevation for it to happen often. No matter the hour, Dad would wake me up to stand outside and watch as the large snowflakes would fall from the heavens, almost as if it was in slow motion. It was hypnotizing to stand out in the yard and stare straight up into the black sky and watch as the white flakes would land softly on my eyelashes and lips before melting. On certain nights, it was like watching *Han Solo* and *Chewbacca* jump into hyperspace and it didn't matter how cold it was, it was a gift that we stopped to savor. We both knew it wouldn't last long - if it even lasted through the night.

I wouldn't dare step a toe out of my bedroom come Christmas morning. Dad had a lot of setting up to do, and I don't mean putting presents under the tree. I mean, making sure that the lights on the tree were on the right colored setting and that the right album was playing over the stereo. Either *Charlie Brown Christmas* or *Alabama*. *"Thistlehair The*

Christmas Bear" playing on repeat. He would then come into my room with the camcorder over his shoulder and a grin from ear to ear, giving me permission to leave the comfort of my bed and enter into the magical world of Christmas morning. As I grew up, I knew it didn't just magically happen. Even I had to put Dad's presents under the tree, but the magic of it was knowing that all of it happened without either one of us seeing the other in action. It left that small possibility that maybe because I didn't see it that maybe it was all done by magic.

I never got a full night's sleep on Christmas Eve. I was always a jittery ball of anxiety and anticipation. So when Dad finally would come in to get me, I would have to rub the sleep out of my eyes with the palms of my hands repeatedly until I could see straight. The blur of my eyesight would result in the twinkle lights on the tree glowing and melding one into another until the focus would come, and yet still they would have a glimmer about them.

Looking back on it, Christmas, as I remember it, is now a jumble of what I can smell, taste, see, and hear. I can still smell the coffee and bacon. I can taste the peppermint in my cocoa and the snowflakes on my tongue. I can see the colorful glow of the tree we decorated with a miscellaneous concoction of *Looney Tunes*, motorcycles, and Disney ornaments, in addition to the traditional red and silver baubles. I can still hear Dad's laugh, like he was Santa himself. He was to me. He even looked like Santa. Long white hair and a red hat, though the American Flag parachute pants and over-sized henley on his bodybuilder frame were very different from a red suit lined with fur.

I can hear the CD player in the cabinet skip to the next album on its automatic changer as it clicked to the next song. And I can hear the crinkle of the paper being ripped into. Each present sparkled under the glow of the tree, enticing me to what perched in its center. However, there was tradition. Number one was that I didn't leave my room until invited and the second being that we would ALWAYS start with stockings. We wouldn't even touch presents until after breakfast.

I can still hear Dad saying, "Slow down Jenesis, savor it. When it's over, it's over."

While that was true, Christmas would always come back around another 365 days later. What ended were my Christmases with him and it was hard to savor it or make it slow down when not all of it was good. Sometimes I needed the day to end. Others were pure magic. It was the roller coaster that I was used to, but when I stop and think of Christmas. . . it is the traditions and the smells and the moments of magic that I think of. It was his warm hugs that consumed me with his twenty-two-inch biceps that I could rest my head on like a pillow and feel safe. That's what I think of. Not of the last Christmas we had together and the redo he died before we ever got to redeem.

45

FLASHBACK
2021

This was our last Christmas.

Not sure what possessed me to think that having Dad sleepover on Christmas Eve was a good idea, except I wanted to recreate a Christmas from my childhood and he lived a little over thirty minutes away. It wouldn't be Christmas morning if I had to call him to see if he was up and on his way. That, however, would have been more preferable to what happened.

"Hey, Jen. Mind if we have some hot-buttered rums while we watch Christmas movies?" *Insert red flag here. ▶

It wasn't a tradition we had when I was ten, (for obvious reasons) but maybe it would be a nice new one we could make. We're both adults.

"Yeah, Dad. One or two after dinner sounds nice."

"Great! I'll be sure to bring what we need. Can I bring anything else?"

It was so nice to hear his excitement. Even over the phone, I clung to it like a child making a wish on a shooting star. I didn't want it to be fleeting. I wasn't nervous about it either. Drinking wasn't Dad's problem. It was the pills and the pain he used to justify taking them. One drink couldn't hurt and that's just it; ONE drink couldn't have hurt, but addiction is excess.

When he pulled up to my apartment door, he was already wasted. Functioning, but wasted. He brought an entire handle of spiced rum. A quarter of it had already been consumed. I think it's safe to say it was being consumed all day.

I didn't want to think about how he drove here. I wasn't in charge of him, but the sudden urge to feel responsible for him intoxicated behind the wheel overwhelmed me. Thank goodness he was staying over I guess, so I could watch him, which I did. I had to change my mindset.

I pulled the sofa sleeper open and set the sheets up for him right next to the glow of the Christmas tree. I made sure the setting was on solid colors. Dad's favorite. My small apartment didn't have a guest room or even a second room to use as an office, but I wanted him to feel cozy and nostalgic. By the way, that's hard to do when you're blotto.

"Hi, Dad." I went in for a hug and could immediately smell the leather of his jacket, the sweat of him, and the rum on his breath. He would only sweat like this when he was under the influence. I knew rum, but couldn't tell if he had mixed his pills in as well. It was always safe to assume so. Although the pills made his eyelids flutter and his words slow and linger. A sentence could stumble on forever. . . if it would even complete at all. Each one would be freckled with an "um" between every other word. He wasn't quite to this point.

Immediate frustration came over me. I called him so many times today to hear his voice and see how his demeanor was. What, did he shoot back shots of rum right before coming here, just so he could be drunk when he got here?

I was so close to asking him to leave, but then I heard, "Oh Thistlehair, The Christmas Bear," pouring through my speakers. It was a moment I wish I hadn't taken as a sign, because it was the first and last nostalgic moment of the night.

He fell asleep, face first, in the Christmas dinner I spent four hours making. He woke up at one, two, and three in the morning. He stumbled around with the TV on, so I went out to see him. "You okay Dad?"

"Where is the bathroom?"

That is all he said, which was concerning because I thought that was where he was going all the other times I heard him up. It was also the room right next to him.

Christmas morning rolled around, and I slept in just a bit. I almost waited for Dad to come get me, but thank goodness I didn't bother. He didn't wake up for a "good morning." Or when I went into the kitchen to make coffee and bacon with peppermint pancakes. Or when I sat under the tree and waited for him to open up his gift and wondered if any of the presents under the tree were for me. I got him slippers, by the way. The kind that are more like boots because he said the ones with no backs slip off so easily.

It wasn't until almost noon that he finally stirred awake. So groggy and pale, I almost ran for a bucket for him. He looked sick.

"I gotta go. I will call you later. I'm just not feeling myself this morning."

I wanted to laugh. *Oh really? You mean the half liter of rum isn't causing the worst hangover a sixty-seven year old man could experience? How shocking.*

Instead, all I did was open the door for him. I didn't bother watching him leave. I cleaned up his bedding from the night before and put my couch back together. I actually cleaned my whole home in an attempt to scrub the bad experience away. Also the musky smell. I lit a pine candle and popped some popcorn. All so I could watch the 1974, *Twas the Night Before Christmas*, movie about a mouse and a clock and bawl my eyes out until I passed out on the couch he had slept on just hours before. The realization that childhood Christmases could never be recreated burned the last bit of magic away completely.

46

LAKE TAHOE
2022

I always did my best to recreate the Christmases of my childhood. The feeling and not so much the exact memories themselves.

I didn't go home like I told Adam I was going to. Not my home anyway. I'm in Tahoe. It is pure euphoria, and also only about two hours from my apartment. However, it snows here! It is yet another locale in Dad's journal. Part of me still thinks I should have read the whole thing before embarking on this tour of his past, but I was flying by the seat of my pants and following the same route Dad did.

After London was supposed to be Tahoe. I took a detour in Palm Desert and going back to Maui to find my brother. To be honest with myself, I wasn't ready to leave Adam just yet. He was right when we said that there was something between us, but it wasn't just friendship and it wasn't quite love. It was this weird in-between where connections grow, but into what, I don't know.

Doesn't matter now. Whatever flower of emotion was budding between us, I squashed and left buried in the sand to be washed away by the tide. I know that we somehow managed to meet and connect in two different states, two different countries and two different continents, but the likelihood of that occurrence recurring is just not likely anymore. Or at least that is what I am telling myself.

Being around him used to make me feel like there was a higher entity drawing us to one another and no matter where I went, this person would be there as well. I started to accept whatever was being given to me and then, in true Jenesis fashion, I threw it back into the void, like I didn't want it.

I didn't want it. Right?

I know that I am not okay when I can't even answer the questions rumbling through my conscience. I have been dodging Jules' calls. I know she will ask me the same thing. She liked Adam. I could tell. I know exactly what she will say.

"What happened? Why did you sabotage yourself? Don't you want to be happy, Jen?"

Maybe it isn't my voice asking me these questions in my mind, but hers. I can't answer any one of them and I don't plan to.

I made myself a fire in the cabin I somehow nabbed on Airbnb. During the holiday season, it was a pure miracle. When I checked in, I immediately looked in all the obvious places for hidden cameras and then I looked in all the not-so-obvious places. There has to be something wrong with it, like frozen toilet pipes or a dead raccoon in the garage refrigerator, but so far it all seems very normal. My last guess is that it is small. Pretty much large enough for one. Ideal for me who plans to spend Christmas becoming a prune in the jacuzzi on the back porch, but not so ideal for someone who actually has family to spend time with this time of year.

Alone on Christmas.

Do I care?

It doesn't feel like I am capable of emotions. I tried my hardest to find something to make me feel better since Dad died. Even if I could just feel the relief that the addict in my life isn't anymore. I cringe every time I think about how many times I would wish he were dead and how much easier my life would be. I could have a life. It hurts me now to believe I ever thought that way. I don't feel relieved. I don't feel like I can finally be happy and experience all life has to offer. I feel nothing. I guess I thought that the life I envisioned would somehow fall into my lap. If that were supposed to happen, it didn't. I even went out looking for it. Or maybe I was looking in all the wrong places. Maybe my future isn't buried in the past. His past.

I've read every entry now. Pretty much after I discovered I had an older brother, I decided to read every entry. I read them all twice. I saw the glaciers he saw in Alaska. I surfed a wave in Maui. Well, I kinda surfed a wave in Maui. I didn't push a double-decker bus up a hill by myself, but Adam and I rode one together and I tried to envision the pure muscle my dad would have had to utilize for that story to be true

(Max swears as a witness it happened.) I even toured Great Ormond Street Hospital and saw the statue of Peter Pan where he posed, not knowing how much I would think of Dad as the boy who never grew up.

I stayed at our condo in Palm Desert and watched the sunset over the desert in the mountains. I even made a few memories of my own. I do feel a pinch deep in my chest when I think of the desert disco Adam took me to. How his body felt swaying against mine and how safe I felt with the heat of the desert and the heat of his body blanketing against mine.

And now I am here in Tahoe. Where my dad taught as a ski instructor. I have a class ready for tomorrow. The irony of him instructing others, but never finding it in him to teach me, makes me laugh. It's the kind of laugh you make out loud so you don't cry. No one is around and yet I still can't face my pain.

Isn't that what all of this was for? Cry Damnit!

I want to cry. I want to cry over it all. The overdose and seeing my dad's decaying body is worth crying about. Finding out I have a half-brother all this time. A family that I could have been a part of, and yet I haven't cried over. Leaving whatever shell of my life behind to gallivant around the world trying to understand who Gideon was before he was my dad and coming up short is worth crying over. All the pain that the pills brought into my life and the moments he was broken or arrested or intimidating me are worth crying over. All the moments that we had that were great, but there will be no more. The moments of greatness that just were too few and far between. Those are worth crying over. Being alone on Christmas in an unknown place is worth crying over. Heck! Even Adam is worth crying over.

The boy who pulled me into his Neverland before I kicked myself out. The man who wanted to put the pieces of me back together and admire them like a Japanese kintsugi bowl. Broken, but put back together with pieces of gold, making it whole, if not better than before. Even with still visible cracks.

I want to feel something more than just a deep ache for these things, but nothing erupts more than what feels like heartburn deep in my chest.

Tahoe was for more than Christmas in the snow and a lesson at the ski resort. I need space to finalize Dad's estate. I need to pick up his ashes that have been sitting in the crematorium for months now. They were kind enough to keep him there while I traveled. I am next of kin. Only kin and they were more than understanding, but eventually, I need to do that. Getting the call that I could come and get his ashes felt so final. More so than death, for some reason.

Even though he was gone and couldn't be rejoined into his body, cremating him felt like it would never be a possibility. He can't come back if his body is dust. It was insanity behind my logic, but even now it still makes sense to me. I don't like to think of his body not being here anymore. I don't like to think that I will never see his *Nightmare Before Christmas* tattoos or my name inked on his back.

The blood had settled in his body before he was found, making it impossible for the coroner to determine what exactly was tattooed on his back. It was purple and swollen, but I will always have it etched into my mind. My name with a Celtic cross covering the remainder of his back. It too is just gone.

I need to make my way back to the cabin and get the remainder of his stuff out. His landlord was also understanding and, in exchange for a delayed move, I told him he could keep the washer and dryer, fridge, and couch for the next tenants. He can charge more rent that way and would make up the difference a few months without rent would cost him. Plus, I know he liked Dad.

When I called him to tell him the news, he was driving. "Hold on. I have to pull over," was all he said before I heard the car turn off and soft sobs echoed through the receiver. I had never met him in person, but knew of him from what Dad said. He was a fair landlord and would listen to Dad ramble on for hours when he would stop by. He offered to fix the door that was broken into when the police came by for a wellness check. Yes, I know they usually don't break down the doors, but they do when the person inside doesn't answer after repeated knocking. Turns out in this particular instance, Dad was just taking a snooze with the TV on too loud and the floor fan running. He didn't hear the officers until they were inside his home. He was also high.

I got an earful from the cops that he was fine and I could tell they were unnerved that I had wasted their time. Dad was always good at putting on a face and hiding the truth. The pills played a bigger role in him not being able to hear the knocks on the door than just the TV on at two in the afternoon.

This cabin feels an awful lot like the one Dad called home. He would like it here and that realization makes my heartburn come back. I know it's there. Deep within me are all the emotions I wish would bubble up to the surface. There is just something in the way.

I brought all the paperwork with me. It was emailed to me last week. The death certificate and the affidavit to get the remainder of his funds out of the bank. Everyone was operating on holiday hours this week and I didn't feel like getting into it just yet. Not with the fire roaring. A level of cozy I haven't felt since Uncle Max's home.

Just like that, the snow outside begins to fall. The sun had set a few hours ago, though in the winter that is still pretty early. I have to go outside. I have to feel it. The little sting of each snowflake as it perches on my face. I crave it, but there is only one way to enjoy it. I rip open my suitcase and pull out the swimsuit I have become well acquainted with in Hawaii and Palm Desert. It is still a little damp from its last use only a few days ago. I unwrap it from the plastic grocery bag I had packed it in and throw it on. I will watch the snowfall from the hot tub. If I had thought ahead, I would have gone to the store and bought a bottle of wine, but something tells me I won't need it.

THE CHILL OF THE AIR ON MY SKIN IN A DAMP SWIMSUIT almost sends me back inside to the fire.

This jacuzzi better be over a hundred degrees.

I am pleasantly surprised as I dip one toe in first to

check that it is even on. The steam that floats into the snow-fall should have tipped me off. One test is all it takes before submerging fully into the warmth. My skin is a bundle of prickles as my cold skin meets the heat in the water. It is most definitely over a hundred degrees.

For a moment it stings so much I think to get out, but almost as quickly as that thought enters my mind, my body relaxes into the warmth. My body aches with the tempera-ture, causing it to feel feverish. My face is still cold with the brisk northern air.

Every inhale chills my throat, only to be immediately reheated. Every exhale produces a cloud of fog in front of me, blocking my view briefly of the dark sky filled with flurries.

There isn't much to see besides white, anyway. It isn't quite a blizzard, but it is way more snow than the dustings we would have in Christmases past. My eyes blink with the memories and the heavy-laden flakes clinging to my lashes.

This is it. This is my moment. I think to myself. *If not now. . . when?*

This is what I ran away to do. Alone in my thoughts. A quiet place to think. I hadn't found silence in my other trav-els. My chest heaves with the weight of it all. I either figure out my life at this moment or stop trying to make sense of anything and live my life half-heartedly from here on out.

I begin to pray. Well, maybe not pray, but I start to talk to the heavens like maybe someone is listening. Maybe he is listening. Unabashedly and loudly talking to silence and listening, begging for a response.

"Why did you have to die?"

Even the nature around me is still. But I wait. And then.

..

"I never wanted to hurt you."

There it is. An answer.

"That's not what I asked. Why did you die?"

"I took too many. I didn't know."

"You didn't know what? You didn't know it would kill you or you forgot you already took some?"

"I just wanted the pain to end."

"Well, it did. And at what cost? You did hurt me. You left me. Alone. How could you?"

"Was I there for you when I was alive?"

"No." I'm honest. He wasn't there for me when he was alive. Maybe in spurts that he would often remind me of in times where he had let me down, but never consistently. I was there for him.

"What do I do now?" The burning question I have been chasing.

Please answer. Please answer me.

"You live."

"Yeah, but how?"

"You do the things that make you happy. You stop living for someone else and their pain. You put yourself first. You find someone to love. Someone you would move mountains for. You find someone who loves you even more. You remember all of our good times and leave what was awful in the past. You never forget, because when we forget, we face the likelihood of history repeating itself in some other way. But you don't carry it in your heart like a weight that keeps you down. You recognize that what happened to you was awful and the trauma you endured made you strong, but it shouldn't have happened in the first

place and it will no longer rob you of your serenity from this moment forward. You pick yourself up and learn how to ask for what you need and take the help that is given to you. You learn to tell our story without feeling like you have to defend all the poor choices, but you also can recognize, that even through all of my mistakes, I loved you more than life itself. Had I been able to do better I would have. I am so sorry Jenesis.

"I want you to live a life that is full. A life of adventure and things that consume your soul. I want you to see and do all the things I let my addiction rob me of and, most importantly, I never want you to feel alone. I want you to stop trying to find me in the pages of the journal I left behind. I'm not there. I am in your heart."

The tears that refused to fall are now beginning to surface.

"Do you miss me like I miss you?"

I can hear his voice so clearly, even though I know this can't possibly be real. Maybe that other gummy Adam grabbed ended up in one of my bags. I don't remember taking anything, but I am talking to a ghost.

"No." If I am giving myself these answers, why would I have given myself a no?

"No?"

"No. I don't miss you Jenesis. Because I am with you. Always."

And with that. I sob.

All of the pain and all of the hurt seems to fall out of me and into the frothy jacuzzi water below. It isn't one of those soft cries. It's one of those ugly cries where snot drips from your nostrils and you almost dry heave from swallowing so much air. My shoulders shake, making small waves in the water, which only remind me of Hawaii and

Adam and how I was so cruel to him. He willingly let out his hand for me to take and I pushed it away like I didn't want it. I do want it. The fear of loving him forced me into a state of retreat. If loving someone hurts this much when they are gone, then I will never love again. How could I feel like this more than once in my life and not just drop dead? Somehow, I know that if I let Adam love me, I will never recover from the compounding grief if it ends up not working out.

I cry for so long that my fingers are now prunes and my throat feels scratchy from wailing. The not-too-distant neighbors must be wondering what animal is dying in the woods next to us because no sound like this could come from a human. Let alone someone on Christmas Eve.

This is a time to be filled with joy. A time to share with loved ones and relish in the traditions of the season. I had purposefully placed myself in solitude and now am wondering why. The weight on my chest has finally lifted and the baggage I've been dragging around from place to place is gone and a need washes over me.

I don't want to be alone.

Still sobbing, though much quieter now, I plunge out of the hot tub and back into the house. Small drops of water and now melting snow follow me inside. I barely have the towel wrapped around me and I move so fast I almost don't feel the cold. . . almost.

My phone sits on its charger on the kitchen island, and instinctively I just start dialing. A few short rings later, there is a voice on the other end. The first sound of life other than my breathing.

"Hey." the voice on the other end hums through. "You okay?"

"No. Not really." I laugh and choke and cry all at the same time. "I'm sorry. Can you come here?"

"I am on my way." is spoken without an ounce of hesitation and I feel warm again.

47

LAKE TAHOE

2022

"I made it!"

Jules shows up at the cabin almost exactly two hours after I make the phone call to her. A little exasperated. She was in the middle of Christmas Eve service with her family, and I felt terrible for tearing her away from them. I told her she didn't have to stay and apologized for crying on the phone to her. To which she very lovingly told me to, "Shut up. You are family, too." This only made me cry again. Once the floodgates are open and all.

I had showered off all the chemicals from the hot tub and made sure to wash my hair free of it as well. Jules being a hairdresser is amazing, but also I am afraid if she sees the state of my hair after so much ocean water and general lack of care, she might bark at me and slap a moisturizing mask over my scalp. That sounds wonderful. I do love a good makeover and I feel like I could use one right about now. A whole-person kind of makeover. Make me new. Cue an early 2000s montage.

My eyes feel so swollen and still burn from all the tears, but when Jules walks in, I can feel my body welcoming laughter again.

"How did you find this place?" She asks as she sets down an overnight duffle in the entry.

"Airbnb had a last-minute deal."

"Always so thrifty." She says it as a compliment. Jules has always been good at helping me indulge a little. Like with the upgrade in Hawaii. She is the best gift giver I know and immediately I see a package under her arm, wrapped in perfect paper.

"I am so glad you could make it over the pass." I sputter into her hair as she embraces me yet again.

"Me too girl, the snow started dumping the second my car engine revved. I think I beat it by thirty minutes. Not sure when we will be able to get home, but what an adventure."

Her hands are still shaking a bit from gripping the steering wheel too tightly. As great of a driver as Jules is, no one likes to drive in the snow at night.

"I knew I needed to be here," was all she said.

"Merry Christmas to me." And I led her to the kitchen for a hot buttered rum.

CHRISTMAS MORNING COMES ALL TOO QUICKLY. PROBABLY because the hot buttered rums were abundant and then turned to spiked eggnog, which resulted in headaches and a groggy morning. Jules and I both slip out of our shared king-sized bed with a plaid duvet cover on it and blaze straight for the high-end espresso machine - it was one of the reasons I gravitated towards this particular cabin. That and the hot tub.

Honestly, starting a Christmas hungover is less than ideal. Both Jules and I are reaching for anything to curb the roiling nausea. Part of that is shoving stale frosted Christmas cookies in our mouths.

"Part of this complete breakfast." I spew with my mouth full and shower Jules with several chalky cookie crumbs.

"Shhhhh. Please don't be so loud." Jules isn't a morning person to begin with, but add a hangover and she is lethal. I'm not too spritely either, but apparently, I am being too loud.

Somehow with Jules here, it feels like that nostalgia I've been chasing. I find the *Alabama* Christmas album on Spotify and play that through my small speaker phone at a very low volume. Not much is uttered between us in our current states, but Jules grabs the duvet off our bed and wraps it around us on the couch. Gently, she drops her head to my shoulder while we sip our coffee in almost silence.

"Could you sip that a little less aggressively?" Jules pinches her face together and places her fingertips on the bridge of her nose like my sipping is making her headache worse.

"If you sip loudly, it aerates the liquid, so it doesn't burn your tongue," I say it with my tongue thick in my mouth so it comes out like I am tongue-tied.

"Burn your tongue for all I care."

It makes me laugh into my next sip. Her words come out as calloused, but her body language doesn't move from comforting me. She's annoyed, but not at me. She loves me and I finally feel like I am ready to let any and all love in.

"You know you are always fixing places in my heart that weren't ever broken by you?" I ask her. I'm pretty sure I saw that on Instagram somewhere. Or something like that.

"Just call me Bob the Builder." her monotone voice not pitching upwards.

"Why Bob?"

"Can he fix it? Yes, he can!" Ironically, Jules shouts this part from the top of her lungs. I may have jumped 20 feet, but that only makes Jules laugh more. "Don't hog the blanket."

"Don't scare me like that and I won't take the blanket with me." We both are just a fit of giggles, and it is more healing to our hangover than any other remedy.

"It's Christmas day, honey. What do you want to do today? We could go sledding on that hill outside. We could watch the snowfall from the hot tub, we could open presents and take a nap, and I could make some waffles. What sounds good?" Jules gets up briefly to go and stoke the fire.

"Definitely make waffles," I say, just salivating at the thought of syrup and butter-filled little boxes. "And, I don't know. Let's do all of that and just pretend like everything is fine."

"Do you want to pretend everything is fine, sweetie?

Because if you do, I will be here to distract you as much as I possibly can. I just am not convinced that's what you want to do."

I don't want to cry again. I place my hands against my lower eyelids to stop the tears.

"I'm sorry. I don't want to upset you." Jules comes back to the couch and wraps her arms around me. "Don't you think it's time, though?"

"He's only been gone for four months." It comes out strained.

"Oh, I know, I don't mean 'get over it.' I don't know if you will ever get over it wholly and I don't think that's a bad thing. What I don't think is serving you, though, is all the hurt you are still carrying around. You are punishing yourself for his choices. I saw you do it when he was alive and you haven't stopped. I just want you to know that if you choose to forgive him and stop telling yourself that you are in any way to blame for what happened, that I will hold your hand the whole time." Without waiting for me to answer, Jules grabs my hand.

"I wished him dead for so long. How do I not carry that shame with me?" It's too sad for Christmas, but it is the birth of the Savior, and boy, could I use a Savior right now.

"I don't think you wanted *him* dead. I think you wanted the cycle of abuse to stop and at a certain point, it felt like only death could bring that. It is okay to miss him and to grieve both what was and what could have been. Please stop denying yourself joy because of it." She pulls stray hair from my face.

"I was so mean to Adam. I made sure that when I left, I

left the entire island burning. I can't fix that. I never dared to go find Keone. I can never ask Dad how he felt when my mom died and when he learned about Kailani. I can never ask him why he didn't tell me about Keone or try to be a father to him. Though I'm sure the pills quelled that desire." I inhale sharply. "I thought this trip was my start to healing, but now I feel like it broke me more. I don't know how to begin. . . again."

Jules sips her coffee and contemplates her next thoughts. "I don't think that this trip has broken you more. I think you are right and that it was the start of your healing. Sometimes you have to make a wound worse to allow it to heal properly." Always my sounding board of good advice. Adam and Jules both have that "fortune cookie" trait.

"I don't know if the 'Adam situation' is fixable or if you even want to resurrect that relationship, but I will say that I like him and I think he is good for you. I can go with you to find Keone and no matter what happens there, you can know that you are doing it for yourself and no one else matters. I think you can begin by saying goodbye. Say goodbye to the hurt. Say goodbye to the person you were. She played a vital role in your life, but now it's time to grow. Say goodbye to any expectations you have for this journey. Healing is not linear. There will be ups and downs. And say goodbye to Gideon, the person he was, and the dad you wished he could have been. It's not going to be easy, but you won't have to do it alone. Are you ready for that?"

Am I ready to not use my trauma as an excuse to not try? Am I ready to let go?

48

THE EULOGY
2022

"Dearly beloved. . ." Do you start a eulogy like you do a wedding? I don't know.

I stare at the lake like it is going to swallow me whole. The Nature surrounding me is the only thing lively in such an environment of death. I stand, more statute than even the surrounding trees do. I can't move. Frozen in disbelief. I know a big part of grieving is acceptance, but seeing the urn containing his ashes and his favorite picture crinkled from my pocket, pulled out and displayed next to it, I am in complete and utter non-acceptance. Jules picked up his ashes on her way up.

Got to rip the bandaid off.

"How are we here, Jules?" She takes my hand. The anchor I need.

"You know I love you more than anything. You are my sister. So, can I be honest with you?"

Like she has to ask.

"Please."

"This wasn't going to end any other way."

I pause. Completely breathless in her candor. But she is right.

"It just happened a lot sooner than I thought it would."

She wipes away another tear of mine like she has been doing for most of our two-decade-long friendship.

"I know, honey."

None of the last few months have seemed real. Jules and I got up early to see the sunrise over Lake Tahoe and scatter Dad's ashes like I knew he wanted. Well. . . he wanted to be scattered at the foot of the *Walt Disney* Statue in *Disneyland*, but when I told him I wouldn't risk being kicked out of the *Happiest Place On Earth* for the rest of my life, he compromised with this.

He talked about dying a lot. It was something that came up in conversation, whether sparked by talking about Mom or how much pain he was in. My desire to honor his wishes are so strong that I was about to book a Disney ticket and risk it all until Jules showed up and everything fell into place. I know this is the moment and I pull out the eulogy I wrote late last night.

How can I begin to eulogize such a person? What if I don't cry? What if I can't stop?

Jules rubs the back of my shoulders like she can read my thoughts.

Gideon Haynes was simultaneously the greatest and the hardest man to be around. My life would have been a lot less chaotic had he been able to kick his addictions. It's hard to eulogize all the good. Do we pretend that the bad wasn't there all along? Do we pretend the bad wasn't what ultimately caused his departure from this realm? Or do we mention the bad and the ugly? Bringing it to an uncomfortable light.

This isn't a round of roasting, although there could be some ill-timed joke about roasting the dead emotionally and literally through cremation.

If I can make myself laugh, maybe that's all that matters.

I brought his leather jacket with me. In part to keep me warm and in part to have an important piece of him with me while I do this. Adorned with patches of past motorcycle memories, it was what he wore most often, an immediate identifier in looks and smell. It still smells of him, radiating leather and the scorching summer sun, mixed with a little musk and the wind. It smells like freedom and I just know that Dad is finally free.

I put it on and it is swimming on me, but I have to feel the weight of its largeness scale me down until I disappear into it. I could hide and become invisible with his lingering presence. It's what I have always done. Why must death dictate the end?

Jules fades away into the background. Giving me the space I need to accomplish this. To say goodbye.

Another presence on the beach alerts me that I am not alone. Sure enough, one, two, ten others begin to freckle the sandy shore. An audience, though no one is paying us much mind. Each living body reminds me that the world is more consumed with life than death. This is it. This is where I share the person I found in the pages he left behind for me. So I begin.

"Forgive me as I stumble through this, Dad. I have never delivered

a eulogy, let alone one for a man as important in my life as you. Gideon Haynes, The Wave, *as he was more affectionately known, was my father. . . well he will always be my father despite the past tense verbiage. I feel a great responsibility to deliver these final words with as much honor and importance as I feel Gideon is owed. And so, as they say, there is no better place to start than the beginning.*

What a cliche. . .

"Gideon was born in 1954, an only child. The minute he entered this world, laughter was abundant. Even sometimes at his expense. However, Gideon steered into all the humor he possibly could. Everything was funny and everything was a joke and everything was a good time. He could brighten a room with his laugh and assume the role of the life source of any social gathering, a.k.a. the life of the party.

"One moment that stands out to me as a story my dad would share is when he was a young boy of about four or five. To evade a beating for being naughty, he ran outside and away. His mother chased closely behind. And my dad, in nothing but a towel around his waist, kept running out onto the suburban streets of Alameda. She snagged the towel in hopes of catching him, but to no avail. Now a very naughty and very naked little boy, with no shame and a loud chuckle, kept running birthday-suit and all down the street for all the passersby to gawk at, but that is who he was. A body confident, trouble-escaping, little boy who had no problem putting on a little show.

"One of his proudest moments was when he was on the original Mickey Mouse Club with Ginny Tyler. His signed postcard was his most treasured possession. He didn't like rules, and this was another moment in Gideon's life where if he had followed the rules, he would have missed out. He often chose experience over obedience. When his dad pulled up with Gideon's team to the Disneyland resort and told him to stay on the bus, my dad felt adventure calling and bailed. It's frus-

trating for many how breaking the rules often led to such a reward for Gideon rather than ruin, but that is just how it was.

"*Moving up in years to high school, the same trouble-maker mentality rang true. No one could tell Gideon what he could or could not do. He told me a story once about wearing cut-off denim shorts to school and being told by faculty that those were against the dress code and to never wear them again. Well, taking that as a challenge, Gideon wore them loudly and proudly the next day. He felt confident, so who was anyone to tell him otherwise?*

"*This is also when Gideon really came into his athletic abilities and fell in love with all things sports. Between football and wrestling and jiu-jitsu and many more, he quickly became very competitive and very accomplished in all areas of athleticism. Gideon was always keen on noticing where he excelled and made sure to put all his time and energy into making himself known, however he could. His time spent as a lifeguard was one of the more fond eras of his life that he mentioned.*

"*He learned the lesson early on to never miss out on an opportunity. It was far better to have a terrible time than regret missing out on all the fun. One story, in particular, was after a long day of scuba diving with friends. He was wet and cold and had just gotten his wetsuit off when his buddies invited him to go on a night swim. He was just beginning to get warm. He hemmed and hawed, but ultimately and begrudgingly squeaked back into his cold wetsuit and got into the water. Whenever he told me this story, he stressed the importance of that decision. It was magic. He swam in the waters that glowed with bioluminescent plankton. With every stroke of his arms wading in the water, the surface would break in a light show that felt like it was especially for him. I got to experience this too, Dad, and it was amazing.*

"*He wouldn't have had that if he had chosen comfort over opportunity. From there on out, he never was one to miss out.*

"We now enter the 1980s where I remember stories being told about all the adventures Gideon had. He was a gypsy nomad living out of a van in Oregon, and he looked like one, too. He illegally worked at a gas station because he wasn't technically old enough yet. Regardless, he became a manager and met many people who had a great impact on his life.

"He was a hairdresser on a cruise ship to Alaska where he would tease and hairspray the lady's hair into beehives so immovable that even the gusty winds on the ocean wouldn't budge the helmets of hair he created, but hey it was the style back then. He balanced pitchers of beer on his head at the Red Dog Saloon in Juneau and didn't spill a drop, even though he was told to knock it off.

"One of the most memorable moments of Gideon's life was when he was aboard the cruise ship and had appendicitis. Many moments in my dad's life were categorized as near-death experiences, this being one of them. After a night of grueling pain where my dad would say he was just begging to let out a fart (excuse me his words) the ship made port and dropped him off to get a taxi. Bent over in the taxi demanding to be rushed to the hospital, the driver wasn't feeling the sense of urgency and decided to take the scenic route of Alaskan highways and show Dad all the notable spots as they drove by. When he finally reached the hospital, his appendix burst on the operating table. The surgeon said a few minutes longer and he wouldn't have made it. I often told Dad that it was obvious God had a greater purpose for him in life with how many times he managed to evade death.

"There were so many other stories that he was sharing with me in the weeks before he passed. So much so that we were planning on sitting down and writing a book together. It was to be called 'Son, Rebel, and Free spirit,' if I remember correctly. It will forever be one of my greatest regrets that we didn't get to accomplish it. I told myself I had many *years, but we never know how much time we truly have left. The title alone, he chose, and I couldn't think of a better few words to sum up Gideon Haynes except for maybe a few. Those being, father, charismatic, and filled with a willingness to love any and all people.*

"Mixed into this timeline was also a stint where he lived in Hawaii and also a time lived in London, England. Maui was spent loving the island and the locals and chronically having a tan, and England was spent with good friends where he pushed a broken-down double-decker bus down the streets of England. Again, putting on a show, but in the best sort of fashion."

I too fell in love with Maui. Now the tears are a river on my cheeks. . . Adam.

"The history of my dad before he became my dad is a little hazy and I wish I had asked him more. I want to hear more stories of Dad, in the younger years.

"We now enter the portion of the eulogy I like to call the Daddy years. In 1992 he married my mother and welcomed me. I am so blessed to have found terrible quality 1990s VHS home videos of my life for me to cherish. He often said he spent my childhood watching me from behind the camera lens. I'm sorry you felt that way Dad, but I also can never thank you enough for making those moments immortal.

"I asked him once if he was sad that he never had any sons, to which he responded 'NO WAY.' God knew he was meant to be a girl dad and I never for a moment felt like he wasn't beaming with pride at being my daddy. He took every opportunity to brag about me and decorated his home with the many photos from our lives. He was sad whenever I called him Dad because it felt so cold compared to Daddy.

"He was also just the coolest Dude Dad alive. He would pick me up from school on the Harley, and I've literally never felt so superior to all my classmates in my entire scholastic career. He would often correct

us all that it wasn't motorcycle, it was pronounced 'motor-sickle.' He scared all my boyfriends and didn't approve of anyone." (I think he would like Adam.)

"Dad brought his childhood love of Disney into our lives in such a powerful way. It was magic, and it was tradition. The last thing I did with my father was watch the last episode of Obi-Wan with Ewan McGregor. It is a powerful Star Wars tribute that I will forever cherish in my heart and rewatch often, pretending he is sitting next to me.

"He loved Star Wars, the Incredibles, Pirates of the Caribbean, etc. He even looked like a pirate a lot of the time. However, Peter Pan was his favorite, probably because he was Peter Pan at heart. He was the boy who never grew up. Gideon used to say, 'You're only as old as you feel and I don't feel old.' To be fair, he wasn't old, in fact far from it.

"When I was little, he took me to Neverland. It's true! I was the first lost girl to be allowed in Neverland. I flew there on a board that Dad and his best mate Max Campton carried to Neverland. I had to have a pillowcase over my head because I wasn't allowed to see anything too specific. However, Peter and Tinker Bell definitely made an appearance, and we saw marks in the gravel from where Peter Pan took off with happy thoughts in flight. There was pixie dust every-where. When I got back to the house from our Neverland adventure, no time had passed at all on the clock. Tinker Bell even made a second appearance at my window when I went to bed that night. It was stuff like that that he did often for me as a little girl that truly did make such magical moments.

"Christmas was also just pure magic. He was an amazing Santa Claus on a motorcycle for a local kids' charity. He was jolly and round enough at the time to ideally portray the jolly elf, only a little more 'bad to the bone.' His years dedicated to the Mio Manz charities and Great

Ormond Street Hospital were deeply impactful for handicapped and terminally ill children. He touched and altered their lives for the better.

"A story I will share briefly of one of the hearts he touched was a child who had very little time left here on earth. He couldn't talk, but he communicated that he really liked my dad's shirt. That's all Gideon needed to hear. He pulled his shirt off and gave it to the kid right then and there. Only a few short years later, Gideon received a letter from the family of that boy saying he had passed wearing the shirt my dad had given him. It just meant that much to him. One of the visions that brings me comfort is my dad and this boy together in Heaven having a grand ole time and neither one experiencing the pain they must have felt here on earth.

"He was a gym owner, a bodybuilder, an avid skier, and took great pride that at his peak physical fitness, he had twenty-two-inch arms! For reference, that is not much smaller than my waist. When I was three or four, he tore his bicep right off the bone while moving some furniture and when he finally got his cast taken off, he left it in our garage and I used it as a tunnel fort to hide in. This man had BIG ARMS! And he also had a 'heart as big as his biceps.'

"Now, I won't stand here and pretend that my father wasn't a flawed man. This is the highlight reel, after all. A lot of people here, myself included, had a complicated and at times tumultuous relationship with the man. And yet it's amazing how when someone dies, all the bad seems to be washed away. I am so grateful that the week he died was such a positive time for us. I never wanted it to end.

"He had just attended his 50th high school reunion. He almost didn't go, but I told him he should, despite missing a few teeth and 'looking like a hillbilly,' he said. He came home a brand new man. He said all his past resentments had been lifted off his shoulders. I half expected him to pick a fight like he said he might, but instead, his heart *was filled with forgiveness and joy. He was almost buoyant, he was so unburdened.*

"In his final voicemail he sent me, he said he felt like his life had come full circle. He could feel the love of those around him and how grateful he was to be alive, despite the ever-increasing gas and grocery prices.

"Dad was coming over to my house often to spend time with me. He would stay for dinner and he was always the best person to cook for. Everything I made that he ate, he would just sit in silence. When I asked if he liked the food, he would say, 'Do you hear me talking?'

"My dad, being the handsome green-eyed man he was, as a child, used to plead to God to give him blue eyes. He was desperate for his eye color to change, but God never changed his eyes to blue. Instead, all of a sudden, people from his peer group would stop and comment on how incredibly beautiful his green eyes were. God didn't change his perfect creation, he just showed him how rare and special his eyes were, as they were meant to be.

"Gideon Haynes was a handsome, complicated, leather-loving, adventurous soul, with a great sense of humor and especially large muscles. He loved The Doobie Brothers and The Beach Boys. He called his friends 'Brother' because he truly cherished his friends like they were family. To tell his story from solely my perspective feels like it falls short of all the greatness this man deserves. How can I say all that there is to say of such an immense lifetime in such a brief period of time?

For Gideon, life wasn't always kind, and as his daughter, I am broken at how quickly he was taken from this world. So many things feel left open-ended. We just have to have faith in our Savior that this was indeed his time. I know he isn't complaining about walking streets of gold and basking in the majesty of God.

"Dad often talked of when he would meet Jesus with great antici-pation and never any fear. In the end, his body was more of a prison that he just couldn't seem to escape. The pain that he felt was consuming him every day.

"I will forever miss you, Daddy, and I am permanently altered by your absence. I am fortunate to know his faith was strong and we will all one day see him again. I see him in Heaven also being the life of the party. My dad, Gideon Haynes, The Wave, all one person, all one incredible man who has left a ripple effect in the lives of all he encoun-tered. He made an ordinary moment magical. As Peter Pan said, 'To die will be an awfully big adventure.' May he rest in peace knowing that each of us is better for having known him and our love and adora-tion of his life here on earth will live on for eternity.

"Thank you all for attending and God bless."

I wrote it as if I were going to be speaking in front of a crowd at his funeral, which I had every intention of doing until I realized this is what he would have wanted more.

"That was beautiful." Jules' soft sobs bury in my neck. It got to her too. "Are you ready for more?"

"I think it's now or never."

"Can you handle what comes next?"

I open the urn and begin to sprinkle some of his ashes in the lake. Watching the clear water wash him away.

"What do you mean?"

"I think Adam deserves a phone call." Jules looks stern, like she dragged me to do this and she will drag me to resolve things with Adam if she has to.

"Adam deserves way more than a phone call."

"There is one more thing I have to do first."

49

MAUI
2022

"I can do this. I can do this." I chant to myself.

Jules was right. She always is, but once she gave me the courage to let go of all my hurt, it felt like I had room in my soul to allow for healing to come. I am not afraid anymore, which I now realize is what held me back from finding what I was searching for. Step one is finding Keone, and that's why Jules and I are standing outside a home on Maui that at one point was the known address of Kailani's family. Who knows now?

"I can do this. I can do this. I can do this." I assume I am talking in my head, but then Jules grabs my hand and squeezes it with a, "Yes, you can," and I realize I wasn't talking to myself.

If this is still the home of Keone, then the family certainly knows how to upkeep. The yard is freckled with thriving tropical palms and a hibiscus bush a size unlike any I have seen before. It's a garden oasis and I must admit it is welcoming. Whether the people behind the door are as welcoming as their front garden, I don't know, but I knock all the same.

No going back.

"Aloha." A friendly, deep voice opens the door. Fully. Screen and all. Back home, I would have maybe cracked the door with my safety chain still attached.

"You," I say.

"You." He says back with a smile and a point. "I remember you. Do you need a ride?"

The driver who took me from the airport to the resort several months ago stands before me and a flash of his card spews in images across my mind. Keone, handwritten over a business card and a personal number for me to call anytime I needed a ride. He doesn't question how I got his address and is unassuming with the actual purpose of standing on his doorstep.

"You remember me?" I ask. Though the answer is obvious. "I do. You're my sister."

I can't speak. I can't breathe. He knows?

"How did you-"

"Gideon sent photos of you every year, along with some money. As soon as you got into my van, I recognized you, but Gideon was also adamant that I never tell you about me. With every check, he sent a plea that I keep myself hidden from you. He wanted me to know you, but my family wasn't the kindest to him when he came by all those years ago. I think he knew that he couldn't come back, which meant that he wasn't going to risk us not welcoming you, as we didn't him. I never cashed a single check.

"I thought about using the address on the checks,

however, to come see him, but my family was still so angry. I couldn't alienate them for a father who ultimately left me and my mom. They blame him for my mother's death. I didn't. . . I don't."

He has the same sincerity in his voice as Adam, and it makes my heart ache momentarily.

"We also met once, but you were young and I never said I was your brother. After my family basically booted Gideon off our front porch, I went to the hotel to see him. He didn't mention you when he came, so I was shocked to see him with a child. I'll admit I almost turned around and left. How he could be a father to you, but not to me, stung. A lot. I just needed to know why. We ended up chatting and then you and I played in the pool for a bit. You were in your own little world and asked me to play mermaids. I did for a bit until you got bored with me and went off to play on your own. You were so carefree. I envied you so much."

"So it wasn't a dream." The recollection still haunts me. "He never told me about you."

"He didn't?" Keone looks confused. "How did you know to find me, then?"

Here comes the part I don't want to say out loud. "He died." I pause. Not for dramatic effect, but because we both need a moment to allow it to soak in. "I found his journal and followed it, well, here." I point to the welcome mat as if I mean this exact geological location and not just a metaphor for how the last few months have gone.

"I'm so sorry for your loss." Keone's eyes brim with tears. He is not immune to loss, but I notice that he says "my loss" and not "our loss." This is a man he only knew because of an uncashed check every year.

"I told him I wouldn't come to seek him out again. That if he wanted to know me, he would have to come to me in the future. He never did, aside from the money. I was too mad to deposit them. I always thought he could have done more than assuage his guilt with money. I just assumed he was too scared of my family to be rejected again, but I forgave him for that a long time ago."

"Funny, you and I both wish he had done more." I laugh and with that, Keone invites Jules and me inside to discuss the rest. The fall of Gideon and the pills, his death, my travels, and all the in-between. Jules, who had been quiet on the porch, is now a vibrant conversationalist. Turns out Keone is single and I think she might have a little crush. She won't stop twirling her hair.

It's hard not to see the similarities between us. We both have Dad's eyes and he especially has Dad's nose. Seeing the pictures he brought out of him as a baby and Kailani, though, proves he looks more like his island mother than our shared father. She was so beautiful. I can't help but tear up at the sight of her.

"I have this one too." Keone leaves the room momentarily. I haven't asked him where his family is. He will offer that up to me if he wishes. I don't ask almost any questions. Keone shares and there is no better way for me to get to know him than to just listen. When he returns from a small one-off bedroom, he comes back holding a yellowed photo. My heart knows what it is before I see it. "It's them, isn't it?" Keone nods.

I take the photo in my hand and cradle it like it might detonate and take with it all proof of their love.

"I only knew her through my dad's words about her. He portrayed her with such devotion I feel like I knew her, but seeing them together, forever frozen in time like this, it's hard to think he didn't do her justice. She is so beautiful, Keone."

"Thank you. I wish I got to know her."

Then I remember that he was a baby when she died. Much like how my mom passed when I was a child.

"I lost my mom too, when I was young." It isn't information I thought I would offer up so easily, but the realization that we both grew up so similarly makes me say it. "You might have envied me, but when I learned of your existence, I envied you. You at least had a big family who loved you. I just had Dad, and it wasn't for very long."

"Oh, really? How long ago did he die? He sent a check only a few months ago. I thought he just gave up because I never cashed them."

"He died in September this year, but shortly after coming here, actually, he found solace and comfort in pills and, well. . . addiction set in after that. I hate to say I took care of him more than he took care of me, but sometimes I feel that to be true. I think the loss of my mother and then discovering Kailani had died coming to find him was all too much in the long run."

The truth doesn't hurt so much to say out loud anymore.

"Honestly, I was afraid to meet you. Thanks for making it so easy." I take Keone's hand from across the small kitchen table and breathe in the humidity.

"I want nothing more than to be in your life from now on, Jenesis. Just because our families couldn't make it work doesn't mean it isn't my immense honor to be your brother."

We both stand and embrace in a hug that feels like several generations are mending with it. "I'd really like that."

The rest of our time together is spent laughing and snacking on some of the best pineapple I have ever had. Had I gotten out of my own way and done this sooner, I could have felt this immense relief much faster. Then again, I know everything comes in its own timing.

Jules is less a bystander now and more involved in Keone. I don't know how eating pineapple can be sexy, and yet Jules is all over it. I am going to give her so much crap for it later.

I left my bag by the front door, but the size of the house allows me to hear a notification go off. I leave Jules and Keone to continue flirting with one another while I go check my device. Still, there is a part of me hoping Adam breaks the silence first. It is the last piece of my puzzle that needs mending, and yet I am still terrified to take that first step. If he did it first, it would save me a lot of anxiety.

It isn't Adam who messages me, but to my surprise, Natalie's Instagram handle illuminates across my lock screen. *What on earth could she possibly have to say to me?*

INSTAGRAM

2022

@BeachyNatitude

Hey Jenesis. I know I am the last person you would expect or want to hear from right now. Or ever. But I had to reach out to you. Adam needs you. Even since you left, he has been in a bad way. I've never seen his heart broken like this. I didn't know the extent of his feelings for you. That doesn't excuse my behavior and I do want to apologize for the role I played in all this, but he has relapsed or "fallen off the wagon" or whatever it is you want to call it. I tried to help him, but you already know the mess I made. He needs you, Jenesis. Can you please come, or call him at least to talk to him? I am honestly afraid of what might happen to him if you don't.

@Wanderlust_0425

I am already here.

MAUI

2022

"Have you ever seen a mermaid?"

I ambush him. I know this. Adam kept true to his promise and left me instructions on how to get to Neverland. I wasn't going to take them, thinking that I would never come back here anyway, but right now I sit at the shore of the lagoon under the waterfall; waiting for him. I knew he would come, eventually.

I can hear someone coming with the crunch of the dirt and some fallen palms underneath what must be sandals. I am not arrogant enough to think Adam is the only person who comes here. (I am sure there are no true secret places on this island.) It's an island for crying out loud, but my heart thunders a little in the anticipation of who will broach the corner into view.

I am amazed I can even hear footsteps over the waterfall, but I am waiting for someone, so that's all I set my ears to. I am waiting for him. My fingers shake with anxiety.

"Have you ever seen a mermaid before?" It's him. I ask

with utmost certainty. I can see his sandy hair cross first into my view.

My question prompts Adam to look at the person waiting at his secret hiding spot. All I can do is smile at him. It is a smile that doesn't show any teeth and doesn't quite reach my eyes. I have to tread lightly. Based on how I left things, I am not entirely convinced he will be happy to see me.

"Hi," I say through my teeth. My previous silly question went unanswered.

"Hi," He says back. The look on his face for once giving away nothing, though his eyebrows are a little more lifted. "What are you doing here?"

His eyes have a darkness brooding underneath them in a puffiness I have never witnessed on him. I had hoped Natalie was exaggerating. I know she has a certain flair for the dramatic, but looking at Adam now, I think maybe she undersold me on how low he has fallen.

"I don't know what to say right now." I don't really answer his question as to why I am here. "I guess I'm here to see if you are okay?" It comes out timid and squeaky. I've been around this before. I know he is not okay.

"What makes you think I might not be okay?" Adam crosses his arms. A very clear indication through body language that he is not interested in being close; both conversationally and physically.

"Natalie messaged me." That's all I need to say.

"I'm going to kill her," Adam mumbles almost inaudibly, but his lips purse tighter. There is a moment of silence after.

My mermaid joke didn't ease the tension like I had hoped it would.

"Oh, are you wanting to know if I am okay since you decided to sleep with me, tell me you're falling for me and then completely rip my heart out and leave yet again. . . Yeah Jenesis, I'm Okay." He says it sarcastically and he also says my full name, which I have to admit is my least favorite name he calls me. "What are you here to accomplish, Jenesis?" There it is again.

"I don't know."

"You flew all the way here to sit there on my beach and tell me you don't know?"

I can feel the rage radiate from him like a slow simmer of a volcano about to erupt. I don't tell him I came here to meet Keone. I don't tell him I want to mend things. Instead, I find myself mute. He isn't full-on yelling at me, but the sullen sharpness of his tone is almost worse. I hurt him and I don't know if he will forgive me for that.

"Natalie said. . ."

"Oh, Natalie said," he mocks in his tone. "What did Natalie say?"

"She said you backslid and haven't been doing well. She said that you have been getting blackout drunk every night and acting stupid in doing so. She said you came onto her and she rejected you because you were so sloppy she realized if the only version of you she could have wasn't the sober one, then it wasn't the you that she wanted. She told me that I hurt you more than she has seen anyone hurt you before and that if I truly loved you, I would get myself on a plane within the hour and get back to you." I am paraphrasing.

We had a full-on conversation over the phone after she initially messaged me on my socials.

"She said what?" Adam's eyes got big, his arms loosening around his middle.

"She said. . ."

"No, I heard you." Adam cuts me off and holds a hand up to me.

"So, are you here to try to save me or are you here because you love me?" There is still very little tenderness in his voice.

"Can it be a little of both?"

"No Jenesis. It can't. It can't be that you love me and want to save me because I can't be saved by someone else. I am an addict. We both know how this works. The only way I can stay clean is if *I* choose to. I can have help, but I can't be saved and unless you are here to admit you love me for real and not take it back, then there is no point in even trying anymore and I don't want you here.

"I've been clean for years until a few weeks ago when you left. I went to the corner market and bought the biggest bottle of rum they had. I finished it before they closed and went back for another. I was so drunk the only way I actually knew I went back and bought another one was because I found the receipt. I completely blacked out. I don't remember walking to the store to begin with, but that pesky memory of you still lingered in my mind. No matter how much I drank, I couldn't get those words out of my head, your words. 'I just don't believe in love anymore.' You said that to me. Right after I made love to you, right after you opened your heart up to me and told me you loved me, you immediately took it back. Ripping out my heart in the process.

"All the times I tried to show you I loved you without saying it. Then all the times I said it out loud to you. None of those instances had any effect on you.

"I have been able to find resolution from my woes at the bottom of a bottle time and time again, Jenesis. You are the only troublesome memory that I can't even escape from with mind-numbing intoxication."

A tear falls down my cheek, and I don't bother to wipe it away. I am not hiding any of my emotions from him anymore.

"So I stopped."

I exhale a breath I didn't know I was holding.

"Yeah. I'm on day three, but I am clean again." He pulls out a coin from his swim trunks pocket. I recognize it as a sobriety chip. "I'm starting over. Natalie doesn't know because the last time she saw me was when she was prying me off of her and laying me on my side on my bed so I didn't choke on my own vomit. She deserves an apology from me. I will not stand here and apologize to you, though. I will not allow your look of disappointment to affect me. I let you have so much power over me and I decided to take it back, but the shame I have in throwing myself at Natalie. . ."

I wince at the mental image. I don't want to hear this. Even though I left with the verbalized intent of pushing them together. The reality of it stings. I can't imagine the man I have come to know being forceful with anyone. His consideration oozes out of every pore in his body. But I can see the shame he has for crossing that line with her.

"I don't need an apology from you. I came here to apologize to you." I stand up finally and work my way over to him. It's been loud with the waterfall, but I have heard every word. I thought maybe he would come to meet me, but the whole point of me coming back is so that I can meet him where he needs me.

I place my hands on the sides of his triceps, his height towering over me.

Adam's hands fall over his face. Hiding. "I'm so ashamed."

"I know. Shame is good, though. Shame means you feel something still." I breathe heavily. "I watched as my dad justified his usage with his pain. At first, I could see the shame. By the end of it all, the shame wasn't there anymore, and he never found relief from his demons because of it. He stopped trying. I still see the fight in you. You refuse to let it win. "

"I don't need an AA meeting from you, Jen." He calls me Jen. One step closer to softness.

"I'm scared to love you, Adam. I'm sorry. You make me feel things that no one ever has and as much as I feel hurt by my dad, I fear you have the ability to absolutely demolish me. It scares me to think about diving into another relationship with an addict. Even one who is clean, which I do commend you for more than I let on.

It's just that you were right. My dad did play the villain in my life and I still love him so much. What if you replace him as the villain in my story and I love you too much to ever leave you? You can make me lose myself completely and I just have begun to feel like I might be coming up for air. What if my love for you makes me drown?

"These are all the fears that have been suffocating me since I left the beach. I thought leaving you might save us both because I know that two broken people do not make a whole."

I can see the pain building up in Adam's breathing as I reopen our wound, making it worse before it gets better.

"But. . ."

Adam loosens all the air in his lungs with relief.

"But I do love you and I can't let my fear of the unknown stop me from living fully in the now."

I barely get the words out before Adam has bridged the gap that separated us. I almost flew backward, his arms so tight around my middle it's the only reason I don't tumble into the lagoon behind me.

Hard shoulder shaking sobs echo into my ear and I can feel the dampness of his tears soak into my shoulder. I haven't cried much since Tahoe, when I just couldn't stop, like I finally ran on empty, but Adam's rawness and vulnerability to cry as he crumbles into me has my eyelids burning.

"I can prove to you that I can do this." Adam muffles into my shirt. "I can stay clean."

"You can't do this for me. You have to want to stay clean for you."

"It is for me." His head pops up and his eyes, even more blue from the tears, stare deeply into mine. "I want to stay clean so that I can be the man worthy of your love."

How do I tell him that he has already proven to be more worthy of

my love than anyone else who has been in and out of my life? How do I
share that I need to learn, too? I need to learn how to love.

Fortunately, Adam does not leave room for more discussion and places his mouth on mine. A kiss so meaningful I almost have to pull away. It makes me feel so much. But, then I remember that I am welcoming all emotions, and letting them be present in my life is what I am trying to be better at.

I thought that I would find Adam drunk in a state where I would feel the savior complex to try and get him clean. It speaks volumes that he had the initiative to do it himself. I don't fear Adam. I fear what time will do to us, but I will just have to take it one day at a time, which I told Adam, and to which he replied that it would have to be the same for him. We will have to earn each other's trust. In time.

"Why do you call this place Neverland?" I ask.

Adam and I have been sitting next to the lagoon for hours just talking and kissing and making up for lost time.

"It looks like it, doesn't it?"

The surrounding waters sparkle in the diminishing sunlight, which reflects the pools in an almost greenish hue. I breathe in the air around me as if to embody the sparkle internally.

"This place didn't hold any real magic until I shared it with you." He admits. "I have a feeling life will be the same now. You have no idea the impact you have had on my existence, and it makes me love you more."

I take his hand in mine and lean into the sun-kissed heat of his body. "What now?" I ask.

"Now, we can go anywhere in the world and do anything

we want. As long as we are together." Adam places a soft kiss into my hair.

"Well, Jules met Keone and I think she is in love. Any chance you have room for two more in that bungalow of yours?"

"Okay, number one, you are just telling me now about how you met your brother and two, did you just ask if you can move in with me?"

"Me and my best friend." I jest. *He knows I am kidding, right?* I decide to make it clear. "I am kidding, you know, but I think moving here is something I could easily convince Jules to do." My heart leaps at the thought of having it all. Every person I love in one place.

"Maybe you should move in. I'd have room for you. Maybe Jules could crash on the couch for a bit. My studio would be mighty crowded and we would have no privacy, but I would do that for you."

"Jules can find her own place." I bump his shoulder.

"Is that a yes?"

Is it a yes? It's crazy to move in with someone I haven't known for a very long time, but if Dad taught me anything, it's cherish love while you have it.

"Yes."

EPILOGUE - ADAM'S POV
PALM DESERT - 2024

"We are going to be so late." I stand halfway between the entry and the outside of our now-shared condo in Palm Desert.

"Please close the door. You are letting all the AC out." Jenesis throws on one sandal, then the other, and hobbles/hops towards the door.

"I wouldn't be letting the cool air out if you were even remotely on time." Even after two years, I have never really been cross with her and she has never been on time anywhere. Some things never change, though so much other stuff has.

"We will see you when you get back," Jules yells from the kitchen. "We will have dinner ready for you guys when you return. I am thinking of making gorgonzola skirt steak and a fresh green salad." It sounds delicious, but I know Jenny won't be thrilled with the stinky cheese. She will eat it anyway because she has never said no to any of Jules' gourmet meals and isn't about to start nit-picking her now. We also haven't had one we disliked yet.

"We will hold down the fort." Keone comes out of the bedroom and meets Jules at the kitchen counter. These two still haven't admitted they like one another, but watching it all play out has been highly entertaining.

"We won't be late unless Jenny here has anything to say about it." I say as my eyebrows narrow.

"Yeah. . . yeah. . . yeah. . ." She grabs her purse and we shut the door. "You tease me so much."

"I just love you." I place a heavy kiss on her lips with such force it throws her head back.

"Now, who is making us late?"

We have been attending AA and Alanon meetings regularly since that day at the lagoon. We both agreed we needed tools because neither one of us was equipped to manage the other. We both have healing journeys that are individual and woven together. Healing isn't linear, but I'd like to say we have been doing well since our reconciliation.

Even when we travel we find a meeting, and I honestly love that about us. I have learned so much and it is amazing to watch Jenesis grow in her own recovery. She has healed parts of me I didn't know would ever be healed and I'd like to think I have done the same for her.

Me, Adam, Jules, and Keone are visiting the condo for the week. Being surrounded by the family we chose, and the lost family she found, I know makes her feel closer to the Dad she still misses every day. Her journey didn't go as planned, but everything unraveled as it was meant to. She found the man she never really got to know in the pages of the journal he left behind. Keone filled in a lot of the gaps as well and he feels like a real brother to us both now, which is why Jules falling for him has Jen cringing a bit. She often teases, "ew girl, that's my brother." I secretly hope they get married one day.

Jen offered to sell the condo and split the sale with Keone as a shared inheritance, but he insisted she keep it and his share can be that he vacations with us once a year. I am so glad that was his decision because the trips we take have become one of our favorite new traditions.

We ended up meeting Keone's family, and they welcomed Jen more warmly than we both expected. I guess they too felt a little guilty for running Gideon off all those years ago. Neither one of us mentioned his addictions. We both would like to leave the hurt in the past and often muse that maybe Gideon and Kailani have reunited once more.

At first, it was hard for her to think that Gideon might have had a greater love than her mom, but now we agree that maybe we all have many loves in our lives and each one serves a purpose at the time. If Kailani and Gideon hadn't been together, there would be no Keone and by extension, Jen too might not have existed. How much sadder would the world be without her. She has become my world. It's amazing to see Keone and Jen mend the hurt of all those years apart. I like to think that Gideon and Kailani are looking down on them, proud that the two have found each other. A generational curse broken.

Jenesis tells me every day how much I remind her of Gideon. Of course it's the good parts she is referring to. Death was so final a few years ago, but even now she sometimes feels like she can see the ghost of a younger Gideon, looking out from the golf course below, or a passerby in the airport. I even thought I saw him on a surfboard once. I took it as a sign that he approves of our relationship. It's hard to ask for his approval in marrying Jenesis, but in my own way, I did. Because nothing we do is conventional, I got us matching golden toe rings as engagement rings and I plan on proposing when we get back to Maui. Our spot, "Neverland," is where I plan to do it. Jules even temporarily stole Jen's mom's ring, which I plan to use if the toe rings backfire. Eh, I will probably use both. Jen would accept a piece of seaweed as a ring and I love her for it.

Selling Jules on moving to Maui wasn't hard. "I can do hair anywhere," were her exact words. I reminded her that growing a new client list would be tricky, and she assured me that it was the right move.

She might have done it because she knew Jen probably would not have moved in with me had she not. I thank her for that. She might have also done it because living in Hawaii is a bucket list item for many people. I've never seen the girl say no to a piña colada. Or she might have done it because of her feelings for Keone. For all I know, it was all the above if it were a multiple-choice question, but I never asked. There was no need for a reason. I was just grateful that she decided to follow.

Jules slept on my couch for about a month while she found a salon and an apartment. She quickly found a gig at a resort that pays well for her to do hair and nail treatments for vacationers, and they even offered her a room as part of her pay. She was so thrilled to be living in a hotel, like some tropical *Eloise*. I reminded her that she wouldn't be in any sort of penthouse to which she just scoffed and swirled her long, thick Portuguese hair. "Do you want me off your couch or not?"

I laughed because, of course, I did. As much as I have come to love Jules, there was very little opportunity to be private with Jen during the entire first month of our living together. "It's growing the anticipation," is all Jenesis would say, but I knew it was starting to drive her crazy. It was for me.

"Get a room," was uttered by Jules often. To which I would reply that I have already and I was waiting on her to "get a room." It was all kind of fun though.

The entire bungalow blew up with stuff that, little by little, we sorted through, organized, and sold off. When Jules moved out, it felt like we had added an entire room to the small tropical oasis. Her presence makes our small bungalow feel more like home than anywhere on earth. Almost like I have "settled down." Even Jen has said the island spirit has welcomed her. I thank Keone for sharing his heritage with her. We still travel often though. Together and on purpose now.

There isn't much we changed. We got a bigger bed, and Jen made sure to add the comfiest cooling duvet for maximum comfort and aesthetic appeal. I told Jen to change anything she wanted to. "Make this feel like your home too, because that's what it is."

I never want her to feel like she is disappearing into my world like she had done before. I want it to be our world. I love how the birds come in through the windows in the morning and she feeds them crumbs from her muffin while we sip *my brewed* coffee at the counter. I offered to put up screens, to which she immediately told me to never suggest that again. Being one with nature on this island is part of loving it here.

Jules and Jen take almost daily walks on the beach and truthfully, they both have never been healthier. A simple diet of tropical fruits and yes, Spam, coupled with surfing and walks on the beach, have us all thriving. We love the lifestyle change.

Speaking of surfing, I got Jen her own board for her thirty-first birthday. It's pink with hibiscus flowers. Natalie rolled her eyes and called Jenny a *"Beach Barbie,"* but she laughed. Despite her sarcastic quip about the girlie board, the two have actually become close friends. Jen may never beat her on the waves, but there is also no longer any sort of competition or jealousy.

She and Zeke actually went out on a date, which made me belly laugh. They haven't gone on a second yet, and the entire group gave them crap for even trying, but who knows what is in store for those two. We are all still friends, though no more campouts on the beach mixed with edibles have happened since.

Jen has decided to remain sober in solidarity with me. We have a dry bungalow, but our cocktails are virgins when we go out with friends as well. I am so appreciative because she knows she doesn't have to, but rather wants to and it helps a lot. She says, "it's the best decision she ever made."

I think the ultimate best decision she ever made was getting on that plane after Gideon died. She had no idea where the journey was going to lead and I never could have predicted the blessings that would intertwine our two lifelines into one.

WHEN WE GET BACK FROM OUR MEETING, JULES AND KEONE are sitting on the couch watching a movie. Kind of. They waited for us to eat and, based on the way, they bolted away from one another like shrapnel, I am assuming that Jen and I just walked into a moment that was more NSFW than PG. *Transformers* is playing on the small TV screen. A great make-out movie because it's three hours long.

I've convinced Jen not to pry and we both agree that they will tell us about their relationship in time. For now, we politely pretend we don't notice anything incriminating.

"Dinner smells delicious." My stomach always rumbles after a meeting. I catch Jen's eye who said she was starving on the drive home. Jules tries to tame her hair as she sets the table, while I swear I see Keone button his jeans. Jen tries so hard not to snicker.

As we sit around the table in one of my new favorite places with all of my favorite people, I can't help but look back at the last two years and think of what led us here. It was a journal that Jen found underneath a couch cushion. It was a chance meeting in Alaska that fate gave us more than one opportunity to accept. It was pain, and it was healing. I've been privileged to read Gideon's words that brought us both to a happiness we never thought possible. The similar leather journal Jen bought in the cafe in Alaska at the beginning of it all is now a place where she chronicles all her past, both good and bad, as well as all our memories together. The *flashbacks* of her past, are documented for memory sake. Stories for her to pass on, maybe for someone someday, to know a version of her they weren't around to know. She's so proud of it and cherishes both journals now with a lot more care than previously. I.E. throwing it at walls.

She told me once, "I know Gideon didn't write his journal with me in mind, but if I could thank him for anything in this life, it's being brave enough to share his story in the pages he left behind. Maybe our daughter can read both journals and in a way know who we are now."

"We have a daughter?" I ask, jokingly because we haven't talked much about our future. She doesn't even suspect my upcoming proposal. I would have done it already, but it has take place in our "Neverland."

That's when Jules comes out of our bedroom, (I didn't even see her slip away), with a pink stick that has two distinct lines on it.

"I think it might be a girl." Jenesis rubs the lower part of her stomach and I fold onto my knees and hug her around her middle. I place a small kiss right under her bellybutton.

"We can't name her Wanderlust, can we?"

"What about a different W name. I was thinking, maybe, Wendy."

AUTHORS NOTE

First and foremost, I'd like to note that writing this story was incredibly therapeutic for me. While a lot of its themes and scenes were born out of truth, the entire compilation of this novel is fiction, a.k.a. not true. . . So much of this was my real life experience and so much of it, I completely fabricated. So if you know me and see yourself in a character, please know that no one character was a hundred percent anybody I know and love. All of these characters are born from my imagination. As readers, especially those who know me personally, you might be able to tell what is fact and what is fiction, but my goal in this was to blend the two. I wanted to take my pain and grief and turn it into the beautiful ending I sadly never got with my Dad. That being said, there is so much I completely made up and I don't like to speak ill of the dead.

A villain is more complicated than we realize. No one person is inherently all bad. I wanted to portray the complexity in loving an addict. The good and the bad. The Jekyll and Hyde syndrome.

Since my father is not around to defend himself, I need to make it clear that I embellished a lot of the horrible things the Gideon character did in this book. Dramatized for, well. . . dramatic effect. While my father was a complicated man, and our relationship was rocky at times, there isn't a day that goes by that I don't think of him and miss him with my whole heart. He was an incredible human being and anyone who met him was touched by his love and his kindness. People used to say that he had a heart as big as his biceps. For a man with 22-inch arms, that is a really big heart. He just also had his struggles that unfortunately rippled into my life, altering me completely.

But isn't that the beauty of a book? We can escape into another reality. For Jenesis, she still lost her Daddy. That was a reality that couldn't be escaped, but she was able to search for the amazing man he had been. While I wish I had had more time with my father, there was an entire side of him I never got to know. He left me clues in photo albums, whereas Jenesis gets to know him in pages of a journal. My dad was no different, and this was my way of traveling back in time, to know the man before the addict became his identity.

In real life, my husband found my father passed in his home on September 7th, 2022. I don't know when he took his last breath. I wasn't there by his side. In the book, Jenesis endures the same hardship that broke my heart in ways I will never be able to fully heal. I can't let all pieces of my dad one day disappear and in many ways, I found him in writing this book. In other ways Gideon Haynes, (my father's fictional proxy,) is very different from my father Mark Hayes.

I find my father in the smell of buttered popcorn, a Doobie Brothers song, and the hum of a motorcycle speeding down the freeway. I can smell his scent still on his leather biker jacket that will forever remain in my possession. Pieces of him still exist all around me.

These characters are not me, nor are they my father, but parts of us can be found within. These are my pages that I have left behind since he is no longer with me.

There was no typical happily ever after for Jenesis and her dad. Much like there wasn't for me. That was the one reality I couldn't rewrite, but have this desire to find beauty in the painful aftermath. Jenesis' journey is much like my own. I too have traveled to places my Dad touched. Recalling the stories he told in these places is how I learned to heal.

Grief is like the ocean. Some waves hit the shore harder than others. Sometimes the tide is soft. Regardless, grief, like waves, is always moving and always changing. Losing a parent young is a wound that never truly closes, but we learn to navigate and alter around the pain. I have a wonderful family I have been able to lean on, whereas Jenesis found Adam, but just like Jenesis, I am still healing from such a tragic loss. Always will.

Sometimes it's hard to find the good in the trauma and sometimes it's hard to admit there was trauma at all. It feels like dishonoring his memory to admit my physical being was changed by the trauma I experienced as a child and into young adulthood. I believe that admitting it was real and blaming the addict is not synonymous. I can admit that it was painful and not okay, while still loving the man who created the chaos. Jenesis has been a great tool for me to work around those complicated emotions.

I wrote this book for all of those who never got to say goodbye. For those of us who didn't get to hold the hand of our loved ones as they departed this world. I don't know if it's better to have it come suddenly or have death make its face known. I believe both leave an open wound, but for us who didn't see it coming, closure is a bit harder to come by. We go from one reality to the next. They exist then they don't and there were no hospital alarms or doctors to tell me the time was near.

I went from having a nice dinner with my father and a movie night to watching him drive away and then never seeing him again. Looking back, part of me knew it was the last time. I remember hugging my father tighter than I have in years and I had an urge to watch his car leave my driveway. I remember feeling so weird that I had done that. It felt unnatural. Now I know it was a gift from God. His spirit told me to soak up every last second because that is what it was. . . the last. For now that is. As my dad would say, "It is always see you later. Never goodbye."

Ok now on to the thanks for the book stuff. . .

ACKNOWLEDGMENTS

~THIS BOOK IS FOR YOU, DAD.

THE MOST OPEN-HEARTED AND COMPLICATED PERSON I HAD THE PRIVILEGE OF KNOWING. THIS ISN'T THE BOOK WE THOUGHT WE WOULD WRITE TOGETHER, BUT I HOPE IT STILL MAKES YOU PROUD. YOU WILL ALWAYS BE A REBEL, WILD AND FREE, WITH A HEART AS BIG AS YOUR BICEPS. I WISH OUR STORY HAD A DIFFERENT ENDING. I MISS YOU EVERY DAY.

I want to thank you, Dad, for loving me as you did and knowing that if you could read this book, you probably would have really liked many parts of Gideon. Those are the parts that remind me of most of you.

I want to thank my sister. For always being there for me. While Jenesis has no one, I had you. Always. Even at the end, when all we had were FaceTime calls, you were always there on the other end, either crying with me or giving me sage advice. My baby sister, I will always appreciate all you do for me. Not to mention, my book cover is fire! You are legit so talented and amazing. Such an incredible artist. There was no one else better suited to design this book cover. In Pages Left Behind is, in part, your story as well. Though you have your own voice, memories, and strength.

To my mother for being there through it all. Who made

my childhood an actual childhood and who tried to shield me from the pain. You broke the cycle. You did the hard work and got the tools needed to make sure that life changed. I don't think I can ever express how much gratitude I have towards you. You are my champion. And if this book is too much for you to ever read in its entirety, I definitely understand. You are always my biggest fan and I want to be you when I grow up.

To my husband, who held me every time I cried, who shielded me from the hurt, and who inevitably said that you would go check on Dad in the end somehow knowing I shouldn't. I cannot express enough thanks. You protected me from what Jenesis endured. I get to remember him as my loving daddy and don't have the image of his death marred on me. I'm grateful to you for so much, but for protecting me from that permanent imagery, I thank you.

To my in-laws for rushing over to be with me and helping finalize all the estate stuff. You did more than you were even asked and I appreciate all of it. To my father-in-law, who has been another Dad figure in my life. You have been such a stable presence. Thank you.

To Bri. You took my phone call when it was super late, and you had two babies at home. You picked me up off the floor when I couldn't get up. You held me and told me it was okay to cry. You were there when I felt alone. I could cry just retelling it. The sacrifice to come and stay well into the early hours of the morning while you had a baby to feed at home. My bosom friend. I will forever be grateful. You also were the first to read this novel and for that too I am grateful.

To Julia. Uh-huh Jules. Thank you for helping me clear

out all of my dad's stuff. For pausing with me when I needed to cry, for bringing me a latte as a comfort. You are my sister in so many ways and I can't wait for our friendship to span another 25 years. Longer, please.

To Melissa, who watched five kids total, for hours, while I took care of business. You never bat an eyelash or texted asking when I would be home. And I knew my babies were so well taken care of. You took worry off of me and gave me the space I needed to compartmentalize the grief.

I have found family in all of you.

It has been a long time writing this book and I have to thank all of my author friends who answered my incessant questions and gave me inspiration.

To Lauren who has author dates me with. Those are some of my favorite things. I can't wait for our next one.

And lastly, to all my readers. Thank you for picking up my sad, romantic story. I hope you fall in love with Jenesis and Adam or Gideon and Kailani as much as I have. Maybe Natalie and Zeke or Jules and Keone need their own novels. . . who know's what the future holds.

RESOURCES

If you or anyone you know has been affected by the disease of addiction, there are programs out there that can help.

- https://al-anon.org/
- https://www.aa.org/

IF YOU ENJOYED IN PAGES LEFT BEHIND PLEASE CONSIDER
LEAVING A REVIEW! AS AN INDEPENDENT AUTHOR, IT MEANS THE
WORLD TO ME AND HELPS OTHERS FIND MY WRITING AS WELL.
FOR MORE CONTENT AND EXCLUSIVE INFORMATION ON WHAT'S
COMING, FEEL FREE TO VISIT MY WEBSITE
JESSICANOELLEBOOKS.COM.

ALSO BY JESSICA NOELLE

Adopting Secrets

In Pages Left Behind

ABOUT THE AUTHOR

Jessica Noelle has worked as a lifestyle journalist in a small town in Northern California. Her writings now center on the compelling themes of love, family, and tragedy. She studied at San Francisco State University and spends most of her time with her husband and two babies at their idyllic farmhouse in the foothills of California. She loves to work in the shade of a palm tree on the beach, however, and uses her many travels to inspire her writing. Her words are at times comic, sensual, complex, and transportive.

jessicanoellebooks.com

Instagram: jessica.noelle
TikTok: @jessicanoelle
Pinterest: jnkonrad
Substack: Jessica's Journal